# THE PRICE

Ron Welling

Book Guild Publishing
Sussex, England

First published in Great Britain in 2012 by
The Book Guild Ltd
Pavilion View
19 New Road
Brighton, BN1 1UF

Typesetting in Baskerville by
Keyboard Services, Luton, Bedfordshire

Printed and bound in Great Britain by
CPI Group (UK) Ltd, Croydon, CR0 4YY

A catalogue record for this book is available from
The British Library.

ISBN 978 1 84624 798 9

# 1

'You built this flash place, man? They tell it's gonna be a hotel.' There was no warning as a blur of black that was a face, hard to see in the early evening darkness, appeared at Harry Stone's side on the warm Caribbean beach. He turned so fast his right foot shot a jet of ink-black water from the sea, soaking his trouser knee. The water was not cold but for a fleeting second Stone felt a jolt.

The voice continued in a low monotone.

'This new building needs protection. Hurricanes hit St Lucia. Blow things down, man. But there's worse can do damage than hurricanes.'

The tone, threatening and contemptuous, brought hot words to Stone's dry lips.

'Who the hell are you?' he rasped, peering for features that might identify the person beside him.

'Call me Columbus or Drake,' the voice said loudly.

'Don't play games with me,' Stone said, his natural aggression edging his voice with rage.

'Me? I don't play games, man. You'll find me dead serious. And if you don't listen you get done. You'll know what that means.'

Stone's thoughts flashed to the bloody beatings he had ordered, and once or twice suffered, in a life not always on the right side of right.

'This hotel's ready to open for business. And nothing'll stop it.' Instinctively Stone turned sharply. He wanted away. But a vice-like grip seized his right arm and spun him round, holding as firmly as if he had been chained to a

1

wall. A long blade glinted and Stone felt a sting at his throat.

He froze, his mind went blank and he found himself speechless. The shadowy face whispered coarsely again as a rain-laden cloud swam low overhead, intensifying Stone's sense of exposure and isolation.

'You need to know more,' Drake sneered.

'What do you want for God's sake?' Stone forced through clenched teeth, furious at this insolent assault, the small movement of his throat shooting needles of pain into his neck.

'Let's see. Two hundred fifty grand'll buy the protection this showy place needs.'

'You *crazy*?' Stone said furiously. 'I don't have money like that.'

'What're you on, man? Only the rich could build a place like this. How many million dollars it cost you?'

The knifepoint pushed a millimetre into Stone's flesh and he felt the grip on his arm pull him back as if about to slice his throat.

'That's none of your nasty business,' Stone croaked, determined to keep his nerve and not give way to this brazen bum.

'Jus' you wait and see, man. I know you people. Millions of dollars swill in your pockets. You drive swish cars. Me and me mates we talk. We know you people got plenty dollars to lose.'

Stone thought he could see a second figure crouched under the wide banana leaves fringing the beach and felt a new twinge of fear. He could no longer doubt the danger he was in.

'You won't get a cent if you kill me,' Stone hissed desperately. 'You'll get life.'

'You 'fraid, man?' Drake asked mockingly, close to Stone's ear.

Stone did not answer but winced as he felt the knife prick again.

'Leave the bucks in ten-dollar bills sealed in plastic bags near Soufriere two nights from tonight. You'll need the road that goes to the sulphur springs near the volcano. At the slope half a mile from Terre Blanche there's the sign to Martha's Cabin. Put the bags in the long grass where the sign hits the ground. And not before seven. It's dark then. Don' be 'fraid neither, man, the volcano's extinct, don't 'rupt no more.' The taunt maddened Stone as Drake glared boldly at him.

With a grating laugh the knife was removed from Stone's throat as quickly as it had been put there. Drake waved it close to Stone's face making him stumble backwards and the gust of sweat and tobacco from Drake's body made Stone retch.

'This point'll cut your throat out next time if you don't do just as I say. Got it, man?'

Stone shook with tension. The grip on his arm loosened and Drake stepped back as if about to free him. With his left hand Stone gingerly felt his bleeding Adam's apple, unsure whether to grab Drake or get away himself. He was still lean and tall at sixty, with the heartbeat of an athlete. Yet shoeless on soft sand, and sensing Drake had at least one other thug with him crouched ready among the palm trees, he knew running would get him nowhere. Stone's impulse was to fight. Yanking his arm free he squared to his shadowy attacker.

'You better hear this. I don't respond to demands from screwballs like you,' he said, trying to hide the tremor in his voice.

'We'll see 'bout that. You got two days to get the bucks. If not, you've problems, man. Big problems. Me and me friends destroy if we don't get what we want. Expect more than a tickle to your throat next time.' Drake drew a long forefinger slowly across his throat with a hideous leer. It left Stone in no doubt about his meaning.

'Don't be dumb. Banks don't dish out $250,000 just like that. So get real.'

Drake pretended not to hear, turned his back and started to walk away. Over his shoulder he said viciously, 'You ain't seen nothing yet, what we can do on a dark night. And all nights are dark in St Lucia. People like you always get money when you want. And I tell you, you want it now. Real bad. You'd better get it and get it quick, man, or you've had it.'

'You won't get away with that gangster crap, beach bum. Scum like you never do,' Stone called back heatedly. 'It's a small island and you'll get caught and put in the slammer for a long, long time.'

Stone only just caught the soft-spoken reply as Drake walked away.

'We know our way around, no problem, Mr Stone. Got friends in London and where we need 'em here in the islands. So do yourself a favour an' don't threaten us. Forget the police, man. They're a joke, and I can buy 'em anyway.'

It was time for Stone to clear out but he was halted by the use of his name. The voice sounded closer again.

'An' you'll need this,' it said.

Something thudded on the sand at Stone's feet.

'It's the instructions about Soufriere, where to drop the stash. Get a map and find it. Quick! I said, *quick*, man!'

Stone unwound the paper from the rock and looking up saw the silver glint of a blade trace a bright arc deep in the shadows next to the hotel. He heard a throaty laugh, then there was total silence, or so it seemed to Stone in his jumpy state, before his hearing filled with cicadas' soothing, timeless chorus. The rain clouds passed and the moon silvered the beach with calm light as if nothing untoward had happened or ever would.

Stone peered into the palms around the hotel and, seeing

no one, allowed a wave of nervous exhaustion to shake him from head to toe in the humid air.

Less than fifteen minutes before, the Caribbean beach had attracted Harry Stone like a magnet. He came to gloat over his triumph, a five-star deluxe hotel built with $3 million of carefully laundered money and soon to be sold on to make the money whiter than Swiss snow. The stylish low-rise structure easily dominated the few banana and palm trees in the newly landscaped garden and was interrupted only by the stately tower that overlooked the beach. It was as if he had built the place with his bare hands and in his mind's eye it was as valuable as some eastern temple covered in a rich tapestry and crusted with gold and jewels. It was not a building, it was *money*, the only commodity Stone traded in.

Touching the drip of blood at his throat, Stone felt anxious, bruised, alone, oppressed by a mere shadow that had threatened violence. He was amazed at himself. Why was he so easily frightened by a chancer who could menace but had no means to do harm? But the thought detained him barely a second. The dark empty beach was no place to be. He turned away from the hotel and, without a backward glance, stumbled over the uneven sand to the rented silver Mercedes coupé he had left on an unmade track. He gasped with pain and frustration as he stubbed a toe and cut his leg on a jutting piece of driftwood. Oddball and loutish Drake might be, but the fear he had so easily and quickly instilled had without warning eroded Stone's steely nerves to snapping point.

Headlights ablaze, Stone wrenched the car into drive and powered erratically at high speed along the empty road to the rented villa in Castries' outskirts. Deep potholes jarred his back as the car sped over them. Stone swore and gunned the engine the more, making no attempt to steer clear. It was now a mixture of fear and high octane rage fuelling him.

Fourteen minutes later the iron security gates with spiky

tops clicked closed behind him and only then did he feel calm return. He barged unceremoniously through the front door and barked at the surprised butler hovering in the kitchen off the far end of the entrance hall.

'Fix me a drink, Combo, one of your Rumbuster specials. And make it quick. I'm parched.'

Stone gulped lungfuls of cool air in the living room where Combo, in his methodical way, had opened the windows in two opposite walls to make a through draught. He held Drake's note to the light and read it through several times. The pencil scrawl was all but illegible on the grubby scrap but '$250K' and 'Soufriere' stood out and Stone heard the mocking voice all too clearly in the slanted 'Sir Francis Drake' signature, as if Drake's malevolent shadow from the beach stood at his elbow. Furious, Stone pocketed the note and paced the veranda decking, looking out to sea. The knife that had pricked his throat shouted to him that Drake was no mere chancer but a headcase who would kill without qualm if he didn't get his demands. Stone shuddered.

His pulsing leg demanded attention. In the bathroom he gingerly bathed, disinfected and dressed the swollen gash and the wound to his neck. His deep annoyance grew at Drake's insolent rupture of his peace and this reinforced a growing determination to outwit him and avenge himself. Arrow Hall! That's where I need to be, he thought, the Essex country mansion where he would be safe, where he could call the shots, well away from the world of crazed no-hopers like Drake. He towelled his torso with a dry flannel, changed his sweat-soaked shirt and consciously slowed his breathing. The effect was tonic and filled him with new poise and confidence. Soufriere was the very last place he would go. He returned to the veranda.

'Your 'buster, sir.'

Combo had appeared with a silver tray and Stone took the drink with a cold glare. Combo made to move away as quickly as he had come. There seemed no way to please this visitor with the icy eyes and rough manners.

A swift swig later Stone spoke curtly.

'Too much sugar in this stuff, Combo. Don't you know by now! Get me a Jack Daniel's, man, quick. No ice.'

Combo appeared to expect the order and took the Rumbuster away, with a resigned look not seen by Stone.

Deaf to the cicadas' continuous trilling in the villa's dark garden, Stone ceased pacing the deck boards. He sat in a rocking chair and stared moodily over the moonlit sea. The rocking made him drowsy. Combo silently reappeared with the whisky.

'Soda, Mr Stone?' he asked as he leaned attentively towards his guest, holding a bottle over the cut-crystal tumbler.

'To the top. Right to the edge, Combo,' Stone said impatiently and stopped rocking long enough to take the glass.

'Stay,' he ordered abruptly as Combo moved towards the door, his tone still harsh with hurt and rage.

The butler froze. 'Sir?'

'Do you have crime in St Lucia?'

'No, sir. You are quite safe here.'

'I know that,' Stone snapped. 'But do people rob each other? Are there guns? Knives?'

The butler looked blank. The question seemed somehow timid from this wealthy and assured visitor.

'I've never had no problem, sir. But there are parts of town I avoid as they say bad things happen there.' Combo paused, not wanting to annoy his important guest by speaking too much. But the precaution was wasted.

'Don't go into some parts of town! Why ever not?' Stone said testily.

'Er ... it's the gangs, sir. And some people don't work. They hang around and drink all day. And that always leads to trouble. But only late at night...'

'Sure, sure, same everywhere,' Stone cut in flatly. 'But the police. What do they do? Are they strong? Are they on the ground? Haven't seen many around since I've been here.'

Combo paused again. He saw himself as an upright citizen, attended Sunday church with wife and daughter. He also rarely saw the police.

'Mr Stone, sir, I'm sure if there was trouble the police would sort it. We have laws and most people keep them.'

Stone, restless again, paced the deck, his darting eyes telling Combo something was on his mind, but the butler couldn't tell what.

'Is there anything I can help with, sir?' he asked, stepping quickly out of Stone's distracted way to avoid a collision.

Stone paused, took a long pull at the whisky and gazed out to sea again.

'No.' He spoke less abruptly, softened by Combo's attention.

But Stone thought, I sure wish there was something he could do. This is a bitch of a place and who knows what might happen next. Of course it isn't safe. Holed up in a huge villa surrounded by a high fence is no shelter from mobsters like Drake and his gang. Stone looked into the dark and a wild thought momentarily took hold. Shouldn't he pay $250,000 for his safety? Then get the police onto Drake. But he'd never paid protection before and the extortion rackets he'd heard of were never stopped like that.

Then the idea of parting with such a sum of hard-won cash brought him back to his senses. Sweat dripped from his brow as the drink and heat infused his thoughts with a kind of fever of self-disgust. He felt he was losing control by letting a lout like Drake get to him with his cheap threats.

Combo bowed and turned to leave, sensing that what bothered his touchy guest was beyond his help.

'Where's Cutlass?'

'Drinking downtown I'd say, sir.'

'I want him right here,' Stone said peremptorily, 'now.'

'Very good, sir, but it'll take time. Bars'll be packed this late. And I may have to search a lot of dives to find him.'

'I need solutions not problems,' Stone rasped. 'I want Cutlass. Go and get him. Quick.'

'I'll leave at once, sir. Can I tell Mr Cutlass why you want him so bad?'

'For God's sake, man. Just do it. Go!'

Stone heard Combo's car start and crunch down the gravel drive. Alone, he hesitantly rubbed his now itchy throat, but desisted, not wanting to restart the bleed. He fell into the rocking chair and drifted to sleep thinking hopeful thoughts. Head site honcho, Cutlass was a six-foot-four giant with attitude, built to boss and bully. A Jamaican, he knew the island and its people instinctively, and wanted his $50,000 completion bonus badly enough to be ruthless with anyone that risked it.

A fleeting dream of Cutlass strangling Drake and hurling him into the sea flickered through Stone's mind, Stone cheering him on from his office window in the Morning Room at Arrow Hall.

Waking an hour later, Stone drained the whisky and refilled the tumbler, leaving less than an inch for soda. Needing no reminder, but wanting the assurance of the words and figures on paper, he reached under the rocking chair for the file. There they were, infallible rows of columns and figures, all in order, meticulously set out in neat bold black columns and rows of computer type. '$3,000,000'. The sum stood out double underlined at the end of eighteen pages of costs. He had laundered it into his new hotel, money slyly creamed from business deals over the years into his secret Cayman account. Stone's eye wandered down the columns, gloating at how concrete the descriptions sounded, of payments to surveyors, architects, interior designers, The

Globe Construction Co., a string of backhanders to officials, insurances, landscaping, trees and plants, water pump, pool, staffing, refrigeration, security, plus almost $30,000 unspent, more than enough for contingency expenses in this place. It said it all, a masterly deal, soon to be cashed in and about to land Stone a new fortune. That part at least had gone to plan.

Thick black clouds had smothered the moon and a squall from nowhere blew gusts of cool rain onto the deck. Suddenly even this enclosed villa, hidden from the outside world, felt inhospitable, perishable, no place for a civilised being to linger. Stone dropped his glass clumsily onto the deck, tucked the file under his arm and wondered hazily why he had not acted sooner. Ignoring the rain gusting through the wide-open windows he grabbed the telephone and dialled James O'Halloran, of O'Halloran Wise, the Manhattan realtors. James's client account of course! That's where the cash from the sale of his building sat at this minute, out of immediate reach, but his as soon as he shouted loud enough. The whisky had done nothing to slake and everything to swell his lust for gain.

'Ready to close deal, James?' Stone mouthed thickly down the line.

'Sounds like Harry. Harry Stone,' James answered evenly as if quite used to such a call. 'How're y'doing, Harry?'

'Cut the small talk, James. This is business and urgent,' Stone said roughly.

'Where're you calling from this time a day?' James asked.

'Where do you think?' Stone barked. 'St Lucia. Working all hours like you should be.'

Stone gave estate agents no quarter. They made money, they took no risk and that was not real to him.

'Call sitting on the beach with a drink and a girl working!' James, cool and mocking as ever, maddened Stone in his tense state but he just about kept himself in check.

10

'Drop the chat, James. I've built the hotel your lot've agreed to buy. Five million, remember? So stop blathering. When can you complete? I need to know. Now.'

'Harry, slow down! If you want to cash your money you'll give me space to do it my way, know what I mean?' O'Halloran hated being crowded by rapacious profiteers like Harry Stone.

'Look, James, I don't have time or patience for the runaround. The building'll be ready by the end of next week and I must have the cash in my Cayman account on the dot of Friday noon.' Why didn't James cut the crap and get on with it, Stone's grasping mind fumed.

'There's papers to sign first, Harry. You know that. Contracts, transfers, title deeds, all need seeing to. So lay off hitting me, will you.'

'There's always Goddam papers, and they're ready! My lawyers've cleared them and they're waiting for you. Trust me.'

'Harry, please say you'll come to New York to pass and sign the paperwork. It's got to be done across a desk where we see the whites of your eyes and know it's you signing.'

'It ain't like that at all, James, so don't be an ass. You know I don't come to you. It's too far, I don't have the time and New York ain't for me. It's too flashy by half.'

'If you want the deal wrapped up quick and no questions like you said, that's the way it's got to be, Harry.'

'Bunkum, James, and you know it. Just do as I tell you and courier the papers right now, DHL. I'll deal with them by return, promise.'

'Okay, okay, Harry. You're a hard man and clearly mean business. But let's meet soon.'

'Sure I mean business. That's why I want action now. There's time to meet later.'

'Harry, another thing. Don't forget. Client insists on full inspection before you get paid. Five million is big bucks and no cash changes hands until the client signs off the estate.'

'So, big deal, they want to see the place. I'm not stopping them. But no nit-picking, understand? It's finished, it's good, and I'll find other buyers double quick if you don't use your option. So no last-minute hiccups, if you want more big deals to come your way. Always remember that, James.'

'Harry, calm *down* will you. You want to sell, we want to buy. That's how it works. These deals take time and it doesn't do to rush if you want your cash safe. A slip could cost you the lot. We don't want that do we?'

'James! For God's sake, what world are you in? I'm in a hurry. I want to get out of this steaming heat before...'

'Before what?' James cut in.

'Before I die of heat stroke. That's what.' The lie dropped naturally off Stone's tongue. 'Now listen a final time, James. This is how it goes or I take my business elsewhere. Surveyors two days. Cash Friday.'

The bluster worked. 'You win, Harry. I'll courier the papers to you in the morning. But I hope we can meet someday.'

'Someday,' Stone said as he put the phone down, smiling at the deferential tone. Amazing how threat of force wins he thought, not for the first time.

Stone flopped into the rocking chair and stared at three large moths darting at the light bulb. He loathed relying on others but had no choice. For another hour he sat alone with his thoughts, the night softened with rhythmic sighs from breakers dying on the beach, shafts of moonlight haloing cloud breaks and frosting the ocean's metallic crests. He poured himself another hefty Jack Daniel's and fell into sullen reverie on the evening's events followed by fretful sleep.

It took Combo two and a half hours to find Cutlass and a further half to pull his beer-soaked frame clear of his mates in The Thirsty Pirate, the dockside bar he found him in, a flimsy shack that looked as if it would blow away like balsa wood in a puff of wind, let alone in a drinker's brawl, though the bar had actually stood there half a century and more against the odds, including hurricanes.

Keeping Cutlass calm and coaxing him home to face Stone took patience from Combo and Stone, furious at the delay, his leg sore and throbbing, was on his feet when Cutlass arrived on the deck.

'Cutlass, where the hell've you been? Tell me you got the hotel site under control.'

It was late, Cutlass's brain was dulled by alcohol, but he knew instinctively how to bluff, especially if a $50,000 completion bonus was on the line.

'Control, boss? Course I got control, Mr Stone. Nobody dares cross me. You know that.'

'And when you're away?'

'I'm always here, Mr Stone, day and night, more or less.'

'You're lying through your teeth, Cutlass,' Stone said, eyeing Cutlass's large face with a deadly stare. 'Like tonight. Where were you?'

'Why you ask questions, Mr Stone? I never let you down you know that,' Cutlass wheedled.

'I've good reason,' Stone replied, now looking away. 'Very good reason.'

'Reason? What reason? Tell me, sir. Ain't I not doing the right job for you? We finish in days, we're on time, site's tidy, and we've had no looters.'

'What about the missing TVs?'

'I told the police. You know I did.'

'And what good did it do?'

'There's been no more thieves, sir. Ain't that all right?'

Stone glared into Cutlass's bloodshot brown eyes. 'I brought you all the way from Clapham to see this through for me, Cutlass, twenty-four hours a day if necessary. I

13

brought you because you know how to get rough when called to. And site security's what I need now more than ever, night and day, every day, is that clear? And you've got a bonus to come but only if...'

'Mr Stone, if I beat up every idler you'd never get your hotel,' Cutlass cut in.

'It's not idlers I'm talking about, halfwit. It's vandals, arsonists – wreckers. Surely to God you know what I'm talking about. So, who's on guard tonight?'

The question caught Cutlass off guard. 'No one ... I've been out with the boys ... we needed the break,' he said dully, eyes averted.

'Are you *mad*, Cutlass! Between now and Friday handover is the riskiest time of all. The hotel's a sitting target to every crook wanting to make a name for himself. Cutlass, wake up! This island's seething with poverty, envy and depraved idiots dripping venom like puff adders, and all you can think of is clearing off for a drink with the boys! What the hell do you think you're doing?'

Cutlass, used to the respect his vast frame and surly expression usually won him, was visibly stung by the tirade. A vein stood out on his forehead, he clenched his jaw muscles and fists and seemed about to strike Stone.

'You should've thought of that before we built yer posh hotel,' Mr Stone,' he mumbled.

Seeing that he had got through to Cutlass and had his full attention, Stone backed off. 'Okay, okay, you just need reminding sometimes. So let's agree here and now, you'll guard the hotel with your life, twenty-four hours a day up to completion. You do know what's at stake.'

Cutlass swallowed, and seeing his bonus safe relaxed his fist. 'Sure, Mr Stone. You got my word.'

'And I don't want squatters or idlers dossing on the site,' Stone added. 'They don't help and they don't make it look pretty.'

The stand-off over and Stone's mind eased, Cutlass tried to cover his back against the unexpected.

'You know the site's impossible to seal off, Mr Stone. The fence is only spongy banana palms.' Cutlass gulped a beer handed him by Combo and suppressed the grin that flickered between the two servitors at their boss's displeasure. Stone missed the moment of insolence and remained deadly serious.

'If I say guard the place, you go to and do it, no half measures. So get out of here and get on with it.'

'Me and you always understand each other, boss. I know how you work and I'll do what you need.'

Cutlass sank the rest of the beer and crushed the can with a spasm of his large hand as if strangling a chicken. This man would never enter the real world, he thought, as he moved to the door, still wondering what had worried Stone enough to insist on seeing him with an outburst of paranoia so late at night.

'I'm off, back to the UK,' Stone announced. 'This humid heat's cooking my brain.'

Moodily he paced the deck again, his slippers sending a stealthy padding sound into the night like a ghost's footsteps, while Combo hovered, not knowing quite what to expect. Brooding, Stone left the deck for his bedroom. He'd made his feelings clear about this place, and he did not look at Combo, as if he were not there.

In the morning the wind had gone and Stone took a quick early walk along the beach. A flight of steep stone steps led to dunes overlooked by the villa and in the glistening light the scene appeared as innocent as Eden with not even a footmark in the sand. Stone walked the wide sweep of the bay to a grove of trees with thick roots that made tangled patterns just above the ground. Bored, with nothing he could do to hasten completion on the hotel, he sat on the sand. A crash of twigs in the undergrowth startled him. Two herons, long legs dangling, heaved themselves into the pellucid air to fly lazily out of sight round the headland. Stone longed to join them. Then it fell still again, ominously so, Stone thought. The sun, not yet high, burned into the sand and soon it was too hot even just to sit, so Stone sauntered back to the villa, seeing nothing but sand and sea as he scanned the shore before climbing the steps. Drake, Cutlass, New York, the tense triangle that cramped his thoughts and threatened his plans, might never have existed. If only.

Later, Stone ate lunch alone on the veranda deck, not tasting the red snapper caught fresh that day, and settled for his siesta. Combo's sunny mood shone in his ready smile, though he sensed from Stone's intense frown that last night's worries still weighed on him. Little did Combo guess that a fellow islander, a tough from Soufriere, had dared to threaten his touchy guest's life.

Waking, Stone changed, took a quick drink and instructed his Cayman bank to pay the last tranche on the hotel to the Globe Construction Co. Moving the cash drew a line under the deal, making it final, and he grinned, satisfied at his astuteness. When a minute after he had put his mobile down on the deck beside him the house phone rang, Stone let Combo take it. His watch showed it was a minute short of three.

'A Mr Roger Garon from London, sir.'

Stone sat up. At last, the real world again. He took the cordless from Combo.

'Great to hear from you, Roger,' he said with warmth.

'Harry. How's it going?'

'I'm coming home. Money's spent. Building's up. Time to scoop profits.' Stone laughed for the first time in four days.

'How much did you put in this time?' Roger asked.

'Three million US, give or take.'

Roger was taken aback, and there was a long pause before he replied.

'No kidding. Where'd it come from? I thought cash was tight.'

'Cash is always tight when you want quality, Roger. But I've a money box in Grand Cayman where I keep small change.' Stone's smirk to himself gave his voice a gloating inflection.

'Cayman Islands? That means no tax, doesn't it?'

'You got it, Roger. So quiet, please. Not over the phone.'

'And now you're laundering it through the hotel?'

'Shut it, Roger. But...' Stone's pride in his own cleverness overrode his caution. 'But, yes, now it's built, I sell it for a hundred point mark-up, take the cash back into Grand Cayman, and so it goes on. It looks legit, and no one asks where the money's from when I filter it back to the UK.'

'It's never that easy, Harry, be warned. You end up several million dollars richer all of a sudden, and don't tell me you can hide it that easily. Someone gets smart, knocks on the door, and you've had it. You're a caged bird for life.' Roger spoke prissily, like a father scolding a tearaway teenager caught thieving at school.

'Don't be so boring, Roger,' Stone said cheerily. 'I've done it before and I'll do it again.'

'Harry! You do know laundering means a long time in Belmarsh, surely? And you lose the cash. Not just you, your associates too. And when it's over there's nothing to come out to.'

'Leave it off, nanny. The game's called risk and you and I play it. It's also a fix I need, so don't spoil it. Anyway whoever got mega-rich sitting on their backside, tell me?'

'Okay, okay, it's your deal, but don't say I didn't warn you.' Roger Garon knew better than Stone what he was talking about. He had built layer on layer of trusts interwoven with corporate entities spread around the world, where

17

shareholders could never be traced if he needed to hide a deal from the authorities. To Roger, Stone's attempts at secret tricks were dangerously naïve, risky, far too direct and open to escape detection for long. Yet he knew that somehow Stone had got away with it for almost as long as he had, and was content to have sounded the now routine note of caution.

'Your call not mine, Harry. Just be very, very careful.'

'Back to reality, Roger. What did you ring about?'

'Obvious isn't it? The next deal. You up for it?'

'You bet. Go on. Make my mouth water!' Stone replied excitedly.

'It's as good as your St Lucia deal and a licence to print money just the same. You'll love it I think.'

'Don't stop!' Stone's lightness belied the greed tightening his throat.

'It's a contract to manage a dozen or more pubs around Fenfleet. That's North Yorkshire. OK? The Fenfleet brewery wants out. They keep the properties and you get to run 'em. You've done it before. You remember the ones you had in Brighton? Two-year turnaround and you can get rid of them again.'

'Sure,' Stone drooled. Of course he remembered Brighton. Some of the cash had found its way to the Cayman account. 'And the properties are all in good nick? No old shacks? When does this happen?'

'A bit above three weeks. Tight but we can do it.'

The St Lucia aggravations suddenly faded for Stone as the rush of a big new killing coursed through his veins. The chance of a lucrative deal was like mayfly to a salmon to him.

'Have we still got the people in place who can look after the day-to-day bits if we get the deal?'

'I'll find them for you. My contacts in that market are always strong.'

18

'Let's go for it then, Roger.'

'Why not for God's sake. But before you get excited there's one little problem you need to know about.'

'When did I ever let a problem get in the way? Spill it.'

'It's the tendering process. Highest bidder gets the deal. The brewery receives bids in sealed envelopes and opens them with a whole committee of hangers-on watching.'

'I know. Like an auction at an abattoir,' Stone said, sounding bored. 'Find me the price I should bid to win and I'll cut you a deal, Roger. Not too much, not too little.'

'You're on then?'

'Course I'm on. Why not? I need a new deal to get into after this place.'

'I'll see to it then, Harry. I'll do the diligence, snoop around and sense the scene.'

'Go for it, Roger. But play on the field, don't break any law and don't get caught at your snooping.' It was Stone's turn to play the prim dad.

'We don't do breaking and entering, in case you didn't know, Harry. Bit of hacking plus a modest wad to buy quality intelligence, that's my style. I'll keep you posted.'

'Sure, sure, spare me the grisly detail. Whatever does the trick.' Stone tried in vain to hide the excitement he felt.

Roger went on, 'Listen. Here's the inside story. You heard of the Trifoni Group?'

Stone wracked his brains but nothing came.

'Trifoni're big. Wealthy. In and out. Secret. Bit like you. Except they're regular in their deals.'

Stone wrote the name on a pad and considered it.

'They main bidders?'

'Only bidders serious enough to worry you. The rest won't get a chance.'

'What do we know about Trifoni?'

'Rick Austin. He runs it. He's well known in flashy parts of London.'

19

'And the Fenfleet brewery? Who's boss there?'

'James Kennedy. Forties. Nothing to pin on him yet.'

The satellite link began to echo. Stone lost patience, decided he'd heard enough.

'Let's leave it there, Roger. We'll run it through when I get home.'

'One thing, Harry. You'll pay my going rate? A thousand quid a day plus expenses.'

'I always pay your so-called expenses don't I? Just make sure you do the job and earn it this time.'

'I can't wait six months again, Harry. On the nail or no deal.'

'Okay. I was short of cash last time and I couldn't pay you from my Cayman account. Too obvious for all to see.' Stone laughed.

The satellite line went crackly, which suited Stone. He'd heard enough to be excited. 'You there, Harry?' Roger called loudly.

'See you in a few days,' Stone called back down the phone, and flung the receiver onto a chair.

Stone stood, stretched and looked out to sea from the shady deck. It was almost flat calm with a deep green reflection where the sun did not burnish it. Stone felt back in control. The world was swimming his way. The Fenfleet pubs were timed to perfection, ripe to be plucked. Chancers like Drake were a world away. First, cash and bank the St Lucia proceeds, then back into another deal, the bonus waiting for him at home. An involuntary grin lit his face.

Combo was noisily loading the dishwasher in the kitchen.

'How do I get to Soufriere?' Stone called to him.

'Soufriere, sir?'

'You heard, Combo. Come on, tell me how to get there.'

'Hour and half drive from here, sir, small village near the volcano, signposted all the way. You can't miss it. But not much happens there, Mr Stone.'

20

'No big shot residents?'

'No, sir, not in Soufriere. A few shacks, fishing boats, rough bananas, that's all. No work. It's very poor, they're all broke.' Combo's puzzled expression said it all. What in the world would a man as rich and powerful as his guest have to do with an end of the road dump like Soufriere?

'I won't find any business there then. Is that it, Combo? Good. That settles it.' Stone laughed. 'Take me to the hotel site, Combo. I want a last look, before I fly home.'

'Yes, sir.' Combo left to get the car keys and soon the two were on their way. Combo made small talk, thinking it the best way to humour his now affable guest.

'How many more days you staying, Mr Stone?'

'Two. Maybe three at the most.'

'Is it cold in England this time of year?'

'How would you know what I meant if I said yes, Combo? There's no such thing as cold in St Lucia and you've never ever seen snow,' Stone said wryly. 'Yes, it'll be a lot colder than here but the UK makes up with hot, cold, wind, rain, sometimes all together. Here each day's the same, hot. And too hot for me.'

'Sir, your new hotel. Friends who work at other hotels tell me how good it is.'

'Have you not seen it?'

'Not yet, sir. Today's first time.'

Stone stared ahead and let the breeze fan his face through the open window. He remembered the glow he had felt for his hotel before Drake interrupted his dream.

'I'll be glad to show it you, Combo. It'll bring work in plenty to you and your friends.'

'We're all most grateful, sir. I wanted to ask, any chance you could help me get a job there? I've applied for beach bar chef assistant. Pay's twice what I'm on now.'

Stone closed his eyes. He didn't care a damn about Combo

or his job hopes and felt hard and cold inside. With St
Lucia behind him he would never return. Running the
hotel was the buyer's job. Beach bar chef assistant! What
sort of bum job was that?

'Yes, I'll do all I can for you, Combo. But the new owner
will make the running.'

Minutes later Stone stood at the spot where Drake had
demanded money. The sun blazed with warmth and
brightness. Stone stared open mouthed for a second at his
glittering creation. Truly it was superb, a masterwork of his
own devising. Yes, the Yanks would love it. The sale was
assured. He saw Cutlass and cheerily called him over.

'No problems, Cutlass?'

'Boss. Problems? What kind of problems, boss?'

'Thugs. Vandals. Squatters. Anyone out to make mayhem.
Remember our chat?'

'Oh, no, no, Mr Stone. Nothing at all like that.' Cutlass
spoke reassuringly. 'All's just as you see it, calm and quiet,
not a thing to worry about, boss. I honestly don't know why
you have us guard it. Nothing ever happens here.'

'Glad to hear you say it, Cutlass. Remember, buyers inspect
day after tomorrow. Keep surveillance on red alert until
they've been. Oh, and ensure the site's impeccable in all
the bits that show, plants watered, pool full, building
immaculate, air conditioning on. You get your bonus the
instant the deal goes through. Okay?'

'Sure, Mr Stone. Can I show you? Want to see inside?'

'No. I leave it in your able hands, Cutlass,' Stone said
crisply. 'But you just remember, drinking and bonuses don't
mix. Right?'

As they shook hands, Stone felt the sweat in Cutlass's
palm. Stone turned on his heel, strode to the car and slid
onto the rear seat through the door held open for him by
the dutiful Combo.

The survey inspection went without incident and Stone,

at ease on the villa deck, signed off the agreements couriered from New York, his signature witnessed by attorneys from Castries. He shared a bottle of champagne with the surprised lawyers and visualised the $5 million cascading into his bank account. Now at last it really was time to go home.

Combo did Stone's packing and Stone pressed ten twenty-dollar bills into the butler's hand, receiving a wide smile and neat salute in return as he climbed into the chauffeured Daimler.

An eager porter met the large car as it drew into the airport, unloaded the luggage and pushed the trolley into the departure hall. Stone's heart missed a beat as he stopped short in front of a coal-black face with a wispy beard, insolent eyes and strong white teeth that flashed as the words left his lips.

Stone felt his neck hair bristle at this most unwelcome intrusion of a threat he had thought to be about to leave behind forever.

'Remember the deal, man, $250,000? Drake says "Hi" to remind you.'

Stone tried to push past, determined to check in and board his flight. But the man grabbed him in a vice-like grip.

'Let me go, you scum!' Stone shouted, yanking his arm free.

But the unwelcome messenger persisted. 'Check your fine hotel before you go to London, man. If you fly away without paying you'll find Drake was a bargain at $250,000.'

With a malicious V sign the man vanished into the crowd around check-in, leaving Stone unwilling to follow. Suddenly his day was drained of excited anticipation of returning to Arrow Hall. He felt shaken, sick even, as he caught up with the porter and watched his luggage being unloaded at the first-class desk.

'Leave it,' Stone told the porter. 'I've a call to make. Stay with the luggage until I get back.' He handed the porter a ten-dollar note.

Stone suddenly smelt the dingy, dark and dusty concourse. A gang of ragged labourers, some with stained T-shirts, others bare chested, was laying new floor. The crowds of departures, arrivals and hangers-on were an amorphous mass, shabby, smelly, chaotic. Stone swore as he criss-crossed the hot building, shoving the press of humanity rudely aside, until he found a grimy old-fashioned telephone hidden away in a dark corner. Urgently he dialled Cutlass and as he waited he felt the humidity soak his shirt with a cloying and malodorous syrup of sweat and water. The phone rang for two minutes before it was answered by a woman's sleepy voice.

'Get me Cutlass. The large Jamaican.'

'Mr Cutlass isn't here.'

'Where is he?' Stone snapped. 'My flight's waiting.'

'I've no idea. He's guest here, not prisoner.'

'I need him urgently. Can you get him to the phone, please.'

'Is there a message?'

Stone thought for a moment. 'No message,' he said and abruptly hung up.

He'd made up his mind. He was going back to London. Immediately.

He fought his way back through the crowd to check-in. Just as he gave orders to the porter to unload his luggage the man with the beard reappeared beside him.

'You better believe Drake's message, man. You'll need to sort y'er hotel first, yes you do, man. You no want to go to London before you get Drake his money or you're in trouble. *Big* trouble, an' time's running out, man.'

Stone looked hard at the man. He was a mere boy, but lithe and wary as a thief. The menacing eyes reminded him sharply of Drake's on the beach. But Stone now had his passport and ticket in his hand and the porter had pulled his three heavy leather cases onto the belt for loading.

'Get out of my way, you nasty piece of trash,' Stone shouted at the young man, impervious of the hundred pairs of hostile eyes that swung on him in the surrounding throng. He seized his boarding pass and passport and frantically barged his way to the final security check to get into the departure lounge, away from the evil youth. It was then, drenched in sweat, waiting for his flight to be called, that Stone remembered that the payment to his Cayman account was not due for another three days.

# 2

Stone flew by helicopter. He sat next to the pilot, who looked no older than the boy who had menaced him at the airport, his palms sweating as the shivering, shouting, lump of metal moved violently in dense cloud. But it descended slowly, nestled onto the beach, and Stone silently eyed the pilot's deft manipulating touch. There was deep darkness with coal-black clouds looming as Stone nimbly jumped from the chopper. But the washed grains of sand slowed him as he ran towards his hotel.

'Jees,' a half word whistled through his heavy breath. A hundred metres off, the scene of random, ugly, chaos pointed accusing fingers at the sky. 'Somebody's going to be minced and fed to the sharks for this,' he finished.

A mechanical digger, a giant clawed animal, had torn into his living temple. The carnivore was precariously reared up, attempting to climb further into the carcass, looking for more morsels. It would bite another chunk if anyone tried to interfere. Stone's eye momentarily moistened.

Only fragments of the strong pink wash now showed on one side of the L-shaped structure, its middle tower pulled to the ground. Jagged lumps of block lay in haphazard heaps over the pristine beach and wispy curtains from the ground floor windows floated limply in the light breeze as if they had been opened just to air the place. Banana trees, never strong, had been trampled messily to a sandy green flatness.

'What for?' he murmured as he stared. 'Why?' His agitation for a moment barred his temper as he surveyed the ruined chaos of his money-making venture.

and it had been stolen. Dollar bills had been thrown in the wind and the full force of a human hurricane had torn them up as useless.

Stone got in the car, ignoring the whiteshirt holding the door. He saw Pemberton as an ineffective man who would make heavy noises but get nowhere. He didn't look back. He had already decided that revenge for him had nothing to do with courts and the slow process of the law. Five years was not long enough for a hoodlum like Drake.

As they moved forward Stone pointed to the radio. 'Turn that racket off.'

The driver looked over his shoulder, the grin went from his face and he flicked the switch. Quietness tempered Stone's anger. He leaned his head on the back of the seat, letting it bump in tune with the uneven road.

In twenty minutes Stone was back at his villa. He rang the agent and arranged to rent it for two more days. Combo had spent the few hours since Stone had left tidying and cleaning, and was surprised to see him back. After unpacking his clothes and arranging valeting and laundry he quickly prepared a Jack Daniel's and soda precisely to the levels Stone liked.

The moon flickered uneasily through the clouds and Stone's mood was volatile as he again rocked on the veranda.

On the cordless phone he punched in the numbers for Claire Watts at Arrow Hall where he knew it was past midnight. Claire was still up.

'Where are you? You should be in the air,' she said as soon as she heard Stone's voice.

'No. Small problem's come up. I've got to stay on for a couple of days. Re-date my ticket for Sunday night and tell Anton to be at Heathrow Monday morning. Sharp. I won't want to hang around.' Stone's voice was tight, unusually so, and it alerted Claire.

'What sort of problem?'

'Don't want to talk about it over the phone. But I gotta clear it up.'

'Of course,' Claire said easily.

'Yeh. And one other thing. I don't want anyone to know where I am. St Lucia's now a closed secret. Okay?'

'That's how it's been all the time. Roger Garon knows. The travel agent thinks you're on holiday.'

'Good. Let's keep it that way. So anything new at home?'

'There's a letter from the Inland Revenue. They want a meeting with you.'

'Meeting? With me? What for?'

'It's from the Special Inquiry Branch. They want you in their offices. In London.'

'When?'

'Wednesday week. They suggest you should take your adviser.'

'Special Inquiry Branch? What the hell's going on? You'd better find what they're on to.'

'I've already rung but they won't say. Just that they need to interview you.'

'Well, I'm not going then.'

'Clive Pontin at Stead White says you have no choice. Otherwise it'll cost big time.'

'I don't want Pontin in on it. Those nosey accountants know too much already.'

'He warns to be careful. That department of the taxman has big powers. Clive says they can take you apart even down to how much you spend on a bottle of whisky.'

'Claire, leave it. I've got enough to sort out here. Stuff the taxman's letter. Fix my ticket.'

Quickly Stone shut the phone down, not wanting to hear more. The taxman was never on his agenda. Sipping his Jack Daniel's he stared straight ahead suddenly feeling hot, his world turning sour, closing in on him. He'd heard of the Special Inquiry Branch, he'd been warned of their methods, they got what they wanted. Unpaid tax, plus as much again. And then they never went away. What did they know?

'Sir, is there anything I can get for you?' Combo was close by, anticipating Stone's mood.

'Get Cutlass.'

'Yes. I've heard about your hotel, sir. Bad news travels quick. I'm sorry I didn't tell you of some of the corrupt people we have here. I never thought...'

'Leave it, Combo. We'll deal with it. In our way.'

Combo moved away quickly and Stone closed his eyes. For a moment Claire's call was blotted out and he saw the depths his revenge would take for the heist on his money. There would be no waiting for arrests and attorneys, there would not even be a struggle, just a cold-blooded, merciless fix, with knives if necessary.

Money! What scoop were the Special Inquiry Branch onto? Cayman accounts? Had he been shopped? The thought made him sweat. Combo handed him his second Jack Daniel's.

Cutlass arrived at 1.00 a.m. He was not offered a beer but was left standing for ten minutes in the darkness of a side room, perspiration dripping freely from his heavy-jowled face as he moved uneasily from one foot to the other.

Yes. He'd heard the news too. And he was agitated.

Stone drained his whisky, savouring the last drop, and in a thunderous voice, his eyes narrowed to slits, he exploded.

'You've lost your $50,000 bonus and you're about to lose your fatarse skin! What've you been playing at while these chancers have their way?'

'Boss, I'm sorry.'

'Shut up!' Stone screamed. 'You're too late to be *sorry*. You got problems. *Big* problems, you bungling cowboy.'

'Do we know who did it?' Cutlass asked timidly.

33

'A man who calls himself Drake. Sir Francis Drake. Lives near Soufriere.'

Cutlass let out his breath heavily. 'Sir Francis Drake?'

'Shut it!' Stone shouted and stood to face Cutlass squarely. 'You don't ask the questions. You listen to me like you didn't before.'

'Mr Stone, whatever he's called I'll go and find the bastard. I'll get him.'

'More than that. Revenge.' Stone's clenched fist, knuckles showing, came close to Cutlass's eyes.

'I know how to do revenge, boss,' Cutlass said, backing off. 'You want some butchery.'

'Quit the details,' Stone said quickly. 'You know how I work.'

'Sure, boss. I know what's needed.'

'This time's final. For you as well if you don't finish it.'

'It ain't relaxed here no more,' Cutlass said, almost to himself.

Stone's stare focused on Cutlass's bloodshot eyes. 'Listen hard or you'll find Clapham's a dangerous place when you get back.'

'I promise, boss, I'm not going home 'til the job's done.'

'No you aren't.'

'Are you staying too, Mr Stone?'

'That's my business, not yours. Okay?'

'Sorry, sir,' Cutlass said, eager to get away.

'Drake's the name. And you make him erupt like the volcano where he lives. And forty-eight hours. Forty-eight hours. For a dumbwit like you that's just two dangerous days.'

Cutlass nodded and after ten seconds lumbered with purpose from the dark, hot deck. He had let his boss down, his drinking was to blame and Stone would show no mercy if he didn't sort it. There was little he remembered of the night when Stone had first called him to the villa. Then

34

his boss had been upset for reasons he didn't know. But that was Stone. This man was volatile – talk about a volcano, Cutlass thought – and to be exposed to his explosive temper in the heat of the Caribbean, where the sun boiled the inner rage, was something he didn't want to think about.

Cutlass drank hard with his mates in St Lucia. Rum washed along with frothing beer straight from the bottle. He knew the Vigie waterfront around Port Castries, all its bars, where seamen and islanders drifted in the torrid heat. But he hadn't heard of Drake. And *Sir Francis Drake*? There had been no whispers of anything big planned or this man's curious name. How had he missed it?

Cutlass's interest in Drake was aroused. Anyone who hit Stone was serious and Cutlass's own animal instinct told him he wanted to examine the whites of Drake's eyes.

*

Cutlass's room, in a small block close by the waterfront with no air conditioning, not even running water, was very hot. Its outlook was not the blue sea but an oil storage farm of glinting metal. But Cutlass slept well that night, and rose from his sweaty bed about eleven the next morning. Without shaving he slipped on a T-shirt with green and red blotchy stains, and his working jeans, which were smeared with a mixture of earth and oil.

An enticing barbecue smell wafted through the open window from the restaurant below as he left his bare cell.

With two of his chosen mates, both oversize, he walked through lethargic back streets to the dockside bars. They were opening slowly with a yawn and those who made their living in night-time ways were stirring.

The sun was high as Cutlass entered a bar fronting the dockside, near the banana warehouse but within sight of

Government House. There was a single-mindedness to Cutlass's stride that said this was definitely a business call.

Corrugated sheets of iron shielding a bare concrete floor, and open wooden sides painted in a mute brown, were not inviting. A mangy dog slept in the shade, motionless as if dead, and inside there were upturned boxes for tables and benches for chairs. Dud unemployables sprawled at any time of day around the doorway in effortless poses and music blared through the still air, summoning attention to its offerings. Alcohol.

Cutlass had never frequented this shack, the 'Sunray Bar', as it was even below his low standards. But he had a warm feeling of being at home in this part of town even with its smelling, rotting, garbage and abandoned, oily trucks. Instinct now led Cutlass and his mates.

They sat on high rickety stools at the bar, facing a row of half-empty bottles ranged on a clumsy shelf out of reach. Dressed sparsely they passed easily as deckhands from a tramp ship, the type of vessel that called any day to unload its crew for onshore adventure.

A lanky youth with a moustache, a toothy grin and a freshly pressed red flowered shirt, too clean to be in this place, served their beers, incongruously in long glasses.

'We've a message for a man called Drake,' Cutlass said. He wiped his mouth of the foam from his beer. 'We hear he wants to get down to Venezuela to join his boat, the *Green Haven*. It's been sheltering the hurricanes.'

The bartender looked up, unsmiling, and said nothing.

Cutlass continued. 'Venezuela's where we're going next and we need a deckhand. So where do I find him?'

There was a shrug of the shoulders, the boy's mouth stayed shut and he walked away. Noise erupted from the other end of the bar, with demands for drinks.

Cutlass watched patiently. They drank their Carib beers in silence, but perhaps more quickly than the languid day would have enticed. It was five minutes before the bartender came to them again, the toothy grin now more muted. Cutlass pushed a small wad of dollar bills openly across the bar, kept his large fist on them, and focused his eyes on the startled lad. He rolled from the stool to show his height and spoke in a strong booming voice above the level of the blaring music. 'Tell me where I find Drake and get paid or get an almighty bust-up in this shack. And a bust-up'll ... you won't find work easy for a long time. Which you prefer, man?'

There was a tight gasp from the youth. 'Okay, mister. You got it. You want more Caribs too? The rum bottle?'

'No. You just tell me what I ask for. Then I leave you alone. Got it?'

'I don't want no trouble, mister.'

'Good. You understand me,' Cutlass replied.

The bartender was cowering, exactly where Cutlass wanted him, and he heaved his large body back on the rickety stool.

The youth continued, his voice a nervous quiver. 'I'm just a good hard working boy. I got a mamma and sister to keep and I only drink Carib. Sometimes.'

He grabbed the unexpected gift of dollar bills.

'I've only been there once, mister, but I listen to what I'm told. Got me? Soufriere Town. Then the road up to the volcano. It's wild up there, man, but a mile on there's a green shack right on its own by the bananas, called Columbus Hideout. You get to the sulphur springs you gone past it. Ask for Christopher Columbus. And please don't say I sent you, man. He don't like no one to know where he lives.' The youth paused and felt the dollar bills, soft in his hand.

A nutcracker was now enclosing the naïve bartender with the white teeth and it would crush him if he moved. He knew who ruled without question in the gangs, who was paid to be in a pocket, but troubles he heard from a distance.

He had a job, hard to get, and he wanted to keep it. His words quickly trailed off, obliterated by the music. He was unnerved by the dangerous demands made by this big black man and his friends.

Cutlass's stare added anger to his bloodshot eyes as he banged his empty glass on the bar with an echoing thud like thunder, shaking the shack.

'Don't play with me, boy. You're making it up. So what you got to tell me that's true and I can believe?'

The youth again saw his future drain away. He blabbered quickly. 'His mates come in here. I give 'em drinks for free. They talk about the big man all the time, sometimes they call him Christopher Columbus, sometimes Sir Francis Drake. They show me pictures of the banana trees he owns over Soufriere and tractors bring bananas down here for the boats. Believe me, mister, it's true.'

Cutlass saw the fright in the bartender's eyes and knew he had got what he needed. He stood, drained his glass, and walked quickly to the door.

'If we don't find Christopher Columbus living with Sir Francis Drake by these sulphur springs we'll take you to some very nasty snakes that crawl in the jungle up there. And then what happens to your sister and your mamma? Got it, man?'

Cutlass's parting words jangled in the bartender's ears and as the three men left he poured a generous measure of cheap island rum. In the bright sunlight Cutlass suddenly enjoyed the menace instilled in the unsuspecting barman whose day had begun with a warm benign feeling. It had all been too easy.

It was sunset when Cutlass left Castries. He hired an old, rusty taxi at the dockside with a driver who did not talk, and rested his arm easily out the window as they drove the coast road winding like a spiral from Castries. It was bumpy, rutted, fit only for farm vehicles and it shook Cutlass and his mates until they became insensitive, irritable and dripping in their own pools of sweat. After an interminable half hour Cutlass closed his eyes and dozed.

The cabbie brooded as he drove on the uneven track. He knew where he was going but the less he spoke the less he would be questioned. As they reached a small wooden shack on the edge of a dense banana plantation, primitive in its roughness and position, and painted vermillion green, Cutlass's humour was malignant. He needed a drink. Two abandoned pickups in the disused garden showed nature was regaining its rightful place, smothering unwelcome intruders. A naked bulb on a long flex swung over an open door and a light wind hummed easily around the dense bananas. This place was as close to nature as it was possible to be, with a creepy, timeless, feel. You could understand why this man called himself by a name from a bygone age.

Cutlass stopped the driver a few yards past the shack.

'Shove off, man. Go have a drink. Be back in half an hour and we drive back to Castries,' he said. He gave the driver five dollars which split his face into a wide grin.

The track was now very dark, the only light coming from the bulb over the cabin porch. Cutlass trampled through the rough grass to the front door with definite purpose. Without knocking he swung the door open and barged in. It was stark. No furniture filled the small room. Rough boxes improvised as seats and empty beer bottles littered each corner. A youth was entwined on the wooden floor with a naked girl half his size, their clothes lying in an untidy, colourful heap by their side. The youth rolled over and looked up, puzzled, into the staring eyes of the brooding Cutlass. And Cutlass showed no embarrassment, he had seen many more erotic scenes than this.

'What you want, man? Why you interrupt when I just get going?'

Cutlass hovered for a moment, kicked a beer bottle and boomed, 'You the famous man Drake? Or Columbus?'

The youth sat upright, his eyes wide, alert to these visitors. He wanted to hear more.

'Why you want to know?'

'I got news for such a big man. But you gotta come outside to get it. Too private in here.' Cutlass stared at the girl who jumped from the floor and covered her naked breasts with a colourful skirt. Her eyes, small and round, widened with fright as she retreated to a back door.

With a grin of pleasure, the youth followed Cutlass. His name had been used, and what was the news this guy had promised? Outside on the small deck enclosed by the fronds of banana trees he was hit in the face by Cutlass's sledgehammer fist. Cutlass's two assistants piled heavily on top, yanked the youth's arms behind his back until the elbows brushed the short hair at his neck, and with a thin rope that bit deep and brought blood to his skin, tied the wrists. Drake made no resistance, he was not allowed to, and a rough rag bound tightly round his mouth, jarring it open to show his teeth, ensured there were no words that could summon mercy. A faint gurgle, like a baby waiting for its food, was lost in the cool night air.

Cutlass pulled the limp body upright by the hair, and Drake stumbled like a drunk as he was dragged into the dense, dark, wet banana grove. The tangled mass of the large leaves, not stirred by any breeze, and damp grassy undergrowth, was all that flourished here and the wide-eyed fear now showing on the youth's face was not seen by Cutlass and his men as they pushed further into the grove. Cutlass had not come just to deal out fear and it excited him as they carried out their real purpose with a single-mindedness that bordered on extreme pleasure. The revenge Stone had demanded was extracted mercilessly and the fear the youth had shown was well justified. In the end he was very quiet.

# 3

Tiredness etched his hollow eyes as Stone touched down at Heathrow. A first-class seat, two glasses of whisky, a sleeping pill, but still he had not slept. Anton, sporting a trendy black leather blouson, newly pressed grey slacks and a smile on his stubbly face, met him in the crowded arrivals hall.

'Let me take your bags, Mr Stone,' Anton said as he grabbed the loaded trolley.

'Thank God you're here.'

'I hope you had a good journey, sir.'

'Tiring. Boring. Let's get out of here. Quick. I hate these crowds.'

'Get you home quick as I can sir. Leave it to me.'

'I don't know how people do this for fun,' Stone said as they walked from the busy terminal. 'That plane was full of noisy holidaymakers and kids shouting and crying. Ugh!'

'I've never done it, Mr Stone.'

'Don't try then.'

'But it's an adventure for them isn't it? I mean not everyone goes to the Caribbean.'

'If that's an adventure you can keep it.'

'Have you missed Arrow Hall, sir?'

'You bet,' Stone said. 'I like it quiet.'

Anton pushed the rattling trolley fast and then waited for Stone to catch up.

'The weather here's been awful,' Anton said. 'Lots of rain. No sun. And with you away Arrow Hall's been very slow. Creepy slow.'

'Come on, Anton. With a house in the middle of the

41

country what do you expect? You want motorways and noise, you live in London.'

'Yeh. But you can spend all day at Arrow Hall and see no one. No one.'

There was silence as they descended in the crowded lift to the car park but once in the claustrophobic concrete gloom Anton continued.

'Was St Lucia successful, Mr Stone?'

'I don't pay you to ask nosy questions, Anton. And I never talk about my business. You know that. Anyway St Lucia was too suffocating hot. I'm not going back.'

'Sir,' Anton responded evenly. He dutifully opened the door of the Jaguar, loaded the bags into the boot, and Stone slumped heavily and without speaking onto the leather of the front seat. They left the airport by a side road and Anton expertly weaved through early morning traffic, Stone's head nodding with the car's gentle movement. His eyes were closed, but he was not asleep, alert to every noise.

Arrow Hall was an hour and a half from Heathrow. Once a grand manor house in the Essex countryside sixty-five miles from London, it had an old exposed timber frame, hardened, blackened, now showing a solidness that could never wear away. Three hundred acres of land, once farmed but now left fallow, with scrub, trees and scampering rabbits randomly littering the area, surrounded the house. Arrow Hall was isolated from prying eyes. And that was how Harry Stone liked it.

Stone made money but never spent it freely. Except on himself. Arrow Hall was decaying, it no longer had an appearance of nobleness and splendour that the long history of the place should give it. Inside, dark heavy oak panelling made it claustrophobic. Outside, plaster flaking from the northern corner had left a scar, and peeling paintwork made it look like an urban slum. Gutters leaked dirty water, staining the walls both inside and out, and the tall, twisted, angular chimneys, patterned with dark red brick, were unused. The original outline of a moat with shallow grassy banks could still be found but it no longer held water or wildlife. The gardens had lost the battle against weeds and overgrown shrubs, a battle which nature always fights against disciplined order if left alone.

Heavy iron gates to the long gravel driveway, rust encrusted, with green mould growing freely and claiming them as part of nature and blending them into the towering trees which shielded the manor house, were stuck permanently open. For several years the estate had slowly rotted. Local villagers, farmers and visitors talked in the pub and church about its owner as a curiosity. Some remembered Arrow Hall before Stone, when it was known for its manicured gardens, rich in colour, and as a house which stood proudly dominant. It had been the noble's house, it had controlled local money and patronage with work, even food.

The Jaguar crunched slowly up the gravel driveway. It was raining lightly and Stone stirred, feeling cold.

'Home, sir,' Anton said brightly.

'Yeh. We start again. And Claire had better be ready.'

Anton sensed Stone's unsmiling mood and silently began to unload the car.

Claire was in her flat in the west wing of Arrow Hall when she heard the car on the drive. She had lavished her own money on decorating and furnishing the wing and it was now elegant, light and airy. Curtains floated at the windows, and soft furniture with deep carpets made an oasis in the dimness and decrepitude of Arrow Hall.

In front of a full-length mirror in the small hallway Claire hesitated momentarily. Dark shoulder-length hair and thick eyebrows made her face look heavy, and her loose-fitting clothes hid a petiteness that could make her alluringly attractive. But being finicky about her appearance was not Claire's style, and there was no time to change.

Claire was easy going, but with an intensity and a perfectionist efficiency in her work which gave her frown lines on her forehead. Working for Stone they had gradually deepened. The cheval mirror looked back at her as she tried to relax her face but the marks showed and even when she smiled the deep lines left traces.

Suddenly feeling that the tempo of life would increase again, she turned away and a smile came to her lips. A new deal in Arrow Hall's intricate money web would return with her boss, she was sure of that, and it stirred her from a fog of inaction. She went to the kitchen. Hot Earl Grey tea strained from tea leaves and left to stew for a few minutes, with a slice of lemon to revive, was what her boss would now want. A barrage of questions from her would be ignored.

Stone pushed through the solid oak door into the cool house, leaving Anton to handle his luggage. Habit took Stone straight to his study where he sank his tall frame into a high-backed leather chair set against a Victorian desk of richly polished oak. The desk was clear of papers, Claire had seen to that, and Stone tilted back, rested his head and closed his eyes. The desk faced an eastern window on the ground floor in a room described by the previous owner as the 'Morning Room'.

The St Lucia deal was dead, he knew that. The dark face of Drake and the steamy intimidation at the airport momentarily flashed into his mind. How had Cutlass finished the job? He didn't want to know and he shut it out.

Another deal was now capturing him. Fenfleet pubs. Yes, there were things to do. Suddenly Stone was wide awake as if pricked by a pin and he shouted loudly as he often did when he needed something.

'Claire? You there?'

Claire kept her relaxed smile as a minute later she placed Stone's tea in front of him.

'Welcome home. I hope you had a useful trip to the sun.
I wouldn't mind some myself.'

Stone did not even look at Claire. 'St Lucia's finished.
It's not a place I'm gonna remember.'

'Was it that bad?' Claire enquired easily.

'I come home tired and with a headache. So forget St
Lucia. We get on with something new. Eh?'

'But Roger Garon said it had gone well.'

'No. He doesn't know yet. Money's lost. Gone. Shan't see
it again.'

'What happened?' Would Stone tell her?

'Some local gangster bust up the hotel. Made it into a
pile of rubble.'

'Why did he do that?'

'I wouldn't give him money.'

'Did the police get him?'

Stone hesitated for only a moment before he spoke, his
voice strong. 'No.'

'And?'

'Cutlass did. He bust him up. Slaughtered him.'

Claire saw a satisfied glint in Stone's eye, a glint she had
seen before when he thought he'd had the last word.

'So, no more trips to the sun? You don't like the heat
anyway do you?'

'Claire, I'm forgetting it. We have to move on.'

'Yes, of course,' Claire said soothingly.

'There's something important we need to get done.'

'You haven't forgotten your meeting with the Revenue
people, have you? The taxman wants to see you. The Special
Inquiry Branch sounds ominous to me.'

'That lot? Forget it. They're just a bunch of power hungry
meddlers so I'll deal with 'em in my own way and in my
own time,' Stone said quickly. He paused and looked at
Claire through narrowed eyes, his thoughts racing ahead.
'Claire, there's something else I want to get on with, a bit

more pressing than the time-wasting Specials or whatever fancy name they call themselves.'

'Another deal?'

'Yes. There's always another deal.'

'You going to tell me?'

'I'll tell you when I'm ready. Something else needs looking at before another deal. And I'll need your help.'

'Oh yes?'

'You don't sound interested. What's up?'

'There aren't many things where you ask for my help. That's all.'

'This is different. Arrow Hall. We're going to renovate the place.'

Claire was very surprised. 'You've only been back five minutes and you want to talk about it now? It's never been a priority before so why the hurry?'

'I've been thinking about it for some time and as I came into the driveway it shouted at me. We gotta do it soon. How's that for a homecoming present?'

Claire looked into Stone's eyes. He was up to something for a hidden reason, but his motives were as impenetrable as the overgrown thickets and brambles that surrounded the house.

'You surprise me,' Claire said with a wondering look out of the window at the soggy summer's day.

'And the gardens,' Stone added. 'I want the experts brought in. We'll find out how it looked when it was first built.'

'You mean five hundred years ago?'

'Why not?'

'Why not?' Claire echoed, feeling excited.

'Yes. The gardens. They're a good place to start.' Stone followed Claire's gaze with a long hard stare through the French windows to the overgrown shrubbery. Pockmarked with rabbit holes, it ran along the edge of the lawn and enclosed two sides of the house. Heavy rain was falling and moved the gloom of the day into the 'Morning Room'. There was no smile on Stone's ashen face, just deep lines of tiredness under his eyes that hid an adrenaline rush at getting Claire tied in. His plan was already running.

'It'll be a big job. So what do you want me to do?'

'Get onto the hotshots who know about these things. No cowboys.'

'Definitely no cowboys,' Claire said cautiously. 'Especially if we're to keep it true to its history.'

'Good. And let's show the woman's touch in a few places too, eh? That's when we choose curtains, carpets and colours.'

Stone was still staring through the French windows at the abandoned garden. Renovating Arrow Hall was definitely on his mind, but Claire, looking at his tired face, found no trace that this was just a manipulating scheme. But it didn't quite add up. Would she really be allowed to help? Unlikely, she thought. Stone didn't work that way. She watched him, instantly suspicious of his motives, as he noisily sipped his tea.

Rain was falling heavily, making little rivers on the driveway's scattered gravel. The June sun had not shone much and the long awaited promise of summer was passing without being seen. Trees and flowers were in full bloom but childhood memories of picnic days by the sea were unobtainable, as if they had been purposely blotted out.

Claire's frown deepened and she spoke slowly. 'If we're to renovate Arrow Hall, I have one condition.'

Stone looked up without smiling. 'I don't accept conditions, Claire. You know that.'

Claire laughed. 'You'll have to accept this one or it won't work,' she teased.

'Oh,' Stone said, unused to Claire's relaxed mood. 'Tell me more.'

'I want your promise that this is really going to happen. That's all.'

'Claire, start straight away. Go and get on with it.'

'Good. Tomorrow.' But Claire paused still uncertain. She knew there was more to come.

'I have another deal,' he said briskly and turned away.

The lines on Claire's forehead suddenly concentrated again. 'Ah. Yes. Something exciting?'

'Business the way I do it is always exciting. And this time ... well wait and see.'

'Of course,' Claire said. 'Should I know more?'

'Some pubs at Fenfleet.'

'Fenfleet? Where's that?' Claire asked. 'I've never heard of it.'

'Up north. You will. We'll maybe go there sometime. But for now we gotta work fast. Like very fast, Claire. This one'll be different.'

'Sounds ominous.'

'No. Just different.'

'I thought Roger Garon was helping you.'

'He is. But we've to put in a bid. It's not a negotiated deal. I can control those. And Roger's too slow. Maybe we gotta find other ways...'

'Other ways? Other ways for what?'

'Getting the right bid in.'

Stone ran his hand through his hair a gesture that told Claire his mind was on a new single track. The tense lines on his face slowly relaxed and even the outline of a smile creased his lips.

'Money, business, it's all murky. And this time it sounds to me as if you're hedging,' Claire said.

'You just be ready to move with me if we have to go without Roger. Be ready to do what I ask. Okay?'

'Sure. But when?'

Stone paused, fiddled with a silver pen, and then looked at Claire, for the first time noticing her fair skin, arched dark eyebrows and absence of make-up. He looked away.

'Soon,' he said quickly. 'But no more questions. They make me nervous.' Stone's cheeks creased slightly and he gave a hollow laugh which rang through the room.

Claire left quickly, not wanting Stone's laughter, however empty, to finish, because it so rarely began.

Stone's wife Sofie had upped and gone fifteen years before. She had put up with his sultry ways and blazing temper for a long time, partly because she had lived comfortably and her credit cards and cheques were met with little question, and partly because she had nowhere else to go. Sofie walked out on Christmas Eve to make the point that life had to change. Particularly at that refocusing time of the year.

Ivy had grown thicker, covering more of the house, weeds had slowly, relentlessly taken control in the gardens and Stone, too busy dealing, barely noticed Sofie had gone. But Claire had felt the change.

She now arranged flowers Stone rarely noticed, and organised the household. His past business deals, only the bits he wanted her to know about, were filed in her neat mind. She was discreet and Stone took her for granted as he had Sofie.

Stone sipped his tea. The time difference on returning from St Lucia had caught up with him and his eyes, red tinged, were heavy, he was ready to sleep. St Lucia was dead and the bright prospect of the Fenfleet deal, with Claire on side, loomed. Exhausted Harry Stone went to his bed.

# 4

The woman with unruly hair, dressed almost entirely in black, stood up. Now she had heard enough. The interview was short, sharp, the beginning of an unstoppable process that would inexorably wear its way forward. She took a final look at her papers, satisfied with her hour's work and that her opponent was in a corner.

'Mr Stone, this is what we call a preliminary meeting. This is a list of the information I require and when you've got it together we shall meet again to review it and see where it takes us. We will contact you very shortly to bring the documents in. You'll be at Arrow Hall?'

'That's where I live. And I ain't going anywhere.'

'No,' she said, and looked over her glasses at Stone. She had seen the cocksure reaction before, it never won because she knew how to beat it, and she had given little away but that this taxpayer was on notice she was after him.

Stone had arrived at the cold, impersonal tax offices confident enough in his own paper trail to ride out the Revenue investigation. They were spongers who deserved the contempt he would give them, little people who would never see through or understand his big business dealings. He was a man of wealth, he had contacts, and this woman had probably never left her comfortable desk to see how the real world ticked.

He had put on a dark suit, blue check shirt and deep-red tie. He looked businesslike, regular, not a wheeler dealer. He was going to see this lot out.

But the balding young male assistant and the middle-aged woman, who constantly adjusted her glasses and fiddled with a plastic ballpoint pen, riled him for the hour long meeting in the sparse interview room. More than once he had to stop himself from walking out. Bureaucracy at any time boiled his temper and more than once he bristled at the officious bullying pressure of the woman and the sullen look of the balding young man making notes at her side. A sharp punch on the nose would loosen their immovably smug features, and a bust-up of the intimidating room so that it could not again be used for interrogation became attractive. But he thought of St Lucia. The Cayman cash. Yes, he knew too well he had to sit this out and control his disdain for all they stood for.

'Why have you called me here?' Stone had asked three times.

'Have you declared all the income from all your business interests to the Revenue?' was the parroted reply. The inquisitor had a script and she kept to it. Closely.

'You've had the forms,' Stone had responded, three times, becoming more irritable and impatient with the process each time, but it had not satisfied the woman who remained impassive and he knew there would be more to come. He wanted to ask her what she knew that had made her draw him in to this stark place, but he held off, deciding to drag it out, to play dumb and innocent.

Like sparring partners in a boxing ring, each was trying the other, searching for an opening to get a jab in the face that would make them open up and give something away. Stone had breached the immovable line before where officialdom was concerned and he would kill it now. All the cash to his Cayman account had been fed anonymously, bundles of untraceable notes by courier, bank transfers from an obscure bank in Andorra, and nobody, not even this colourless woman, would find the trail, he was sure of that. But what did she know? Why had she not told him what she was really after instead of teasing him with rehearsed questions that gave nothing away?

Fuming inside, his face tinged red, he finally strode from the room, dissatisfied, still clutching the long list of detailed information she required. Outside the grey building he took a deep breath and swore he would beat this lot. With the noisy traffic buzzing around him he called Anton on his mobile to bring the car.

\*

Stone never idled his time but now he was distracted and he could not concentrate. He lolled in the chair at his desk, he walked aimlessly in the garden and drank many cups of Claire's tea. He had his usual Glenfiddich in the evening. He was brooding in his own silent way.

Sleeping fitfully, Stone went to bed late, watched films, even black and white films, until his eyes no longer stayed open. One night he woke abruptly from a snoring sleep. Instinctively he looked at the clock which showed a few minutes before three. A heavy gust of wind waved the curtains at the open window and instantly brought Stone to full wakefulness. He sat upright and felt the hairs at the back of his neck tingle as if somebody was running their hand up them the wrong way. He'd heard something. The stairs creaking? Or an unseen presence, something from his past that might arrive in the darkness to torment him? In the middle of the night his thoughts were not rational.

He remained rigid, listening. It was quiet, it was still, except for the whispering of the wind brushing the trees. After a few seconds he got up, quietly padded to the window and peered through the curtains. Darkness flooded the grounds, silhouetted trees towered against an orange glow in the sky towards the west reflecting the street lights of the nearby town.

Nothing moved, not even a rabbit scampered in the grounds which were as quiet as a cemetery. He looked towards the garage block where Anton had a room, but nothing moved. Stone let the curtains rest, moved to the door, squeezed the handle and crept onto the landing. Emptiness, with only the inexorable, comforting ticking of the grandfather clock in the hallway below. Time was moving forward as normal.

Claire's flat along the landing showed no light or noise. Her door would be locked, and she would not creep around the house in the middle of the night making the stairs creak.

His hand dragging on the wall, Stone awkwardly trod the long stairs. Each step grated, and the threadbare carpet did nothing to dampen the noise from vibrating into the darkness. In the hallway Stone stood still, alert, tension in his neck, but he saw nothing. The front door was locked, the latch chain rattled securely as he swung it. His study was dark, cold, with a strong draught, but, in the darkness, as if to conceal any unseen presence, he closed his eyes. He was being brainless.

Solid in the middle of the room stood Stone's desk. Nothing had been moved, not even the tray of silver pens he collected. He slumped into his leather swivel chair.

Suddenly a wild thud echoed through the house. His heart pounding heavily, Stone stood and froze. The wind gusted and the crash was repeated, now sharper. Something was in the room.

'Jees!' Stone cried. 'What the hell...'

Impulsively he flicked the light switch. The French doors were open, dragging the heavy curtain which flapped in the windy gusts zipping around the garden. Quickly he slammed the doors shut and wedged them with a chair. He ran his hand over splintered wood and the scratched glass of one door. The latch had been forced. Someone had been in the house and a racing pulse stiffened his shoulders as a cold feeling held him. He'd been watched while he slept. Who would want to do that? He had no answer.

He plucked the whisky decanter from the sideboard but his mouth was too dry and stale for drink. A brooding anxiety gripped him and he sat still for a long time, staring at the window and listening for noises that no longer came.

In the morning Stone felt a lingering, tense, nervousness which he thought he could keep from Claire and Anton. Nothing was missing, there had been no violence, it was just an eerie mystery, but somehow expected.

The deal for the Fenfleet pubs was gnawing at him, added to by the pussy sore of the bossy tax inspector. It stirred his restlessness, rushing his adrenaline.

And it rubbed off on Claire. She was bright and busy but also perceptive. She confronted Stone in the morning room.

'Something's on your mind,' she said.

He looked away, annoyed at Claire's attention. But he spoke with an even tone.

'Yes. Lots.'

'Anything I can do to help?'

'No. Nothing.'

'Is it St Lucia?'

'Maybe.'

'How much did you lose there?'

'The numbers are too gross, obese, to talk about.' Stone looked sullen, answering quietly.

'What happened with the taxman? You never told me.'

'That lot are just trying to frighten me. They've given me a list of their demands for information, it's in the top drawer of my desk, so get Clive Pontin to gather everything together and then I'll go and see them again myself. It's better that way. It'll go away if we tell them enough to keep them happy. But make sure that Pontin's fees are tight. I don't want his lot having a ball on it too.'

Stone relaxed, sure that he had this unwelcome intrusive bureaucracy under control. Nobody would get at his secrets, they were too well covered, and any amount of probing would not get beneath the cover on his deals.

Claire turned away, knowing she was being kept in the dark as Stone played his own game. That was how he worked – she had never liked it but she had learnt to live with it.

'Perhaps I can tell you about Arrow Hall,' Claire continued.

'Don't push it, Claire.'

But Claire wanted to talk. She wanted to change the dull, sombre mood of Stone *and* Arrow Hall. She sat opposite him and looked into his eyes.

'I do need to tell you. I've found its history. There's a lot recorded in the town library. Did you know it was built in the fifteen-hundreds by a Sir William Wholinge, who seemed to be a Protestant friend of Elizabeth I? And James I stayed here in 1610. I wonder which room he had.' Claire looked for a reaction.

'Claire. In time. When I'm ready,' Stone said testily, not returning her stare.

'The other day renovating Arrow Hall was urgent. What's changed?'

'Be patient.'

'I'm always patient. Why can't we get on with it? What's holding you back?'

'The Fenfleet deal, Claire. Remember? Fenfleet pubs are urgent too.'

'You're keeping me on a piece of string with Arrow Hall. What's it all about? There's something you haven't told me.'

'We can't stop doing business. The world won't stand and wait while you do the easy bits. Be real, Claire.'

Stone was playing for time. He had no intention of renovating Arrow Hall, he just wanted Claire hooked into it, bait for a bigger catch.

Claire was suddenly disappointed, an inside anger growing. She stood and noisily strode from the room.

Late that afternoon she hovered by the door until the shouting down the phone, which Stone had down to a practised art, subsided. He was scribbling on a file of papers. She said nothing as she placed a letter on an empty space of his desk. The white envelope had no stamp, it was well handled and dirty, and it was addressed to 'Mr Stone' in a spidery scrawl. Claire had not seen it delivered to the box by the high iron gates and her curiosity was aroused. She wanted to tear the thing open and see what was inside.

Stone said nothing, not even acknowledging her presence, and Claire left slowly, closing the door quietly, afraid to upset the shadowy stillness.

Alone, Stone threw the schedule of figures he was inspecting onto the desk and poured a large Glenfiddich. He sipped it neat. Without opening it he impatiently brushed aside the letter Claire had put in front of him. Letters came every day and, unless they brought cheques, most times he did not want to know. Sharp phone calls were his way of communicating.

Glass in hand he moved to the window and peered into the rain as if he was definitely searching for something in the overgrown garden. He scowled when he saw nothing but trees and wet long grass stretching endlessly into the misty rain that created an ephemeral fog around the old house.

The grandfather clock in the hall chimed five, its deep resonance bringing a momentary tinge of life to the room. But it faded quickly as if its intrusion was unwelcome. Stone did not hear the sound and continued to stare, hypnotised by the drizzle and mist, as he swallowed half the whisky from his glass.

He picked up the figures on the Fenfleet deal again. Each time it looked better, its bonus was the cash that flowed like a benign stream through the business and which could be diverted at his own bidding. After St Lucia he needed that money. Like a druggie needing a fix Stone was drawn irresistibly, irrationally, to Fenfleet and he would do whatever it took to get his fill. He sniffed as if he had an advancing cold and refilled his glass, not seeing the large measure he poured. He picked up the phone and shouted.

'Claire. Get me Roger Garon.'

A smirk of expectation spread over his face like a child who has just been rewarded with sweets for good behaviour. He fingered the Fenfleet file and his eyes glinted with pleasure as if he was already handling the fruits of the deal. His mind ticked uneasily on the taxman's demands for incriminating information as he sank more whisky to edge his frustration away.

Roger never visited Arrow Hall and although he advised Stone on his deals it was from an office, small but elegant and technically efficient, in South Audley Street, Mayfair's smarter part. Roger was a refined professional, sharp, accurate, the opposite of Stone's ruthless bluntness.

'Roger,' Stone said sharply. 'I've been to see some woman at Revenue and Customs.'

'Whatever for?'

'They're asking questions.'

'What do they want to know?'

'That I've declared all my income to them. And a list of all my business investments over the past six years with full accounts, audited, as well as all bank accounts, deposits, currents, loans I've had for the past years and who can sign on them.'

'Call the guys who look after your books, Harry.'

'Already done it. And it'll cost a fortune on greedy accountants just to satisfy that bloated bureaucracy called Revenue and Customs.'

'Knowing how you deal, this sounds a bit serious to me.

The taxman has some mind-boggling powers and once they've got you they don't let you go for a long time.'

'What the hell, Roger, whose side are you on? Do you know how much tax I've paid in the past few years?'

'Taking that attitude won't help when they get their claws into you. I'd even call your lawyer if I were you. You do know they can levy pretty hefty penalties, even send you to prison if they find anything wrong. And with your affairs ... well, rather you than me, mate.'

'Hold it, Roger. I told 'em it's all on the forms they get each year. It's not as if I've ignored them.'

'Just listen, Harry. What do they know you haven't told them?'

'Don't know.'

'Cayman accounts? The deals you do on the side? Cash swills in your pockets, and that'll interest them. Take my advice. If the taxman gets his claws into you you're as good as dead. Banks won't lend. Then what?'

'Then what?' Stone echoed.

'No Fenfleet pubs. You still want to go down that road?'

'Why not? We've waited too long already. I do it my way, Roger. Hadn't you noticed I always win? Just help me forget the leeches at the Revenue. Get me your report on the Fenfleet bid in twenty-four hours. I want to know the price, how much down, how much each year, how it stacks up, and that means all the inside info on anyone who's out there who could stop us cornering the deal. I don't want Trifoni Group to get it. You got the picture?'

Roger hesitated for a couple of seconds. 'Look, Harry, first clear the Revenue investigation. Give them what they ask for.'

'I'll deal with that lot in my way. So you fill me in on Fenfleet. It's urgent. Got it?'

'You know damn well Fenfleet can't go ahead just like that. I'm working on the figures. There's a lot of detail, sums, calculations you wouldn't even understand and we've no chance of getting it right without going through them. And if we don't get it right you'll bid too high. Then you lose a fortune. A fortune, Harry.'

'Forget fancy calculations. Computers don't work for me. You should know it's always the dodgy competitors you keep your eye on. It's what they offer and nothing else matters. I thought you'd been following this Rick Austin and his Trifoni lot.'

'It's not that easy. People guard secrets when they're worth money. I've been trying since you were in St Lucia to find how big Trifoni are bidding but so far nothing I can believe has come. I need more time.'

'Listen to me, Roger. We haven't got loads of time. This thing is going to walk away if you don't get it done like quick.'

'Sure. And I'm working on it. Even hacked at their computers.'

'So give me the bottom line. Does this Rick Austin take the decisions? Has he got the purse strings in his paws? Is he the one who'll decide how much they bid?'

'You heard of Apollo Searches, Harry?'

'Don't waste my time with fancy outfits.'

'You want to dig the dirt, they do it. They've traced all the directors at Trifoni Group. And Rick Austin's top of the pile. We know where he lives, where he does his wining and dining, who he does it with, but you try to get through the front door of Trifoni and you hit the security barrier. Wham.'

'So this Apollo lot aren't effective, eh, Roger?'

'Look, you can't go and ask what they're bidding. Is that what you want?' There was gloating sarcasm in Roger's voice which Stone ignored.

'Leave it. What about Fenfleet's director? The guy who says where the contract goes.'

'James Kennedy. Been there since a boy when he made the tea. Knows how it works and likes to tell everybody he knows,' Roger replied.

'Can't he be nobbled, bribed to give us the deal?'

'Yeh. Anybody can be nobbled. But Kennedy's run the Fenfleet pubs for a long time and he knows how these deals work. He's got to follow the highest bid with a whole committee of people up his backside to see he does.'

'You're too fragile to be in this business, Roger. If we're to win we've got to get to the bones, and cut through the crap. And that means doing it my way.'

'Yes. I know your methods, Harry,' Roger said.

'I play to win. I do whatever it takes. I'll buy off this Kennedy guy at Fenfleet. And then we'll get closer to Rick Austin at Trifoni. I'll find what he's bidding even if this Apollo lot can't get close. I'm gonna cover both ends of this deal. So watch me.'

'All that in the few days that are left?' Roger asked.

'I've already started, I know what I'm going to do. And who's going to do it for me.'

'Sure,' Roger replied testily. 'But how'll Kennedy respond if you dangle cash? What if he runs to the police?'

'Don't make me laugh. You know damn well he won't be making real money as a crappy pubs' merchant. So we'll make him rich beyond a few drinks. We'll make him want to give us the deal. You never seen people's greed at work?'

'You give sweeteners, you be careful. That's my advice. And it's for free.'

'Kennedy's ilk are only in it for the money.'

'Harry, kickbacks are dangerous and I'm not doing it with you. Do you hear me?'

Feeling confident, Stone drained the rest of his whisky and looked at his glass.

'We'll get into Trifoni Group first, right inside,' he said. 'No security's too strong to break.'

'Let's give Apollo a couple more days. It's the most likely route.'

'Stop whingeing, Roger.'

'I'm not whingeing. I just talk straight. And you need to get straight too. Do you know how long bribing gives you behind bars? And with the taxman getting a sniff at you you've got enough problems already. So don't add to 'em.'

'Being negative won't win this. Remember why we're doing it. I take the risk, maybe I make money later, maybe I don't. Either way you get a fat fee. Okay?'

'Harry, slow it!' Roger shouted.

'No. We do everything necessary. My way.'

'I'm beginning to wish I'd kept this deal to myself. You're too hot headed.'

'You don't understand why I get up in the morning.'

'I know why, Harry. Money. There's nothing else is there?'

'Not much.'

'Listen carefully. Fenfleet's good at the right price and on the right terms. Overbid and you've got problems. It'll drain you dry. Take your shirt. And once you're in the place there's no way they'll let you walk away if it doesn't work. Like you did...'

'Shut it,' Stone interrupted. 'Risk, risk, boy. That's me.'

'I know all that. But let's be sure of our facts before we throw money away.' Roger's voice sounded tired with the argument he knew he wouldn't win.

'Twenty-one days. That's all we've got. So we'll fix it tomorrow,' Stone said sharply. 'Arrow Hall. Make it evening. Say eight.'

'How do you know I'm free tomorrow evening?' Roger was playing for time.

But Stone ignored him.

'Don't be late. Time is very precious.' There was raw insistence in Stone's hard voice that didn't invite argument. It had an intensity that stated he had finally moved on from

St Lucia and the pub deal was the only thing in his world that now mattered. Even the probing irritation from the taxman was momentarily blotted out.

Stone threw the phone down as if it might infect him and silence enveloped the large sullen room. The rain had eased and as a tentative ray of sun broke over Stone's desk it pricked the dull atmosphere that surrounded him, and the sweet-smelling mustiness that pervaded every corner of the house wafted by.

Claire did not notice the mustiness. She lived with it every day. She placed a bone china cup of mint tea in front of Stone.

'A bit early for a drink,' she said, looking at his whisky glass.

'Helps me concentrate,' he said, looking away.

'You want me to take it away?'

'Yeh. Why not.'

Claire scanned his desk. She wanted to know what was happening.

'You haven't opened the letter I brought in earlier. Shall I do it?'

'Don't *fuss*, Claire. Clear out. Leave me alone. I've more important things than greasy letters.' He waved her away with an impatience she had come to expect and which she had learnt to ignore.

'I'm leaving for the evening then,' she said. 'I've got dinner with friends.'

'Wait. Hold half an hour. I may have something else.' Stone's demand was just a selfish impulse, a need not to be in the house on his own.

Claire said nothing. Yes, she could easily wait and as she left the room she had a sense that Stone was plotting. But what?

Stone sat forward, grabbed the grubby white envelope that had rested untouched on his desk for the last hour and with a long silver paperknife deftly slit it. He ran his hand through his hair in involuntary agitation as he quickly scanned the roughly pencilled scribble that filled the paper.

*Stone,*
*St Lucia not finished. Me revenge. Me mates in London money. 250 grand you owe. Don't pay you get killed. Get money ready. We're coming for it.*
*Drake's boys.*

Stone breathed in heavily. Drake was as dead as his Caribbean hotel. Cutlass had finished him. Feeling a clammy sweat in his palms and with a clean glass Stone poured another Glenfiddich, and ignored Claire's tea. Unbelieving he read the scrawl again. He had turned off from the Caribbean, he was onto something new. Fenfleet. So what was this about?

He swore out loud and stared through the window at the dense shrubbery at the edge of the garden. Who was out there? He drank the whisky noisily, his hand shaking wildly from a rush of adrenaline.

# 5

'Where's this come from?' Stone shouted. The noise hit the walls of the gloomy 'Morning Room' and disappeared into the stale air. Shouting released a small spurt of tension but worry lines showed on his face as he stood and started to pace the uncarpeted floorboards.

He ran a hand through his hair as he stopped by the French windows. With his palm still sweating he fingered the unstamped letter and re-read the spidery writing, but it was only a nervous impulse as he already knew what it said. With a gulp he finished the whisky, feeling it burn momentarily as it passed his throat, and his hand involuntarily touched the point on his skin where Drake's knife had nicked him.

How had Drake, unseen, found him and delivered this threat? Wasn't he hiding in his large house isolated in the Essex countryside which always gave him solitude away from prying eyes? Harry Stone was unusually ruffled, he knew he was now on notice, and an acrid smell of violence whiffed in the air.

He stuffed the note back into the envelope and pushed it aside as if it was a malignant wart that would take its own revenge if touched too much. He sat silently at his desk in absolute stillness for two minutes. The phone didn't ring, nothing stirred. He shuddered.

Nervous tension wouldn't let him sit still for long and he slowly rose, walked to the French windows and took a further look into the overgrown garden as if he expected to see Drake or the youth from the airport lurking in the shrubbery.

But there was nothing, only the rain falling from the heavy grey clouds of the darkening sky, the hovering dreariness reflecting Stone's leaden mood. He paced slowly around the room, disturbed, distracted, unsure, and twice he stopped at the French windows. He tried the handle. It turned easily and he stepped into the still air of the garden, listening, alert, as if he needed to search and find who was out there.

A minute later, feeling cold, he returned to the room, closed and locked the door with the sliding bolts at the top and the bottom which Anton had fitted only yesterday. It still did not make him feel secure.

Who had padded around this room, and who was now watching him from outside? Stone's cold eyes flashed across the starkly furnished room. He saw the two faded Constable prints on the walls, and he smelt the room's oppressive, claustrophobic atmosphere. Feeling snared, trapped like a hare by hounds, he could no longer stay here. He had to get away, he had to think clearly, to play with the cunningness that had always moved him forward when he sensed trouble. Cunningness that had always helped him avoid violence too – that he knew he couldn't deal with.

Stone placed the scrawl from Drake in his briefcase. He could shut it away now and decide if he needed to deal with it later when his temper had subsided. He opened the top drawer of his desk and took out a file on the Fenfleet contract. He flicked it open, read several papers briefly and then placed it too in his briefcase. A calendar rested on the side of his desk and he looked at it intently as if it held some secret for him. Roughly he marked with a red pen the Fenfleet bid deadline and leaned back in his chair as he considered it. He breathed heavily and swore that nothing, not even demands from cranks like Drake, would ever stop him making that deadline date.

Stone picked up the phone that was his umbilical cord to Claire. He spoke in a tone that contained total irritability.

'I'm going to Claridge's. Tonight.'

'Are you all right? What's the matter?' she asked.

'I said I'm going to Claridge's,' Stone said loudly, ignoring Claire's concern. 'Get Anton to take me there by six.'

Claire looked at her watch. It was nearly five-thirty and she tried to contain her surprise.

'You want me to call them and make a reservation?' she enquired. 'You'll need a suite, I presume. Anything else?'

Stone thought quickly. 'Yeh. A suite on the top floor. And check with the manager that their security is tight. I don't want to be interrupted.'

'How long will you be staying?'

'Book for ten days. It may be more, may be less.'

'Why Claridge's? You sure everything's all right?'

'I gotta get away from Arrow Hall. There's a lot to do on the Fenfleet deal.'

'But you can do that here,' Claire said.

'No. I'm not staying here,' Stone said firmly. 'I need to be somewhere I can feel the pace of the deal unfold, be with it each minute, and Arrow Hall's just too quiet for that.'

'I'll call Anton to be ready,' Claire said.

'Yes. Half an hour and I want to be away.'

Claire breathed in deeply. Stone's move was odd but as usual she would meticulously make the arrangements. She asked no more questions but she was puzzled. Stone's privacy was part of her job and she guarded it as closely as he required it.

Quietness again surrounded Stone and he tilted his chair backwards. His eyes darted round the room for the tenth time in the last few minutes, and he looked through the windows to the utter stillness of the grounds outside. It was warm, wet and windless, and this was not a place to stay until he'd cleared Fenfleet. Then ... he wasn't sure.

Stone dressed up to go Claridge's. He could be imposing and noticeable with his penetrating blue eyes making it difficult to ignore him. His hair was smoothed and combed and even though it was straggling over the collar of his white shirt, as he looked at himself in the mirror he was satisfied.

Yes, he was powerful and it was not only his ego telling him. He had the money, connections and motive to deal with Drake. In his own way. In his own time.

At just after six he left Arrow Hall.

'I'll call so leave your mobile on. And that's at night too,' he shouted at Claire as he climbed into the Jaguar.

She waited until the car had moved past the high iron gates and then went to the study and switched the lights on. She wanted to find the unstamped letter she had placed on Stone's desk and which he had not wanted to open. She was sure there she would find the answer to why he was moving so quickly.

But his desk was as clear as the room was quiet and not even the envelope remained. She opened the drawers but there was no envelope, just the untidy mess of Stone's own papers which he would never let Claire touch. She too now felt uneasy.

She turned the light off, shut the door tightly and went to her flat. The four large rooms in the west wing was where she felt secure. Stone dealt in odd ways, she knew that, and many times he'd dealt ruthlessly with rivals who lived east of the Tower of London, and who knew when they might call? For a few moments Claire felt cut off from the world, and Stone's departure for Claridge's had left Arrow Hall very quiet, its stillness intense. She flooded her flat with light, switched the television on to kill the silence and fastened the outer door firmly. What was it Stone had not told her? What was it he thought it best she should not know? What was in that letter? Claire pondered these questions as she began to get ready for her dinner date.

\*

The Jaguar was skilfully handled by Anton as he weaved through the familiar country lanes and headed for the motorway. Stone relaxed, closing his eyes, his head gently rocking with the movement of the car. Anton knew he should only talk if he was spoken to and he fixed his mind on the quickest route that would take them to Claridge's. Suddenly he stabbed his foot on the brake pedal. The road was wet and the surface shiny. The rubber of the tyres tore into the tarmac with a deafening screech and they held the car in a steady straight line as if it was on rails. But the approaching white Ford van, old and dirty, carrying a ladder on its roof, had no chance. It left the road without reducing speed and like a diver entering water it plunged bonnet first into the grassy ditch that lined the country lane.

Stone jolted awake as the Jaguar slid forward. From the corner of his eye he glimpsed the van move past his left shoulder and heard the thump of metal and the jingle of glass as it bounced heavily into the ditch.

'What the hell!' Stone shouted, and his eyes widened in a moment of panic. He sat bolt upright and tugged at the seat belt which was now clamping him tight across the chest.

'What the hell!' Anton echoed as he instinctively gripped the steering wheel tighter and brought the Jaguar to a clean halt. He turned and stared at the crumpled van lying on its side in the ditch with steam hissing quickly from its bonnet.

'Whoever's in that mess is hurt,' he said. 'You all right, Mr Stone?'

'Yes,' Stone said and he breathed out heavily as he just stared ahead.

'I'll go have a look,' Anton said as he picked up his phone to call 999.

He slipped his seat belt and started to open the door to investigate the crumpled metal. But Stone's hold on Anton's arm was solid.

'Drive on. Leave it in the ditch. Get me out of here.'

'But, Mr Stone . . .'

'Shut up,' Stone snapped. 'When it's wet if they wanna be reckless and drive so fast on these small roads then they deserve what they get.'

'But they're probably hurt in that van,' he persisted. 'We can't just leave them.'

'I said get me out of here. I don't care what's happened to them.'

'Mr Stone, we should report an accident like this to the police. Or at least call an ambulance.'

'If you don't drive on I'll do it for you. And then you don't work for me any more.'

Anton did not argue. He saw the wildness in Stone's eyes and he felt his grip on his arm like a vice. Panic had overtaken his employer and he didn't understand why. For a moment he stared at the crumpled and now silent van in the ditch. There was no movement. Not even a cry for help. And for only a moment Anton was undecided what he should do.

Then he obeyed Stone's command. He put the Jaguar smoothly into drive and moved forward at an urgent but controlled pace.

Stone hunched his shoulders tightly. His eyes searched every car they passed. It was as if he felt the same threat would come again – he was a target to be hit – and it was not until they reached the motorway that Stone spoke.

'Okay, Anton. You'd better forget that little incident. We'll never speak of it again. You understand?'

'But the van just skidded on the wet road taking the bend.'

'Didn't you hear what I said?' Stone persisted.

'But that guy was driving too fast. Most delivery vans do. And wham! he ends up in the ditch.'

'Listen, you fool. Your pay packets keep coming and they're good aren't they?'

'Yes, sir,' Anton replied.

'So I said we'll never speak of it again. And that's final. Got it?'

'Yes, Mr Stone. I understand. It's just that I don't like the idea of leaving people injured and without help.'

'Shut up!' Stone screamed. 'Get me to Claridge's. Quickly. Then you can go back and sort it.'

Anton, his hands firmly holding the steering wheel, understood. Nothing his boss said or did surprised him any more. And you didn't argue when your whole lifestyle was on the line. Anton liked what he had got.

They arrived at Claridge's forty-five minutes later, Stone still belligerent, frightened and now with a gnawing tenseness in his shoulders.

He snapped at Anton before the car had stopped at the front entrance.

'Get my bags in quick. And find out about security. I want to know they don't let anyone wander around this place.'

'Sir,' Anton replied, calmly, not rising to Stone's angry mood. Stone passed a fiver to Anton.

'Give it to the concierge and don't let him fuss around me.'

'Leave it to me,' Anton said as the top-hatted doorman opened Stone's door.

'Welcome to Claridge's, sir,' he said.

Stone nodded quickly in acknowledgement and stalked to the reception desk. Within five minutes he was escorted in silence to his suite on the fourth floor by a tall tail-coated receptionist half his age. Stone was by now no longer visibly shaking. The concierge received another large tip when his bags were brought to his suite.

'I don't want visitors,' Stone said.

'That can be arranged, sir. I will make sure security and reception are advised. How long are you staying?'

'I've checked in for ten days.'

'Can I arrange a special time for the housekeeper to clean your suite each day? So your stay is not interrupted.'

'No,' Stone said sharply. 'I'll call if I need anything.'

The concierge saw the angry look in this guest's eyes and backed away, closing the door quietly.

Alone, Stone paced the room and without thinking in a swift movement he poured a double malt whisky from the bottles arranged neatly on a sideboard in the sitting room. As he slumped heavily in an armchair he took a large gulp from his glass. It was as if he was now confined like a caged lion aware of its fate.

There was nobody else in the room but Stone spoke out loud.

'God, I'm being irrational,' he said. 'Why am I running like this from an invisible madman who was chopped in St Lucia?' He sipped his whisky and intently looked at the glass as thoughts ran wild in his mind. That uncontrolled van shooting in front of him was a threat. He knew that. The threat from Drake and its demands flashed in his mind. He shuddered.

It took Stone half an hour to calm down. But his frustration was rising. He was unsure how to deal with Drake and he paced the large, elegant room, not even stopping to peer through the heavily curtained windows as he would have done at Arrow Hall. Two minutes later he called Roger Garon from the bathroom, driven by an irrational feeling that he would be less likely to be overheard from that smaller space.

'I'm staying at Claridge's. I want you here in half an hour.'

There was a pause before Roger answered.

'But Jennie and myself are having dinner with the Rebers at home here. The Canyon Building east of Brighton town centre. You'll remember that for its problems I hope. Fred

Reber we have to cultivate.' The sarcasm in Roger's voice rang easily down the phone.

'Roger, the Canyon project finished several years ago, we bought 'em all off so why're you playing with that lot still?'

'It's called tidying up. We might need them again sometime.'

'Never. And if we do, then we'll buy 'em in again.'

'Be more subtle than that. It costs less my way.'

'Move on, Roger. If you're not here in half an hour I don't pay your fees any more.'

'But I've just told you...'

'You have heard of Claridge's? It's in a nice part of west London.'

Roger ignored Stone's arrogance but he couldn't ignore his call.

'I thought we'd arranged to meet tomorrow, Harry. What's changed? What's going on?'

'Nothing. I want you here. And maybe tomorrow also.'

'What's so urgent?' Roger's voice was controlled and strong.

'Everything's urgent.'

'Okay, I'll come. But don't let me find you don't need me when I get there.'

'While I pay your fees you come when I call, Mr Garon,' Stone said with a sneer. 'But don't leave it beyond half an hour. We've got to act fast.'

'Why Claridge's, for God's sake?'

'I like it. It's a good place to do business.'

'It's not your style, Harry. What you up to?'

'It's not about image or style it's about the pressures I'm putting on the Fenfleet deal. Nobody's going to stop me getting it.'

'For goodness sake, Harry, there's only the Trifoni Group as a bit of competition and we'll soon sort them.'

'You been to St Lucia?'

'No, and I'm not likely to. I don't need to deal in fantasies, Harry.'

'You go and do the hard stuff some time. Like getting your hands dirty on a deal.'

'You mean *lose* some time.'

'Yeh. Not some time. *Big* time. I did. So I know what failure is like. And that means you get here quick so we get Fenfleet fixed.'

'You promise not to be so moody and tetchy and I'll leave in ten minutes.'

A tingling sensation bristled around Roger's neck as he put the phone down. It was his usual frustration surfacing which always came when he was dealing with Harry Stone.

\*

Roger had his own views on how to corner the Fenfleet contract, and they did not agree with Stone's. They never would because Stone's methods were too unsubtle, too shady, and that was not the way Roger Garon worked. But you had to humour Stone – the arguments could come later – and Roger was good at that. But tonight he now had to walk out on Jennie and that was something he didn't like doing.

Taking a deep breath he quietly closed the door of his study and prepared to face Jennie. He walked casually into the kitchen where she was sipping a sherry as she supervised the supper preparations.

'Who was that?' she asked brightly.

'Harry Stone.'

'What the blazes does he want this time of the evening?'

'Darling, I have to go out for an hour.'

'But the Rebers'll be here soon!'

'Sure. Give them plenty to drink. Just for an hour. I'll be back before ...'

'Where are you going?'

'Claridge's.'

'What on earth for?'

'Stone's staying there. Don't ask me why.'

Jennie took a long hard look at her husband and moved swiftly away to the other end of the large kitchen.

She shouted. 'You're running to Stone! He yells, you jump. Don't you see he bullies whenever he likes?'

'Darling, it's not like that,' Roger pleaded.

'I know *just* what it's like. You leave me to keep sweet some difficult clients while you go off just because Stone wants to talk. If our guests tell you what they think of your business I won't blame them.'

Roger knew he was bungling forward. He could not argue with Jennie, she was right, but he was unthinking, insensitive to anything other than Stone's call. The yank from Stone was real. Roger liked the tug of business and he wanted the fees. He hovered at the end of the kitchen for only a moment and looked at Jennie, but she turned away. He was torn but he knew where he was going.

He didn't say goodbye. He went into the hall, took a raincoat from the cupboard, slammed the front door as a farewell, and walked quickly to his car.

An hour later, after being cleared by the hotel security, Roger hung his coat in the hall of Stone's suite. The ashen-grey pallor was Stone's natural colour but Roger was surprised at the excited, animated look on Stone's face, which was usually flat of expression, giving nothing away. Tonight his mouth no longer sagged at the edges, he looked tall and strong. He was very ready for getting at the next deal.

'Drink?' Stone asked, moving to the bottles on the sideboard.

'Whisky. Malt. Neat,' Roger stated crisply.

Stone poured a generous measure and Roger sat with an

audible sigh in an armchair facing Stone. He watched Stone's eyes dart in an almost uncontrolled sequence between the door and the windows, and then his hand ran roughly through his lightly greying hair.

'For God's sake what's the matter, Harry? You look as if you're expecting something to happen in here.'

There was a pause. Perhaps Stone welcomed the question.

'Got problems. Something you ought to know about.'

'The taxman?'

'No. Nothing new there. They can just fry for a while and we'll see who blinks first.'

'That's dangerous with the Revenue. Rather you than me.'

'I'm being pursued by a crank from St Lucia. Known as Drake. He did me over there and he's not gone away. Got a letter from him with demands.'

'Oh yes?' Roger said, sipping his drink and enjoying Stone's unease.

'And a van shot across us coming down from Essex. Like a bullet from a gun. It wasn't an accident.'

'You think it was this Drake?'

'After his antics in St Lucia he'd do at least that here.'

'Cars carve you up everywhere. Haven't you heard of road rage? You're imagining things.'

'Not this time. I'm being watched. And Drake's demand was for money.'

'Blackmail?'

'No. The usual protection racket.'

'Harry, how did you get yourself in this mess?'

'I tore him up in St Lucia, and now he's coming back at me. Simple as that.' Stone was uneasy and it showed in his continually darting eyes.

'Is that why you've come here to this classy place? Feel better with people around you?'

'Maybe.'

'Why don't you tell the police if you're sure you're being hunted? Protection demands aren't exactly legal.'

'No. Never.' Stone's reaction was sharp, emphatic. 'I'll never talk to the police. Don't like 'em. Don't trust 'em. And I've got too much to hide with the taxman chasing me. Eh, Roger?'

'You maybe. But not me.'

'I lost a lot of cash in St Lucia. It took me ten years to skim it off and get it out there.'

'I don't want to know about that,' Roger said, holding up his hand. 'Don't tell me and I can't tell the police.'

'No, I won't.'

'Anyway you shouldn't have made the Cayman deposits in the first place. Then you wouldn't be in this mess, skulking like a fox.'

'Lots of other people do it,' Stone said.

'Forget it, Harry. Let's move on. What's for now? Tonight.'

Stone shrugged. 'I'm going hard for the Fenfleet contract. And I got ideas to make it work.'

'And the reason for the hurry? You're frightened someone'll slug you before you do the deal?'

Stone thought for a moment. Had he said too much? 'Only you know about this Drake madman. No one else. Let's keep it that way.'

'Sure,' Roger responded. 'But you just called me here to tell me that?'

'No. I've planned for something special on the Fenfleet deal,' Stone said. 'And it's got to be done carefully and quickly.'

'But we've decided already. Don't you remember? I'm searching for the inside information you need. Apollo Searches. They're doing some telephone tapping, mobiles too, even looking in dustbins that hold their waste, and I've also got a contract hacker probing their computers. That's a lot of effort, Harry, and a lot of cost, so hold off and see what comes.'

'You're not quick enough. There's other ways of getting there. You'll see.'

'Why don't you leave it to me, Harry?' Roger persisted.

'Look. The Fenfleet deal's urgent. Dead urgent. And when it's done I'll go somewhere until that nutter from St Lucia has been dealt with.'

'Harry, you're stupid. Go off somewhere *now*. Leave Fenfleet to me.'

'No. I'm not waiting around for you to get results.'

'Why add to the havoc you've already caused tonight? You know you've killed my supper with important guests.'

'There are bigger things than your boozy supper. St Lucia's threatening on one side and there's a tight deadline with Fenfleet on the other. I'm not going to get caught in the middle like some nut in a cracker.'

'You're really worried about getting done over, aren't you?'

Stone did not answer but refilled his glass without looking at Roger. Distracted he left it on the sideboard and paced the room while Roger watched. Stone looked angry, his eyes narrowing, ready to spring at anything given half the chance.

'Harry, calm down. Fenfleet isn't the only business we can do. Deals are sloshing around all over the place looking for backers and we'll have some excitement somewhere else.'

'No. I don't want other deals. Fenfleet'll be quick and easy. And remember pubs swim in cash as well as beer.' Stone talked enthusiastically. The glint in his unsmiling eyes and the tight set of his jaw showed the irresistible force that was now driving him forward. A single-minded force that Stone obviously could not control.

'It's your call, Harry. But I'm telling you to take it steady. Get it right.'

'We'll get it right,' Stone said. He sat and stared at Roger who noisily crunched a crisp before draining his glass.

Roger was emphatic. 'My advice is that this is not the sort of deal you go in on blind. That's unless you're prepared to gamble lots of gold.'

'How many times do I have to tell you I don't have time? And you know very well I'm not gambling. I never do.'

'Harry, hold on a minute.'

But Stone interrupted. He was in no mood to hold. 'Don't you ever listen to what I say? Have you forgotten we have to tender to a tight deadline?'

Roger retreated from Stone's irritability by saying nothing, and relaxed more deeply into the chintzy chair. All he could do was stare at Stone and it was then he decided Fenfleet was Stone's own money not his. If Stone wouldn't listen, well...

'Step one,' Stone said, his face again becoming animated. 'We enter Trifoni Group and look closely at Rick Austin. You haven't found out using your fancy outfits what this guy's bidding so I will. And when I know the size of their money I cap it. Not by much but by just enough to control the deal.'

'What do you think I've been working at these last few weeks? I've spent a fortune on taps and bugs at Trifoni and on Rick Austin. I can tell you about his bank account, his credit cards, where he eats out, where he buys his wine, even where he buys his suits, but I still haven't quite got what we need. People like Trifoni and Rick Austin guard their money with tight fists.'

'You're playing at it.'

'What do you mean? I've done an expert job. But you don't get results overnight.'

'I'll get somebody right inside their operation. Up front where they take the decisions. Alongside Rick Austin. That means in his office sitting with him. So close he won't even know they're there. And then we'll move to step two.'

'What do you mean step two?'

'I told you. We bribe James Kennedy. He's the real key in all this. There's always someone who holds all the power in a deal and it's him. Kennedy is Fenfleet. Don't you see?'

Roger walked to the sideboard and filled his whisky glass. He wished at that moment he was at home with Jennie. He had disappointed her tonight and now he wondered why he had walked out on her and their guests to be with this hothead Harry Stone. The man was obsessed, his own ego was blinding him to reality and he was in fantasy land.

'How much are you going to spend buying Kennedy?' Roger asked.

'Kennedy'll be as greedy as the rest. Don't know yet. Fifty grand, hundred grand. Maybe more.'

Roger looked away. 'Keep me out of it.'

'You're too soft. That's peanuts.'

'Forget it, Harry. I'm going home. But tell me who you think'll be fool enough to act as your spy right in front of Rick Austin? It'll cost you more cash than Kennedy's bribe. And what about the short time we have?'

'I've got my ways.' Stone was impassive as he spoke.

'You'll lose control if it goes wrong.'

'It won't go wrong. Not the way I do it.'

'Well cough it up. Who's going to do it?'

'There's one person intelligent enough to understand the secrets we're after.' Stone raised his eyebrows and a flicker of a smile crept over his grey face. 'And there's one person who Rick Austin won't know because she works for me. So we can move quickly.'

'I'm not taking this seriously, Harry. There's nobody I know who'd be stupid enough to start spying for you. And as for bribes...'

Stone moved towards the door as if he was inviting Roger to leave.

Stone smiled. 'Does your wife still run her salon in Mayfair? The one that works on women's appearances?'

'Why the hell do you ask that?'

'I've got another client for her.'

# 6

Roger left Claridge's in a hotel car just before midnight. His earlier tiredness had gone, replaced by irritation at the real greed in Stone which now showed as plain nasty. Out of earshot from the driver, he activated his mobile phone.

'I know the time, Dave,' Roger said quickly, 'but I have to be sure on your search into the Trifoni Group.'

'Aren't you satisfied with what I've done?' Dave replied placidly.

'Yes. Of course. But my client wants more.'

'Your client sounds a bit too demanding to me. So make sure you keep him off my back.'

'Yes. I'll be your buffer but we need results on their inside info. Quick.'

'I'll get more. In time,' Dave said. 'But I guess your client's never hacked himself.'

'No, that's what he's paying you for,' Roger said, knowing that Stone wouldn't even know how to switch a computer on.

'I've got other work on just now. Work that doesn't keep me up all night and goggle-eyed for the next day. There's easier, safer ways to make money.'

'Sure. But my client pays good,' Roger coaxed. 'Better than your day job.'

'I've gone into Trifoni Group once for you. And that took too long.'

'So you could get into their system again?'

'Do you know how many systems they've got? Eleven at the last count.'

'So it's eleven. Take them one at a time.'

'You don't understand. Getting into them is a long job. You've got to find passwords and last time they were changing them once a week. A bit like my underwear.' Dave sounded tired, disinterested and did not laugh.

'Okay, Dave. I'll pay. How much?'

'It's not the money. You don't even know what you're looking for. So until then, what's the use?'

'I've already told you I want everything on their bid for the Fenfleet contract. How much they're offering, when they'll pay it, who's running the deal at Trifoni, any conditions attached to their offer – like the pubs are as good as the sellers say they are.'

'I don't understand big business, I'm just a simple computer whizz. Anyway, it's only the systems that run the business that I get into. Not info that'll be stuffed in a drawer that you're talking about.'

'So that's it?' Roger asked.

'Yes. That's it.'

'I'll send you some cash. Thanks for what you've tried, Dave. Until the next time.'

Roger flicked the phone off. He closed his eyes and rested his head on the seatback. Yes, with Dave that *was* it, an expensive try and probably the only way that would extract from Trifoni their hidden secrets, whatever Stone thought. Tomorrow he would call Stan at Apollo Searches to close them off. That would leave Stone on his own, isolated in his underhand search for what he saw was a golden rainbow. 'To hell with Stone,' Roger said to himself, and yawned noisily. Tiredness enfolded him. It was an hour's drive home, and he felt depressed, which was unusual for him. The feeling was heightened by a sense of being useless, being ineffective when dealing with Harry Stone. For a few brief moments he nodded asleep as the car raced along an almost empty M4. But he woke with a jolt. He had to face Jennie and he now didn't have the patience for an encounter that could end in a fight. Stone was enough for one night.

Roger paid the driver and let himself into his house on the edge of Newbury. The lights were on, it felt hot but quiet, welcoming even. The Rebers had gone and before he faced Jennie he decided on another drink to see him through tonight and then he'd sleep, turn the whole sordid mess off. He walked into the wide lounge, his shoulders hunched, frowning deeply. Facing him full on was Jennie, and the room suddenly became small, intimate, a place from which there was no escape. She was in a flowery, patterned dressing gown, her feet on the sofa, cushions surrounding her, and with her make-up removed her face was sharp and pallid. She averted her eyes – she was ready for sleep too, but intimacy was not for now.

'I'm not going to argue,' he said firmly. 'Just listen to me for a minute. I've something to tell you.'

'It's more likely you've got to listen to me!' Jennie shouted. 'You do that to me once more and we're finished.'

'I've never done it before, you know that, but tonight had to be different. How do you think you live in this luxury if I don't attend to business? Money doesn't grow on trees. It has to be earned with a bit of sweat and sometimes even inconvenience.'

Jennie shuffled her feet on the sofa as if she was ready to leave.

'We don't want money at the expense of enjoying our friends,' she retorted, not looking at her husband. 'And particularly if you're kowtowing to the demands of Stone. He's a blatant cowboy, he has no manners, no sense of anything but his own big, wide ego. He loves his arrogant self, no one else, and he's coarse. Coarse as the jungle that he has run from at Arrow Hall. You know I don't like that man.'

She moved her feet more securely onto the sofa, satisfied

her rant had exposed her hostile feelings for Harry Stone, a feeling Roger would have shared but for the large fees he extracted for advice that was rarely taken.

'Nor me,' Roger said quickly. 'But pieces of silver...'

Jennie cut him short, she was not yet finished. 'How many businesses has he meddled with in the last few years? How many lives has he ruined without caring a fig?'

'Not ours,' Roger said evenly.

'Tonight's the start.'

'Look, darling, we've been through all this before. Stone pays big fees and that means sometimes he calls the tune. And when he does I have to dance to it. That's all.'

'He doesn't run your life does he?'

'Of course not. I don't like it any more than you do, honey. But if I want his business that's the way it is.'

'Don't be weak and for God's sake don't always follow that clown Stone,' Jennie said.

'You've got it wrong,' Roger shot back. 'Sure tonight was killed off by Stone but don't muddle what you like to see as weakness with my success.' Without taking his coat off he sank onto the other end of the sofa. He kicked his shoes across the floor to show he was home, relaxed even. But Jennie rose quickly and moved to the door.

'You better know the Rebers weren't impressed. You won't get them back again.' She tousled her hair in a mixture of frustration and anger, her high-pitched voice showing strong emotion.

It was too late for Roger to argue about something he knew he could not alter. Yes, he knew Jennie was right. Stone was a bully, a cowboy, and he just kept on dealing with the guy as if he was normal. Sliding deeply into the sofa he looked at Jennie as a wan childish smile crept over his tanned face. He had some good news as well, something positive to end the night with.

'You want another client for the salon?'

Jennie took her hand from the door and turned to face him. 'Don't change the subject. It won't help.'

'Jennie, I'm serious. It's Claire. Stone's PA. She needs a makeover. The whole thing. Clothes, hair, whatever it takes with no money spared to get her looking good. She's quite pretty anyway so it should be a doddle.'

'I don't know this Claire,' Jennie responded. 'What if I don't like her? And if she's anything to do with Stone that might be the case.'

'You'll like her. I promise you that. She's serious, good at her job, bright, friendly and refined, not coarse like Harry.'

'I'll think about it,' Jennie said.

'Don't take too long. She may be sent somewhere else. Stone needs quick results and he doesn't hang around.'

Jennie's mind raced. There was silence in the large room and, sensing that Jennie was calming, Roger heaved himself up and walked to the closed drinks cabinet in a corner.

'Want one?' he asked, holding the gin bottle for Jennie to see.

'You don't win that easily,' she replied testily. 'No,' she added a moment later. 'I'm too tired. And you look as if you don't need one either.'

Roger ignored the comment that was meant to stop him in his tracks, poured a large measure of malt whisky and again slumped onto the sofa. He closed his eyes as he took a long thirst-quenching sip.

'Jennie, I need to know. If you want a new client you don't have time to think about it and you don't have to teach me a lesson. I've already learnt it, honey.'

'Don't let Stone come near me, he's not a man I will ever deal with.'

'Claire will come to Mayfair. Day after tomorrow,' said Roger. 'About midday. Okay?'

'What if I've got other clients the day after tomorrow, midday?'

'Make another date. Jennie, work with me,' Roger said. 'I promise you'll like Claire.'

'So what happens to the poor girl when I've finished?'

'Let's leave that for now. It's a long story and it's too late tonight.'

'What? You mean she's being softened up for something big? Part of Stone's grand scheme?'

'Jennie, please. Claire's sensible. Let her make her own mind up what she wants to do.'

'You've got to promise me one thing.'

'What's that?'

'I don't want any pressure from Stone put on her. Sounds as if she's in enough trouble already.'

'Promise,' Roger replied as he stifled a yawn, finished his drink and placed the glass heavily on a side table.

Jennie had started the salon on a whim five years before, and because she was creative and independent it had been a success. It was upmarket, chic, trendy and expensive. Helping women of varying ages to become elegant and stylish was engrossing, it excited her and she was good at it. But several of Jennie's regular clients had moved from London and coupled with the powerful uncertainties of an economic recession where purses, even in Mayfair, were more tightly held, clients with open budgets were becoming more difficult to find. The prospect of a new client was enticing.

And Stone? No she didn't have to see him. But secure in the warmth of her large house she would not have cooperated and nor would Roger if they had known where Stone would lead Claire.

*

When Roger left Claridge's Stone pulled the curtains across in the lounge. Earlier he had sent housekeeping, who normally carried out the ritual as well as turning the bed down, away and had sharply told them not to come back that evening. After all he never had such close attention at Arrow Hall. Now alone, for several minutes he lay on the sofa and stared at the ceiling pensively, satisfied with his evening's progress on Fenfleet. But suddenly he knew his day's work was not finished and, pricked into action as a result of his paranoia, inside the inner hallway he put the security chain on the suite door and then picked up his mobile from a low table. He never knew where Cutlass might be living as he moved around London often but after fumbling through a list the second of the numbers he held found him.

'Where are you?' Stone demanded without announcing himself.

'Going to bed.'

'You in London?'

'It's Mr Stone, isn't it?'

Stone ignored the question. 'How long you been back from St Lucia?' he barked.

'I left the day after you did, boss.'

'What happened to Drake?'

'I did him over, took revenge like you asked.'

'So was that drug-soaked thug dead when you finished with him? Did you kill him off like he did my hotel?'

'Don't know. Me and me mates laid into him, he tried to yelp but we shut him up. There was a bloody mess round his mouth when we'd done and he weren't moving.'

'I don't want details,' Stone said, stopping Cutlass quickly. 'But I need to know if he ever got up again.'

'It was dark, we needed to get away. But he was very quiet and still when we left. I didn't get his pulse, I'm not a doctor.'

'Was he breathing?'

Cutlass hesitated. 'Don't know. Don't care. I know how we beat him though.'

'Why don't you ever finish a job properly? You even foul up on ordinary beatings! I know you've never had a brain but now you don't even have any guts to cut up rough,' Stone shouted.

'We did the job you asked for, Mr Stone. We beat him up good and proper. He must have had at least some broken bones.'

'Did the police know about it?'

'Look, boss, back in Castries we saw the boy who told us where to find Drake. Told him Drake had an accident and they should go look for him. Then we caught the next plane home. If he's dead and we'd been caught, well...'

'A few years in jail. That's all you'd get. That's if they ever found you.'

'We did him over, you didn't say you wanted him killed. So why you ask now?'

'He might come at me again.'

'But he's in St Lucia. And you're a few thousand miles away in London. So how's he coming at you now? Eh?'

'Something's going on because you didn't finish it like you should.'

'What?'

'The Caribbean's still rumbling, as bad as it did when we were in that sizzling heat.'

'You can forget Drake, Mr Stone. Like I told you we busted him. He ain't gonna come at you no more. Not for a long time.'

Stone spoke quickly, pouring the words out with nervous ferocity. 'There's things to do. Like finish the bust-up you didn't do right first time. You've now got to go out and be more bloody, and when I say bloody I mean bloody.'

'Is everything all right, boss?'

'Don't question. Okay?'

'You're not telling me everything are you, Mr Stone?'

'You know enough. For now.'

'If Drake's still alive he'll be broken. Bad. I know what we did and nobody gets up quick and walks away from that. They don't come back for more.'

'How many times do I have to tell you, the job's only half done, you fat arse? You should've stuck a knife in his throat like he did to me. Made him cringe until he sweated for mercy. Sounds to me you've crapped out like you did in guarding the hotel.'

'Leave off, boss. I did what you wanted, I did it quick and I don't want no trouble.'

'You ain't got trouble, not yet. You're just a lazy fool, but you'd better be ready.'

'I don't wanna go back to St Lucia. What happens if…'

'Shut it,' Stone shouted. 'I'll call when I want you. And that'll be soon.'

Stone disconnected. If Drake was alive where was he? The hope he was dead with a broken skull that oozed blood from a beating by a savage was not now real and it killed his earlier satisfaction that he had moved sharply on the Fenfleet deal with Roger. Stone got undressed, hanging his suit carefully, and drank from the bottle of water in the minibar. Fenfleet and his plans with Roger were obliterated from his mind and he went to bed feeling very edgy, the tomblike quietness and solitude of Claridge's leaving his mind to whirl without direction or interruption as he drifted into a fitful sleep an hour later.

# 7

Before 5.00 a.m. it was getting light and Stone was wide awake. Quietness pervaded. For a moment Claridge's – chosen irrationally and in panic as a hideout – was unreal compared with the steamy heat of St Lucia, the thug Drake and lost laundered money.

An inner urgency drove Stone. He got up, called room service for a light breakfast, and switching on the TV flicked through the news and cartoons before throwing the remote control onto a sofa and turning his thoughts to other matters. He nibbled at a warm croissant and drank two cups of strong black coffee as he walked round the room with a distracted stare in his blue eyes.

At 5.30 he called Claire in Arrow Hall. A minute and a half later his impatience was bursting when the phone was answered, but with Claire he would keep his voice calm and soft, without intimidation. Rarely would Claire fight back and now – when he needed her help – was not the time to encourage it.

'I don't call you early unless it's necessary, Claire.'

Claire, flustered, sat up in bed. 'You woke me,' she said.

'Yeh,' Stone said dryly. 'I guess I did.'

'Why so early? Are you all right?' Claire switched the light on and ran her fingers through her hair.

'It's business, Claire. Something very important has come up. I need to talk. I need you at Claridge's. Quick.'

'I'll get dressed and come straight away. But why so urgent, can't we talk on the phone?'

'No,' Stone said emphatically. 'I need you here.'

'Any papers you want? Anything else I need to bring?'

'No. Come as you are. Just get here quick.'

'You sound flustered. Are you sure everything's all right? You did leave Arrow Hall quickly the other day.'

'Sure, everything's okay,' Stone said smoothly as he nibbled at another croissant. 'And don't forget to lock the house when you leave.'

'It'll take over an hour to get to Claridge's,' Claire said. 'It's a train ride and then the Underground.'

'Get a cab from Liverpool Street. It's quicker. Claire, I need you here like fast.'

Claire reacted to Stone's urgency as if on auto-pilot. She dressed quickly, ignored any make-up and gulped a bowl of cornflakes in the large cold kitchen. Propelled by Stone's abrupt command she checked the locks on the two side doors and pulled the oak front door hard shut, twisting the key until satisfied it was securely locked. She often wondered why there was no alarm in this isolated and vulnerable property.

Claire boarded the first train of the morning for London. Despite the early hour the carriage was busy, and continued to fill up as they approached the City. Gradually the lush green countryside gave way to grimy urban areas and eventually to the concrete of London. Sitting two seats away was a dowdy young girl, dressed in a black leather jacket and skirt, both of which matched the colour of her Afro-Caribbean hairstyle. Her eyes were closed. Her face was totally blank of any expression and Claire had no reason to give her more than scanty attention.

In the surge of people at Liverpool Street and the windless warmth of the City Claire was flustered as she hurried from the concourse and queued a few minutes for a taxi. The cloudless sky promised real heat that would be overpowering in London. Claire's day was often fast, but crowded hustle was never part of it and London was just not her kind of place.

The dark-haired girl from the train followed her. She lit a cigarette and watched as Claire climbed into the cab. She needed to know where Claire was going, who she was meeting, because that was what her bosses demanded. But following a cab in the sprawl of London was not possible and for some hours her day was now dead. But so what? she thought. Like much of her life this could now become another day spent aimlessly lounging around, smoking, drinking and just waiting.

The taxi moved away, and the Caribbean girl crossed the road to Starbucks where she could begin to idle the hours away until the girl from the country returned for a train home. Her bosses would shout at her for letting her quarry get away but she would ignore their strong words in the fug of cannabis and amphetamines that were a normal part of her life.

The rush-hour traffic clogged the streets, slowing Claire's cab to a crawl at times, but eventually it deposited her at Claridge's, where the flags of different nations hung limply over its canopy. Ordered luxury pervaded in the lobby, with large eye-catching flower arrangements placed conspicuously and much attentive, discreet movement. Even the bright air seemed to be spotlessly clean and no speck of dust showed in the light. It was very unlike the decrepitude of Arrow Hall.

The concierge smiled easily at Claire and only after he had phoned Stone's suite for clearance was she escorted to the lift where she smoothed her hair and took a deep breath. How could Stone live with the stark contrast between drab brownness of Arrow Hall and the smooth luxury of Claridge's? But soon Arrow Hall would get the attention it craved and then it would be a lot better than this flash place.

'You got here quicker than I thought,' Stone said. Unusually he smiled in greeting and looked deeply into Claire's eyes.

'I caught the first train after you phoned. But London's not my place, too hot, too crowded,' Claire said.

'Coffee's coming,' Stone said.

Claire took a biscuit from a plate on the sideboard and sat at the end of a small chintzy sofa. She watched the rare animated look on Stone's face as he paced the carpet and wondered what was coming next.

Business in Arrow Hall was never routine. There were calls to bankers, to lawyers, to anyone who could influence a deal. Letters, never written when a call could be made, were always abrupt, fired off like missiles to those who had crossed Stone's path. Apologies and money as recompense were demanded when he felt aggrieved. The word 'please' never crossed his lips and often his letters were in a language that Claire toned down before posting. She told him more than once that it was an offence to send obscenities through the post. And he just laughed at her.

But she knew how to handle Stone. This morning, though, it was time for Stone to learn how to handle Claire.

She took another biscuit and watched as Stone ran his hand through his hair as if it needed smoothing. The sharpness in his lined face had softened and the upward curve of his mouth even suggested that he was trying to maintain the smile he had greeted her with. Her boss was after something.

Stone spoke abruptly. 'How long you worked for me, Claire?'

Claire's arched eyebrows showed her surprise at the question. 'Eight years. Why?'

'I need to know you're happy in your job.'

'That's an odd question after all these years. Of course I'm happy in what I do, otherwise I wouldn't do it.'

'Good. There are some exciting times coming up.'

'More deals like the Caribbean?'

'No!' Stone snapped, and immediately wished he hadn't.

'No,' he said more calmly. 'The next deal's here. Fenfleet. North country pubs.'

'So? Why are you suddenly concerned about me? What's changing?'

'Claire, listen. You have a rent-free apartment in Arrow Hall and there's not many people I'd give that to. There's something special I want you to do for me. I can't do it myself, and if you're successful ... well let's do the job first.'

Claire sipped her coffee and studied the delicate array of fresh flowers on the sideboard. Her natural curiosity was rising and she spoke confidently in response to Stone's unexpected move.

'I'll do most things. As long as they're not dangerous. So try me.'

'That's the confidence I like to hear.'

'I haven't said I'll agree to anything yet.'

'Sure. We take this slowly. But remember, when this little deal is over we'll breathe some new air into Arrow Hall. We'll follow up what I said the other day, we'll do whatever we have to do make it look like it should. I know you'll find that exciting.'

'Yes, I'd like that. It's run-down and it needs big money thrown at it. But you've got to promise we'll do it.' Claire stared at Stone, searching for a clue to what this early morning call was all about.

'Sure, sure. But let's clear the air first. Get Claridge's out of our hair, eh?' Stone laughed nervously.

'You'd better tell me more.'

'I want you to change your appearance.'

Claire put her coffee cup noisily on its saucer. 'What?'

'I don't mean you don't look fine already. I just want you to look completely *different*. City-like not country-like, so you can fit unnoticed into a different role somewhere else for a while. And when we're both satisfied that the appearance of Claire Watts has been changed we'll look at the next part of the deal. It'll be fun I promise. Will you go along with me and give it a try?'

'I need to know more,' Claire said frowning.

Stone lied easily. 'I can't tell you yet. I've not worked it out.'

'Where's all this leading? You run to Claridge's for no reason you'll tell me about, you call me early in the morning and you make me an unusual offer. You need to be more open with me.'

Stone smiled widely, a gesture Claire instantly distrusted.

'Wouldn't any woman accept a makeover? Make-up, hair, clothes. Nothing too flashy, just a different style with the same efficient Claire underneath. Okay? And there's no limit on the budget.' Stone spoke smoothly, at his persuasive best.

'When did you last spend money on a woman? Any woman?'

'Claire, trust me. I know what I'm doing.'

Claire thought for a moment. 'New clothes? Style change? What then? Arrow Hall makeover?'

'Yes, Arrow Hall makeover too, that's definitely part of the deal,' Stone said. 'But if we can't change your appearance to City girl, we forget it. Go back to business as usual.'

'When does all this start?'

'Tomorrow.'

'But I've got other things in the diary for tomorrow. Like chasing the rents on the Southend flats.'

'You can put that off for a day or two, this is more important.'

'What is it you're after?'

'You know. Fenfleet pubs. I need your help to get that deal.'

'It should be simple. Between you and Roger you've done that sort of deal many times, so what's so complicated now?'

'Don't question my motives, Claire. Anything we do, we do together. Okay?'

'You've not told me about what went wrong in the Caribbean yet.'

'I'm not going over old ground. I've made an appointment for you to see Roger Garon's wife. Jennie's her name. Midday tomorrow. She has a salon in Mayfair for ladies who wish to review their style.' Stone placed an address card on the table. 'I pay for everything and the cheque book's open. But I want results.'

'And what follows from all this? The less glamorous bit? The bit that gets you the Fenfleet deal?' Claire persisted.

'I'll tell you when I've made some other arrangements. It's all got to be tied together.'

'Other arrangements? What? When?'

'Soon.'

'And what happens to my work at Arrow Hall while all this is going on?'

'Leave it. Nothing else matters until we've done this.'

'How long do we play this game?'

'Claire! Stop this questioning. Trust me. I know what I'm doing.'

Claire did not trust Stone. She had made up her mind on that some time ago, but it had never been something she was prepared to say. And now was not the time to start.

'Do I have your promise that we'll renovate Arrow Hall? Soon? The surveyors, renovation architects and the experts in garden design. We'll take them on?' Claire asked.

'Why not? It needs money spent on it and that's what we'll do. So, Fenfleet first, Arrow Hall next.'

'That is a fixed promise?'

'Look, one thing at a time. Make money first, spend it second. Will you go and see Roger's wife?'

'I've never met Roger's wife. Who says I'll agree with her ideas? It's my style, not hers. Or yours.'

'She's got an expensive reputation. She knows what she's doing. So what's your answer?' Stone's tone was becoming sharper.

'I need time to think,' Claire replied.

'Deadline's this evening. Call me from Arrow Hall,' Stone said.

'Is that all you've asked me here for?'

'Yeh, that's it. Nothing more today.'

Claire was immediately annoyed by the arrogance of Stone's clipped manner, contrasting with the false smiles of half an hour ago.

'Okay, I'll call,' she said airily, desperately trying to sound indifferent to Stone's unreality.

'Good. I'll be waiting.'

Stone held the door open. He had no smile and Claire felt sucked into something she did not understand but could smell was not right. Stone's methods of dealing with people she had seen many times, and they had often offended her in their sharpness. Now she was being squeezed tight until she did his dirty work. It was not how she had expected the day to be.

Her head was buzzing as she walked through the hotel lobby and climbed into a taxi. At Liverpool Street she bought a ticket and then waited an hour for the next train. The buffet was hot and stuffy and she sat alone, had a coffee at a cluttered, stained table, and considered Stone's proposal. Arrow Hall was often quiet but it was busy, and never dull, always something new. Today London had contrasted with that familiarity and its newness made Claire anxious. The prospect of change and its uncertainties loomed large.

Before boarding the train she headed to the ladies' room to apply some make-up. There she peered in the mirror. She saw no fault with her appearance, but maybe her hair could be restyled, after all she was thirty now and shoulder-length was less fashionable. She liked the deep-green suit she was wearing but of course she had bought it for the country, where she lived and worked. She noticed now that it was showing wear, gradually moulding to her body more tightly. Her handbag was large and floppy, and her shoes were flat, designed for walking more than elegance.

Claire applied make-up, ran a quick comb through her hair and then walked purposely to the train. There was no rush, the carriage was empty except for half a dozen scattered passengers, and Claire stared through the window at the passing summer countryside. The colourful fields, yellows of rape contrasting beautifully with the deep-green of the trees and hedges, was a scene with which Claire felt comfortable. Nature was predictable, everything was in harmony and at that moment she did not want it changed, whatever her boss's grand plan.

Two rows away in the open carriage sat the darkly dressed Caribbean girl, but Claire had no reason to notice her. And the girl did not look at Claire but was quietly satisfied that she had made contact again. Arrow Hall was her trail and then ... perhaps hitch a lift to Chelmsford where the pubs would be welcoming and she'd find a bed for the night. Unable to light a cigarette in the carriage she chewed her fingers out of habit.

Half an hour later the train crawled into the country station that served the hamlet near Arrow Hall and Claire left the carriage, the coloured girl mingling with the few other travellers on the platform. Alone Claire ambled down the winding country lane, pleased to be back in her own familiar territory. With the sun on her back her mood lifted. The offer of a no-expenses-spared makeover was enticing. Why not let Stone spend money on her? And then on Arrow Hall. The renovation she desired so much to be a part of.

At the Hall Claire picked up a pile of letters from the box at the gate. Inside, Stone's study was chilly and she shivered as she placed them on his desk. The phone rang, startling her. She listened closely to the caller for almost a minute. It was a cold, stark message about an unexpected death.

Saying goodbye, Claire sat in Stone's chair and hurriedly made some notes. Her mood becoming gloomy, she leant back and she felt the dreariness of Arrow Hall surround her. Yes, she decided, she should get out of this place for a while, but was Stone's offer the route to follow? She did not know. She looked at her watch. It was time to meet with the architects who were calling. Whether Stone was ready or not, she would push him, drag him if necessary, into the renovation, and these two guys now entering the gravelled driveway would be the start. And then whatever Stone wanted from her would have a price.

She sorted the letters and decided the death she had to report to him would wait until later.

*

Claire's visit to Claridge's left Stone upbeat. He was inching closer to the Fenfleet pubs, a deal that was drawing him as unstoppably as gravity pulls everything down to earth. But his elation soon wore off and he began to feel like a caged lion needing the width of the savannah. He re-read three times the scrawled note from Drake – as if he needed to be reminded of the menace – and each time he shuddered.

To divert his thoughts he called Roger Garon.

'Claire's okay. She'll call your wife tomorrow. They can then get on with it together.'

'Has Claire said yes? To the spying bit I mean.'

Stone hesitated. 'Not yet. But she will when I follow it up,' he said. 'Midday tomorrow. And I want her treated like a real client.'

'Of course, of course, Harry. Whatever you say. Jennie'll be there to deal with her. But don't push Claire too far. And don't take her for granted.'

'She'll like the pampering. All women do.' It was said with a finality that did not invite argument. After a short silence Stone snapped into the phone, 'You still there, Roger?'

'Yes, Harry. I'm still here. I'm listening to your mad scheme.'

'Good. Because I want something else. I want the name of Rick Austin's secretary at Trifoni Group.'

'Rick Austin's secretary?' Roger echoed. 'What for?'

'You don't ask the questions, Roger. Go and get on with it. Time's passing. Quickly.'

'Harry, don't be so impatient. I'll find out who she is. But Trifoni Group's a big operation. And you won't want me to pick the wrong one.' There was sarcasm in his voice.

'I'm just asking you to earn your fat fee. So far you've not done much. And now you've got to be quick and accurate. Got it?'

'My fee gives you value. Doing it my way,' Roger replied.

Stone did not let up on his barrage. 'Have you been to see James Kennedy at Fenfleet yet?'

'No. It's too early, until we know what we're going for.'

'I want you to corner him, Roger. He's the key to this deal.'

'I'll do it my way when I'm ready.'

Stone ignored the comment. 'See if he's bribable. Get a feel for the sort of money he's looking for. For God's sake, Roger you know what these deals are all about.'

'If there's bribing to be done, you do it, Harry. I've told you that.'

'Put some spine into it,' Stone said. 'You haven't even met him yet.'

Before Roger could reply Stone put the phone down. He poured himself another coffee and could feel sweat on his neck and forehead. His suite was cool but his pulse had increased from an adrenaline flow. Manipulation was Stone's game. He enjoyed it, he was good at it. And most times it worked. There was a sudden glint in his eye that showed his excitement. Stone re-read Drake's threatening letter yet again. For a moment he wished he had been part of the beating that Cutlass had given out in St Lucia, been there to direct it and listen to the screams for mercy. But he hadn't and Drake had survived. He was mysteriously still around. But where?

Later that afternoon Stone took a shower and through the noise of the water did not hear the phone ring. He shaved and dressed slowly, bored with inactivity and the deathly quiet in his suite.

Then he heard his phone whirring, indicating a missed call and because few people were allowed his number he picked it up instantly. It was Claire.

Immediately he rang her. There was a tightness to her voice as she answered.

'What did you call for?' Stone asked sharply.

Claire's voice was even. 'Letter from the taxman. Demanding another meeting in three days. Same place as before. Thought you might need to prepare for it. I'll get everything dropped by Claridge's. Clive Pontin says he should come with you to the meeting. He should know all the answers. What do you want me to say to him?'

'No way,' Stone replied petulantly. Tell him I go on my own to deal with that lot.'

'Okay, whatever you say.'

'You got an answer for me about Jennie Garon?' Stone demanded.

'Yes, I'll take up your offer. I'll meet her.'

'Good. I thought you would,' Stone said smugly.

'That's not what I really called about.'

'Oh?' Stone was surprised at Claire's tenseness.

'Do you have a brother, David?'

'Yes,' he replied.

101

'He's been trying to contact you.'

'But I haven't spoken to him for twenty years. What's going on?'

'He rang just after midday. He thought you should know. Your mother died three days ago. Her funeral is tomorrow.'

# 8

Stone sat down. 'What did she die of?'

'I didn't ask. But she was eighty-eight. Not many people live that long.'

'When did you last call the nursing home?' he asked.

'Last month. The nurses told me she was fine then.'

'How long have I been paying the nursing home fees?'

'Ever sine I've been working for you.'

'Yes, it's a long time. And it's been a lot of money. But I'm not counting.'

'I expect you'll have the funeral expenses.'

Stone ignored the comment. Something rankled with him.

'She never said thank-you, you know. All I ever got was a Christmas card with "Best Wishes" written in her shaky hand.'

'It's been a long time since you last saw your mother,' Claire said.

'Yes, it's fifteen or more years,' Stone said.

'Did you keep in touch before she went into the home?'

'All I remember is that she was a bit sprightly then. But she smoked heavily and became cantankerous in her old age.'

'Most people get a bit dogmatic as they get older.'

'Dogmatic is the wrong word. The old girl was totally immovable. Even when I was a kid we used to row and fight over the smallest thing. So I just kept away. My sister used to say soothing words to me after a row. We only had lino on the floor when I lived at home and the walls were bare.

It made shouted words even louder and it was only a small terraced house. Anyway, my family became jealous of me. Still are for all I know. They knew I had money and they thought I should share it with them. And they listened to too many rumours about how I'd made it. They thought I'd nicked it. In London's East End that's not done.'

'Who's left now?'

'Two brothers and my sister. They all live together like a clan in the East End.'

'That's how families are,' Claire said.

'My sister Jane's the only one I'd really care about. She was pretty. I wish I'd kept in touch with Jane.'

'And your father?' Claire enquired.

'He was an alcoholic. Died thirty years ago. I don't even remember him. Just his alcoholic rages. And they were a time to keep out of the way too.'

'Are you going to the funeral?' she asked.

'Where? What time?'

'Tomorrow. Ten o'clock at East Ham crematorium.'

Stone thought for a few moments. 'The family won't want to see me. There's too big a gap now. It's been too long.'

'So you're staying away?'

'No. I'll have to go. But I won't stay long.'

'Do you want me to arrange a wreath? Or some flowers?'

'Definitely not. What use are they?'

Claire had no answer to that, so she let it go, not surprised at Stone's cold indifference.

'Don't forget the date with the tax people,' Claire said lightly.

'How could I?' Stone replied and put the phone down, gently for once. He rarely thought about death and the end for his mother, although sudden, he could take. She had been old and cantankerous and her passing, the end of an era, would have no effect on his life. It would even save him money. His memories of her were dim. His family had never been close and would now be driven further away, but that did not bother him. He had moved on, he would treat the funeral as no more than a pointless ritual.

His attention shifted to the tax inspector. He had much to hide and she was persistent – she wouldn't disappear and die, to be finished off in a crematorium. He knew he had to be careful, he had to play the bluff game with officialdom as he had always done, mixing truth and half-truth into a seamless mesh that appeared as reality. For the next ten minutes he made brief jottings on a small pad from his briefcase. He knew exactly where money had come from and where it had gone, and by reminding himself now he could be sure he would give no secrets away to officialdom, however hard they tried to crack him.

Top of the list was his Brighton pubs. Regular cash flowed from them, personally delivered each week by George, one of the managers, who always received a hundred notes for his trouble, and which Stone had then carried in a briefcase and banked into an account of an anonymous company set up with false passport and papers. He reckoned he had taken nearly £200,000 over five years from that.

Next on his list was the large backhander for 'Services Rendered and Advice Given' clearly stated on the invoice. This had come from a building company which had bought a property from him that was ready for redevelopment and overpaid in the process. It allowed for some of the price to come as a regular deal but with the balance as an anonymous backhander. Sure, the backhander had avoided lawyers and relied on trust or mutual thuggery if it had gone wrong. The developer had gone bust a year later and Stone was now confident enough dust had settled for the money ever to be traced. He pencilled £450,000 on his pad, remembering it was paid indirectly into the Cayman account without his own name on the paper trail.

Now he recalled the trucking company deal in Kent, Lorry

Loads Carting, with a cash pile in its bank. Stan Murphy was the guy who bought it and Stone smiled to himself, sure that was not his real name. He was a little fat, round man, but he was as hard as Stone at the leverage game. Stan received a sweetener of £100,000 in £5 notes to keep the deal tight but Stone cleared half a million. Bags of notes said that Stan was never going to grass on him as everybody had too much to lose, and Stone knew that Lorry Loads still rolled today under Stan's guidance. Stone wondered how much Stan had made in notes since the deal.

He eagerly made a note of the next deal, this one close to home: a row of six terraced houses in Plaistow, East London, bought in a fake name, where a mate of Cutlass's collected the rent each week in cash from unsuspecting Bangladeshis making their home there. But the tracks were always hidden through a network of false identities, bribes when necessary, and faking accounts to lawyers to show that the deals were genuine. Stone even let the taxman take a bite from the cake. Just to make it look right.

Stone immediately felt refreshed. He tore up his jottings, sure that the track-marks of his deals were obliterated, however much the tax inspector searched.

A few moments later he left his suite and took the lift to the foyer. He took a short walk along the uncluttered streets of the block around Claridge's. A few people ambled along, a taxi rushed past, but he saw nothing unusual, and he stopped and window-shopped several classy antique shops.

Unpriced furniture and pictures almost enticed him to enter and browse further. Arrow Hall needed offerings like these and what better than antiques to keep Claire interested? But this was too classy and he left it. At the next corner he bought an expensive black silk tie to see him through tomorrow and left the shop quickly.

As he threw his purchase onto the bed in his suite his

instinct reminded him that times were changing, and the ice he was walking on was becoming thinner. Fenfleet, Drake and the taxman crowded in his brain. If only he could knock them down one by one.

*

The next morning on his mobile Harry Stone summoned Anton. It was time to meet with his family after many years of coldness, inertia, even hostility.

Anton drove Stone slowly and with care as if his boss's temper would suddenly erupt if jolted. But Stone was silent and even as the comforting and familiar surroundings of East London enfolded him he could not discard an unusual feeling of solitude, isolation, of not belonging here.

The crematorium in East Ham was close to a rail line and the distinct rumble of electric Underground trains regularly disturbed the peace and quiet that was the ordained order for the well-tended lawns and blooming roses. 'This is just creepy, a film set built for today,' Stone thought as Anton drew up close to the chapel.

Undeterred, he walked purposefully into the small building. A misty drizzle barely slipped to the ground but stayed suspended in the air as if it had stopped just to allow this ritual. Stone was late, as he had planned, and the coffin and family mourners were in place. The stark chapel was hushed, slow, but its purpose was not comforting.

In the front row he saw his sister, Jane, dressed totally in black, her head covered with a scarf, flanked by his two younger brothers, David and Alf. Behind sat a dozen vaguely remembered people, and alongside them presumably neighbours, nursing home staff, people he did not know at all.

Stone sat through the short service and mouthed the words of a hymn. The end of the ceremony came quite abruptly with the vicar announcing a blessing which made no impact on Stone. The moving coffin creaked as it disappeared from the view of the gathered mourners. Now was the time for Stone to slip out quickly, even though he wanted to speak to Jane. But if he stayed it would lead to difficult conversations, awkward silences, and Stone was not up for that. He did not know why but he hoped his presence had been noticed. At that moment that was all that mattered.

On the lawn, twenty yards from the chapel's entrance, Anton waited, standing rock still with his arms folded. In the mist he was almost indistinguishable, with his cap and dark suit, from the undertaker, who stood by a large black car waiting to whisk the family mourners away. They would soon meet elsewhere and the place would be cleared before the next mourning procession arrived.

In these unfamiliar surroundings Stone was uncertain as he left the chapel. Piped organ music filled the air with an unusually spirited tune and the faint rumble of a passing train held him back on the marble steps for a few unclear moments. Perhaps he knew it was the last time for meeting with his family. Maybe he should stop and speak to Jane. Maybe he should...

Stone did not even see the face. He just heard a sharp voice over his shoulder and it startled him just as he had been startled on the warm St Lucia beach.

'Harry Stone, eh?'

Stone spun round.

'Drake says to tell you he ain't forgotten his beatin'. Just like you he's got mates and a big family in the East End and he's after you. It's no use hiding. It won't work. You better pay up. Here's how.'

A short, squat, coloured man, old, in dirty jeans, waved a sheet of paper in the air close to Stone's face. Forcefully he stuffed it deeply into Stone's coat, roughly pushing him forward a few steps. Then a hard thud came as the intruder's fist made contact with Stone's neck, spinning him round and flinging him to the ground. He fell fast, a movement he could not stop.

Water from a small puddle oozed through Stone's coat onto his back and he felt the coldness tingle his skin as he lay momentarily dazed in the mist that enclosed this ethereal place.

He looked up, his surprise quickly turning to fright. He saw the hunched shoulders of a dark-haired man in a torn brown leather jacket straighten and stride away towards the rose garden where he was soon hidden by a large yew tree as solid as the chapel building itself.

Stone sat up and staggered to his feet. This time it had been a cockney from the Caribbean whose tones had been blurred into the true notes of London's East End. This time there were no knives to the throat but a sharp punch to the neck. It still hurt.

Anton, facing the other way, had missed it all. Now he turned and saw Stone heaving himself from the ground and ran to his side, holding his cap in his hand.

Stone staggered forward slowly like a drunk, brushing water and gravel from his coat. He straightened his tie.

'You okay, Mr Stone?'

'Yes. Let's get out of here. This place gives me the creeps,' he said, pulling Anton with him by the arm as he walked breathlessly away.

Family and other mourners were coming slowly from the chapel into the misty drabness. Stone saw Jane from the corner of his eye, a handkerchief held to her eyes. He averted his gaze with a tinge of regret that he could not wait to see the one woman with whom he had ever felt at ease and who was the only person who had ever really loved him.

But Stone was now in a hurry. He looked back and saw his family standing together on the marble steps. Had they seen him fall? Would they have done anything if they had? These thoughts increased his haste to get away.

'Did you see that guy?' he asked breathlessly. There was a darting look in his eyes.

'No, sir. I saw you fall and I rushed across, like quick.'

'Keep your eyes open next time. He hit me and I could have been killed. You're supposed to guard me aren't you? That's what you're paid for.'

'Mr Stone, I came as soon as I saw you fall. What happened?'

'Punched me in the neck.'

'Who was it?'

'Nobody you'd know.'

'I might,' Anton replied. 'I know a lot of people in London.'

'Shut up,' Stone snapped. 'Let's get out of here.'

Drake had been finished off in St Lucia and he wasn't supposed to be strong enough to kick back. But the stark truth of a fist to his neck now told Stone differently.

With excessive care Anton helped Stone into the car. He said nothing. Stone tore his tie off and threw his wet coat onto the back seat. For a moment he sat still, dazed, a deep frown highlighting the lines on his face. Retrieving the piece of paper that had been thrust into his pocket he read it quickly.

*Stone,*
*Two hundred thousand used notes. 3.27 next Tuesday afternoon. Hammersmith Tube station. Platform two. Third seat from the signal end there's a bin. Stash the money in it. No police you get no problems. You'll be done if you don't do it.*
*Drake*

Stone stuffed the paper back in his pocket. He stared thoughtfully through the windscreen, rocking gently with the movement of the car as it left the crematorium. Another arrow of pain hit at his neck and he swore under his breath.

His breathing quickened as Anton drove slowly along a jammed road towards the City and momentarily he forgot his discomfort as he barked instructions to his driver.

'Make sure we're not being followed,' he said as they passed a muddled jostle of traffic at some lights.

Anton looked in his mirror. 'A red mini, Mr Stone. A few cars behind left the crematorium with us. Can't do much to clear it in this traffic.'

Stone's neck stiffened as he tried to turn round. 'Get to the City and I'll dodge them there,' he said sharply.

Stone was agitated and twice in the next five minutes he questioned Anton about the red mini. Twice Anton broke the silence to confirm it was trailing a few cars behind. The pursed lips on Stone's face showed that tenseness was biting at him.

At traffic lights at the Bank Underground station, and with no warning to Anton, Stone suddenly left the car, slamming the door heavily as he looked behind. He saw the squat dark man from the crematorium leave the mini a hundred yards behind and run to catch up. In a moment of panic Stone stood still, mesmerised, but adrenaline then drove him down the wide stairs that led to the trains. Few people impeded him but he was breathless when he arrived at the hot and stuffy circular booking level. Stone ran quickly past a small queue of people at the ticket counter and at the toilets he locked himself in the first empty cubicle. What the hell is going on? he thought as he caught his breath.

It was twenty minutes before Stone left the cubicle, peering tentatively around as he opened the door. There was no one about. He breathed in heavily and walked quickly to the booking hall where he bought a ticket that would take him to safety.

The station was crowded, a strong dusty wind blowing

down the tunnel. Stone, now sweating heavily, kept to the rear of the crowd and felt his neck, which was aching with a dull pain. Two minutes later he was on a train and as it rattled noisily through the tunnel Stone stood and swayed by the doors, keeping his face to the window. He stared into the tunnel. It was dark. It was noisy. Again he wondered how this madman had found him at his mother's funeral.

The train came to a screeching halt minutes later at St Paul's station. The carriage emptied and Stone took a seat. He stared at nothing as the train moved urgently forward. Yes, he'd got away, he was now more composed and in control of himself. Of course he would never pay the crass demand for £200,000 . . . Then he felt cold as he remembered that that was exactly what he had decided in St Lucia. In the rumbling carriage, staring vacantly into space, he knew he had to take action to stop this menace getting any closer.

There was urgency in his step as he emerged into the now sunlit day at Oxford Circus, where he took a cab back to the quietness and safety of Claridge's. There, almost as a ritual, he tore up the note demanding cash and flushed the pieces of crumpled paper down the toilet. He would deal with Hammersmith tube station in his own way and not as a knee-jerk response to Drake's crazed threats.

He knew it had been a mistake to go to his mother's funeral. He should have left it well alone, let his family get on with it, even though the bill would land with him. Except he again thought of Jane.

He took his time changing into a newly-laundered white shirt and freshly pressed trousers before he called Roger Garon – a lifeline he had to keep open, a lifeline that could deliver the Fenfleet pieces of silver that were luring him.

'Tell me how your wife's getting on with Claire.' His loud voice showed irritability.

'Hold on, Harry,' Roger replied. 'These things don't happen overnight.'

'I want it done quickly.'

'Don't you know what women are like when buying clothes? No. Perhaps you don't,' Roger said almost to himself.

'Mrs Garon got Claire ready for her real job yet? The one at Trifoni.'

'Not yet. Push 'em too hard and it won't happen. Hold back is my advice.'

'Don't be negative, Roger. And I hope you haven't told your wife all that's going on.'

'Of course not. Only as much as she needs to know. Just like you've told Claire.'

'Have you found the name of Rick Austin's secretary?'

Roger tried to play for time. 'If you want to do something nasty to Rick Austin's girl then let's pick the right one.'

'I want to get on with it. Like now.'

'Harry, for God's sake you sound more rattled than you did the other night.'

'I'm not rattled!' Stone shouted. 'I just have more urgency about things than you.'

Roger ignored the comment. 'It's a Gail Crayshaw. She's been at Trifoni working for Rick Austin for a long time. Five-foot-five, blonde hair, late thirties and drives a red VW Beetle.'

'Registration number?'

Roger gave the personalised number G 246 which Stone wrote down eagerly.

'And she lives in Islington. Where else?' Roger added sarcastically.

'Right. I'll deal with it,' Stone said.

'That's just what worries me,' Roger added.

'It's not Gail Crayshaw, it's her job at Trifoni that we're after. So what about a little accident that'll keep her out of work for a few weeks?'

'Harry, you're playing with fire. Why do you have to do these crazy things?'

'You watch, it'll be quick and efficient, eh?' Stone said smugly.

'You thought of the downside?'

'There's none. Claire fills the gap, gets what I need to know to corner Fenfleet, then she comes out.'

'And if she gets caught in the middle?'

'She won't.'

'Cayman accounts. Taxman chasing. And now this. Why?'

'I want the Fenfleet pubs.'

'You don't need 'em that much.'

'Have you made a date to go see James Kennedy?'

'He won't see me until next week earliest. His secretary kept me on the line but she wouldn't let me speak to him. It was the brush-off, Harry. You know how that works, for God's sake.'

'Ring him every day. Ring him at home. Let him know it's to his advantage to see us.'

'And talk openly about bribes? On the phone? Harry, you're crazy.'

'You want your fee paid. You get me a date with this guy. And it can't wait.'

'We're working on it fast. So have some patience.'

'Call me tomorrow, Roger. Call me with better news of progress.'

There was a snarl in his voice, a coldness with his demands, that Roger had heard before. But he let it pass as all in a day's work advising this man.

Stone poured a glass of Glenfiddich and after his first taste took a small pocket book from his briefcase. The number of a man whose full name he did not even know but was listed as 'Bonso' was on page six. It had been ten years since they had spoken. Ten years ago Bonso had done a job for him and he recalled it as clearly as if it had been

114

only ten days. The decade had passed quickly since he had tried to get planning permission to convert a disused Victorian church into shops in the middle of a prosperous East Anglian town. The planning committee had been behind the deal to enliven their blighted town centre, except for two vociferous members. At every turn they opposed Stone, wanting to preserve the past no matter what.

No one saw the coincidence but Councillor Jeans, one of the opponents, arrived home one evening to find her neat house on a trim estate smouldering as firefighters damped down the embers from a blaze which had gutted the place. 'Electrical fault' was the cause identified by the forensic investigators.

Two days after the fire the local paper proclaimed that a violent mugging, which put Councillor Harries in hospital after being left in a side street with a broken leg and badly bruised ribs, was the work of 'drunks'.

Stone took another satisfying draught from his Glenfiddich as he remembered that after such traumas both councillors had other things on their minds than Stone's plans, which were rubber-stamped by the committee a week later. It had been a smooth and efficient job for Stone, brute force had worked then to get his own way, so why not now? He dialled the number.

'That you, Bonso?'

'Yeh.'

'You remember me? Harry Stone? You did a job for me a few years ago in East Anglia.'

'Tell me about it.' Bonso was guarded.

'Want another job? Good money. In cash. No questions.'

'Keep going,' Bonso said.

'A business called Trifoni Group. Flashy offices up West. You'll find the address in the telephone book. I want a secretary removed for a while.'

'Name?'

'Gail Crayshaw. Five-foot-five, drives a red Beetle. Reg G 246. Not difficult to remember that, eh?'

'I'm writing it down,' Bonso said.

Stone thought for a moment then added. 'Nothing too drastic. Off the scene for about six weeks would be enough.'

'How much?'

'Three grand.'

'Make it five. There are expenses, you know.'

'Okay. Five. In used notes paid into the bookie on Union Street in London E12.' Stone paused for a moment then added, 'Like it?'

'A broken leg would do,' Bonso said coldly.

'Whatever you think.'

'How soon?'

'Urgently. Tomorrow or the day after at the latest.'

'Why's everybody in such a tearing hurry these days?'

'Do you want the job?' Stone asked testily.

'We'll do it. But it might take more time than you ask for.'

'Just do it quickly, Bonso. I'll ring by the weekend to see how you're doing.'

Bonso replied gruffly. 'Don't forget the notes. Because if you do . . .'

Bonso's voice drawled on and sweat was staining Stone's shirt as he put the phone down. The raw end of life in its total nastiness somehow always bothered him, and coming at the end of a day which had marked his mother's funeral his mood sank, swamping his hopes that the Fenfleet deal was nearly his. Then a thought struck him. Anton. He was the answer. Anton was big, tough, with a brutal streak running through him bred from looking after himself in a hostile world. In the morning he'd call Anton and give instructions to get Drake finished off.

Stone put his jacket on and descended to the foyer. He walked quickly to the cashier's office where he presented two gold credit cards to a smiling, dark-haired Asian man. The discussion was brief, the commission payment high, but Stone's request was granted without further question. The cashier did not look at Stone as he deftly counted out the notes. One thousand pounds in used fivers. The bundle was surprisingly small and Stone easily stuffed it into his jacket pocket.

Slightly breathless he securely closed the suite door, and looked at the Glenfiddich bottle. No. He'd celebrate when Drake had been cornered and smashed. He'd celebrate after Claire had moved unnoticed into Trifoni.

Methodically Stone undressed, showered and was ready for bed. It was only 9.30 p.m. But before he climbed between the crisp white sheets and because he could no longer bear the thought lingering from the grey morning in East London of her mourning alone, he rang the receptionist and arranged for a large bouquet of flowers to be sent to Jane. Anonymously. That small action settled his mood. But he did not know then what would happen at Hammersmith Tube station next Tuesday or how Rick Austin at Trifoni was getting ahead of him on the Fenfleet deal. However, the gesture of the flowers allowed him to drift into sleep satisfied that he had thought of his sister in the middle of problems she would not understand at all.

# 9

Le Matin D'Or nightclub was in an empty Paris backstreet off the Champs Elysées. There was nothing outside that indicated what went on inside, just a large brass number 21 on a heavy wooden door. Rick Austin tentatively tried its handle. Nothing moved. He knocked heavily with his fist.

There was no window but a small square covered with heavy wire mesh had been cut out at eye level. A latch slid open from inside and a throaty voice said, 'You have a reservation?'

'I booked a table from the Intercontinental Hotel. My name's Austin,' Rick said in fumbled French.

The latch slid shut with a loud click.

Rick turned to James Kennedy who was by his side and smiled. 'Getting into a nightclub here is like getting at the gold in Fort Knox,' he said.

'It's not getting in that worries me. It's getting out that might be more difficult.'

'They let you out when you've had a bucket or two of champagne and you've paid the bill. But don't worry, I'll deal with that when the time comes.' Rick laughed, as at ease in a nightclub as James was at a football ground.

Rick and James had already shared a bottle of champagne over dinner at the Intercontinental, close to the Tuilleries and the Louvre. They were in good spirits and Rick was determined that they would make the evening a long one. Whatever the cost.

Suddenly the heavy door swung half open and the two

118

men were invited into the cavernous and dark interior. It was warm and a perfumed aroma met them as they were greeted by a leggy, bare breasted hostess. There was a false, fixed smile on her face as she led them to a table close to the cabaret floor. Disco lights flashed in a blurred sequence. The room was very enclosed with a low ceiling and thumping music instantly surrounded them. Hazy darkness pervaded everywhere including at the corner bar. The place had a faded luxury that showed in the unlit chandeliers and erotic gilt-framed pictures on the walls. It was already crowded.

As they sat down they were approached by another topless hostess who also had long legs that were too thin.

'Gentlemen, welcome. What shall we drink together?' she asked in broken English.

'Dom Pérignon,' Rick ordered. 'Make it very chilled.'

'Steady,' Kennedy said. 'We've already had one.' He stared unbelieving at the girl.

'That was with dinner. Anyway, you can't come to Paris and not drink champagne. That's what the place is all about.' Rick laughed.

This was what Rick enjoyed. This flashy over the top entertaining was expensive, particularly with the private jet that had brought them here. But what the hell. He'd get the payback. In time. Fenfleet was a glossy deal at the right price that fitted well with another brewing business he already had, and Trifoni had cash which could swallow anything – jets and Parisian nightclubs included. Think big was Rick's motto and that would not change in cornering James Kennedy.

The hostess brought the champagne, opened it with a large pop, laughed loudly as if it was the first time she had done it, and three glasses were placed on the table. One for herself.

'Je m'appelle Collette,' she said with a contrived giggle.

'We'll enjoy ourselves tonight, so you boys just relax and leave it to me.'

Rick looked at James with a broad grin as Collette sat close and smiled widely with flashing eyes as she filled the glasses. There were no more words. Her fixed smile, the crossing of her long legs, and the exaggerated sip from the champagne said everything that was needed.

'Here's to Paris,' Rick said as he raised his glass in the air and took a long fill.

'And here's to our business tomorrow,' Kennedy replied.

'Let's leave tomorrow until it comes,' Rick said. 'Enjoy ourselves first, James, that's the agenda.'

Rick knew the softening-up process had to be gone through. Fenfleet pubs was the excuse for coming to Paris, not the purpose. If he enticed James to indulge himself, tear off his inhibitions and then in a week or two remember where he'd been when the deal was about to be closed, that would be enough, money well spent.

Collette filled their glasses before they were half empty and Rick and James drank freely. They could not talk in the crowded, noisy cavern but talking was not their purpose. Le Matin D'Or was a place to watch, to drink and to feast the eye on unexpected erotica. Rick soon ordered another bottle and the cabaret music started. Lilting and soft at first, it gained rhythm and out of the darkness six girl dancers, just enough covering them to cause excitement, appeared from almost nowhere. They stripped with theatrical fervour to the increased tempo of the music and like naked statues stood for a moment in the full glare of a spotlight on the cabaret floor. It was impossible not to watch their hypnotic movement.

Two girls came close, tantalizingly close, to Rick's table, showing their perfumed naked bodies as if they were models on a catwalk, their movement slow and rhythmic, just naked moving limbs to excite the mind.

The hostess sat closer to James, filling his glass as quickly as he emptied it. The popping cork of another bottle soon delighted James's eye as much as the dancers. A Parisian *boite de nuit* was new to him, beyond his reach, but he was now drawn in and he grinned stupidly at Collette as she kissed him on the cheek. James's face looked hot and blotchy and his eyes were becoming less focused. He slurred as he whispered to Rick, 'What would your wife think of this?'

'Don't have one,' Rick replied. 'And yours?'

James looked at Colette. She had heavy make-up which only partly hid a lined face. Her blonde hair was so stiff and so long it had to be a wig.

'I won't tell her,' he said. 'She thinks I've come to Paris to talk about pubs. Not play in nightclubs.'

The dancers continued to gyrate for another quarter of an hour, a teasing time with the drink flowing easily. They entertained to the four sides of the cabaret floor as if it was a personal show to the audience. James, now with his arm around Collette, was hooked.

The dancing girls suddenly finished their routine, leaving a moment's silence in the smoke-filled room before it filled spontaneously with clapping and cries of 'More!'

His jacket off, a permanent smirk had fixed itself on James's face. Unsteadily he rose and tottered across the dance floor to the cloakroom. Collette stayed and helped herself to more champagne, now fixing her smile on Rick. He returned it fleetingly. He was not interested.

James staggered back five minutes later and slumped into his seat. He drank more champagne as if he was suddenly thirsty, and Collette again edged close to him. Coherent speech was now almost impossible for James, but he leaned nearer to Collette's waxlike face and Rick watched as he whispered in her ear.

'Where are we going?' he slurred.

Collette kissed him on the cheek. Slowly she rose and

pulled him from his seat. James, unsure on his legs, not knowing where he was going, waved to Rick as they left the hot, dark, stuffy room.

Rick sat back for a moment and thought about the evening. James had got himself into the erotic scene, but wasn't that part of the plan? He was now on the hook, his memory would never let him forget this place, his own part in it, and that left Rick in no mood to stay in the *boite de nuit* on his own. Ten minutes later he looked at the bill which included the champagne, Collette, an entrance fee and an exit fee. He could hardly see it in the darkness, even with the flashing disco lights, but he knew it was a few thousand euros. He settled it without argument from a wad of notes and left a large tip. For Rick Austin it was not difficult to get out of this Fort Knox and there would be another time.

In the taxi back to the hotel Rick was content. James Kennedy had suggested Paris when Rick had spoken to him and satisfying Kennedy at this time was all that mattered. And tomorrow? He doubted that Kennedy would be in any state to talk of anything by then. Let alone business. He would have the most almighty hangover.

Rick slept for a few short hours and without breakfast took a walk around the Tuilleries Gardens, enjoying the fresh air. He breathed in heavily, called the pilot of the jet to be ready for early afternoon, and rang Gail, his PA, to make sure a car was waiting to take Kennedy up north when they landed.

Kennedy appeared just before midday as Rick was enjoying a coffee and croissants, his face turned to the sun at a pavement café.

'Great night, Rick,' James said with surprising brightness, taking a seat out of the sun.

'That's what we came for, glad you enjoyed it. Something to remember,' Rick replied.

There was a moment's quiet. James lit a cigarette and

blew smoke calmly into the fresh air. He spoke without looking at Rick.

'There's something you can do,' he said. 'I wanna fix a date to meet you in Geneva. Last night was good but Geneva could be better.'

'Want to enlarge?' Rick enticed.

'No, but I'll call when I'm ready, so we keep it quiet until then. Okay?'

'Sure,' Rick said, but he was unsure of the hard glint he saw in James's eye.

James should be hung over, not suggesting more days out. Rick knew that his softening for the Fenfleet deal was not yet finished.

# 10

Claire arrived at Liverpool Street ahead of her own imposed schedule. She took the Underground to Bond Street. It was crowded, hot, uncomfortable. She had no eyes for other passengers as she sat in a corner and anxiously counted the stations on the wall map as they inexorably came and went.

As the Tube noisily rumbled in the dark tunnels Claire questioned what was driving Stone. The tax inquiry? No, never. Stone's withering contempt for bureaucracy would be no different this time. St Lucia his money-making deal had gone flat and he wouldn't talk about it. Was it that? And why Claridge's? A place he would never normally approach without cynicism and inverted snobbery about its customers. As she finally emerged into the sunlight of the West End Claire had many nagging and unanswered questions.

The evening before, Claire had located Jennie's address on the A–Z map and there was a tinge of excitement in her step as she walked the three blocks to the salon. But the shadow which had been behind her for the past two hours she never saw. A dark-haired girl, dressed in torn jeans and carrying a well-worn shoulder bag had been a few seats and a few steps behind her since she had left Arrow Hall earlier that morning. The shadow now crossed the road and watched from a few yards away as Claire opened the door of the salon. When Claire had disappeared the girl fumbled in her bag, lit a cigarette and for a moment stood and read the nameplate over the door. She wrote on a scrap of paper the address and stuffed it carelessly in her bag with her cigarettes. Beauty salons were not for her, they

124

were way beyond what she could afford anyway, especially in this flashy part of London. The girl walked away, unwilling to loiter in this money-bags area as there were other places to visit. Particularly Soho. There she could meet people she knew, have a drink and more cigarettes before going back to Liverpool Street. There was something from this trail, something to tell her employer about the movement of the girl from Arrow Hall, and that added a small amount of zest to her otherwise aimless life. She would now get paid for more cigarettes and perhaps even get a spliff or two. She crossed the road and strolled towards Soho through the maze of roads that she knew so well.

Unlike the girl, Claire was in strange surroundings. She entered the salon timidly, but it was an inviting place, with fresh flowers and soft music. It was elegant but informal, with a positive aura of comfortable hauteur and she immediately felt cosseted, relaxed and welcomed. Heavy ceiling-to-floor curtains at each window blended with chintzy chairs and light pink carpets. Coloured prints of ladies' fashions in Paris of the 1850s covered most available wall space with only a few mirrors intruding, there more to reflect light than to act as looking-glasses. Claire was dazzled. But would Jennie be somebody who would want to dominate and control her? Claire was cautious, determined that she would not be pushed into areas she did not want to go.

Jennie greeted Claire with a warm smile and held her by the arm.

'Claire, it's good to see you. I'm sure we have a lot in common.'

'Thank you,' Claire said hesitantly. They shook hands gently.

'I really feel I know you,' Jennie said. 'You will call me Jennie won't you?'

Claire smiled in return and the frown on her face momentarily relaxed.

'Has Harry Stone spoken to you? Has he told you what this is all about?' Claire asked.

'No. I've only ever spoken to Harry Stone once and that was about ten years ago. But Roger's told me about you and that's all I need to know. So let's have fun at Harry Stone's expense.'

'I'm uncertain. Why don't I have some beauty treatment my boss says, which is not him at all, and all of a sudden I find myself here. It's all a mystery to me.' Claire's frown returned.

'It's a mystery to me too. But give it time and we'll find out what's going on.'

Jennie ceased smiling for a moment. She took Claire's coat and led her to a sofa. Jennie sat opposite and looked at Claire's face, where she saw innocence. Claire momentarily felt hot and wanted to get up and run but Jennie took her hand in a soothing gesture.

'You look apprehensive, and that makes me feel really concerned for you,' Jennie said.

'Concerned about what?'

'Harry Stone doesn't do anything without a motive. And as far as spending money on his personal assistant's appearance which is perfectly all right anyway... well I just don't know.'

'He was very insistent I came to see you. I pressed him to find out why but he wouldn't tell me. Did Roger tell you *anything*?'

'No. But Harry Stone can be devious. I've seen it before.'

'So have I.' Claire laughed. And it broke the ice.

'Even more reason to know what he's up to, then,' Jennie said easily.

A phone rang.

'Sorry Claire. I'll have to deal with this. Be with you in a minute.'

Jennie was gone for less than thirty seconds. She returned

126

with the phone in her hand and gave it to Claire.

'It's for you,' she said. 'A woman. She wouldn't give her name but she sounds a bit gruff and short.'

'Nobody knows I'm here,' she said. 'It's a hoax or a wrong number.'

'She asked for you by name,' Jennie said, and then left the room to give Claire privacy.

Claire spoke tentatively. 'Hello? Claire Watts.'

'I know who you are,' the woman's voice replied. 'And I know where you are. Now I gotta know where your man Harry Stone is. Are you going to tell me?'

'What's this all about?' Claire asked, her face quickly turning a blotchy red.

'You can make it easy by telling me where Harry Stone is hiding. He's not at Arrow Hall is he? And somebody I work for wants to know where he is.'

'He's away on business.'

'Where?'

'I can't tell you,' she said. 'Anyway it's none of your business.'

'You'll find out it is,' the woman said.

'Who are you?'

'It doesn't matter who I am. We need to get to Harry Stone. Quick.'

'If it's part of his business interests you can tell me about it and I'll pass the message on.'

'No. We gotta find him.'

'That's not possible,' Claire replied firmly.

'Harry Stone can hide but you can't,' the woman said. 'So if you won't tell me, watch out. I'll be around.'

The phone went dead and Claire felt flustered even though the call had only lasted a few seconds. A moment later Jennie returned.

'Claire? What's the matter?'

'I don't know,' Claire replied. 'That was an odd call.'

'You look ruffled.'

'Someone asking where Harry Stone is,' she said. 'Almost demanding. And how did they know I was here?'

'You've surely told someone you're coming here.'

'No. Only Harry, Roger and you know. Nobody else.'

'Well, it's only a phone call asking for Harry Stone. Don't bother yourself about it. We've other things to do today.' As far as Jennie was concerned that was the end of the matter.

Claire looked thoughtful. 'Harry's been acting oddly lately,' she said. 'Running and hiding in Claridge's at great cost is not exactly him.'

'He's an odd man your Harry Stone. Full stop.'

'You can say that again,' Claire said.

'Okay. Let's just agree that we don't trust him.'

'Sure,' Claire said thoughtfully. 'But I can handle him, you'll see.'

'Good. Because my services will cost him a few thousand. So watch out for the payback. It'll come when you least expect it.' Jennie laughed easily.

Paybacks. There was suddenly something deep and sinister in the air which Claire did not understand.

Jennie spoke. 'Tell Stone about the phone call. Let him know someone wants to find out where he is. It'll do him good to think somebody's after him.'

'Yes, I'll tell him,' Claire said.

'One other thing,' Jennie said. 'I've got a flat. It's just behind Harrods. Small but comfortable. Feel free to use it as you want. I use it if I have early morning or late night clients and there's none of them coming up soon.'

Claire was genuinely surprised. 'Why should I need your flat?'

Jennie hesitated. 'Don't you think Stone'll have you running around for him after this? And the flat'll be a good place to hide when you want privacy. Don't give Stone the address and don't let him know where you are.'

'But I'm not leaving Arrow Hall. My own flat's there.'

Jennie handed the key to Claire. 'It's central for shops, you'll enjoy Knightsbridge and even Oxford Street. And you'll find it quite different to Arrow Hall. Make yourself comfortable.'

'Another flat, another place, that's enticing,' Claire said as she put the key in her handbag. She laughed nervously.

'If Stone's got something nasty going on and at any time you need to come and talk, well, you know where to find me. I'll be here. Or in Newbury.'

'Jennie, why are you doing all this?'

'I want to help you.'

'But nothing's happened.'

'Sure.' Jennie smiled. 'So, no more Harry Stone today. We won't even mention his name again. As you said, nothing's happened.'

As the day progressed Jennie worked skilfully and Claire wondered why she had never had a beauty treatment or even visited a spa for a day. She didn't need Stone's money, she had her own. Gradually she relaxed, blotting out the menacing phone call that, alone at Arrow Hall, would have made her very wary.

Jennie looked at Claire's make-up, toning in her natural colours, softening her angular face, and suggesting different hairstyles that would suit her. She gave Claire ideas for darker-coloured suits that would certainly make her more noticeable. Country was out and town was in, but the real Claire would still show through.

An appointment was made for early the next afternoon at an expensive and exclusive hairstylist that even a few celebs from the stage and television were known to visit. After that Jennie arranged appointments at two boutiques where Claire would find the right clothes to complement the rest of her style change.

'Isn't all this going to be a bit expensive?' Claire asked.

'Harry Stone said there's no budget limit as long as we get it right. So let's get it right.'

'But we don't want Harry to say no when he sees the bill.'

Jennie laughed. 'Stone's problem. Not yours. Not mine. Relax, Claire. And I'll sue if he doesn't pay up.'

The afternoon ended quickly and forgetting the gruff telephone call earlier Claire left for Liverpool Street feeling good about herself.

She arrived back at Arrow Hall just as it was getting dark. The place was empty, Stone was not there, Anton was not there and not even the wind blew to make a welcoming noise around the old house. Claire felt its eeriness almost touch her on the shoulder.

She turned the lights on as she entered the hallway just to make it more friendly and then out of habit went into Stone's study.

The message light was blinking on Stone's answerphone. Claire pressed the play button and with pencil and pad ready prepared to take the necessary notes. Stone's voice was the first to speak.

'I want you to come to Claridge's,' it said strongly. 'Tomorrow evening. Be here by seven o'clock. There's something else to talk about.' The phone clicked, the message ended as sharply as it had begun.

In the gloominess of the room Claire suddenly felt tense. There were no more messages. The solitary voice of Stone with its inevitable demands was one she could not argue with, but it reinforced her decision to leave Arrow Hall and find a hotel room for the night. She did not want any more unnerving calls from people she did not know.

*

The few hours away from Arrow Hall passed quickly and Claire felt again a tingle of excitement the next morning.

She got up early as the sun shone through the lightly curtained hotel room and carefully prepared herself for a long day.

Claire drove back to Arrow Hall and wondered when she would next make this journey along the familiar lanes, in countryside she knew well and which seemed gently to enfold her.

But as she entered the gravelled driveway she shuddered. The whole place suddenly looked stark, a decrepit mess with its unmown lawns, pockmarked with rabbit holes, and its overgrown shrubberies. She loved it here, though, and Jennie's flat could never be like this with its open freedom to nature that had many colours and scents. Claire then knew it would be a growing part of her plan to force Stone to renovate Arrow Hall and the estate. To bring it back closer to its history of long royal and noble connections. If Stone would demand payback for beauty treatment, so could she.

She took a deep breath as she entered the familiar front door and spent the rest of the morning at her desk catching up on papers she had ignored for two days. At midday she packed a large case, called a cab to take her to the station and left Arrow Hall. She fingered the key to Jennie's flat several times as she travelled to the West End, aware that options were now opening for her. But what was Stone after?

In the afternoon as arranged Claire and Jennie visited the hairstylist. It took an hour and half. She was disappointed not to see any celebs, or at least none she recognised, and Jennie would not let her see the bill or the tip that was added as they left the salon. Claire liked the restyle, felt good, even confident that, facing Stone later that day, she would be on more equal terms than usual.

And then there were the shops. The first boutique took an hour and cost Stone well over £3,000. The second was

£4,500. All Jennie knew were Stone's instructions that Claire should look different, chic, efficient, with no budget on the job. Carrying several elegant designer bags with some items to be delivered to Jennie's salon, Jennie was happy she had achieved her mission by the end of the afternoon.

But there was one final call. To a jeweller.

'Jennie, this really is too much,' Claire protested as they examined several exquisite, top-end price pieces of jewellery.

'Put it round your neck. Here, let me fasten it,' Jennie said as she held up a pearl necklace. The pearls were translucent, reflecting the bright light onto her pale skin.

'I could certainly wear that, but I really couldn't have it. It's just taking too much advantage,' Claire said, examining the piece in the large wall mirror.

'That is a very unusual row of pearls,' the male assistant said. 'They are the finest you will find anywhere. As you would expect they're not cultured or indeed glass. They come from pearl oysters in the Indian Ocean. Each pearl has been hand-picked. They are the very best that nature can provide.'

'That dark blue Prada suit you bought. They will nicely touch it off. They're not flashy but very sophisticated. Claire, they're you all the way.'

Claire looked again, felt excited, but also hot. An unlimited budget to spend in London's West End was a new experience. And Jennie was going over the top. Stone wouldn't stand for that.

But as Claire looked into the mirror she liked what she saw. These pearls were exotic, contemporary, an exact match to her skin colour, and with the clothes quite beyond her own purse. Stone was rich, he could always find the money if he needed to. And today with Jennie supporting her he would need to.

'No, I don't think so,' Claire said after thinking for several seconds and fingering the tight row of pearls. 'Maybe just too rich.'

'We'll take them,' Jennie said to the assistant. 'My credit card.'

'Of course, madam. Do you want them insured?'

'Yes,' Jennie said quickly. 'Full replacement value, please.'

The assistant carefully placed the pearls in their own padded box and Claire looked on anxiously, saying nothing. Jennie was showing no restraint, and where would that lead?

But Claire now trusted Jennie and she tried to hide her unease as they left the shop and walked in silence along the crowded pavement. Claire was uneasy, deep in thought. Stone's reaction would be sharp, he would know he had been taken for a ride and he would someday strike back. But Jennie had relished the experience as much as if she were buying everything for herself and this left a wide smile on her face.

On the next corner they took a cab to Jennie's flat.

'You'll be very comfortable here,' Jennie said as she quickly showed Claire around the small apartment.

'I'm sure I shall,' Claire responded. 'But I doubt I'll need to spend much time here.'

'Knowing that man Stone he'll have you running around. Use the flat and hide in it is my advice. Stay tonight. Why not, if you have to be in London.'

An hour later Claire, alone in the flat, unpacked her new clothes. She had a long bath, put on a dark green suit, one of the cheaper ones she recalled, and tried on the expensive pearls in front of the mirror. Carefully she took them off, still concerned at the extravagance, put them in the padded box and locked it in a small safe in the bedroom. Perhaps better not to flaunt them in front of Stone at Claridge's in an hour's time.

At 6.30 precisely, the excitement of the day gradually subsiding, she left Jennie's flat. She took a taxi to Stone's

133

hideaway at Claridge's, her curiosity growing as to what Stone was really up to and what her role would be in his plans.

In the marbled foyer Claire felt good, confident that no one would question why she was here. It was quite different to the first time when she had been flustered, overawed even. The world was after all a big place, she wanted to see more of it and was suddenly excited to make up for lost time spent at Arrow Hall.

As she entered Stone's suite she saw him quickly stuff a crumpled piece of paper in his pocket and he stood looking ruffled. His strained, pallid face surprised her.

'Is everything all right?' she asked lightly.

'Sure,' Stone replied and ran his hand through his hair – a sure sign that it wasn't.

Claire knew he was lying and turned away as his lips curved into a half smile. She was instantly wary.

'You look good,' he said, as if he wanted to change the subject.

'I feel good. Thank you for the clothes and hairdo. It's been fun with Jennie Garon.'

'Mmm, she's done well. So now we move forward.' Stone's smile disappeared as he spoke.

Claire sat on the deep sofa and watched Stone. He was dressed in a freshly laundered shirt and not in the scruffy patterned sweater that he wore at Arrow Hall. His authority showed. He picked a slip of paper from the coffee table and passed it to Claire.

'Three employment agencies,' he said. 'In London. They'll all give their right arm to have you on their books. There's a special job coming up that you're ready-made for.'

Claire glanced at the paper, surprise in her eyes. 'What have I done to deserve the sack?' she asked.

Stone laughed. 'No sack. You keep working for me and I keep paying you. But your new employer won't know that and he'll pay you too. How's that for a deal?'

134

'Where's this job?' she asked, a frown arching her eyebrows.

'An outfit called Trifoni Group. Offices in a posh part of the West End not far from here.' Stone paused and watched her reaction. He knew she could still say no.

'How do you know this job's coming up?'

'I have a source. Let's leave it at that.'

'I know what you're after. You want me to find out what they're doing on the Fenfleet tender. Then you'll use it to outbid them. That's it isn't it?' Claire was perceptive, and direct when she wanted to be, and the starkness of her words made Stone flinch for a second. It was as if she was telling the whole world of his secret plan and he did not like it.

'Okay. Well let's get on with it then. I don't have much time. There's only just over a couple of weeks to make the bid.'

'Hold on a minute, this is a big move. If I get the job at Trifoni what's the detail?'

'You said it already, Claire. You find out everything they're doing on the Fenfleet deal. The bid price they're going to offer, slush money, presents and anything else dropped to James Kennedy, the big shot at Fenfleet pubs. They'll be entertaining him with champagne in flashy places. They'll be throwing money at the guy like confetti to get favours. Probably paying for foreign holidays and ... well, Claire, for goodness sake, you know how it all works. Everything that Trifoni have put into their bid that we might need to match, I need to know. You got the picture?'

'And if I'm clever enough to get into Trifoni Group, who's got all this information tucked away?'

'A guy called Rick Austin. He's their CEO. The job's in his private office, his PA just as you're mine, and once in you start burrowing. Quietly, of course, so it doesn't show.'

'You want all that done in just a couple of weeks?' A deep frown spread across Claire's face.

'Don't get like Roger Garon. He's negative. He just sees too many problems.'

'He probably disapproves of your methods too.'

Stone gave Claire an intimidating glare. 'Are you going to do this for me or aren't you?'

'I'll try,' Claire responded nervously. 'But I doubt I'll get results. Especially if it gets anything like dangerous.'

'There's no danger to you.'

'You're being chased aren't you?' Claire asked, inquisitiveness overtaking her normal reserve.

'Why do you ask that?' Stone replied, avoiding Claire's eyes.

'You didn't move to Claridge's for nothing did you?'

'I have my reasons.'

'Okay, listen to this. Yesterday in Jennie Garon's salon I had an odd ugly phone call. Somebody demanding to know where you were.'

'Did you tell them?'

'Of course not. But what's going on that I don't know?'

Stone turned away and the same tight lines that came when he was tense made his mouth pucker. His only way to answer was to ignore the question.

He stood and started to pace the room. The smile had gone from his lips and he looked agitated as he continued to avoid Claire's eyes.

He held up his hand, he wanted to move on quickly. 'Try the Stargel Agency first. Near Leicester Square and top of that list. I happen to know they have contacts with Trifoni Group. And just believe me. I know what I'm doing.'

'But the agency will ask all sorts of questions about me. Where I've worked, where I live, why I'm looking for work.'

'I know all that,' Stone said. 'I've got some names for references. Let's say you've worked for them. A couple of years each.' He passed another slip of paper to Claire. She looked at it and read the names of three people. She'd never heard of any of them.

'But these are all made up fakes,' Claire protested.

'Sure,' Stone said. 'Happens all the time. Just don't hesitate and then it's no more difficult than telling the truth.'

'I've never acted as a spy before,' Claire said. 'So what happens if it goes wrong?'

'That's negative thinking and you're just too clever to let that happen.'

'This is very murky water you're asking me to jump into,' Claire protested.

'I'm not going to argue over this. You look the part of a top PA, I've paid for all of that, so you now act the part. Got it? Your job will be just to listen and observe what your new boss does. That's not illegal. And that's not dangerous.'

*Not illegal* and *not dangerous* were the sneering words that rang in Claire's ears. She sat silently.

'That's all,' Stone said. 'Keep it simple. Keep it tidy. And you'll get results.'

Stone rose from his chair. 'I'll be staying here a little longer,' he said. 'It's nothing important. Just some unfinished business from St Lucia I need to deal with.' Unsmiling, Stone walked to the door of the suite. 'Call and let me know how you go.'

Claire was confused. She asked no further questions as she left because she knew Stone would not answer.

# 11

Gail Crayshaw and Claire Watts had never met. Nor were they likely to. The only common thread was that they were equal in their intensity to be one step ahead of their boss.

Gail was in her mid-twenties, blonde, stylish, with as many boyfriends as months in the year. Even so, she still gave her all to the fast-paced demands of life in Rick Austin's office. She was close to the action, she knew what was happening in every secret corner of the business and Rick never stood still. Business moved fast, deals came and went speedily, and Rick and Gail directed it all. Trifoni bought property, offices, factories, unused land as investments, they bought businesses that weren't working well, tidied them up and then sold them again. And mostly at a good profit. It was all carried out with an air of relaxed calm, as if it was all just for fun, but like an ants' nest it was busy beneath the surface, busy with a serious and organised purpose.

Unlike Arrow Hall, with its musty chaos surrounded by the overgrown garden, Gail's office was modern, with hidden high-tech gadgetry, soft carpets, plush curtains and wall lights which took away starkness. Gail had personally chosen the landscape pictures on the walls showing Loire countryside where she went often, where she drank the wine with her friends. The room where Gail worked was not an office but almost a second home to her.

On her direct line she lightly touched the number pad. Her thin elegant fingers, with no rings, were well manicured and she rested them easily on the desk as she waited for her call to be answered.

'This is Gail Crayshaw, Trifoni Group,' she announced. 'May I speak to Mr Kennedy?'

'And it is in connection with?' the voice enquired.

'Mr Kennedy will already know Rick Austin of Trifoni Group,' Gail said forcefully and then waited a minute before she was connected to James Kennedy.

'Ah, Mr Kennedy,' she said. 'We speak again.'

'Nice to hear your voice,' Kennedy replied. 'We'll meet one of these days. What goes?'

'Rick has asked me to call. I believe you wish to discuss some points with him on the Fenfleet tender.'

'You got it,' Kennedy said. 'But we can't talk over the phone. Not in your office and not in mine.'

'Where to this time?'

'I've already told Rick we go to Geneva. There we talk real business.'

'Can I ask what the outstanding points are? I'm sure Rick'll want to know.'

'No.' Kennedy's voice was sharp. 'I said we meet in Geneva. And I mean Geneva.'

'When?' Gail enquired, her pencil poised in her hand.

'Well, today's Monday. So let's say Thursday. I'll call later to let you know where in Geneva and the time of day. Okay?'

'That's fine, Mr Kennedy.'

'You can call me James if you like.'

'Thank you,' she said. Gail had heard men talk like that before but she did not respond.

As she put the phone down Rick came into her office and saw her excitement showing through the smile on her face.

'You look happy,' he said. 'What's new?'

'Geneva. I've spoken to James Kennedy and he wants to meet you in Geneva. On Thursday.'

'When he said Geneva in Paris I thought he was drunk. Did he say why?' he asked.

139

'No, and I didn't ask. But he was insistent that the meeting be there. Not here, not Fenfleet.'

'He wants some more entertaining. That's it.' Rick laughed.

'Will you go?' Gail asked.

'Of course. The Fenfleet contract is one I want. And if it takes a trip to Geneva to puff James Kennedy up again, well, let's go do it.'

'Geneva's more serious than Paris,' Gail said. 'Not so many nightclubs there.'

'It's not called "nightclubs" it's called *entertaining*. And it has to be done.' Rick's laughter now filled the room as he remembered Kennedy tottering away with the lanky hostess in Paris.

'I'll book your ticket then,' Gail said.

'Book one for yourself too while you're at it. I might find it just too boring to go on my own. And anyway James Kennedy likes to see a pretty face.'

Gail leaned back in her chair, the grin on her face widening. Although she had never met James Kennedy she had a mental picture of him. She saw him as ostentatious, an arrogant show-off who would have an ego big and fat. Rick had already looked after Kennedy, throwing money at expensive entertaining. London theatres, Ascot racecourse, a few nights in Paris where suites at the Intercontinental were not cheap, but she knew this was how it worked and that thank-you letters were not on Kennedy's agenda.

She knew Rick was gradually hauling in his catch, having played the fish easily, and was looking forward to his meal. So a trip to Geneva to meet the man who could make these demands on Rick and who had asked her to call him James suddenly set her pulse racing.

'I'm off to lunch,' Gail said as she put her head round Rick's door a quarter of an hour later. 'I'll get the Geneva tickets on the internet as soon as I'm back.'

'BA and Club, please,' he said. 'Or should we take a private jet?'

'Do you know the cost last time we chartered to Dublin and Paris?'

'Okay. We do BA Club,' Rick replied. He was busy with some papers and had a sandwich in one hand. He could take it or leave it, Geneva would not be like Paris, from where he already had a hold over James Kennedy's indiscretions. This time it would be real business. It was time to close the deal.

'Chartered jet another time perhaps?' Gail knew that Rick only ever travelled in comfort.

'Yes, another time soon. And don't forget we have to sell the Kent car company this afternoon,' he said. 'So be back in time.' Rick was moving on.

'The lawyers have been on the phone this morning about that deal so I put them through to Graham Cuckney when it got technical,' Gail said.

'Yeh. He's the man for the detail.'

'Did it make money?'

Rick leaned back in his chair and put the sandwich on his desk. 'Not a lot,' he said. 'But we've had the wrong management running it. I changed them twice but it still didn't work.'

'I thought you were selling the business to the management.'

'That's the deal,' Rick said. 'We keep the property, collect the rents and let the management deal with the trucks and cars. What do I know about motors anyway?'

'Will Fenfleet be different?' Gail asked.

'Much simpler. Get the right management, give them some money to spend, be polite to customers and then we collect the takings.' Rick picked up his sandwich and began to read the papers on his desk again, his nonchalance visible.

Gail took her car from the underground car park and

141

drove carefully along the West London road, glistening in the sun after a sudden shower. As usual all was well in her world, and a trip to Geneva to deal with James Kennedy would be fun. It might even be exciting if a large contract was argued over. She liked to see a successful deal almost as much as Rick.

The midday sun, high in the sky, came through the windscreen, momentarily blinding Gail. She slowed and pulled the sun visor down, but suddenly a thud shook her as her car bounced a yard sideways and she was showered with glass from the shattering of her side window. Gail's head slammed sideways, hitting the doorpost and then bounced back hard against the headrest. Instinctively she twisted her head to look at the broken window. A large green van loomed over her, its engine revving as if in a panic. She had been rammed as accurately as a fast bullet aimed at the right spot.

Her car stopped suddenly as if it had hit a brick wall but Gail's seat belt held her secure. She turned her head and felt a searing pain shoot down her back. Her hands were still on the steering wheel but she was suddenly aware that she was facing sideways. The sun was no longer in her face.

She sat still, bewildered, mesmerised at the speed of the collision. She tried to ease herself from her seat but stabbing knives of pain in her back and neck prevented any movement. Tears rolled down her cheek as she gripped the steering wheel, her knuckles showing white. Stunned, she rested her head gently on the headrest in submission, a tear falling the length of her cheek.

The road was soon clogged with traffic, impatient horns sounding from all directions, and all Gail could do was sit still and listen. She looked for the van that had hit her but the vehicle, with its heavy bull bar, was not to be seen. It had reversed into the side street from which it had come and its driver had disappeared into the maze of Mayfair roads.

By the time an ambulance arrived Gail was unconscious. Pain and shock had taken their inevitable toll. She woke as the paramedics skilfully lifted her onto a stretcher. She immediately felt intense pain at the top of her back where her neck joined her shoulders. She cried out and clenched her hands.

With lights flashing the ambulance cleared its way through the clogged roads. Gail, confused and unable to speak, felt this had to be a dream. Strapped on the low stretcher all she could see was the roof of the ambulance as the pain now shot like poisoned arrows down her back. The whirring siren noise increased the urgency and blared into her head in the enclosed space.

She was quickly wheeled into the casualty department of Hammersmith Hospital and within two minutes had been examined by a doctor. Her condition was not life-threatening, he decided, but he immediately arranged for specific X-rays. He then gave her two painkilling injections.

Gail relaxed on the hospital trolley, and as the pain wore off so did the shock. She had an exciting few days ahead. There was the trip to Switzerland with her boss and she had never been to Geneva before. Maybe she would stay on for a few days on her own, hire a car and...

Gail drifted easily into sleep.

An hour later she woke. There was bruising where the seat belt had done its restraining work and her back was again feeling painful as she tried to sit up in the bed. She pressed a bell to call a nurse for some water.

'When can I get up?' Gail asked croakily.

'The doctor will be here in few minutes. So just lie still and relax.'

'But I need to get back to work.'

'We may have to nurse you for a little longer. But the doctor will talk to you about that.'

The nurse's words were soothing and as Gail found any

movement painful she did not argue but stared blankly at the high ceiling.

A young smiling doctor in a white coat arrived five minutes later. Without saying a word to Gail he studied several X-rays with a professional intensity that suggested to Gail the news would not be good.

'You've had a bit of a smash,' he said at last. 'There are some very severe small bone dislocations around your neck and also you have a broken collar bone, broken cheek bone and several ribs are dangerously collapsed towards your lungs. All will give you pain. The dislocations we can repair easily under an anaesthetic. But the collar bone, cheek bone and ribs I'm afraid will take longer. They'll heal in nature's own good time.'

'But I have to be up and back at work,' Gail protested.

The smile had gone from the doctor's face. He spoke in an authoritative tone.

'You need surgery and we will arrange that today. And then I cannot recommend you leave your bed in under ten days. Beyond that you'll need complete rest until all the bones and muscles are healed.'

'So, how long will that take?'

'A couple of months is ideal. Maybe longer because if you exert yourself too early the collar bone will not heal properly. And cheek bones are even more delicate. I'm afraid you certainly won't be in a fit state to drive for some time.'

Gail closed her eyes in resignation. She let her head rest on the stiff white pillow as that was the least painful thing to do. She then heard the doctor give instructions to the nurse for the necessary treatment just as easily as Rick sometimes dictated programmes to her in the office. Gail was not going to Geneva to meet James Kennedy and she knew it.

\*

Claire Watts arrived at the Stargel Agency just off Regent Street by appointment. It was at exactly the same time as Gail Crayshaw was feeling pain and undergoing her series of X-rays. The attention Gail received from the medical staff in the hospital was as thorough and professional as would have been received anywhere in the world, while, not far away, Claire was quizzed in a manner that made her increasingly irritable.

She sat in an uncomfortable chair facing a tubby, heavily made-up middle-aged woman. She took a deep breath and tried to relax. Earlier she had filled out an application form on which she had told lies as instructed by Stone. Claire was uneasy, she did not know what to expect but she was determined not to be controlled by this interview. She could just walk out if it got too difficult, she had already decided that.

There was no attempt at Christian names even though a plastic nameplate, 'Barbara Spooner', rested on the desk in front of Claire. Barbara Spooner pushed Claire's completed form aside and started questioning. She noticed Claire's chic hairstyle and expensive, businesslike new grey suit.

'What's your address, Miss Watts?'

'I have a small flat. Number 4b Argyle Street. It's tucked in a small road behind Harrods. I find it useful to be at the centre of things.'

'How long have you lived there?'

Claire thought quickly. 'Just over a year.'

'And do you live alone?'

'Yes. I'm not married. I like my independence.'

'Where have you been working recently?' she asked.

'I haven't worked for payment for some time,' Claire lied.

'Not worked for money?' the woman asked with obvious interest.

Claire sweated slightly, the words of the interviewer

unnerving her. If the agency woman did her job properly her story could be blown away.

'I've worked unpaid for several charities and other good causes. You'll see them listed on the application form.'

'I presume that means you come and go as you want.' Barbara sounded hostile.

'No. I'm disciplined. I always work to get the job done and never go home until it is.'

'So when did you last do real work? I mean for a salary.'

'About a year ago. I worked for my uncle who has his own investment business in Essex.'

'What did you do for him?'

'Usual secretarial work. He had a busy office.'

'Why did you leave him?'

'He died and the business was sold. Anyway, I wanted to go travelling. As most young people want to do at some stage in their life.'

'Oh. And where did you go?'

Claire hesitated. She had only ever been to France and Spain and that had been on school trips, neither of which gave her authority to talk about the rest of the world.

'Mainly in Europe and the Mediterranean. I like the sun,' she said.

'Do you speak any languages?'

'No,' Claire said quickly. She didn't want this subject probed further.

'Why are you looking for work now? Do you need the money?'

'No. I've just got bored. I need something more demanding than I've been doing. And I want to meet some new people.'

'So what type of work are you looking for?'

'Top-level secretarial,' Claire said. 'I have excellent speeds and I know how to organise.'

'We'll check those in a moment. But your background doesn't look very promising for high-level work.'

146

That comment made Claire seethe and she could feel the palms of her hands getting sweaty.

The speeds were duly checked and though Claire was very nervous in front of the word processor she measured up easily to the standards an employer would demand. Barbara was surprised at the result and as she looked at Claire's work she even managed a smile. Claire did not return the smile, she was too irritable and tense.

Claire sat in the uncomfortable chair once more and Barbara flicked through the application form, without taking much notice of it, as if she had seen too many in her time. She pushed it to one side again.

'Can we call these references?' she asked.

'Yes, of course,' Claire said.

'They all know you well enough to give a reference?'

'I'm sure they'll all tell you I'm capable and honest.' Claire would have liked to shout at the woman but she controlled herself, hoping that the tone of her voice would convey her irritation at the question.

'All right. I don't think there's anything else. We'll call you as soon as we have something suitable,' Barbara said. 'At your flat if something comes up quickly? Or a mobile number?'

'Call the flat. The answering service works very well if I'm not in and I leave the mobile off as much as I can.'

Barbara Spooner closed her file, rose from her chair and indicated the interview was over. Claire was ushered to the door. The woman had been cold, offhand, and Claire felt uneasy. She had started the lying process and she had not been sure she had been convincing. There had been a certain look in Barbara's eye that said she believed this girl, Claire Watts, and her record of good works, were just not quite true.

Claire sighed deeply with relief as she emerged from the cramped offices into the bright sunlight of Piccadilly, her whole body now feeling a degree higher in temperature than it normally did. At that moment she was sure that Stone's grand plan was not going to work and she would be the cause of its failure. What then?

For a tense moment Claire stood on the pavement, a busy throng of people moving past her. Standing a few feet away Claire's eye caught a short, shabbily dressed girl, almost entirely in black, with only a large silver earring in her right ear giving any sense of colour. She was in her late teens, with a distinctive Afro-Caribbean hairstyle that showed much of her scalp. She stared straight at Claire. Claire stared straight back. It was like two animals sizing each other up before a fight and it added to Claire's growing unease.

Within a few seconds Claire turned away and walked along the crowded pavements to the openness of Leicester Square. She stopped and browsed in several windows and each time in the reflection she saw the girl standing on the edge of the pavement a few yards away.

Claire hurriedly crossed the road with the girl only a few steps behind. There was a tacky tourist jeweller's shop and Claire stopped and took a lingering look in its window. The drab girl was almost by her shoulder, obviously not caring if she was noticed.

The discomfort Claire felt grew into coldness and she shivered at this unexpected, claustrophobic closeness. She looked at her watch which told her it was twenty minutes to her next appointment, and she still walked quickly into Regent Street where she found the office for the next part of the charade, the same game that she played at the Stargel Agency.

She barged through the door and looked over her shoulder. The Caribbean girl was still there, a cigarette in her hand and a penetrating look in her eyes. Claire was unnerved by this girl's closeness, especially as something suddenly registered in her memory that maybe she had seen the girl

148

somewhere before. And there had been the odd menacing phone call about Harry Stone when she had met with Jennie Garon. Claire shuddered, feeling hot and sweaty as she faced the teenage receptionist. She gave her name in a very flustered manner.

The appointment at the Executive Agency lasted longer than the Stargel Agency but only because Claire was kept waiting in a dingy office for over twenty minutes. It made her very irritable and she was more aggressive when she was quizzed over her spurious career. She repeated the same answers to the same questions which had been put to her at the Stargel Agency and she found lying easier the second time. She could feel from the middle-aged male interviewer's constant gaze that her appearance had made a direct impact. But was she not being seen as a fraud? She did not know.

When she left the agency the pavements were just as busy as when she had arrived. London never stopped, it was always filled with people and traffic, the noise incessant, and for Claire overpowering. Why was she doing this? She had had more than enough for one day.

She scanned the road, the tenseness that had been building in her head making her feel giddy. The dark girl had gone but her absence was just as unnerving as her presence. Maybe she was just hiding, lurking until the next time. Or perhaps she had been dreaming, there really was nobody out there looking at her. The tenseness in her head gradually relaxed its grip as she moved on.

She made straight for a boutique off Bond Street. She had in mind a particular designer dress in a deep russet colour that had caught her eye when she had been shopping with Jennie. Buying it with her own cash would satisfy a growing need to prove to herself that there was life beyond what Harry Stone could offer and one very expensive outfit would establish her new independence beyond doubt.

The experience of having her credit card accepted for

£1,500 was new but, in her suddenly light-headed mood it was not difficult to do. Claire left the Bond Street boutique feeling important. But amidst the crowd on the pavement she was suddenly wary, her eyes alert. There were dark-skinned women around but none took any notice of this elegantly dressed girl walking along the West End pavements.

Claire quickly decided she would prefer Arrow Hall that evening, even in its solitude, to the unknown dangers of staying in London. She held the bag carrying her dress tightly as she took a cab from Bond Street.

It was early evening just after the rush hour when Claire caught the train back to Arrow Hall, travelling in first, something she had only done once before when she had accompanied Stone to a meeting in London. This time she paid for the ticket herself and for a while relaxed in the less than usually crowded carriage. The only other passenger two seats away was a middle-aged man in a neat grey suit, listening on his mobile.

The sun was low when Claire reached Arrow Hall and its total loneliness and tranquillity helped her to believe that her world was back to its normal rhythm. She could forget London for a while, the noise and hustle and even dark-faced girls who might be wanting to get too close. But she did not sleep well that night. The house always creaked somewhere and each time there was a noise Claire was awake. Daylight came surprisingly quickly and in her dressing gown Claire went to the large kitchen and prepared a leisurely breakfast.

The morning was now hers and with little work to do for Stone she set about completing a necessary part of Arrow Hall's renovation. She went from room to room and methodically made a list of the furnishings and decoration the building would need. It took her two hours and her list was several pages long, and although she wanted to get agreement from the architect the mere act of getting something done gave her deep satisfaction, as if she had already transformed the place.

Slowly she walked around the garden close to the house and drew a sketch map of the area. There were parts that showed through the weeds where lawns had been and these she marked. A Victorian summer house stood in a corner by some shrubs and she withdrew at the rotting mess she found inside. The roof leaked and old garden furniture wallowed in damp on the floor. Mice had been at play and the canvas of a deckchair was well nibbled. No wonder no one went there any more.

Back in Stone's study, sitting at his desk, Claire looked at her lists and drawings and then put them in a file. Ideas bubbled in her mind of what she would do to renovate the estate but first she had to be able to hold Harry Stone to his promise to spend the money. He would wriggle but she would corner him soon.

Claire tidied a few loose papers on Stone's desk and even though there was a draught floating through the room from an open window the atmosphere was very heavy. It was weighed down by the complete quietness and stillness but this was Arrow Hall as she often knew it and she felt comforted by its familiarity. Claire placed the folder on a corner of the desk, satisfied with her morning's work and eager to push Stone into spending the money. If he could throw money at her image change then Arrow Hall...

The phone rang and Claire straightened quickly.

'Claire. Is that you?'

'Jennie. How did you know I'd answer?'

'Stone's at Claridge's still. You're not at the flat. I don't have your mobile number. So where else?'

'Yes. Good old Arrow Hall,' Claire replied brightly.

'I've some good news. But I didn't know you were leaving Stone and looking for other work.' From the speed of her speech Claire knew that Jennie was excited.

'I'm not looking for other work,' Claire said.

'Well, I went to the flat earlier, just to collect some mail, and when I was there the phone rang. Somebody calling themselves the Stargel Agency. They asked for you. I said I'd take a message.'

'What did they want?'

'You're to call them back. They said as soon as you could. Do you want to tell me more?' Jennie coaxed.

'Harry Stone sent me to the agency,' she blurted, confused. 'He believes a temporary job is coming up at one of his competitors. And he wants me to get it.'

'For God's sake why?'

Claire drew in her breath. 'He wants me to spy. He wants me to find their figures before he bids for a deal.'

There was a pause before Jennie spoke slowly. 'So that's how he's using you.'

'Could become a bit of a mess,' Claire said. 'I daren't think what would happen if I got caught.'

'I've told you before. Walk out on it all. Find yourself another real job. Start a new life. You've proved the agencies are interested in you.'

Claire thought for a moment. It was not something she had considered before.

'This will only be temporary work,' she said. 'When I've done searching for Stone then I'll return to Arrow Hall, get it sorted out. That's where I want to be.'

'Stay away permanently,' Jennie said strongly. 'There are other places than Arrow Hall and other people than Harry Stone.'

'I can't walk out now. I'm in too deeply. Remember the pearl necklace? How many thousands was that?'

'That's nothing,' Jennie said. 'Stone can afford it and you know it. Go and call the agency. Find out about what they've got to offer and then decide if you want to follow it up. It may come to nothing anyway.'

'I lied to them, badly, about my past,' Claire said.

'So what? Everybody does when they're job hunting. You take the job whatever it is. Get away from Stone. That's my advice.'

'That's easier said than done.' Claire felt hot and wandered to the window with the phone.

'If the Stargel Agency want you, will you take it?'

'Maybe.'

'Good. Let me know how it goes. Roger'll be interested too.'

Claire put the phone down with a tingle of excitement. She sat in Stone's chair and fingered the long silver paperknife that rested on his desk. This was decision time. If she did not call the Stargel Agency Stone would never know.

Feeling fidgety, Claire stood, walked around the room and then went to the kitchen where she mixed a hot drink which she took back to Stone's room. For a few minutes Claire stared through the window. She would be subtle. It was late. She did not know if Barbara would still be there, but she called anyway. Within thirty seconds she was connected.

'Something's come up unexpectedly,' Barbara said. 'Quicker than I thought it might. How soon could you be free?'

'I'm visiting friends in the country, but I could come back to London soon. Can you tell me what's on offer?'

'Have you ever heard of the Trifoni Group?' Barbara asked.

'No,' Claire answered surprised at how easily she could lie.

'They're a prestigious employer. Prosperous, go-ahead, with many different business interests in the UK and Europe. A great name to have on your CV.'

'Where are their offices?'

'In Mayfair. Not too far from your own flat.'

'And what is the work?'

'We have supplied them with many temporary people over the past few years. But none quite at this level. It's temporary PA to their CEO.'

'What does that involve?' Claire asked. She was already becoming apprehensive at the proposition.

'Total secretarial support. Travel and diary arrangements for a very busy man. Keeper of his door too, I hear. In fact everything from your CV that you've done before.' Barbara laughed in a less bossy way than when they had met.

'Why the vacancy?'

'The CEO's PA, poor girl, has had a car accident. She came from us two years ago and has done well. But yesterday somebody ran into her car. Nothing too serious but she'll be off work for a few weeks. Are you interested?'

'Yes, of course, but as long as it's understood it's only temporary,' Claire responded.

'Good,' Barbara said. 'The CEO's a Mr Rick Austin. Could you meet him tomorrow morning, nine-thirty at Trifoni's offices? He'll be expecting you.'

'Of course. I'll be there.'

Claire suddenly felt very alone in Stone's study as she put the phone down. Her adrenaline pumped, her heartbeat quickened and she walked to the kitchen, a smile loosening the frown on her forehead. Get the job and she could now play this game her way not Stone's. That would be a first, she said to herself.

# 12

Stone heavily dumped a file several inches thick onto the bare desk of the income tax inspector before he took a seat facing her. The young male note-taker from the previous meeting looked as smug as before as he sat at her side fiddling with a pen.

Stone looked straight into the eyes of the inspector unflinching in his stare.

'Thank you, Mr Stone,' she said. 'I am surprised you come to these meetings alone. It is more usual and helpful we find if the taxpayer brings their advisers with them.'

'What for?' Stone snapped.

'Advisers, lawyers, accountants, usually have all the information we need. And some of it is technical.'

'Nobody knows my business better than me, and anyway they cost too much to waste time on 'em,' Stone said.

'I hope you don't see this necessary inquiry as a waste of time,' the woman said, now not so calm as when she had started. 'It'll give us both the opportunity to clear up any unresolved areas in your tax affairs and that definitely is not a waste of time.' She sat back, shuffled her papers and returned Stone's fixed, intimidating stare.

'Look, you've had everything about me and my businesses already. Sent to you on time, taxes paid as demanded, questions answered. No fuss, all up straight.' Stone sat more comfortably in his chair.

'I'll go through the papers you have brought later. But is there anything in this file that has not been shown to this office before? Anything new not declared?'

'No.'

'Let me put it this way then. Does it include details of your bank account in Jersey in the Channel Islands which I believe you have held for the past eight years?'

Stone sat upright. 'That's in Jersey. Not here,' he said. He suddenly felt hot, the inspector's comment was unexpected, barbed, and it hit him.

'You are still required to disclose it. Can I presume therefore that details of your Jersey account are not in your papers here?' she said, and her colleague made a copious note.

'Didn't know I had to tell you of it,' Stone said.

'Your duty is to disclose everything to the Revenue. Worldwide income that is. Ignorance is no excuse for non-disclosure.'

Stone twisted his hands. He knew his duty as well as the inspector but bluff, innocence, ignorance was all he was left with. He chose bluff.

'Okay, so I've made a mistake.'

She ignored the comment and looked down at her papers, her tight features relaxing into a satisfied half smile.

'Is there anything else you need to tell about your affairs? Anything else missing from your file of papers?'

Stone looked at the ceiling for a moment. 'No, you got it all,' he said. But of course they hadn't, he knew that, there was nothing about the Cayman account. Well that was loads of cash, no paper trails, no security checks at airports because he had used private aircraft flights, couriers, parcels in the post and the inspector would never get at any of that.

'I want full details of Jersey and any other offshore accounts. You will find this checklist helpful to make sure you miss nothing,' she said, handing Stone several sheets of A4 printed paper.

Stone took the list and carelessly stuffed it in his pocket

without looking at it, a gesture well noticed by both the inspector and her scribe.

'I will call you again soon. I will study your papers but obviously we have further matters to discuss,' she said ominously.

Stone did not respond, annoyed at being caught out and not understanding how. But he knew that Jersey was mere petty cash, isolated, disconnected from Cayman and his real deals. Intimidated but still sure he could push it away, he left the dull offices a few minutes later ignoring hands held out to shake in civility.

Inside Stone was boiling, in a foul, rancid mood as he took a cab to Claridge's.

\*

'Be outside the front door of Claridge's in half an hour.' Stone's voice was sharp, the words demanding attention.

'Sir, I'm ready when you are,' Anton replied.

'The concierge'll ring my suite to say you've arrived. So don't hang around looking too obvious,' Stone continued. 'Half an hour. Get to Claridge's. Got it?'

'I'll be there, Mr Stone,' Anton responded smartly.

Stone put the phone back firmly. It was late morning and there had been raw urgency in his voice. Anton had heard the insistence before but this time it was shorter, sharper and Anton would do as he was told. Quickly.

Anton was in a very modest two-star hotel two miles north of Mayfair but close enough to be instantly available. It was even within shouting distance if Stone wished. But Anton was bored. He could not drink in case he had to drive and his dingy hotel bedroom was overlooked by a tall block of flats. It was even too small to relax in and watch television. The food was no better either. The allowance that Stone had given him was meagre and Anton had nibbled once or twice on a pizza and a disgustingly stale croissant, alone in a small café close to Euston Station. Even by Anton's standards this was not a place to be. He did not know what to expect from Stone's call but he was relieved that it had come.

Stone paced the room, brooding. Events of the past couple of days were biting at him, killing his feeling that he was in control, that he could manipulate anything, and even though his plan for Fenfleet using Claire was now running, other wild, unexpected threats loomed to disturb his progress. The bland tax inspector had in an instant almost stopped it dead and he punched his fist into his open palm, swearing loudly to release his frustration.

Anton took the Jaguar from its secure car park and left it on a meter a short walk from Claridge's. Dressed smartly in slacks and a grey jacket he hurried into the hotel foyer. It was within half an hour of Stone's call that a security guard escorted him in a service lift to Stone's suite.

Anton was hot. But Stone's suite was cool, its ambience totally foreign to Anton. Arrow Hall did not have this polish and he could only guess at how much it was costing his boss to stay here. Whatever, Anton did not understand the reasons for it all. Nor did he ask. He could see consuming agitation in Stone's darting eyes, the same agitation that he'd already heard in his voice over the phone. He stood firmly in the middle of Stone's room, and as the sun filtered through the curtains Stone began his instructions. Just like a schoolteacher talking to a miscreant pupil.

'You'll remember how you let me be assaulted after my mother's funeral. You'll remember how you weren't paying close enough attention to protect me. Well . . .' Stone paused and looked into Anton's eyes momentarily. 'I was given a threat when I was knocked to the ground that day. We've now got to deal with it.'

'Mr Stone, I can see you've got problems. I'll sort 'em for you.'

Stone again looked into Anton's eyes as if he wanted to hypnotise him and then continued to pace the carpet.

'You want me to take revenge against that guy who knocked you to the ground?'

'No. More than that. I've had blackmail demands. Six-figure money. And then threats of violence if I don't give 'em what they want.'

'Nobody's going to touch you. Not while I'm around, boss,' Anton said forcefully.

'Just listen. I want their precise instructions followed up. Understand?'

Anton's face tightened. 'Surely, sir, you're not going to give in to blackmail? If you do they'll just keep on asking for more. They'll bleed you dry. I've seen it happen, I know how they do it.'

'Shut it,' Stone said testily. 'First I need to know what's going on. I need to get their threats checked out and then we'll frighten them off. Do you understand what I'm saying, Anton?'

Anton was standing rock solid in the middle of the room. His face had reverted to the usual deep lines that showed when he was trying to think. Despite the coolness of the room he was sweating profusely, he felt uncomfortable, but he replied easily.

'Sir, you want me to go check out blackmailers, you've only to tell me and I'll go do it. Like quick. Blackmailing's dirty business.'

Stone moved to the sofa and stooped behind it. He grunted and then a moment later he held a white plastic shopping bag in the air as if it was a trophy he had won.

'Okay. There's a thousand in used notes in this bag. You take it along and show it to the bastards like a little teaser to test the system. And I want to see who bites. And then when I know I bite 'em back. Like hard.' For a moment Stone smiled as if he was already winning in this low business.

'Yeh, I can do that,' Anton said. 'How soon? Where?'

'Hammersmith Tube station. Just ten minutes from here. You go there tomorrow afternoon. Platform two. Third seat from the signal end. Next to it there's a rubbish bin. You're to watch that bin as if your life depended on it. That's for ten minutes before 3.27 and for as long as it takes after 3.27. Until somebody comes to collect.'

Anton for a moment looked baffled. Precise times had never been part of his life. Stone saw the look and continued more slowly.

'You put this bag with the money inside that bin ten minutes before 3.27. Just ten minutes. No more, no less. And you'd better understand what I'm saying or you'll get done over yourself.'

'Sure, sir. That ain't difficult.' But Anton's face was screwed into a taught lumpiness showing he was agitated. It was heightened by his unease in this flashy place and what he saw as his boss's crass demands.

'You foul this up and you no longer work for me. So don't think you can walk off with the thousand quid and never be seen again. You know what I mean, don't you Anton?'

Anton looked puzzled, affronted, and sweat trickled down his face.

'Mr Stone, you know I wouldn't walk out on you. No way, sir.'

Stone was not sure about that but he continued calmly. 'You just keep it simple, keep alert. Okay? I know that's unusual for you so don't mess it.' Stone rasped his demands, as he had done to Cutlass, as he did to everybody when he wanted it done his way, and ignored Anton's hangdog, hurt look.

'I already said you just have to tell me and I do it. Ain't that enough?' There was fight back in Anton's voice as if he was about to explode, the low deferential tone momentarily lost.

160

'Okay, so far I've told you the easy bit so you'd better listen even more carefully now. Somebody will come to that bin and you watch to see how they search it. Watch to see if they take the money and if they do you follow them and you know what I mean by that. You follow and get the money back and then teach 'em a lesson with your fists. A lesson which says don't fool with me. Then you find out who they are, where they come from, just so I can frighten them right off. Now you'd like to do that, eh?'

'Yes, boss, I understand it all. You can trust me to get it done like you ask. You'll get your grand in notes right back here. You'll see.'

Anton was becoming cold to instructions given by a boss who paid well but who he thought was eccentric. The orders were routine, the sort of job he had carried out many times in his nomadic wanderings through London and other cities, responsible to no one but himself. And if it meant a fight then that would add a great lump of excitement to his life which he felt had become slow and routine working for Stone.

For a moment Stone stared at Anton satisfied that his orders had been understood and handed him the plastic bag carrying the used notes. He spoke again. Loudly.

'You look a bit smart dressed like that. Tomorrow put some rags on so you're not too blatant or too obvious to these thugs we're dealing with.'

Anton looked down at his trousers, clean and freshly pressed. Yes, he would prefer sloppy stained jeans any day.

'Sure. But you wouldn't want me showing up here like that,' he said.

Stone paused for a moment not rising to Anton's jibe. 'Okay that's it. You can go,' he said. 'Go and get on with it.'

Anton did not reply. He thought he understood everything and he was pleased to get out of this flashy place where he felt uneasy. Two minutes later he left Claridge's by a side door, a sense of purpose in his stride, as if he was on a mission he could warm to and the plastic bag with used fivers easily tucked under his arm. He was interested in following up Stone's demands.

\*

Anton felt breathless, out of condition, as he walked quickly the two blocks to the Jaguar where the meter had run out fifteen minutes ago. In the car he sat still for several minutes to regain his breath, to anticipate the deal he had to close for his boss. He gave no thought to why his boss was in this corner, just that tomorrow would kill the boredom of the last few days as messing with blackmailers was right up his street.

Settling further into the leather seat Anton smiled to himself in the rear-view mirror and turned on the radio, loudly, as he always did when Stone was not with him. He threw the money on the back seat with his jacket and was in a good mood as he drove the car straight to Arrow Hall at his usual fast pace. He knew the journey backwards and with only light traffic it took him less than an hour.

Anton parked the car by the front steps to the old house, something he never did when Stone was there. Stone had this hang-up about keeping the front of Arrow Hall free as it spoiled the aspect from the driveway gates and he was quick to say so. Both Claire and Anton had privately laughed at this, seeing the irony missed by Stone.

Grabbing his coat and the plastic bag Anton noisily slammed the car door. Crunching across the gravel he took out his key but he was surprised to find the front door open. Claire met him in the hallway.

'What are you doing here?' she asked.

'Did you think I'd left for good?'

'No. But I didn't expect you back. Not yet. The boss got you running around?'

Anton smiled. 'You got it. I've been let out. Got a special job to do for him.'

'I'll put the kettle on,' Claire said. 'Then you can tell me what's happening.'

Anton followed Claire down the dark hallway into the kitchen. He removed his tie, threw his coat and the money onto the table and slouched into a chair in a corner. Claire noisily filled the kettle and jingled cups onto their saucers.

'Mr Stone's hiding isn't he?' she asked.

'Don't know what he's up to,' Anton responded. 'All I do know is he's acting strangely. And he seems frightened. Bit unlike him.'

'Frightened of what?' Claire asked.

'No idea. But he's got this hang-up that somebody's after him. Even a van sliding across the road in front of us when I took him up West seem to frighten him. Then he's being followed he says, even at his mum's funeral. And he has this barmy idea that somebody's demanding money or else they'll do him over. Ever since he came back from St Lucia he's been acting odd if you ask me. It must've been the heat out there. Or a deal's gone up the twist.'

For a moment Claire stared blankly through the kitchen window as sudden images flashed into her mind. That menacing telephone call in Jennie's salon, demanding to know where Harry Stone was and then the darkly dressed girl loitering across the pavement with that cold, constant, stare in Leicester Square, reminded her that something was going on that she did not know about.

'Why've you come to Arrow Hall today?' Claire asked.

'Change of clothes,' Anton said easily. 'Got to meet somebody tomorrow to do a little negotiation for him, and he don't want me dressed a bit posh, thinks I might give too much away like that.'

163

'Where?'

'A London Tube station.'

'You're being evasive, Anton,' Claire said. 'You know you can tell me.'

'Listen, darling, it's just better you don't know all the details of what is man's work. Not yet, anyway. We'll talk when the job's finished. Promise.'

'Fine,' Claire said. 'Okay by me. I'm too busy myself at the present to be worried about what our man's got you doing.'

'You've had your hair done. Looks good,' Anton said, changing the subject.

'Yes. Thought I needed a new look. So I splashed out.' Claire could be evasive too.

'Suits you. Except it makes you look older.'

'*Sophisticated* is the word,' Claire chided easily.

Anton detected a strange tone in Claire's voice. She was not relaxed in her usual way when at Arrow Hall and she was avoiding his eyes. Anton sipped his tea and looked around the kitchen as if he was searching for something.

'What do you want?' Claire asked.

Anton stood and smiled. 'Just to get on with the job for the boss,' he said. 'With the boss sitting in six-star Claridge's and me sitting in a half-star doss house so I can be close by waiting to be called ... well that's not what I can put up with for long.'

'I'm off to London tonight,' Claire said.

'What for?'

'Got to do some work, like you, for the boss.'

'Our man's hiding. Who'd believe Claridge's was a safe house?'

'Safe from what?' Claire asked

'Safe from himself if you ask me. So it don't really matter.'

'Good. You know your bit, I know my bit. Let's leave it at that. Okay?' Claire laughed nervously. Something was going on but the kitchen of Arrow Hall with the day closing was not the place or time to pursue that line of conversation.

'I'll take you to London,' Anton said.

'Fine, I'll just go pack some clothes.' Claire replied, ruffling Anton's hair as she passed his chair.

Alone, Anton felt his nerves tingle at the coming action and he ambled away to his own room across the yard over the garage block's converted stables. It was small and dingy but to him it was home for now. He didn't linger long. Quickly he changed into a dirty sweatshirt and torn, greasy jeans which he used for cleaning the car or any other odd jobs demanded by Stone or Claire. Glancing briefly in a small mirror he decided that with runaway, uncombed hair and worn trainers that were badly stained with grease, he was now an everyday labourer who enjoyed his own puddle of mess.

Carefully he emptied his trouser pockets of two credit cards that would show who he was and slid them into a small table drawer. He found a strange comfort in anonymity. It was the way he had always worked when confronting underhand crooks and tomorrow afternoon at Hammersmith would be no different.

Ten minutes later he returned to the kitchen and browsed a London Underground map which he found in a drawer and which always fascinated him although he already knew it well. He put his finger on Hammersmith Tube, stood back and decided he would get excitement from carrying out his boss's instructions. He fingered the money in the plastic bag he had left lying on the table as if it was pure gold running through his hands. Used notes were always good money to play poker with.

Anton noisily pulled open several drawers in the large table and opened the kitchen cupboards until he found a knife small enough for his pocket but sharp enough to inflict damage if it had to. It had an edge to one side but was blunt on the other and until now had only been used for peeling apples or potatoes. He fingered the blade gently as he paced the room, his impatience to get on showing.

A few minutes later Claire returned.

'You're not meeting somebody for Mr Stone looking like that are you?' she asked.

'Why not?'

'Shouldn't you have those trousers and shirt cleaned? Haven't you got something better to wear?'

'What's the use? They'll only get dirty again and I don't have to be careful when I'm dressed like this.'

'Careful of what, for goodness sake?'

Anton looked away. Of course he wasn't sure what he was going to meet when sorting Stone's mess but that did not matter because he could cope. He did not answer.

'Come on, darling, let's me and you go to London and we'll leave it at that for now. Okay?' he said.

'Okay,' Claire echoed.

Claire smiled. She didn't always understand Anton but she liked him even though he was raw and lived in a different way to what she was used to. He had never told her about his past life but Claire had responded to him with concern the previous winter when he had a bad bout of flu. She had shopped for him and bought medicines which she made him take and Anton had laughed at her for being so fussy over a mere cold. A few times they had enjoyed the odd drink together at the local pub and discussed nothing in particular. Not even Stone or Arrow Hall had come into the conversation.

In return Anton had always shown a fatherly gentility, concern even, towards Claire which made a bond of understanding between them, perhaps fostered by the fact that they both worked for a difficult and demanding man. Satisfying Stone's ego was not easy.

Stone bullied Anton like he bullied everybody, whoever

166

they were, Claire knew that, but she could see Anton did not take any notice of it. Insensitive to moods, he got on with his job whatever Stone said to him and Claire liked Anton for that.

With the early evening gloom settling around the estate they left Arrow Hall an hour later. In the car they were both strangely quiet, each absorbed in their own different webs of manipulation for Stone, but neither knowing where the events unfolding around them would lead.

As directed Anton dropped Claire close to Claridge's.

'Got to call on the boss,' she said, lying easily.

'You're not going back to Arrow Hall on your own afterwards I hope?'

'No, I'm staying with a friend. I'll get a cab later,' Claire said.

'Be careful, honey, London can be dangerous at night time,' Anton said.

Claire shut the door of the car and Anton drove off with a wave of his hand. Neither was sure when they would meet again.

Claire went straight to Jennie's flat, her own secret from Anton and Stone. That evening she spent alone preparing herself for the interview the next morning. Just the thought of Rick Austin and Trifoni Group made her nervous and she sipped a glass of wine, her mind buzzing and anxiety taking a gripping hold. She was unsure she could pull this off and that night she did not sleep well, waking early as the sun streamed into the bedroom.

At 9.25 precisely the next morning Claire entered the Trifoni Group offices. She was wearing a new elegant grey suit. She was nervous but a growing determination not to be beaten and to show Stone she could do it drove her forward. Trifoni reception was new, spacious, bright, clean and it carried an ordered air of efficiency and wealth about it. Claire was unused to this sparkle and, taking a seat, she felt the pressure mount and again questioned whether she really did want to be here. How would she live up to all this powerplay?

The flowers on the low table in the cool air-conditioned space were fresh, arrayed in a professional bouquet. They showed elegance, an elegance Claire unsuccessfully had tried to emulate around Arrow Hall. But when it was renovated ... the thought floated tantalizingly close but she'd believe it might happen when Stone gave her the cash to spend. For now she contrasted this place with Stone shuffling around in his slippers in the decrepitude of Arrow Hall, a vivid, stark and unnerving picture. She sipped coffee with a hand that trembled and felt cold moisture under her arm which even her meticulous personal preparation had not prevented.

Five minutes later she met the fifty-seven-year-old Rick Austin. His tanned face, fringed with lightly greying hair, was almost unlined, and without a jacket a bright red tie contrasted with a cufflinked white shirt. Austin exuded a mature authority, he looked totally as if he knew what he was doing. He was calm, unruffled, efficient. Was it like that under the surface, Claire wondered.

Claire sat in a deep armchair. Her nervousness persisted but she still managed a smile, meeting Rick Austin's eyes. She tried to look alert but relaxed, and rested her hands easily on her lap. Austin owned a big slice of Trifoni Group, he was its undisputed boss, and having got this far she was not going to be intimidated and let this chance slip away. But she knew her answers had to be ready and convincing.

'The agency report is good,' Austin said with a flicker of a smile spreading over his face, his clear eyes now meeting Claire's. 'But they always are, whoever they send,' he added, looking away.

'I have a lot of PA experience. I've been around and I

know what makes people tick,' Claire said, a statement she had rehearsed many times that morning.

Austin again looked directly at Claire and decided she looked mature, confident, even elegant. Stargel Agency rarely sent people like this, he thought.

'I see you live near Harrods. Argyle Street.'

'Yes, I have a flat there.'

'Coincidence,' Rick said. 'I have a flat five minutes from Argyle Street. How long have you been in that area?'

'About eighteen months.' Claire was surprised how quickly and easily she lied but she began to feel hot.

'It's a convenient spot. But it's a bit dead on Saturdays if I'm not working,' Rick said.

Claire had no idea what it was like on Saturdays, and she did not reply.

Rick sensed Claire's indecision and gave her a probing stare as if he could tell she was uneasy, but he moved on.

'So how do you think you could help me?' he asked.

'I've dealt with busy people at the top, I know what is needed and I just get on with it. I'm a good organiser too.' Claire was now on sure ground, what she had said was true and she smiled at Rick, looking at him and making sure their eyes met. It had the right effect because he looked away.

'Why did you leave your last job?'

'I haven't worked full-time for at least a year. I'm sure the agency will have told you that.'

Rick flicked over a page of the faxed report from the Stargel Agency.

'You sure that hasn't left you a bit rusty? This is a busy office you know.'

'I'm young enough to be flexible. And the agency checked my speeds.'

'Sure, but when did you last do real work that kept you looking at deadlines? It might look relaxed round here but pressure can get strong. And often does,' Rick said.

'Fifteen months ago I worked for my uncle. It was in his investment business but he died. The business was sold and he left money to me.'

'What was your uncle's name? Would I have known him? We're in similar business.'

'George Fenn. He was very secretive, traded privately, so I doubt you would have known him,' Claire said quickly with her prepared response.

'No, I don't know everybody. But tell me the sort of deals he did.'

Claire wanted to move away from this probing but she responded with more confidence than she would have thought possible a few hours ago.

'He bought into companies, sent someone in to trim them up and then sold them on. The last one he did before he died was a group of pubs and property near Brighton.'

Rick looked interested and sat forward in his chair.

'Coincidence, eh? I'm looking at some pubs just now. Maybe I'll do it, maybe I won't,' he said almost to himself. And then to Claire's relief he moved on quickly.

'Did your uncle's office keep you disciplined? Were you always in at eight in the morning and stayed until he'd finished? Eight, nine at night?'

'Of course. My uncle was not an easy person to work for. He was a perfectionist. That's how he made his money.'

Rick leaned back in his chair and again looked at the faxed form from the Stargel Agency.

'What about pay?' he asked.

'I don't need to work but I do need to be with interesting people. So pay is what you want to make it.'

'You do know this is only temporary work?' Rick asked.

'Yes, of course.'

'My secretary's had a car accident. A bit nasty by the sounds of it but when she returns I'm afraid you'll have to go. But that'll be some weeks away.'

'I'm only looking for temp work. It suits my lifestyle,' Claire replied with a smile. 'And a few weeks would be fine.'

Rick Austin was a man who made quick decisions, often letting gut feeling override sober thought. He was also in a fix with his faithful Gail languishing in a hospital bed after her accident and he needed secretarial help urgently. Claire Watts, a smartly dressed, confident young woman with an impeccable record, if unchecked by the agency, was worth a try. If it didn't work she'd go. Quickly.

Rick's decision was made.

'When can you start?'

Claire ceased smiling, leaned forward and without strain looked serious.

'Whenever you want.' She looked at her watch. 'It's ten o'clock now. Is it too late this afternoon?'

Rick Austin stood, his signal that the interview was over.

'I'm on the 10.30 BA flight to Geneva tomorrow morning. Meet me at Heathrow Terminal Five. Shall we say nine-thirty at the ticket desk? Bring your passport and I'll give you instructions from there.'

'A day trip?' Claire asked.

'A day trip,' Rick responded.

They shook hands firmly and Claire left this spider's web that was now enfolding her within thirty minutes of entering it, but not before she had again stared Rick Austin straight in the eyes. She received an acknowledging smile.

Claire descended the six floors alone in a rapid lift and left the efficient Trifoni Group offices with a sense of excitement dancing lightly in her head. But it had been too easy just lying and flashing her eyes, and she knew the follow-up of delivering Stone's deal would be the difficult bit that could floor her. Either way Claire smiled with relief as she entered the Mayfair street happy that the first part of her ordeal was over.

Suddenly Claire was alert with a watchful eye to see if

she was being followed. She stood still for a moment, close to the Trifoni building, and scanned the street, but it was as clear of lingerers or darkly dressed women as the lanes around Arrow Hall had been when she had left with Anton yesterday evening.

Feeling light-headed, she walked slowly to Jennie Garon's flat with the warmth of the morning sun on her back and the day to spare. She suddenly felt free of Harry Stone, free to make up her own mind on how to play this game he had started, free to tell him whatever she wanted. And he would have to take it or lump it as the puppet strings were now in her hands.

Inside the flat, Claire called Stone at Claridge's.

'I've got the job at Trifoni. Tomorrow I fly to Geneva with Rick Austin. Their offices are very ritzy, palatial even, and everything looks new and clean. It even smells efficient. Perhaps we should have more flowers in Arrow Hall. It does brighten a place up,' she said all in one breath.

There was a pause before Stone answered.

'Okay, Claire, enjoy it. But don't forget this. Plush offices mean they're spending too much on the wrong things. I've seen it many times. You need to be lean and mean in business because that way things get done. And let me remind you why you're in Trifoni Group. Information. Inside information that I need double quick. So no playing.' Stone spoke in a torrent that poured from the phone into Claire's ear. The unexpected harshness of his voice made Claire flinch and she held the phone a few inches away as she replied.

'Hold on. Just a moment, please. You've asked me to do something and even though it's right on the edge I've said I'll do it. So leave me alone and I'll get on with it.'

'Give me a call when you're back from Geneva. And don't get carried away. If they're flaunting it they're not making it.' Stone gave no inch, not even to someone he knew he needed on his side. Claire for a moment felt a tear in her eye as she sat in an uncomfortable rocking chair in the small kitchen of Jennie's flat and drew in her breath. Yes, she would play this game her way, especially as she recalled the dark Caribbean girl who had followed her in the street and the intimidating phone call that Stone denied. Stone was holding back, he knew more than he was saying and she shivered. She walked to the window. The view of cramped buildings in a narrow road was not Arrow Hall, it was depressing, too enclosed, too grey, lacking the vibrancy of colour that the country bestowed. A tear moistened her cheek and her mood was made worse by being alone.

'Damn Stone,' Claire shouted. But there was nobody to hear her.

# 13

Anton was not a deep thinker. He took each day as it came, mostly made his own luck, but he definitely would never have made the rendezvous at Hammersmith with used notes in a plastic bag if he had known how it would end.

He got up late, which was difficult to do in his hotel because of the noise which constantly surrounded it from early morning to late at night, dressed in his well-worn, dirty clothes and made for the café on the corner two blocks away. He had a greasy all-day breakfast, the café's main offering, and sat for an hour at the bare wooden table. He wanted to smoke but that would mean going outside, so he read the *Sun* from cover to cover, and more than once obsessively fingered the white shopping bag full of used fivers.

At 2.30 he left the sparse, half-full café, bought a ticket at Euston Square Tube a hundred yards away and felt growing excitement and an unusual dryness in his mouth. The idea of being busy, physical, violent if needed, was enticing.

The train to Hammersmith took half an hour. It was mostly empty and the plastic bag rested innocently on his lap like any shopping would. Anton casually thumbed at his newspaper and even though the day was hot he was relaxed, eager to get on with it. When he reached Hammersmith it was 3.12 exactly on the station clock. He had timed it perfectly. Slowly he walked the length of the platform and found the seat and waste bin described by Stone. His movement was deliberate, obsessive, even as he looked hard at the seat and the bin. Yeh, that was the right one, he told himself. He sat a seat away and pretended to scan the sports pages. But even though he was now bored with a routine job, every few seconds his eye focused on the waste bin as if it might erupt if he didn't get the timing right.

A few seconds before 3.17, Anton took a deep breath, wrapped his newspaper round the plastic bag and nonchalantly dropped it all into the third bin from the station end. The bundle fell to the bottom of the empty bin with a thud.

A thousand quid in a rubbish bin. Harry really was hallucinating on this one, he thought. Ten minutes to go and the emptiness of the station strengthened his confidence that he would soon be able to get it all back.

Two trains passed. Anton watched the station clock inch forward, and at 3.26 he was impatient for action. In blackmail there was always activity, at least a voice and sometimes someone out there lurking, eager and greedy for the pay-off. And then there would be a next time. Blackmailers hid anonymously but he knew they always had to show up for their pay day. Where were they this afternoon?

Anton looked at the overhead clock for the fourth time in a minute, and walked slowly away from the bin. He went towards the exit stairs and, to waste more time stood and studied a poster that explained the closure of the station for repairs in a few days.

He gained a vital minute. On the first step of the exit stairs he glanced quickly over his shoulder but there was no movement, only a few people standing like soldiers at attention on the parade ground.

Anton walked slowly until he was halfway up the stairs where he was surrounded by a sudden flow of passengers exiting a train. Against the flow he swung round and pushed his way down the few steps to the platform. He was suddenly breathless, a gust of wind hitting his face for a moment and making him feel cold.

When Anton reached platform level it was 3.27, the exact rendezvous time. A train rumbled noisily into the platform and jolted to a stop. People poured from its opening doors and Anton lost sight of the prize waste bin. He kept calm as in his pocket he ran his thumb along the sharp knife he had brought from Arrow Hall. He was in control of this operation, and he would deliver for his boss.

Anton stood rock still on the edge of the platform and within a few moments it was clearing. The bin was again in view but he tried not to stare at it. A few school kids, some on their mobiles, others shouting and jostling each other, mingled with passengers waiting for a train going west and Anton stared hard again at his watch – 3.28, one minute past the time given by the blackmailer. He slumped heavily onto a seat a few yards away from the waste bin, frustrated at not seeing the hood looking for easy money. But then he froze as he saw one of the school kids flip a chocolate wrapper into the bin. A boy picking up the bait was not in the plan, never on his agenda for using knives. What then if he looked in?

The boy sauntered away to join his noisy mates and Anton sat tensely, arms folded. The platform slowly cleared like a mist blown away by the wind. A mist that had momentarily obscured but had now evaporated without incident.

Anton suddenly felt conspicuous, naked to anyone who cared to look. He had been on the platform for twenty minutes, long enough for anyone watching to see who was there to catch a train. Or who was there for some other purpose.

Another train arrived within thirty seconds and Anton moved forward to board, an event carried out by thousands of people that day on that platform. He pushed his way through the open doors into the train. He was really leaving.

Inside he walked the length of the carriage and within seconds of entering stepped out again onto the platform behind an old lady who with her stick and shopping bag was slow in her movement.

The waste bin with the used fiver bait was over twenty yards away and Anton was now feeling hot. A station cleaner was emptying the contents of the bin into a black plastic sack and he bent to retrieve a waste chocolate wrapper and Coke can lying nearby. This black trash collector was dressed in a dark anorak with tracksuit trousers and dirty trainers.

A station cleaner? Anton asked himself.

The cleaner walked slowly and deliberately towards the exit stairs carrying two more black bin sacks. He moved with a speed that said he had all day to do his work. Anton followed, joining the small number of straggling passengers slowly climbing the exit stairs. The anorak with its bundle of plastic bags dawdled and Anton, to slow himself down, took the arm of the old lady with the stick.

'Can I help you up the stairs, darling? Carry your shopping?' he asked.

'No thank you. Left on my own I can just still do it. But it takes me time,' she said. She giggled contentedly and Anton laughed with her.

Anton increased his pace and at the top of the stairs he was just behind the anorak. The black sacks were tucked easily under the man's arm and he pressed a ticket into the barrier gate. Dustbins cluttered a corner next to the exit and the cleaner threw two of his sacks into the pile of debris. But there was a small black bin bag under his arm as he left the concourse of the station and joined the surging traffic of the main road. The sun was throwing heat onto the road and Anton saw the anorak stride ahead with the apathetic nonchalance of someone going about their everyday work.

Making no attempt to hide himself, Anton followed a few

177

yards behind. His target sauntered casually along the noisy road, oblivious to Anton and uncaring that anyone might be tailing him. This was going to be an easy snatch and punch up, Anton thought.

A hundred yards on the man's pace picked up as he turned into a side road that led to a row of three-storey flats with steep steps leading to the front doors. A cul de sac – cars lined each side of the road in a jumble that jarred against what was once an elegant row of Victorian houses. The street was gloomy, cold and empty. But to Anton the run-down dirtiness of the place was London as he knew it.

The man suddenly stopped and without looking round fumbled with a key to a white Transit van double parked and facing the exit. Anton drew in his breath and ran the few yards to be beside the vehicle, drawing level as the cleaner threw the black bin bag onto the passenger seat.

'I want you. You've got something of mine!' Anton shouted and tugged hard at the sleeve of the anorak. His quarry forced Anton heavily against a parked car. The dark face had wild bloodshot eyes, a deep scar bisected the left cheek and it hovered menacingly over Anton exuding a nauseating stench of stale sweat.

Momentarily winded Anton pulled himself up and flung his fists with speed, getting in a sharp blow to the eyes. The two men threw punches wildly in a struggle of speed and ferocity that took the wind from Anton. A knife flashed, momentarily glinting even in the dullness of the road and the two men clung together for several seconds as if in a life-saving embrace that would keep them both upright.

With a loud gasp of expiring breath, Anton, despite his size, slipped almost gracefully to the ground. Blood spouted from a tear in his shirt close to his heart and the dark red liquid gradually oozed to form a stain on the pavement.

His opponent stood over Anton for only a few seconds and then jumped quickly into the white van. The engine immediately roared to life and with a noisy urgency and a gust of smoke it raced down the quiet cul de sac.

Anton lay silent, face up, eyes closed, with blood still spurting freely onto his sweatshirt. Oblivion held him, and his body was only disturbed by a gust of wind that caught a discarded newspaper, tossing it carelessly in the air.

*

At six o'clock Stone paced his suite at Claridge's, annoyed that he had heard nothing from Anton. Yes, he'd been double dealt, he thought, the guy had skipped with the thousand pounds. Gone with the money as if it was a parting present.

He poured a large whisky and after a full taste he flicked the television on to see the early evening news. Only half listening at first he heard the woman newsreader drone on about a vicious West End killing. For a moment the starkness of the picture on the screen, of a dismal road in London mesmerised him, like a rabbit caught in headlights. Awareness came suddenly as he heard the words 'Hammersmith Tube', and he froze.

Nobody was shown but the description of Anton as the victim of the killing was clear. He heard the closing words of the newsreader as she came to the end of the forty-second piece.

'The victim has not been named. No papers were found on the body and police suspect this was another gangland killing. There have been several recently in London and they are appealing for witnesses to come forward as they say unless they can identify the victim it will be very difficult to solve this violent crime.'

Stone flicked the screen to blank. He refilled his glass and began to pace the room, more than once running his hand through his hair in an agitated gesture. Anton was big, strong, tough and knew how to look after himself. So what had gone wrong? Who were this lot Drake had sent to demand money and how could they, in the light of day, kill a man like Anton so easily?

Stone was confused, jolted and his palms sweated. Draining his whisky glass to half empty, without thinking he felt his neck. The bruise from the punch he had received at his mother's funeral was still there. It hurt. He sat down and stared straight ahead, seeing nothing. Fists to the neck he could take, but knives to the heart?

Who was next?

Stone drained his whisky and refilled his glass. Sitting in a deep armchair he cursed out loud that he had ever gone to St Lucia. The lure of washing his Cayman account on a sun-drenched island in the Caribbean had been strong but the thugs who had now cornered him left him faltering. Suddenly there was nowhere else to run. He walked to the windows and stared out at the early evening.

Had Anton suffered pain as he died? Or was it swift, sudden and uncomplicated? And who would bury Anton? If he remained unidentified what would happen to him? Would the police leave his body in the mortuary until they had solved his murder? These morbid thoughts ran wild in Stone's mind ... would *he* have to do something about it? At least claim the body?

Never, he decided quickly. Fuelled by his whisky Stone wanted a fight with this lot. But on his terms. He fumbled with his mobile to a list of telephone numbers. His eyes narrowed as he put his finger on the digits he needed. His meticulous paranoia to corner Drake and see him dead as well for a moment overtook any anxiety. If only for his own safety, Anton's vicious killing in a dingy London backstreet he would repay.

He punched the call hard into the phone and waited as he stared at the ceiling.

'I want to speak to Cutlass,' he said a few seconds later.

There was a grunt from the phone and Stone waited for half a minute before his demand was met.

'Cutlass, you been working since you left St Lucia?' Stone rasped.

'Mr Stone, me I'm always working. And I'm always looking for work. You got something to offer?'

'Drake, the madman from St Lucia, is still around. Find him and sort him better than you did before. But you get paid only when I'm satisfied you've done the job right. Do we understand each other?'

'How much?' Cutlass asked.

'Two grand.'

'And expenses, Mr Stone.'

'I don't do expenses,' Stone spat at the phone.

'Travelling, taxis,' Cutlass persisted.

'Listen to this, Cutlass. We're not playing. Expenses are out. Do you want this job or not? I can always find another layabout who'll snatch at it.'

'Mr Stone, I'll do it. I'll put St Lucia right for you. What goes?' Cutlass's tone was deferential, he knew where he stood.

'You listen to this carefully. Keep off the drink for as long as it takes, make no mistakes, and you might stay alive.'

Cutlass gave a grunt of assent.

'Drake's in London. Trying to get revenge for what you didn't finish in St Lucia.'

'Drake's in London?'

'Didn't you hear what I just said, you fool? Drake's got contacts right here and he might even be here himself. And like they did in St Lucia they're making threats.'

'Violence?' Cutlass asked.

'You got it. They kill.'

'Who they killed?' Cutlass asked with relish.

'None of your business. You just take it as nasty,' Stone said.

'What do you want me to do?'

'You know how the Caribbean works in London. You know where these people hang out don't you?'

'Sure. But I've not been around much since I got back.'

'Well get around now. Quick. Dig around in the pubs, keep your ears open. Ask questions if you have to. But discreetly. You understand that word?'

There was silence for a moment as Cutlass thought. Stone's call was unexpected and he was confused. He spoke slowly.

'So what you want to know, boss?'

'Who's working for Drake. Who can stick knives in so we can fight 'em back.'

'Sure, Mr Stone. You're the boss.'

'Yes, I'm the boss. And never forget it. And it better not be like last time. I want real hard stuff that'll put Drake and his lot out of business. Forever. Understand?'

'Sir. I've got it.'

'Good. One other thing. If you get caught fouling this up you've never heard of me. You're on your own. I'll call in a couple of days to see how you're getting on.'

Stone did not wait for Cutlass to respond. He leaned his head back in the armchair and took a deep breath. For a moment he felt edgy and hot, still stunned at the suddenness of Anton's death. He had not really known Anton well, but a death was a death and he'd now had two of those in a few days.

In his diary he counted the days he had been at Claridge's and then counted the days left for the Fenfleet tender. Barely fourteen to go. With Anton dead and Claire enjoying Geneva, pessimistically he wondered how it would all end.

Too nervous to be bored, Stone walked to the sideboard and poured another large whisky. His arm quivered as he sipped it noisily, now uncertain that he had any control over what was going on around him. It was not a position that he had ever allowed himself to be cornered in before and it heightened his anxiety.

# 14

Claire got up early for Geneva. She had slept for three hours, dozed for two, and by 4 a.m. wanted to get moving. She drank coffee and nibbled at a slice of burnt toast in the growing daylight of the kitchen. Her pulse raced more with excitement than nervousness. She dressed slowly in a dark green suit and spent twenty minutes in front of the mirror. The television talked away in a corner of the small kitchen and she took no notice of the breakfast news of a vicious knifing of an unknown man in West London the day before. With Geneva beckoning, why should she?

The weather forecast was for a hot sunny day with eighty degrees at least over the whole of Europe promised. Claire's excitement made her flustered. Would the suit she was wearing be too hot in Geneva? She walked to the bedroom and looked at herself again in the cheval mirror. What the hell, she decided, she was only doing this for Stone for a short while, Rick Austin had no idea who she was, and anyway the suit was good and it was now too late to change. Ten minutes later she took a deep breath as she slumped into the seat of a pre-booked taxi to take her to Heathrow.

Claire checked her passport several times, counted how many euro notes she had and then read the expiry date on her credit card. Life was moving fast, she was not used to this type of travel and if things became difficult she might need to get away from Geneva quickly.

The taxi was caught in a snarl of traffic as it left the motorway and approached Terminal Five at Heathrow. They inched forward at a snail's pace and Claire sat on the edge of her seat, passport clutched in her hand.

A quarter of an hour later she paid off the cab and entered the hustle of the terminal. A jumble of people confronted her but she soon found Rick by the ticket desk, pre-checked in with boarding cards in hand. Importantly to Claire he greeted her with a smile. Claire forced one in return.

'I hope you're ready for a long day,' he said.

'That's no problem to me,' Claire replied.

As they passed through security Claire could sense Rick looking at her. He turned and spoke with a smile of approval.

'Claire, call me Rick from hereon. We don't stand on ceremony at Trifoni and you'll find it easier if we use Christian names.'

Claire was surprised but not embarrassed.

'You're the boss. I do what you say,' she said. They both laughed.

'Good. We'll have an interesting day in that case.'

'Geneva's a new city for me. I'm looking forward to it.'

'Do you speak French?' Rick asked.

'No. But I can understand it. A little. Why do you ask?'

'Just curious. My secretary is fluent and as I'm not it helps. Particularly if you want to understand what's being said behind your back in a meeting.' Rick laughed.

They had little time to wait before they boarded and Claire was easy with the silence between them. Once in his seat Rick brooded over a manuscript from his briefcase and then relapsed into close scrutiny of all the pages of a newspaper.

Breakfast was served. Claire nibbled a dry croissant and sipped a fruit juice. Half an hour into the flight Rick turned to her.

'You're not hungry for breakfast?' he asked.

'Watching my weight,' she said.

'You don't look as if you need to.'

'Do we lunch today?' Claire asked.

'Yes. And it'll be on me.'

Rick passed the *Telegraph* to Claire and rested his head on the seat back.

'London's a dangerous place,' he said suddenly.

'Oh. What's happened now?'

'It's in there,' he said, pointing to the paper. 'Some guy got himself killed. Knifed to death in a fight yesterday afternoon. In Hammersmith. In broad daylight.'

'Don't tell me that. It'll be dark by the time we get home tonight.'

'A drugs fight by the sounds of it.' Rick added. 'And it was in a road where I used to have a flat many years back.'

Claire opened the paper and the headline leapt out. LONDON GANGLAND KILLING. She turned the page quickly and skimmed the other news. Had she known that the article was about Anton's death she would have been very frightened and would without hesitation have walked out on Geneva, Rick Austin and Harry Stone. Anton was a close friend and knowing that he had been lethally knifed working for Stone would have driven her to blow Stone's scheme wide open.

Claire closed her eyes as the aircraft, enveloped in thick cloud, hit turbulence crossing the Jura. Breaking through the cloud Claire saw a shimmering lake at the foot of the snow-capped peaks of the Alps in the distance. It was an open, grand, vista.

They were met by a chauffeur and in a limousine half an hour later were heading for the city centre. Claire saw a smile return to Rick's face. He lowered the car window and spoke as he breathed in the fresh, sweet air.

'I don't like flying. A bit unnatural if you ask me. And as for the crowds at the airport...' Rick waved his hand in a dismissive gesture.

'Do you fly often? Do you have much business abroad?'

'No, thank God. Today's unusual. But necessary.'

'Can you tell me what we're here for?'

'Chasing a deal. With someone who wants his business kept quiet.'

'So you travel to Geneva,' Claire said.

'Where else? Everything's neatly tucked up here. No rough bits showing.' Rick's tone was heavily sarcastic.

The limo halted at traffic lights on a road bordering the lake. The sun shone brightly, the water sparkled in the wake of a lake steamer making for a pier ... it was inviting, and Rick knew it.

'You do know my business is confidential, don't you?' Rick suddenly asked.

Claire left a few seconds before she replied.

'I hope that would go without saying, Rick. I've worked tight deals before. Many times.' Her response was well prepared, and she had been surprised that the question had not been asked sooner. Claire was confident in her answer.

'What you mean is that I have to take you on trust.'

'Like the rest of your staff.'

'Sure. But you'll see the inside bits of deals that I don't show the world. You'll see and hear things that are very hush-hush. Keep it close, Claire, is all I ask. It makes it more exciting that way too.'

Claire watched the spurt of water from the Jet d'Eau on the lake, aware that Rick had hit the raw spot in this deal.

'Just what do you want me to do today?' she asked.

'Ah, yes. I'm meeting a James Kennedy with his Swiss lawyer, Dr le Borge. You'll hear of James Kennedy a lot in the next few weeks. I'm trying to do a deal with him. He controls some pubs at Fenfleet near Sheffield which I'm after so I need to keep him sweet. James can influence who gets the contract up there.'

186

'I'm not an expert on pubs,' Claire said.

'Didn't expect you to be. Just be alert. Don't take notes, that's too obvious. But I may need you to remind me later what was said.'

The limousine drew up outside an old green-painted town house, three storeys high, in Geneva's Vieux Quatre. The top did not overhang the bottom like Arrow Hall did in places but it was old, with irregular angles as if it had hidden treasures inside. It reminded Claire of the sort of house Dickens would have lived in and she was curious at what she might find inside.

The window of the door displayed a sign in faded gilt: 'Dr Gaston le Borge, International Lawyer'.

They were ushered into a small, dark-brown waiting room. Claire was bemused. How could international lawyers practise from such a place?

Five minutes later a receptionist led them into the lawyer's paper-strewn office. There were no computers, just papers and green-backed files. Dr le Borge moved from behind his desk with a greeting as sparse as his untidy room.

A fat little man, Dr le Borge waddled rather than walked as he moved to close the door. An acrid smell of cigar smoke pervaded his clothes and body. Claire disliked him immediately. There was something sinister about his podgy face, his eyes were set too close together, and the way he dismissed her presence by not looking at her as if she was an unnecessary intrusion into his business left her cold. Claire's intuition took hold and she knew immediately that this place was hostile.

*You know my business is confidential.* Rick's command in the car rang in her ears. Claire looked at Rick. She saw no slyness in his eyes, as she often detected in Harry Stone's and now saw in this fat little lawyer. Where did Rick fit into all this?

'Meet James Kennedy my client,' Dr le Borge said with

an air of total apathy. James Kennedy, tall but slightly overweight and with an easy smile that exposed a row of perfect white teeth rose from an armchair almost hidden by papers.

'Rick and I know each other well,' James said.

Rick and James shook hands and there was a relaxed smile between them.

'We won't talk about our last meeting. Let's just remember it as strictly business,' James said, and laughed easily.

'Sure,' Rick said. 'Paris was hard work.'

The lawyer turned away, disapproving of this show of friendliness, but James looked at Claire, a young woman dressed in chic style, and quickly held out his hand as if it was the gentlemanly thing to do.

'Are you Gail?' he asked.

Rick interrupted before Claire could respond. 'Gail's had an accident. Got rammed in her car so she's off for a few weeks. Claire's standing in for her.'

James smiled. 'Pleased to meet you, Claire.' He looked at Rick with an arched eyebrow.

'James, Claire understands total confidentiality.'

'Would you prefer that I left?' Claire asked.

'That won't be necessary. I read trust on your face,' James said. He laughed but Dr le Borge breathed out noisily, his demeanour already showing boredom.

The lawyer sat at the head of a small table and rested his fat hands on a dog-eared and stained blotter pad.

'Okay, let's get on with the business,' he said. 'You will already have worked out how much Mr Kennedy's pubs at Fenfleet are worth.'

'I'm "James" to these people,' Kennedy interrupted. 'Let's leave the formalities aside.'

'As you wish,' Dr le Borge responded, not distracted by the request. He continued bluntly, looking at his dog-eared blotter. 'You make money if you are successful in the tender bid. And my client, James, should make money too. That's today's agenda.'

The lawyer paused and James looked away over the jumble of rooftops that was the Vieux Quatre. In the distance the sun shone but it did not reach Dr le Borge's room and the gloom remained.

After a few seconds of silence Rick spoke. 'I understood that this deal was with the Fenfleet crowd. James doesn't own that lot does he?'

Dr le Borge fiddled with his pen. 'No. But so what?'

'Okay, let's have it. What do you want?'

'I have a list of things that you will need to offer my client. First there's this.' The lawyer passed a sheet of paper to Rick. 'James will require payment into Switzerland of this amount.' Dr le Borge paused and waited for a reaction. There was none from Rick and the lawyer continued. 'I will arrange the bank, the numbered account, everything.'

Rick read the note quickly, raised his eyebrows in surprise and then folded the paper neatly onto the table.

'That's a lot of money,' he said. But he did not state how much and it made Claire curious. She needed to know.

'You make money if I get you the deal,' James interrupted quickly.

'And what do you do to make sure Trifoni gets it?'

'I know how the system works. I've done it before and I can do it again. Trust me.'

'Sure,' Rick said.

'So, do we have a deal?' James probed.

'Are you prepared for the consequences?' Rick replied. 'Slush money isn't easy to hide. Or at least not that amount.'

'Come on, Rick. Put this in perspective. You'll find the payment to me lost in the ocean of what you can make.' James's face was unsmiling, showing no emotion. Not even greed or fear of being found out flickered there.

'Numbered accounts. I didn't think you were that sort of guy,' Rick said.

'Secrecy. Secrecy is what you get in Switzerland. Don't you know that?' Dr le Borge said irritably.

'I know how Switzerland works.'

'I send you an invoice for consultancy services. Shall we say ... unspecified consultations on how to tender for the contract. You then arrange payment to me in sterling and James's name will not appear anywhere.' This was all in a day's work for Dr le Borge.

'Yes. I know how it happens. But if I pay to a Swiss account I want a guarantee I get the deal. Tender or no tender.' Rick had a frown on his face. He was uncertain about the idea of paying James Kennedy anything. He'd already paid to entertain this shallow man and now a large backhander into Switzerland was definitely distasteful.

'Rick, why don't we look on it as a sort of partnership? We make cash together.'

'What about the other bidders. Do they give you cash too?'

'You took me to Paris, we had fun, so I'm talking to you and only you. Any other sweeteners would help your case too.'

'What do you mean "sweeteners"?' Rick was becoming annoyed at James's cockiness.

'Other bidders might come bearing gifts ... so you might just like to take out, shall we say, an *insurance* with a little extra.'

'If you want more Paris nights out that's fine by me.'

'Gaston, you tell Rick the other ideas,' James said.

'Right. Ten cases of Dom Pérignon to this address. Then the account at this hotel in Mauritius settled by you for up to £20,000 next April. Also, the petrol account at this garage whatever amount for the next twelve months.' A smile gradually creased Dr le Borge's round face.

But James's face was blank, glazed rigid as if such wealth

was beyond him, and he stared at Rick defiantly. Disgusted, Claire looked away. Stone would screw a deal in exactly the same way, she knew that. She shivered at the whole sordid thing.

'Let's get this straight. I pay a large amount of cash into a Swiss account. I pay these bits out of petty cash and on top of that I have to tender for the pubs. So what's the tender price then?'

'You work that out for yourself,' James answered quickly. 'But make it big enough to look real.'

'How big is big enough? One million? Two million?' Rick asked sharply.

'Rick, I can't tell you that. You've done your homework, otherwise you wouldn't be here. You know what'll make you profit.'

'I can guess at it. But my guess might not fit with yours.'

'Then add a bit. And be realistic,' James said sharply.

'Okay. So I pay up big or small and take a chance that I get it right. That doesn't seem like a good deal to me.' Rick began to fold the papers in front of him with a determined air.

'Not quite so quick,' the lawyer said. 'James can put you at the top of the list. That's what you want isn't it?'

'You want it all your own bloody way,' Rick said, becoming angry.

Claire secretly wanted to repeat that comment but she just rested her hands on her lap and sat more stiffly upright.

'A partnership, Rick. That's what we're working at.'

'I don't see this as a deal. I gotta have some idea of the value when I pile cash in,' Rick said.

'Okay, let's say if somebody comes in higher I'll let you know. But they'll have to add much more than I've asked for today to be successful,' James said.

The ingratiating smirk on James's face made Claire shudder.

James looked at his lawyer. 'Right. We understand each other's business needs. You want the Fenfleet pubs and I can help you get them with some modest cash in the pot for me.' James stood and for a moment his height dominated the room. 'I'm hungry. Lunch,' he said, as if that was all he had come for. 'I know just the place where we can celebrate our new-found wealth.'

'Hold on. Before we go I must know if we have a deal,' Rick pressed.

'There's plenty of time to talk,' James replied. 'I'll do what I can, I'll spill the other bids, then it's up to you.' James turned to Claire. 'I'm sure you'd like some lunch, honey. You must have left home early this morning.'

Claire forced a smile, unsure what response to make. She did not take to James Kennedy. He was greedy and his lawyer was arrogant. And Claire did not want lunch, she was too tense. All she had heard was firmly fixed in her mind and now she had to relay the details to Stone.

But what details? Champagne, visits to expensive Mauritius hotels, petrol accounts? Claire knew that was just trivia. What about the cash needed to win the tender? And how much was the bribe to a Swiss numbered account paid through the dingy offices of Dr le Borge? Claire had a lot more digging to do.

The restaurant was on the shores of the lake. Claire picked at a large Dover sole, sipped pink champagne and wondered what Stone would make of all of this. He surely would not tolerate it and might have even thrown a punch or two by now. Big money deals were not new to Claire but in these surroundings she suddenly felt the contrast with Arrow Hall and as she looked out over the shimmering water of Lac Leman it heightened her determination to see the old house changed. She sipped her champagne and the thought quickly left her – the only way that was going to happen was if she could relay the inside deal to Stone.

Rick was playing a poker game, she could see that, but Dr le Borge looked in control, sure they would get their way.

Attacking a lobster which refused to yield to a large pair of crackers, his face reddening from several quick glasses of wine, James spoke.

'Shall I give Rick a price for the contract? A price we can definitely do a deal at?' He shot an enquiring glance at his lawyer.

The lawyer pushed his half-eaten steak away and scowled. 'Why?'

'He's trying to help us. And I'd like to help him back.'

'It's your deal. You do as you wish. But my advice is...'

James cut him short, a wide all-knowing smile on his face. He was teasing and he liked it.

'Okay. We keep quiet.'

'That's right.' Dr le Borge moved his large body in his chair, uneasy with a client who mouthed off too freely.

'You heard it, Rick. I do as my adviser tells me. Eh?'

'You do what you want, James. And I'll do what I want. That's how the world works.'

'Rick and I'll do business. We both want it enough, so it'll happen,' James said loudly to no one in particular.

Dr le Borge looked over his glasses at James as if defying any further stupid conversation, but the messy task of picking at the lobster was all he saw from his client. The lawyer then glanced at Claire to see if anything flickered in her eyes, anything that registered interest at this unusual meeting in Geneva. But Claire's face gave nothing away. All he saw was her contemplative look across the lake to the far snow-capped mountains in France. There was innocence in her eyes, Dr le Borge thought. Innocence that said she would not understand the complexities of business or Swiss bank accounts that were hidden. Women dressed like her never did.

Lunch finished at three o'clock. Dr le Borge picked up the bill and called a taxi to take Rick and Claire to the airport. James's face had a smirk as he shook Rick's hand.

'Good to meet again. A bit different to last time,' he said and laughed.

'Sure. But you've taken a difficult route. There is a limit I can live with.'

'I've taken advice, Rick. Gaston knows what he's doing.'

'It may not be quite so easy for me to make the payments you request. I do have other people who sometimes look over my shoulder and who might ask awkward questions.' Rick's frown showed he was irritated. It was time to step back several paces; he wanted to get away.

James shook Claire's hand. 'I hope we meet again sometime,' he said. 'When this deal is sealed we'll celebrate properly.'

Claire shuddered, Rick saw her gesture and held the door of the taxi open for her. He was pensive as they drove to the airport.

'What do you think of that lot?' he asked, not looking at Claire.

'You don't give in to the brazen blackmail of James Kennedy do you?'

'I might buy him. I don't call that giving in.'

'But his demands are outrageous. Champagne? Hotels in Mauritius?'

'You disapprove, Claire?'

'It doesn't matter what my feelings are. But will you really pay a bribe into a Swiss account?'

'I'm not walking away at the moment. But if he pushes too hard and his price gets too high I might,' Rick replied.

'I didn't like that lawyer. He looks sinister,' Claire said.

'Is that why you've been so tense all day?'

Claire hesitated at Rick's perceptiveness.

'I'm just wary. It is my first day, remember,' Claire replied.

Rick let it go. The flight to Heathrow was as quiet as the one taken earlier that morning. Claire reclined her seat, closed her eyes and tried to relax, but she was uncomfortable at the reality of the web she was now entangled in. Would she be able to keep her deception hidden?

At Heathrow Claire promised to be in early the next morning even though she was feeling tired from the tensions of the day. Her hope was that a good night's sleep would cure that.

Alone in the taxi to the Mayfair flat Claire took a notebook out and stared through the window, deep in thought. She had decided she would write down everything she found for Stone so that later she could present it to him in her own way. But from today what could she say? Fenfleet pubs had a price, but what? And the bribe into a Swiss account ... yes, but how much? Claire closed her notebook without writing anything as they drew up outside the flat.

She had a long, hot bath. Gradually she felt refreshed. She was hungry and she searched in the fridge for food. She put a ready-made snack in the oven and curled up on the sofa with a glass of wine. Flicking through the pages of a newspaper she found the television section. There was a play that would start in a few minutes and she would watch it to unwind further before going to bed.

The ring on her mobile startled her. It was Harry Stone.

'You promised you'd report all that's happening. It's half past eight and since you've not reported I presume nothing's come up.' His tone was forceful, enquiring, demanding.

Claire was instantly on guard. 'Listen, I can't *make* things happen. I've only been here a day so please don't push where I can't deliver.'

'So you've been to Geneva for nothing?'

'Nothing I can tell you yet. Nice lunch, but I need lots more details to make sense of it all.'

'Who was there?'

'Rick Austin. James Kennedy from Fenfleet, and his Swiss lawyer. A fat arrogant little man, a Dr le Borge.'

'How much is Rick Austin paying for the Fenfleet deal?'

'Don't know. Wasn't discussed.'

'Look, Claire, I need information and facts. Don't wait for it to come to you. Go and find it.'

'For goodness sake, lay off. I've not had a chance to find anything yet.'

'Why were that lot together? In Geneva of all places,' Stone asked.

'Swiss bank account for James Kennedy. That's why. But don't ask me for details because I haven't got them.'

'You mean Kennedy's receiving slush money?'

'Call it what you like.'

'How much?'

'Don't know. I wasn't told.'

'Claire, I've got to have detailed information and I've got to have it quickly. Don't you understand Fenfleet aren't going to wait for you to take your time!'

'Damn Fenfleet. I've had a difficult day digging for you. If I put a foot wrong it'll blow the whole thing wide open. And that'll be curtains for both of us.' Claire's throat was tight as she forced the words out.

'All right, but don't take the pressure off.'

Claire had known this prickly impatience from Stone would start unless she produced instant results. She flicked on the television with the remote control and reduced the noise to a small rumble as she let Stone drone on in his selfish voice.

'These are your instructions,' he said. 'Tomorrow you go into Austin's office and find where he files all this information. Look it up and let me have it. Times, places and amounts of money. Got it?'

'I know exactly what you want and I'll get it. But you've

got to give me space to do it my way.' Claire was becoming annoyed and though she knew this was pure Harry Stone she was in no mood to take it now.

'I'll call again to see if *your way* is working. Soon.'

Stone finished abruptly like a tap being turned off. The call unsettled Claire. She began to think that the Essex mansion and all it stood for in its decrepitude had dragged her down too. In the cosiness of the Knightsbridge flat she suddenly had an overwhelming feeling that she had had enough. Next morning she would go to Claridge's and tell Stone she was no longer doing his dirty work for him. He'd better find someone else.

As Claire prepared for bed she handled the other clothes Stone had bought her and wanted to wear them. Soon. Impulsively she took the row of pearls from the small safe and held it up to her neck. In the overhead light of the mirror they sparkled gently and felt warm, even soft. The clicking noise as she locked the safe a minute later reminded her that she was now in the middle of Stone's wild game and she shivered. After expensive shopping and Geneva she was in too deep to go back on the deal now.

# 15

'What's up?' Bluebell asked as she saw the wide grin on Cutlass's face.

'I've got some work to do tonight,' Cutlass said.

'What kind of work?'

Cutlass hesitated.

'Well, I gotta find some information for Mr Stone, a man I looked after in St Lucia a few weeks ago.'

'Information? What does that mean?' Bluebell asked.

'I need to get round the clubs and pubs, ask questions, listen to gossip and see what I can pick up. Someone treated Mr Stone bad over there and now we're home ... well, he wants it sorted.'

'Sounds like an excuse for you to go drinking.' Bluebell was perceptive and direct.

The smile momentarily increased on Cutlass's face and he replied easily. 'It'll be quick money. Stone pays good. Then we can get out of this place.'

'So you come off the dole on Friday?'

Cutlass thought for a moment. 'No,' he said firmly. 'This is just a few extra pounds. In cash.'

'So do I keep claiming as well?' Bluebell asked.

'Look, if we want to get out of this place we gotta have money. That means we both need work sometime.'

'Your drinking's already at dangerous levels. You know that.' Bluebell had a frown as she spoke.

'I've not been drinking for some nights. Well, not hard. And tonight it's work.'

'You be careful, Winston. You can make enemies too if you go snooping.'

'I know what I'm doing. Get me a clean shirt.'

Bluebell waddled away willingly. She retreated to the very small bedroom at the back of the flat where it was cold and there was no carpet on the floor. There was a small cupboard in the corner where she kept her ironed washing and she took satisfaction in the tidiness and cleanness of the fresh piles of clothes.

In the living room at a small table covered with a colourful embroidered cloth Cutlass sat and wrote on a tiny scrap of paper a list of the clubs and pubs he would visit. The drinking places were all within walking distance of Cutlass's flat, hidden in dingy, dark, side streets. They did not advertise their presence, the locals and others just knew they were there.

You could play pool or poker for high bets, and there were slot machines with silver coins. The drink was cheap. And with all that there was the blaring thump of reggae and rap music. Strangers were unwelcome and visitors were only comfortable if they could merge with the alcohol haze unnoticed. And that was not easy in the wooden and plastic starkness that was the hallmark of these places.

But they served a purpose. They kept the likes of Cutlass out of their homes, the gloomy buildings where they slept, and they were the crossroads of gossip and underground information. You wanted something done, you went there to find someone or to join in.

Claire was finishing her day as a mole for Stone and Cutlass was preparing to start his. But for Cutlass there would be no tasty lunches in flash places, just the physical menace that Anton had already felt, until the knife that penetrated his heart wiped it away.

Cutlass's expectations of physical comfort were never high and Harry Stone's call to sort out Drake's contacts in London with cash to go with it made the Jamaican very excited. Mostly out of regular work, he rented a squalid four-roomed flat south-east of the Thames which he shared with his latest partner, Bluebell. She was a Caribbean lady almost as wide round the middle as Cutlass, but she was proud, meticulously tidy, and she dressed in bright clothes as if she was living in the radiant sun of Jamaica.

Their flat was in the middle of a grey terrace in a narrow road, flanked with cars, with no view and no sun ever shining into its grim rooms. But Bluebell kept it tidy. She put net curtains at the windows, she was constantly dusting and hoovering, but she never really beat the battle against squalor.

Perpetual noise penetrated from dogs that barked two blocks away and the bins that lined the road among the cars were always full. This was a depressing area.

Cutlass shaved and dressed carefully. It was an odd ritual for him but he took his time over it, making sure his large face was free from stray grey hairs. He was excited that for a short while he now had a definite purpose in his life, a purpose that would earn him some much-needed cash that maybe could buy him freedom.

It was 8.30 p.m. when Cutlass left Bluebell watching the television. Rain was now persistent and he walked as quickly as his size would let him while holding his jacket collar close to his neck. The first club on his list took twenty minutes to reach and he was seriously out of breath as he entered its front door. He had been there before, just once, some two years ago.

Inside it was gloomy and deserted. A cheap drink that provided an easy escape from life for a while was the only reason anybody ever went near the place. Even talk was not possible above the high decibels of the music that blared from two large speakers on the ceiling. An old coloured man with a wispy grey beard sat in a corner and did not even look up as Cutlass entered. He had a pint of beer in front of him on a table stained from drink and cigarette burns and he stared at the floor. Cutlass nevertheless remained alert.

The barman approached. He was tall, thin and coloured. Cutlass did not know him and there was no greeting offered, not even a smile.

'Large rum. And one for yourself too,' Cutlass said.

There was no response. Just a nod as the man went away to pour the two large measures.

'I'm looking for work,' Cutlass said as he took a long sip of rum a moment later.

'What sort of work?'

'I do anything. Building sites. Driving.'

'Don't know of anything going,' the barman responded with disinterest.

'What about other things?'

The barman looked bemused. 'We don't get much else in here,' he said.

Cutlass took half his drink in one gulp and immediately began to feel a little uplifted from the exertions of his walk.

'So there's nothing going on? No mob work that I can get into? I need some quick cash. Got it?'

'If there's anything being planned nobody talks about it in here.' The barman had a dull voice and it was as void of life as the bar itself.

'I'm not from the police,' Cutlass said. It was time he made sure there was no misunderstanding.

'I can see that,' the barman said. 'But I still don't know of anything interesting like you're looking for.'

'How long you been here?' Cutlass asked.

'On and off two or three months.'

This place was a waste of time, Cutlass thought. He finished his rum quickly, looked in the corner at the old man who had hardly moved and had not touched his beer, and decided to leave. He pulled his jacket collar around his neck and prepared for another walk in the rain.

'I'll call again next week. Keep your eyes and ears open for me. You know what I'm looking for,' he said.

The barman only nodded and turned the music up as Cutlass left.

Cutlass let the front door slam behind him. He had already fixed in his mind his next call. He was cold as he walked through the deserted, cobbled side streets. He fingered a wad of notes in his pocket.

He had made an allowance for each stop and had under-spent at the first one, so he could indulge himself later. For a moment he felt reassured.

Cutlass entered the second club, just south of Tower Bridge. The last time he had visited was for a celebration. He had just split up with his partner and he had met Bluebell. He had drunk excessively and he had little recall of the night or the place.

Tonight he pushed the door open more to keep dry than with expectations of either drinking heavily or finding anything for Stone. Cutlass was wet and cold. The Hellshire, named after a range of hills in Jamaica, was an appropriate name for one of London's starkest clubs. The loud music was regularly interrupted by the rumble of trains passing overhead, as if it were constantly thundering.

In Jamaica the Hellshire hills hide ancient caves where sunlight seldom penetrates and this club had almost deliberately been carved from the jungle just south of the Thames to remind drinkers of that desolate place. But it still held a fascination for some people who had nowhere else more welcoming to go. It was warm and noisy, it was always crowded, and after a few drinks talk was wild, especially in the later hours.

Suddenly Cutlass remembered the run down shack in St Lucia where he had asked for directions to find Drake. The Hellshire was just like that shack except the warmth of the Caribbean sun was not here and nobody lounged around its doorstep. But at that bar in St Lucia he had found what he wanted. He had got to Drake.

Cutlass was now thirsty again and a growing depression momentarily lifted as he took a seat at the drink-stained bar, nodded to the owner, a fellow Jamaican, and fingered a cigarette which he did not light.

'It's Winston isn't it? Winston Cutlass?' the barman enquired.

'You've got a good memory.'

'I never forget a face. But it's good to see you back again. It's been a while. What are you drinking?'

'Usual rum. And one for yourself,' Cutlass replied.

'Why not? I feel dry.'

The barman skipped off, the rumble of a train thundered overhead and Cutlass swivelled half round on his stool to assess the other drinkers in this unlovely place. It was crowded, it was stuffy, it was noisy. A pool table was being used at the end of the room with seriousness, as if everything depended on the outcome. Probably there was big money at stake. In a corner to the right of the bar a group of three men sat. Young, in their mid-twenties latest, one had a prominent gold earring that he constantly fiddled with. On the table was a half-empty bottle of rum. They were oblivious to anyone else in the bar and their conversation was becoming animated and loud.

Cutlass did not recognise their faces but he saw coldness in their eyes and the dirtiness of their clothes confirmed his view about how messy life could be. He took a quick gulp from the rum that the barman had now put in front of him.

The man sitting in the middle of the group and directly

facing Cutlass was speaking loudly. The deep tone of his voice penetrated the continuing blare of the music and Cutlass turned his gaze away, feigning disinterest. But he strained to listen and he heard clearly.

'I've been to see a posh place down in Essex. It's got a bit more room than this patch.'

'Why you wasting your time there? We've got enough to look after here.'

'There's money down there.'

'Antiques? Is that it?'

'No. Antiques are dead. Too easily traced if they're worth anything.'

'So why're you interested?'

There was silence for a moment as they each filled their glasses from the rum bottle and then drank.

'Got a cousin in St Lucia. He's known as Drake but that's not his real name. The man who owns this place in Essex has been building this hotel in St Lucia and it's like a palace. Or was. My cousin Drake smashed it up.'

'Smashed it up?'

'Yeh. He wouldn't pay cousin Drake to look after it.'

'So who's this geezer in Essex with cash he won't share?'

The three men laughed together and drank more of their rum.

'Called Stone. I think it's Harry.'

'Is he on our patch in Essex?' the second man asked.

'No, he's way out in the country. But he's scared. Like, he's run away from his large house. So I'm chasing him.'

'You got him in a corner yet?'

'No. But I'm taking over where my cousin Drake left off 'cos this man needs protection.' There was loud laughter followed by wide toothy grins from his two friends.

'You going to hit him?'

'Sure. Cousin Drake got beaten up bad after he did Stone's hotel over and cousin Drake's not good. Broken up without getting the money from this rich 'un. So I'm taking revenge. For cousin Drake's hurt. Okay?'

'Revenge? How?'

'I've made demands for some readies.'

'How much you got from him then?'

'Nothing. But this man's got it all right. With the help of our friends over the river we'll get him to share some of it. This place in Essex is unguarded, in the middle of fields. The man himself is unguarded, so it'll be easy. You see?'

'How you know he's unguarded?'

There was a slight pause before the first man spoke. Cutlass strained through the rumbling noise of a train and kept his gaze from the trio. He stared hard at his drink on the bar.

'You heard that guy got killed at Hammersmith the other day?'

'Yeh. Got knifed. Saw it on the telly. But that weren't on our patch.'

'No. But that was this man's guarding gone. He was playing with me so I stuck a knife in and it hit the wrong place.'

'And you got away?'

'Yeh. Nobody saw it and the police ain't come knocking yet.'

There was a look of wide-eyed interest from the other two men as they listened closely. Maiming people who got in the way was nothing new, but killing was different and the details held a fascination as if they might come in useful again some time later.

'Is this man Stone around?'

'Can't find him. But I've got some trails on his girl who lives in this big house.'

'This lot don't sound very promising,' the second man said. 'I reckon we stick with places like this. They're easier.'

205

'Listen. Hussain at the bookies told me that Stone's mother just died. So I went to the funeral.'

'You what?'

'What I said. Big brother Harry would be there wouldn't he? And he was. I hit him.'

'At his mama's funeral?' Disbelief rang in the voice.

'Was just a warning. And a reminder for readies.'

'He paid yet?'

'No. But he will. Or he gets done over again. Harder.'

'I like that. Hit him 'til he pays.' The second man refilled his glass as if he wanted to toast the thought.

'There's a sister too. Lives down East. Near Hussain's bookies. In E6. Renfrew Street. She's on the list.'

There was loud laughter from the corner as they each held their glasses in the air. The rum bottle was finished and they were well satisfied with their talking. A moment later the first man spoke again, eagerness in his voice.

'The young bird that lives in the big house in Essex is staying up West. One of the girls is looking after her. She'll lead us to big brother Stone. See, I'm closing in on him.'

'How much can we screw out of this?' The third man who had almost been asleep was now wide awake.

'Hundred grand. Two hundred. Stone's got millions, we hit hard, he's frightened, he'll pay.'

'And if he don't?'

There was a pause. 'We get more violent,' he said slowly.

'Knives?'

'Yeh. They're quieter than shooters. And we go for his posh place in Essex just like his palace in St Lucia got done by cousin Drake.'

Again there was a pause as the thought of inflicting pain sank in. The oily smirks on their faces said they would not hold back given the chance.

Cutlass, on his third rum, had heard enough. He slid

heavily from his stool and without looking at the three men in the corner nodded again at the bar's owner.

'Gotta go. Maybe I come back soon,' he said.

'We don't see you much these days,' the owner said.

'Been away, haven't I?' Cutlass replied.

'Been away?'

'Not inside,' Cutlass added quickly.

'I'm sure you're too clever to go inside, Mr Cutlass.' The owner laughed and jigged away as the music blared.

Cutlass grasped the wad of unspent cash in his pocket for reassurance, but even after several relaxing drinks he could feel menace. In St Lucia he knew how to handle it but here in London he was alone, he had no protection from those who might kill and then openly boast about it.

And what had he done in St Lucia? He had personally beaten 'cousin Drake' until he was practically lifeless and now this gang were looking all over the place for revenge. With his large size he was easy to recognise, so what if they found him?

Blood pressure rising, Cutlass left the bar. There was no glance back to the group in the corner and he just hoped that he looked and spoke like any other Jamaican who had lived in London for many years.

Cutlass was now tired, his excitement at finding the net entangling Stone tinged with nervousness. It was raining heavily, the night was pitch black under the railway arch, but as fast as he could Cutlass walked to a pub a quarter of a mile away. It had welcoming light beaming from its windows and there he would decide his next move.

Inside Cutlass ordered a double rum which he drank neat within a minute and in the starkness of the saloon his pulse quickened. This place had no noise, few customers and bright lights reflected from dusty mirrors behind the bar. He saw his reflection in a mirror and wanted to hide. By chance he had stumbled onto what Stone needed but the whole thing was more intimidating than he had thought it would be.

Cutlass took another rum but drank it more slowly. He stared at himself again in the mirror and tried to reason his position. But his brain, never sharp, was now muzzy with alcohol, his thoughts slow.

It took ten minutes to make up his mind. He looked at his watch. It was midnight and the publican had deliberately yawned twice in front of him.

From the warmth of the pub Cutlass lumbered in silence through the depressing rain, back to Hellshire. He entered the club, confident that he could again mingle easily, unnoticed. It was just as crowded as when he had left and just as noisy. He sauntered to the bar, shook the rain from his coat and grinned at the owner.

'You're back quickly,' the barman said.

'I've still got some money left, haven't I? Need to spend it before the missus gets her hands on it.'

They both laughed easily.

The barman was pouring a rum as Cutlass took a seat at the bar. He sipped slowly from the glass and wiped his mouth on his sleeve. The music was lower and somehow the place seemed more welcoming than before. Cutlass looked around. The men in the corner had gone.

The barman was hovering, ready to talk after seeing in Cutlass's eyes an enquiring look that said that unspent money was not the real purpose in returning so quickly.

'I overheard some interesting things when I was in here earlier,' Cutlass said.

'Forget the talk in here. Sometimes there's too much,' the barman replied.

'Who were those boys in the corner?' Cutlass nodded his head backwards to indicate where he meant.

The owner drew back slightly from his posture of leaning his elbow on the bar.

'You want drugs, hard stuff, Winston? I didn't think those things bothered you.'

'No. Drugs ain't for me,' Cutlass said emphatically. 'But who were those boys? I haven't seen 'em before.'

'I've nothing to say except keep out of their way. Take my advice.'

'I'll do that. But who are they?' Cutlass persisted.

'Listen, but keep it quiet. They don't like it to be known so I haven't told you. Okay? They lead some boys who call themselves the Rex Gang. They hang out at The Dram in Camberwell but sometimes come here to drink. You know what I mean?'

Cutlass had never heard of the Rex Gang but he knew the reputation of The Dram in Camberwell. He nodded.

The owner continued. 'I pay 'em some readies to keep this place going. Otherwise they'd break it up. And I never ask 'em to pay for drinks 'cos that'd be too much. So don't get in their way, Winston. If they want something nothing stops 'em. You know what I mean?'

'Okay.' But Cutlass was now concerned. Drugs were definitely not his scene, never had been. He'd seen people killed for drugs, he knew that ground was all a boiling cauldron, with powerful dealers who shouldn't be crossed.

'Forget I asked. I don't want no trouble,' Cutlass said.

'Good. Nor me. This is a good business,' the barman said.

'Yeh. I'll go to Camberwell if I want 'em.' The enquiring look had gone from Cutlass's eye and he laughed with the barman as if it was a joke.

Cutlass finished his drink slowly. It was now early morning, his eyes were red with tiredness, and his body ached from his fill of alcohol. He nodded to the owner.

'See you another day,' he said.

'Don't leave it too long,' the owner said, relaxed that Cutlass understood about people like the Rex Gang and their methods. It was just part of ordinary life in these places.

The rain was falling heavily again and Cutlass pulled his light jacket closely round his neck as he trudged his lonely route back through the side streets to his dingy flat. Deep in fuzzy thought he was disturbed at what he'd discovered.

He arrived home very wet, his eyes aching with tiredness, and he was cold. He let himself in and sat for a while alone in the small front room that Bluebell kept special and clean in case somebody visited.

Slumped in an armchair his memory of beating Drake in a St Lucia banana grove became vivid in its detail and his mind whirled. The Caribbean was an easy-going place and from there he had escaped by catching a plane with nobody to follow him. But in London there would be no escape, especially from druggies. These boys ran gangs and had large unknown, unseen, armies of runners and enforcers for manipulating and working their patch. And for results they paid well, they could always afford to.

Half an hour later Cutlass undressed in the small bathroom and then climbed into bed next to Bluebell. She did not wake.

He was uneasy at being dragged into areas he knew were dangerous and it was 2.30 before he slept, his brain still whirling with thoughts for Stone's protection and his own. His light and fitful sleep was full of real images of beatings, knives, and banana groves with Drake squealing for help. It made him hot and sweaty.

*

Four hours later his phone rang. He swore, rolled slowly and went to answer it.

It was Stone, with no apology for calling so early and he was sharp.

'What you found?' he demanded.

Cutlass cleared his throat with a deep cough before he replied.

'Lots.'

'Let's have it then.'

'Drake's got a cousin in London. He's chasing you.'

'Don't tell me what I already know. Is that all there is?'

'He knows where your family live. They share the same bookie. And they talked about your sister too. Renfrew Street E6?'

'I don't need to know all that crap. Who's this thug chasing me?'

'A nasty one, Mr Stone. Nastier than Drake in St Lucia. Don't stand in his way.'

'He needs to get out of mine.'

'And there's a girl who works for you at your big pad.'

'Yes, Claire. But she's safe enough. Doing some work up West for me.'

'It's a drugs mob. Call themselves the Rex Gang. They do nasty things to people if they don't get what they ask for and they don't talk politely like me and you. Have they stuck a knife into one of your mates? Someone working for you?'

'Yes. Anton got killed. Runs around for me. But it wasn't for drugs. He was frightening them off like I told him to.'

'Are you hiding, boss?'

Stone thought for a moment. 'I don't hide, Cutlass, but I move around when I need to.'

'Okay. But keep moving. They're watching your girl working up West to see if she leads them to you. So my advice is don't play with this lot. Just pay up and do as they ask.'

'I don't pay blackmail or protection money. You know that from St Lucia,' Stone snapped.

Cutlass grunted. This man wasn't listening so why shouldn't

211

he let Stone's arrogance get him killed too. But for a reason which at that moment he could not define Cutlass knew he would not do that.

'You calling from your Essex place?' Cutlass asked.

'Why?'

'They were talking about it. They're watching it. They intend to get even, boss. Please take them seriously.'

Cutlass had a pleading tone which Stone had not heard before. It was early on a cool morning but Stone suddenly felt uneasy. Nestled in the secure luxury of Claridge's he got the message clearly that a serious menace was now confronting him. As he put the phone down his arm trembled.

Cutlass's head was spinning. A visit to The Dram at Camberwell was out for ever and the next time Stone asked him to do his dirty work he would definitely say no, however much cash was offered.

# 16

'Your Jersey bank account,' were almost the first words from the tax inspector, who was today dressed entirely in black like a judge about to pass sentence.

'Was a mistake,' Stone replied quickly.

'We understand you had £175,000 in it as recently as last month.'

'Could be,' Stone said.

'Have you brought all the statements on the account for me?'

'No. Don't keep things like that.'

'We shall need to see them.'

'I'll ask the bank who told you all about this to send them on.'

'Good. Now tell me where did the money come from? What was the source of such a large amount?'

'Gift.'

'Gift? Who from?'

'A Frenchman.'

'You're not being very helpful, Mr Stone,' the woman said. 'It might be easier for everyone if you gave us all the details as it will save time and might even ease any penalties, if you cooperate. So please you tell me now without all the questions first.'

Her assistant, his pen poised over an A4 pad, stared at Stone as if defying him to ignore the request from his boss. Stone moved in his chair and ran his hand through his hair.

'Like I said it was a gift. I did a favour for a guy who

lives in Paris, helped him acquire some rare antique furniture that was about to be auctioned and as part of the deal he gave me a finder's fee. In the real world it happens all the time.' Stone had rehearsed this statement many times and he was satisfied with the ease that it slipped out.

'Antique furniture? I cannot see from our files that you have ever dealt in antiques before. I know you have been involved in many different businesses so is this a new business venture?'

'It wasn't business. I told you it was a gift and since when did I have to pay tax on a gift?'

'We'll come to that later,' she said emphatically. 'Was anything put in writing for this deal?'

'No,' Stone replied. 'I didn't ask for anything, he just gave it to me. I'm hardly going to send it back, am I?'

'That's not what we're examining here. I get the feeling that you don't understand that undeclared bank accounts are a serious matter with very severe penalties.'

'Listen. I just happened to hear of something from a house clear-out that was going on, I passed the information on and cash follows.'

'So where was this house clear-out?'

'In France. Near Reims. I buy wine there sometimes and heard about the sale. Not my scene, so I tell someone who might be interested and he gives me a present for it. Simple as that.' Stone's tone was raw with impatience.

'A hundred and seventy-five thousand. That is a big present.'

'The guy made a lot of money. It was a chateau full of Louis XIV furniture which was worth over two million. I got less than ten per cent.'

'Did you already have a Jersey account to receive this money?'

'No. Never been there 'til a few years ago.'

'So why pay the money into Jersey?' the woman asked.

'Why not bring it to your account in London? I see you have several with different banks.'

'I'm allowed to keep it where I like and I don't have to answer to you or anyone for that,' Stone snapped.

The woman looked over her glasses at his clenched fists as if she expected him to move closer to her. But she had seen aggressive responses before and knew she would be the one who would win this contest.

She continued calmly. 'That is of course true, Mr Stone. But it might help us to understand what has gone on here, and of course what you *do* have to do is tell us how you got it and how much interest it has earned while on deposit.'

'I've told you how I got it. Give me a chance and I'll tell you how much interest it's gained.'

Stone threw a slip of paper onto the table which the woman took and inspected. Dismissively she passed it to her assistant who gawped at it and then folded it into a file for future reference.

'That good enough?' Stone asked.

'It'll do for the moment,' the woman answered. 'But I'd also like the full name and address of your contact in France who gave you the cash. Details of the bank transfer to Jersey and there may well be other details too of this transaction that we shall need before we come to a conclusion.'

'I'll send his name and address on,' Stone said, playing for time.

'Good, I'll look forward to receiving it. I presume you have no other offshore accounts? That's in Jersey or anywhere else in the world,' she said.

'No. Never. I like to know where my money is and to get my hands on it if I need it.'

The woman for a brief moment closed her eyes, paused as if she was making up her mind on something, looked at her watch and then spoke wearily. She had another point to make.

'When we find something that has not been declared we are likely to suspect that other matters have not been declared too, so once we have finished this inquiry you will be asked to sign a Certificate of Full Disclosure stating that you have made a full and total declaration of all your income and assets. And that means there are no more hidden accounts anywhere in the world which the Revenue should know about. You are aware, I presume, that we have extensive powers to search premises when we believe that to be necessary and that you could be prosecuted if you give false information? Please think on that, Mr Stone.'

Stone leaned forward and stared at the woman as if to return the intimidation.

'Come and search my house, Arrow Hall, as soon as you like. There's no skeletons there. Anyway, you've had everything I can tell you, there's no more, so give me the paper and I'll sign it now,' he said.

'We're not at that stage yet. I shall need to assess the information we receive from the address you give us in France. That might of course lead to further enquiries.'

For the next dreary half hour the woman fired questions at Stone, flicking over pages in a brown file, looking at him with squinting eyes as he responded flippantly, the scribe all the while making furious notes. But nothing she asked got her close to the Cayman account, not even a sniff that she was on the right track.

'I believe that this matter is far from complete as I am not sure that your answers are either satisfactory or convincing. We will call you again when we have the next piece in the jigsaw,' she said in exasperation as she decided to draw the meeting to a close.

'That it then?' Stone asked.

'For today, yes. But there will be more.'

Stone did not respond but stood, ready to get away, and the woman folded her arms as if in defiance at Stone's attitude. It had been terse, and there were no civilities from Stone as he left. His story had been strong, straight as if it was true, and with the thought of Louis XIV antiques ringing in his head he was sure he could stop any trail at the French end. What the hell, he thought, if this bumbling, bureaucratic woman didn't believe him, he just needed to play the bluff long enough, then they would get tired of it and stop the game. Anyway, he had been threatened with the law, received nasty bits of scribble about legal actions many times, and they had never been worth the paper they were printed on, so why take intimidation seriously now?

The Revenue woman and her mute scribe easily evaporated from his thoughts as he found an empty bench by the river and alone, deep in thought, stared out at the busy pleasure boats. This was his kind of place and he drew in a deep breath that gave life to his feeling that Fenfleet was getting closer, more real. But sudden heartburn, the result of an over-quick breakfast with too much black coffee taken earlier, made him pause for breath and he crunched two indigestion tablets, leaving his mouth tasting like chalk.

Tourists noisily ambled past him but he ignored them and suddenly, involuntarily, his mind flitted to Drake and his mob, an invisible menace, merging with the darkness as it had in St Lucia, and even with the daylight, as it had at his mother's funeral. In this placid place, with the open space of the grey river in front of him, he suddenly sensed the threat of impending violence like a dark storm-cloud about to send down a flash of lightning. It was not the sun which was on his face that made him feel hot, and his palms sweated.

It was a few minutes later that the discomforting indigestion subsided and Stone breathed out heavily, staring vacantly ahead at the speedy movement of a police launch on the river. His hand involuntarily went to the bruise on his neck where the thug had hit him at the crematorium.

The news from Cutlass was a warning, the garrotte squeeze was on. Could he ignore it? Sure he could, couldn't he see Fenfleet looming, a money spinner of a deal still in his grasp, his to take? With Claire sorting out the necessary, he'd easily grab the whole thing and not overpay.

He grabbed his mobile and punched in the numbers for Roger Garon. 'Claire's been to Geneva with Rick Austin,' he said as soon as Roger answered.

'So what?' Roger said.

'Rick Austin and Claire met James Kennedy there. Trifoni are getting ahead on the Fenfleet deal. Faster than we are. He's got in close just as we should have done. That's what.'

'Hold on, Harry. What's Geneva got to do with Fenfleet pubs?'

'You heard of Swiss bank accounts?'

'Oh, so that's the route. How much?' Roger asked.

'Don't know. Claire wasn't told but I'm pushing her to get it.'

'Go gently, Harry. The way you've set all this up makes Claire the key, so don't push her over the top and then get nothing.'

'Yeh,' Stone replied, his eye on the constant movement on the river.

'So sit and wait until she comes back with news. And until then take my advice and try not to get too impatient with her.'

'No, we can't wait. We gotta go see James Kennedy. He's got to know we're interested in this deal and that we will top anything this Rick Austin's up to.'

'He *knows* we're interested,' Roger snapped. 'How many times do you think I've rung him?'

'I don't care. And I don't like it that Austin's getting ahead.'

'Look, as long as our bid is in on time and is good then

Kennedy and his mates at Fenfleet will have to consider it. Like all the rest.'

'No. We feed Kennedy money with a large dollop in his own pocket. Switzerland, Cayman Islands, I don't care. But that means we've got to be talking to him direct. Just like Rick Austin's doing.'

'You mean openly bribe?' Roger shouted. 'I'm not going there. It's too dangerous if it goes wrong.'

Stone ignored Roger's outburst. 'Make a date, Roger. We'll go see Kennedy and talk this through with him.'

'How many times have I told you, *Kennedy won't see us.* He's got a gatekeeper who keeps blocking me.'

'You're not persistent enough. Or subtle by the sounds of it.'

'Harry, I've called five times and he's always in a meeting, on the phone or out. And he don't call back, take it from me.'

'I'll get him,' Stone snapped. 'He'll listen to me and one day I'll let you know how to do it.'

'Fine, but until then let me tell you something. I've been working out how much it'll cost to get it all up and running if you get this deal. Capital investment it's called.' Roger had wanted to make this statement for some time, knowing it would annoy Stone.

'How much?'

'A million. That's the minimum. And that's before you've paid Fenfleet for the pubs. And now Kennedy's bribe. Had you thought of that? Have you got that kind of cash? Several million?' Roger's voice was even, flat and immediately it had the right effect of annoying Stone.

'Why are you so negative? You know I can always find cash if I need to. And if Fenfleet makes me as much as I know it will well you just stay at home on your own and I'll go to the party. And remember this. The upside's in coins and notes, loose cash to run through your fingers. I don't pay tax on loose cash.'

219

'You do what you like with the upside, but watch the downside,' Roger said. 'And certainly don't involve me if you run cash out of the country. I don't want to know about Cayman accounts, Swiss accounts or the rest.'

Stone's patience was short and his irritation showed. He shouted. 'I know what I'm doing, Roger! I'll call you with a time to meet with James Kennedy. So be ready.'

Stone sauntered to the next empty bench in the shade and then called James Kennedy at his Fenfleet office.

'It's important I speak to Mr James Kennedy,' Stone said politely.

'Who is calling please?' a woman's voice answered.

'My name is Harry Stone. That's all he needs to know.' It was blunt but accurate.

'May I ask what you wish to speak about?' she asked.

'Tell your boss I've got interesting information for him. Tell him too it'll be very much to his advantage if we speak.'

'I will see if Mr Kennedy is in,' she said. 'Please hold the line.'

Stone waited patiently for less than thirty seconds. He knew exactly what was happening at the other end even though he could not see or hear.

'Mr Kennedy is engaged at present,' the woman's voice suddenly said.

'Give him a message then. The pub deal should not be done through Switzerland and I've got a better deal to put to him. He can call me on this mobile number. That means I can pick it up anywhere and at any time.'

The woman repeated the number as she wrote it down, but her voice was bland and mechanical at the end of what she saw as a useless conversation.

Stone sat silently after he had put the phone down, oblivious of any movement around him. He was not sure how long he would have to wait but he knew it would not be long and the sun warming his face calmed his frustration. It took just five minutes for James Kennedy to return Stone's call.

'Mr Harry Stone?' James enquired tentatively.

'That's me,' Stone said feigning disinterest.

'You called me.'

'Understand you're interested in a deal in Switzerland?' Stone said gently.

'Never been there. So how can I help you?' It was a flat, rehearsed response which hid his surprise that Stone obviously knew something about Switzerland, which he thought had been kept secret. If it was raised again he would give the same response.

'Listen carefully, my friend. I shall bid for the Fenfleet contract,' Stone said. 'And I'd prefer not to talk on the phone. So when do we meet?'

'I'm very busy just now, Mr Stone,' James said sharply.

'I'll leave it to you, Mr Kennedy. But take it from me, I'm not wasting your time as trips to foreign parts might be. Okay?'

James ignored the comment and replied easily. 'Shall we say next Tuesday? Eleven-thirty in my office at Fenfleet.'

'That's good,' Stone said. 'I'll bring a colleague. You won't regret it.'

The call was short, to the point, but Stone had got the meeting he wanted and from James Kennedy's quick response he knew it would not be difficult to get him on the hook. The grub of greed had worked before, it would work now, and he would reel Kennedy in at his own pace and in his own good time.

Stone left the bench and walked slowly along the path beside the Thames, feeling oddly satisfied with his morning's work. Keeping the tax inspector at bay and his temper in check was easier than he had thought and now he had secured a meeting with James Kennedy that would push him to the front of the queue on the Fenfleet deal, just where he wanted to be.

London was hot at midday as Stone walked back towards The Strand. Stone caught a taxi and directed the cabbie to an address in London E6. It was a part of London which he had not visited for twenty years but he had known it, even liked it, in his youth. Stone settled back on the uncomfortable seat and tried to relax as the cab slowly moved through the halting traffic of London's East End.

Stone watched carefully, alert, even wary of being followed as fifteen minutes later they arrived in a maze of short streets with terraced houses. To Cutlass they were dark and depressing, but to Stone the drabness and dust that blew in gusts gave a warm welcome. He had been born here and even though he had long since moved beyond its confines to Arrow Hall the whole place held him as one of its own.

He stopped the driver as they entered Renfrew Street E6 and gave his instructions.

'Drive to the other end and wait for me. I'll be ten minutes.'

'What number are you going to?'

'None of your business,' Stone replied curtly. He slipped a twenty pound note into the cabby's hand. 'That's on account,' he said.

The cabby decided against arguing. He knew his fare could just disappear but he thought it unlikely, although he did wonder what this man with the polished shoes and smart suit was doing here.

Stone slammed the cab door and walked slowly away. Behind parked cars, on the opposite pavement, number 24 stood out brighter than the other houses, its front door freshly painted in a deep blue and its small front garden clear of the wheelybins and debris that choked the adjacent gardens.

Stone stopped and stared for a moment. He wanted to cross the street, he wanted to knock on that front door and say hello to his sister as he had not been able to at their mother's funeral. But he felt an immovable barrier that he could not clear.

His own life had gone on too far, they had drifted apart and he would not know what to say if she came to the door. Nevertheless, his heart ticking faster, he suddenly walked quickly across the street and using the heavily polished brass knocker banged noisily on the door of number 24. There was no impatience, only apprehension as he waited a minute for it to be opened.

Jane McAvoy was a slender woman in her late forties. She had prematurely greying hair but her face was only lined from an almost constant smile that lit up her eyes. Jane always dressed in bright colours as if she wanted to be seen and her red top today matched the warmness of the noonday sun. She looked good.

There was surprise on her face when she saw her elder brother, Harry.

'Jane, I thought it was time I came to say hello. Especially after mum's funeral,' Stone said. He bent forward to kiss his sister but she withdrew before his lips could touch her face. For a moment he felt embarrassed. A car sped noisily down the road and it gave a momentary distraction which both Harry and Jane welcomed.

'You'd better come in. We can't talk here can we?' Jane said.

Stone had never visited his sister in this house but he knew exactly what to expect. He had been brought up in one just like it. The East End was peppered with terraces of similar shape and size.

The hallway was narrow, shadowy but not gloomy, and Harry followed Jane into the living room. Bright, small, tidy, it had a certain elegance with a few colourful prints of

London scenes scattered on the walls and fresh flowers in the bay window.

'Time for a cup of tea?' Jane asked easily.

'I'd like that,' Stone said.

In the small kitchen Jane quickly busied herself with the tea-making, avoiding her brother's eyes.

'Mum's funeral was sad,' she said. 'It was a pity you couldn't stop and say hello then.'

'I'm sorry. I should have done. But I didn't want to create any embarrassments at such a time.'

'Did I see you fall on the steps of the chapel?'

'The steps were very slippery,' he said. 'And I was a bit overcome by the service.'

'But you always rowed with mum,' Jane replied. 'I used to creep away sometimes when the fights were going on. Neither of you would give in, that was the real problem.'

'Let's not talk about the past,' Stone said. 'That's happened, we can't change it now. And anyway, I just called to see how you are. Do you know it's almost twenty years since we've spoken?'

'I'm fine,' Jane answered quickly as she handed her brother a cup of tea. 'Let's go into the other room. It's more comfortable there.' She knew quite well it was twenty years since they had spoken and although she had never counted them exactly it suddenly felt like a very long time.

Stone settled into an armchair that was relaxing as it enclosed him. He looked at his sister and knew instantly that he should not have let the last twenty years pass without contact.

'You look as if you're doing all right,' Stone said as he glanced round the room.

'If you've come to offer me money, Harry, I don't want it. I don't need it and even though Jimmy left me four years ago I have a good job and...'

'Jane. I haven't come to offer you money. I've come to say hello. To make sure you're okay.'

'Why now?'

Stone hesitated. He wanted to tell her of Drake and his threats. He wanted to tell her to be careful in case Drake found her and not him, and then took his revenge in a nasty way. But he couldn't. It would be admitting defeat and he was not going to do that after so many years letting her see how much he'd made.

'Look, Jane. Mum's dead. I saw you at the funeral and I felt it was right to follow you up. To make sure you're okay. It's no more than that,' Stone said.

'Did you send the flowers after the funeral?'

'Yes. You looked sad and I wanted to cheer you up.'

'Harry, you've never done anything without a reason. You've come here for a purpose, I can see it in your eyes which always give you away. So why don't you tell me what it is?'

Stone sipped from his cup, his throat tight, and he looked away. A moment's silence separated them.

'Some people think I've got money. And they don't like it. The same people know you're my sister. Just keep your wits about you, Jane. You may need them.'

Jane looked at her brother and a smile came to her face. 'Nothing changes, does it Harry? I can't remember a time when you didn't face problems.'

'You don't understand, Jane,' Stone said.

'Of course I understand. You've got a guilty conscience over your life and it brings you here.'

'Let me tell you something,' Stone's voice was emphatic, 'I guess you heard on the news some guy got killed near Hammersmith Tube last week.'

'But that was drugs,' Jane said quickly. 'I didn't think you were involved in that sort of thing.'

'Of course not. But you'd better know that the same men

who killed at Hammersmith are stalking me too. And they know you're my sister. They were at Mum's funeral. Watching.'

'You just do your business as usual, Harry. I'm quite capable of looking after myself.'

'Sure,' Stone soothed. 'But make sure you do. And if you need any help give me a call. I'm at Claridge's for the next few days on business and then back at Arrow Hall.'

Stone put his cup on the small table by the chair, and stood as if it was time to go. But Jane would still not look him in the eye.

'I knew you had a reason for coming,' she said. 'Make it a nicer one next time, and give me a call before you come. I'll be more prepared.'

Stone walked slowly to the front door. He turned and faced his sister in the small hallway.

'Just remember what I've said, Jane. I've come for your own good.'

Jane laughed with a mocking tone and for a moment it reminded him of his mother, their rows and her scorn that he was ambitious for money. As he left the small house without saying goodbye he knew he had got it all wrong. He had been pressed into this stupid situation by no more than a gang of chancers whose threats he could hide from and so what if they hit somebody else? Jane closed the front door with a finality that he expected before he had taken the few steps to the pavement.

Annoyed with himself that meeting his sister had not gone as he had hoped, Stone walked slowly to the end of the street. The East End did not change, it was unforgiving and it had its own way of dealing with its sons and daughters who left it behind.

Deep in his own thoughts he reached the end of the terrace and had no reason to notice a coloured girl dressed in dark clothes, cigarette firmly in her mouth, sitting on the low front wall of the end house. The girl did not look at Stone as he passed within a few feet of her but she guessed who he was and she took out her mobile phone. She would report this visitor to those who paid her and maybe that would mean an extra tenner or two at the end of the week.

Stone stood for a moment at the corner and took a long look back down Renfrew Street. Suddenly it now looked dismal, he wanted to get away and he was angry. He barked instructions to the waiting cabby. Gripping indigestion returned and Stone stuffed two tablets into his mouth. It was a penalty he paid more and more often these days for his aggression and the heartburn, when it came, never helped his mood.

The cab moved slowly through the congested City. Red traffic lights confronted it constantly and it took forty minutes before it arrived at the hustle of Fleet Street. Jane had not taken him seriously, Stone thought, but she should have done, she was an easy target and it left him unsettled, concerned as to what violence the Rex Gang might try next.

The cab dropped him at a building as old and grey as his sister's house but somehow the area seemed affluent despite this. This was middle London, sophisticated, with hidden prosperity. Here he would give instructions and they would be strictly carried out even though, as always, there would be a cost.

George Latham, his lawyer, was a man of similar age to Stone. He too was unused to spending money on his own luxury. Or at least on his own workspace.

Stone was kept waiting only a few minutes in a small, windowless reception area. He had called without an appointment but George knew his client well and he dropped everything to see him.

There was little greeting between the two men as Stone was shown into Latham's office and the lawyer dismissed his assistant, a pretty young woman in her late twenties, without introducing her to Stone. He knew Stone would not wish anyone to be present at their meeting whatever was to be discussed.

The leather chair Stone sat in was uncomfortable and made him sit upright. He fidgeted, unsure whether he was doing the right thing in coming here.

'You haven't been to see me for some time,' Latham said. 'Business good?'

'You know what it's like. Sometimes you're up, sometimes you're down. But you have to make it happen, nobody's going to do it for you.'

'So I guess there's something new to bring you here.'

'I want a favour called in.'

'Always happy to help as long as it doesn't push me beyond where I can go,' Latham responded.

'You remember I helped a client of your Paris associates to fix a deal for some property in Docklands a few years ago?'

'Sure I remember, but I never knew the details. It was between you and the client. I never even knew his name. All I did was introduce.'

'I liked the deal. He'd jumped into a big hole without seeing his way out and I dug him clear. Called a few people I know and even put some cash around to lubricate the wheels.'

'I don't think you should tell me too much, Harry. Just let me know what you want me to do and I'll see if it's possible. Okay?'

'I'm about to give your Paris associate's name, address and telephone number to the taxman in London.'

'You in trouble?'

'Nothing serious. A few questions being asked.'

'About the favour you did?'

'Could be.'

'Harry, if I didn't know you better I'd be reporting you to the money laundering people so just tell me what to say. And remember nothing goes in writing.'

'It never does with me unless it has to. You know that. So just get onto Paris and tell 'em to keep the story straight if they hear from the London taxman. When I got their client out of the mess we agreed if they were ever asked they would say any payments were for finder's fees. Remind them of antiques too. Nothing else. They'll know the rest.'

'Finder's fees.' Latham leaned back in his chair. 'Nothing wrong with a finder's fee. I know lots of people in the property game who do just that. Even for antiques.'

'Not quite as simple as that. But your Paris mates will know all about it.'

'And the taxman's going to call them?'

'Maybe. Okay?'

Latham made a note.

'I'll make a phone call, Harry. That's the best I can do. Otherwise keep me out of it and we never had this conversation.'

'No, George. This conversation never took place. And anyway, it's not why I've come today.'

Stone was satisfied. The Revenue would get nowhere further on his Jersey bank account, and they would now find a dead end if they pursued it to its source in Paris.

'What's the real story for today then?'

'I've been thinking,' Stone said.

'Oh?' Latham took his glasses off and looked at Stone.

'My will. I want it altered.'

'I can't remember what's in your will.'

'Arrow Hall was going to the National Trust. I now want it left to my personal assistant, Claire Watts. I rent an apartment to her in the west wing and as there's no one else interested in the place it should be hers if anything happens to me.'

'Yes, I remember Claire. Is she well?'

'Mmm.' Stone was not interested in small talk.

Latham raised his eyebrows as he looked at Stone. He knew the man well, he knew his family background, and he was surprised at the request.

'Does Claire know of this?' he asked.

'No,' Stone said.

'Why not?'

'Don't ask the questions, George. Please just do it. I don't want her to know unless she inherits. And get on with it please. You never know in this world how long you might be here.'

'You're not expecting to leave us just yet?' Latham asked.

'Who knows? There are some nasty people out there and I'm not getting any younger.'

'Any other changes? All the other legacies stay in place?' Latham asked.

'No, that's it.'

There was finality in Stone's tone and Latham did not look up from his pad as he made a note.

'I'll send you a draft. Next week be okay?'

'Sure. But no later,' Stone said.

'So what are you working on now?' It was an easy opening to see if there was any new business to be had.

'Bidding for some pubs. Like I had before.'

'Sounds interesting.'

'This is a big one, George. My bid goes in next week.'

'You want me to draw up a contract?'

'You got it,' Stone said.

'Usual tight clauses? Penalties if you don't get what you expect?'

'It's the only way it works. The bastards'll get it all their own way otherwise.'

Stone spent the next ten minutes outlining the deal to Latham. As he spoke he became more excited. It was always like that when he knew he was in the hunt for money.

Stone suddenly sat upright in his chair. They were now into detail which was boring and he couldn't be bothered with that. That would be Roger's area.

'Right, George. That's where we leave it. Send the documents on. I'll get somebody to read them.'

'Arrow Hall?' Latham asked.

'Yes. Where else?'

Stone walked to the door and they shook hands. A young woman lawyer was hovering outside and she smiled as Stone passed but he ignored her.

Stone took another cab and within half an hour arrived back at the haven of Claridge's. It was four o'clock. He walked across the foyer and bought a newspaper. For a short while he sat in the open lounge skimming the paper and people-watching, mesmerised by types he would not normally give a second thought to. He ordered a pot of tea.

He'd had a good day, he decided. He was beating off the tax people without the inspector getting to his Cayman cash. And anyway, he reasoned, the Caymans had made him nothing, just given him a headache, Drake had seen to that, so why did the inspector need to know about the Caribbean? It was good enough reason for him to keep it all hidden.

Harry had been born with a confident arrogance that now allowed him to deny the existence of anything he did not like. Sipping his tea in the glitzy lounge he did not linger over the questions of whether he would survive if Drake with his London mates got close to their real target or what would happen if his bank accounts were dried out by the Fenfleet deal.

They should have been thoughts threatening enough to

disturb him and make him recoil like a snail into its shell, but instead all Stone could see was that his good days would continue to roll and his inbuilt arrogance left both Drake and Fenfleet dangerous in ways that he did not yet understand.

# 17

Claire glanced down from the first-floor window of the Knightsbridge flat to the street and then quickly recoiled behind the curtain. A young woman, cigarette in hand and dressed in the same dark clothes as the girl in Leicester Square, sauntered slowly along the narrow pavement. Many girls wore black but with an untidy mass of hair, tight-fitting trousers and high stiletto shoes this girl was different, out of place in this plush part of London. She was in a hurry to go nowhere and even though Claire could not see her face she began to feel this was no coincidence. The girl stopped and took a long stare at the front door of the flat with determined interest.

Double glazing made the flat as quiet as Arrow Hall on a windless day. But silence in Knightsbridge was impersonal, unusual, and Claire felt isolated, picked out for unwanted attention.

Claire peeped from the window again. The girl stood for a moment, lit another cigarette, and as if she had all day to kill leaned against a street lamp and continued staring at Claire's front door. She didn't care if she was seen, perhaps she even wanted to be.

Claire stared back but felt intimidated and trapped. Trapped in a game she did not like or understand. On an impulse she tugged the curtain across the window and then ran down the steep stairs to the front door. Fumbling, she released the chain noisily, opened the door wide and strode into the street. The fresh early morning air caught her and she stopped. She looked each way but the girl had gone.

A tense frown creased Claire's forehead. Was it her imagination leading and deceiving her, was the newness of London and following up Stone's plans making her oversensitive to anything unusual, or was something else going on? For sure this was not how she felt at Arrow Hall where she found calmness even when Stone shouted.

She closed the door, went to the bedroom and prepared for her day. Thirty minutes later, dressed in a dark-blue suit, stylish low-heeled shoes and make-up that complemented her colouring, Claire was ready to leave for Rick Austin's office. But first she took another tentative look at the street from behind the curtains. There were no dark girls.

She set out to walk the maze of small streets for the mile to the Trifoni Group building, but crossing the road within two corners of leaving her flat she saw the Afro-Caribbean girl. She froze. Helplessness ran through her and she trembled. The girl stopped too, twenty yards behind, staying on the other side of the road. She lit a cigarette as if that was the natural thing to do. She made no attempt to hide from Claire's gaze.

Claire walked faster, clutching her handbag tightly, ignoring shop windows and the bustle of people around her, and then ran the remaining few yards to the glass frontage that was the entrance to Trifoni Group. Inside, Claire stood breathless, hot and flustered, and looked back into the street. The girl, who was standing close to the glass frontage, returned her stare.

Quickly Claire turned away, swiped her security card and took the lift to her office. She sat at her desk, and after a deep breath felt calmer but still frazzled by the dark girl's interest in her. What was going on? she asked herself. Who had sent this tail? She had a right to know.

She punched the number for Claridge's into her mobile phone. Within seconds she reached him.

'I'm being followed,' she said breathlessly.

'Yeh?' There was disinterest in Stone's voice.

'There's a dark-dressed, dark-skinned girl. Caribbean I would say.'

'There's lots of coloured people in London,' Stone replied.

'So you've seen one of them. For goodness sake don't let your imagination run away with you.'

'Please don't keep on ignoring me! You brushed aside the phone call I had at Jenny Garon's place. I've seen this girl several times in the street, and now this morning she followed me to Trifoni's offices. She wants to know where I am and where you are, so you'd better take me seriously.'

'Nothing's different in my life,' Stone said dismissively.

'Why are you hiding at Claridge's then?' Claire's tone was sharp and insistent.

'Look, I don't know if you're being followed, there's nothing I can do about it if you are, so I suggest you get on with the job, find out what I've asked for at Trifoni and then get back to Arrow Hall as soon as you can. That's what we both want isn't it?'

'If this stops me doing the snooping you want, just don't blame me,' Claire retorted.

'Call back when you've got some more positive news. And don't leave it too long,' Stone said.

Claire snapped her phone shut and hid it in her bag. Stone was blatantly lying, something was going on that he wanted to keep from her, but that was not new. This time though she was close to it, she'd find out and sling the mud back at him. Two could play at this game, she promised herself.

*

Claire was alert but she did not see the dark girl again. Stone was right. In London many people were black and

235

wore dark clothes. Claire varied her routine each day, going to work variously by bus, cab and on foot.

At the Trifoni office, the work was fast, deadlines were tight, but it ran smoothly with Rick pulling any strings necessary to hold it together. Rick spent all his time dealing with two complicated deals – selling a large property in Edinburgh and a jewellery shop business in Birmingham, where the buyers were being awkward and pernickety. It left no room for the Fenfleet contract, and Claire heard no follow-up from Geneva and the ghastly Dr le Borge, and there were no phone calls that gave any clue as to where to look next for the information Stone required. Fenfleet stubbornly remained hidden.

Rick was always at his desk when Claire arrived each morning and he was always there when she left in the evening. Keeping a twelve-hour day by arriving at 7.30 a.m. and leaving at 7.30 p.m. did not free her of his presence and Claire began to wonder if he had any life outside the office.

Security in the building was tight. Entry at the front and the use of lifts was only gained by using her swipe card and there were little unobtrusive video cameras tucked in corners as if they were lights. Claire counted at least six between the front door and her office. Where were they connected to and who looked at them? Were there any cameras in Rick's office? She looked every time she went in and saw none, but they could be hidden, little traps soon to expose her if she pried into the wrong place.

Later that morning a chance came without warning as Rick entered her office with a smile on his face. Claire looked up from the document she had been preparing and smiled back.

'Claire, get me a cab in half an hour. And book me a table at the Runnymede restaurant. The one west of Heathrow. Ask for a table overlooking the river.'

'And can I ask who is going to enjoy lunch with you today?'

'James Kennedy. You remember Geneva?'

'Of course. It seems a long time ago.'

'Kennedy likes the flashy style. So Runnymede on the river will be a good place to make him feel important.'

'You've not mentioned Mr Kennedy since we came back from Geneva.'

'He's not easy to deal with,' Rick replied. 'So I've let the deal sweat for a while. It's the best way. Don't let them know you're too interested.'

'Will it be a good deal?' Claire asked.

'Maybe,' Rick said. 'At the right price.'

'And how much is that?'

'Not sure. But you heard what happened in Geneva. Kennedy wants favours for himself before we get a look in. Greedy bastard.'

'I don't think I like Mr James Kennedy,' Claire said.

'Nor me. Feed his greed and you don't know what you might get.'

'Are you going to give in to his demands?'

'Competitors might. Kennedy tells me he's meeting some of them in a couple of days.'

'And who are they?' Claire's inquisitive questions were easy office conversation, just showing interest in her job and she hid her anxiety for answers by fiddling with some papers and not looking Rick in the eye.

'You'll never have heard of them, they're a bit obscure. There's a guy called Harry Stone. He's a multi-millionaire, or so the story goes. I know he'd like to get hold of this deal. There are probably others but none as tough as Harry Stone.'

Claire blushed at the unexpected mention of Stone's name. This was unreal, like a dream which had to end to be understood. Suddenly she hated her betrayal of Rick, she despised Stone for sending her here, and she knew she had to change the subject or she'd get found out.

'And today's lunch?' she asked.

'Kennedy's in London and he wants to be entertained. Nothing more.'

'Do I need to phone Mr Kennedy to tell him of the arrangements?' she asked.

'He knows. I spoke to him last night. He's coming down on the midday flight.'

'What time will you be back?'

'Maybe after you've gone. Kennedy likes a long, late lunch. French style. And his wine. Didn't you notice in Geneva?'

'Yes, I did. He does seem to know what he wants.'

'Sure, but he might get more than he wants if he plays it too hard.'

'His demands in Geneva were a blatant bribe. I mean, Swiss bank accounts?' Claire said as if she disapproved.

'Don't you remember? They're not a bribe. The good Dr le Borge said they're "payments for consultancy services". Happens all the time.'

With a phone call Claire quickly made the arrangements for lunch but the morning dragged slowly and she felt a nervous twinge as Rick left for the meeting an hour later. For the first time since Claire had worked for Trifoni she was now alone in the Aladdin's cave of Rick's office suite. The soft carpets, elegant modern furniture and rows of richly-polished wall cupboards, from cocktail cabinets to bookcases, were now hers to explore and plunder. And she believed – hoped – that, other than a few ceiling spotlights, the only thing looking down on her would be the framed originals of newspaper cartoons that lined an internal wall.

She waited for half an hour after Rick had left. Her nerve would now be tested to its limits. This was it, her only chance to get the job done and get out. Being followed round London could then become a distant memory.

In Rick's office everything was in a set place, everything knew its order. If a paper or file was moved and not exactly replaced it would be very obvious.

The suite was completely silent. Even the air conditioning, which came through slatted vents in the floor, whispered unheard into the rooms. She checked that the entrance to the suite was closed and with her heart pounding slowly opened the door to the small windowless anteroom which led to Rick's office. Claire had been in there many times in the last few days but now it was different, as if she were trespassing on forbidden ground. She saw the computer screen which stood silently on a side table in a corner away from the windows. It flickered with an relaxing pattern. All she needed on Fenfleet could be stored there but under a password she would never know. She could be close to it but it would be safely locked away from her.

She stared for a moment at the screen, mesmerised by the red ball of fire that rolled into each corner. This was not her area of expertise and outside help would be needed to access any data.

Rick's desk was a large modern affair with slender legs and thin drawers at each end. She could cope with that. A few papers in two neat piles lay together on the top of the desk and she quickly thumbed through them, but nothing she did not already know came to her notice. She replaced them carefully, exactly where they had been left by Rick.

She carefully tested each of the four drawers. They were all unlocked. She pulled on a pair of light cotton gloves which did not impede her nimble fingers and, even though her hands trembled and her palms were sweaty, worked quickly. She fumbled through the first drawer and found no files, just the debris of an everyday working desk – combs, loose stationery, airline timetables and a personal address book. She quickly opened two more drawers but an unused

239

diary and world atlas was all that they contained. Making no noise she slid them gently back.

Suddenly she heard the opening click of the outer door to Rick's office. She froze, her heartbeat again quickened. Her leg and neck muscles tightened and although she wanted to run from this madness she was powerless to move as she shivered in the stillness of her own guilt. She craned her neck and just stared at the open vista from the windows. She had already mentally prepared herself for being caught. If somebody walked in she would smile gently and casually saunter away from the desk – after all, there was no reason why she should not be in the boss's office, she did work for him.

A minute passed before Claire crept quietly to the door and dared to look out. Nobody was there. She breathed out heavily, sure now that the noise had been in her head, her mind playing a trick on her nerves. Or at least that's what she hoped.

She wanted to get this over with, so she set purposefully about rifling the rest of the desk. Fear of being interrupted, caught in the act, had now gone, replaced by the stimulation of rushing adrenaline. To search was why she had come to this place, and these few minutes could give her information useful to Harry Stone. The inside information on Fenfleet would be but a bargaining chip and whatever she found would have a price.

Suddenly she smiled as she withdrew from the final drawer a thin file titled boldly on its side PROJECT FENFLEET. There were three sheets of paper clipped inside and each had notes written in Rick's spidery scrawl.

At the back of the file she found a neatly folded form. Quickly she withdrew it and held it to the light. In heavy print it was headed TENDER – FENFLEET PUBS. Claire flicked the form open and eagerly scanned six pages. In the bottom corner on the last page she saw the figure £1.5 million.

It was written in Rick's hand, boldly in black ink. The form was already signed and dated by him, two days ahead.

Claire scanned the form more closely and finding nothing more that would help her carefully replaced it in the file. If £1.5 million was the Trifoni bid she decided it was not a hard figure to keep in her memory.

She took a quick look at the notes in the file. The figures showed scrawled costs, sales, profits, rents and how much was needed to get it all going. Claire wrote them quickly in her notepad. Then she saw that the notes referred to a computer file called PROJECT FENFLEET, where the real figures were presumably held, and turned again to face the flickering screen in the corner. The hard figures, the detail worked up by the accountants, would be there. But there was no clue to the password and without it she was sunk. PROJECT FENFLEET on the computer was unreachable.

Carefully Claire replaced the file, closed the drawer and took a long hard look at Rick's desk. After a few seconds she was sure that she had not upset even by a tiny fraction the tidy order she had found at the beginning of her search. Wiping her gloved hand over the surface of the drawers and the desk top gave her certainty that there were no smudges and she breathed out heavily, satisfied with her work. She moved to the window and scribbled some quick notes of names and addresses she had found that could be useful to Stone. She took her gloves off, put them in her jacket pocket and took a last look around the room.

She froze. She had been exposed. Again it was a noise that caught her. Nothing else.

The private line on Rick's large desk rang like a shrill siren giving warning to all who might hear it. Her instructions were never to answer it but she wondered who else might come in, if only to be inquisitive. She stood still for a full thirty seconds, her sense of guilt heightening and making her scalp tingle.

241

As suddenly as the noise had started it stopped, leaving her in deafening silence. She walked quickly to the door and with a final glance at the flickering red balls on the computer screen and Rick's large desk she sidled away to the solitude of her own office. Nobody had seen her and the carpeting was so soft nobody could possibly have heard her.

Sitting at her desk it took Claire half an hour to calm down and feel composed. She made a cup of strong tea in the kitchen off the corridor and, after running a comb through her hair, brooded uneasily on the search. Her thoughts on the last half hour ran vividly. Had she ransacked the room, had she betrayed trust, could she ever do it again? She was getting too close to the edge and she sipped her tea to clear the dryness in her mouth.

Rick would be back sometime and to show him she had been attending to business in his absence Claire spread papers across her desk and then typed two letters on the computer. Her brain buzzed with doubts and a thumping headache had begun. She took two paracetamol tablets and sat still, gradually becoming more in control as they took effect.

An hour later, brooding and feeling unhappy at betraying Rick just to satisfy Stone, Claire cleared her desk ready to leave. She wanted to get out of this place, back to her normal routine, back to Arrow Hall where she was safe, not followed, without pressure. She had not coped easily with this day.

Claire took a last flip through her notebook to check on what she had found. She sat and considered it for a minute. Of course there was something missing. There was nothing in the file on Rick's visit to Geneva, nothing on the Swiss account opened for James Kennedy or the amount of the bribe.

Had she missed it in the eagerness of her search? Stone

242

would want to know and suddenly she had a driving compulsion to have another delve and finish this off once and for all while Rick was out. But the tenseness in her neck returned and she knew it would lead to a migraine which would show in her running eyes.

Claire again spread some files over her now empty desk, switched her screen on and tore off a clean page from her notepad. Without hesitating she walked towards the closed door of Rick's office but halfway across the thick carpet the outside door to the office suite abruptly opened. It was Rick.

She stopped and turned, thrown off balance by Rick's unexpected return. Her face became blotchy red, she was flustered and she fought to control herself. But she managed a smile and looking straight at Rick's eyes she said, 'You're back early.'

'Kennedy had to catch an early flight, thank goodness,' Rick replied without looking at her, heading for his office.

'How did lunch go?'

'Fine. Kennedy drinks too much but if you just let him carry on he soon runs out of steam.'

'Get anywhere with the deal?'

'No.'

'You look unsettled,' Claire said, her own agitation subsiding.

'Kennedy's trying to keep me on a piece of string and I wouldn't put it past him to play me off against the other bidders. He's not one to trust.' Rick slumped into the chair behind his desk and looked at the ceiling for a moment as if he was unsure of himself.

Claire stood still and stared at the desk top, a nasty feeling of guilt stirring inside her.

'Anybody rung?' Rick asked as if he expected somebody should.

'No. But I thought I heard your private line ring while

I was making some tea. Of course I didn't answer it,' she said.

'Good, I'll pick it up later. That one's personal, non-business use only.'

'There's these letters to sign.' Claire handed him a folder.

'That all you've done while I've been out enjoying lunch?'

Claire looked shocked but Rick tapped her hand and smiled.

'That's a joke, Claire. Never take me too seriously after I've had a drink or two entertaining the likes of James Kennedy.'

As Claire moved away from Rick's desk the touch of his hand on hers lingered with a slight warm tingle.

'I hope you're enjoying your time here,' Rick said as he set about signing the letters.

'It's very exciting, something new each day,' Claire said as she glanced at the drawers and the desk she had just searched. She wanted to get away but Rick hadn't finished.

'I'm going to embarrass you, Claire. I'm very grateful to you for filling the gap so well. No fuss, no complaints. You've given the efficient help I need. And after today's lot with James there's more to do. Next weekend I agreed to take them to the Cotswolds. Mrs Kennedy's a horsey woman, never met her but she likes that part of the country so I said yes,' he added sarcastically. 'I'd like you to help me take them on.'

'Does the Fenfleet contract mean that much to you? You'll really give up a whole weekend entertaining Kennedy?' Claire's voice showed surprise and her eyebrows arched.

'Sure. Why not?' Rick replied quickly. 'Anyway, will you come?'

'Of course. I like the Cotswolds too. But I'm not so sure about James Kennedy.'

'Good. But don't worry about Kennedy, I'll look after him.'

'When do we leave?'

'Friday afternoon. Before the traffic builds up.'

Claire turned to leave.

'Claire,' Rick called after her. 'As compensation for giving up your weekend how about dinner tonight? A sort of thank-you celebration before the event. I've got nothing on, have you?'

Claire swung round and looked hard at Rick, returning his smile.

'Yes, that would be fun,' she said, but she knew she was lying.

'Right. I'll pick you up at your flat at seven-thirty. Not too early?'

'No, that's fine.'

As Claire replied she knew that Rick Austin, the man she had been sent to investigate, even undermine, was dazzling her and her earlier nervous tension had gone, replaced with an exciting buzz. This new life was feeling great but could she handle it? And dinner tonight with a man she was blatantly betraying?

An intricate spider's web was inexorably dragging her into its dangerous inner core and she was unable to resist.

# 18

Today Stone was on the hunt for prey. Rising early as the dawn was breaking was no problem to him and he left Claridge's just after five, eager to unfold his carefully laid plans for the day.

As he climbed into the rear seat of a Mercedes, the chauffeur holding the door for him, Stone felt his adrenaline surge as it always did when a deal was beginning to take shape. He did not need his tailored suit, freshly-laundered shirt and bright red tie to give him an air of importance and power. Hungry for the chase he browsed the daily papers that had been left for him on the back seat and at precisely six o'clock he arrived at Roger's house near Newbury.

He had never been invited there before – Roger always kept him at a distance – but Stone was now diverted by the house's elegance. The lush green lawns were wet with dew and the wide expanse of garden had a crispness that hinted at constant attention. Stone always knew Roger's fees were high and when he saw the grandness of the rambling red brick house he knew where much of that money had gone. Arrow Hall and its run-down state flashed before him and he shuddered. But he reminded himself that today he'd corner Fenfleet, then he'd get Claire back and get the hall renovated as he had promised her. There was just a quick 'Hi' from Roger as he threw his briefcase onto the seat and the car sedately moved off.

Stone waited for the chauffeur to be concentrating hard on the traffic before speaking.

'You ready for it?' he asked. 'We don't hang around today.'

'It's too nice to go north,' Roger replied. 'It'll be a waste of time and I've got a lot of pressing things to deal with at the moment.'

'Why can't you be more positive? Can't you see today's a day we go to win? Make some cash.'

'Sure, but it isn't going to be easy.'

'Look, all we've got to do is decide how much for Kennedy, get him hungry. That's what we're after. Simple.'

'So you've got all the information you need to sew this up?'

'No. We play it by ear.'

'I call it going in feet first.' There was sarcasm in Roger's voice.

Stone looked through the window at the heavy traffic as they joined the M1. He spoke slowly. 'These pubs are a big deal. I offer big money and I make big money.'

'Go carefully is my advice. This deal may not be quite as you expect. Perhaps I shouldn't have rung you in St Lucia to dangle it before you.'

'Think big and follow me, Roger. You know how I work.'

Roger pensively watched the traffic crawl in the opposite direction.

'What sort of mood was Claire in when you last spoke to her?' Roger asked.

'Claire's always in a good mood,' Stone lied, but it was easier than getting into a discussion about Claire and her moods.

'She hasn't come up with the numbers yet, has she?'

'She will,' Stone replied.

'Don't press too hard. She's new to this way of working.'

'She's fine. A bit of pressure won't hurt her.'

Roger did not pursue it. Jennie had told him all about Claire and he had no intention of letting on to Stone what was happening to her. If Stone did not want to consider the position he had put Claire in and the likely consequences then that was Stone's problem.

He changed the subject. 'Tell me the numbers. How big are you going?'

'You've done the sums. You tell me.'

'My calculations show £1.5 million. And that's top side.'

'Come on, you make a lot of assumptions when you do sums. You could be wrong. Anyway, I keep telling you, you're a downright pessimist.' Stone was testing Roger in his usual way.

'Don't chase this one too hard. And remember it'll cost you cash if you get it. It needs investment.'

'What's wrong with you this morning? Do you know something I don't?' Stone's voice was sharp.

'No. But I just don't understand why you pay my fees if you don't take my advice.'

'I haven't said I won't take your advice. I'm just questioning it.'

'You don't like £1.5 million do you? You don't think it'll get the deal.'

There was silence for several minutes as the car raced north.

'Trifoni Group will add a bit for prestige when they bid. Where's our prestige? Who looks at us and says we're serious with big backing? No, we have to make up for that with the other bits.' Stone was insistent.

'So, what price are you offering?' Roger asked.

'Don't know yet. But it'll be more than £1.5 million.' Stone's face broke into a thin smile. 'The key is James Kennedy. That guy holds the balance where this deal goes, so if we don't get him on our side first you can forget even thinking about the bid price.'

'Don't go there, Harry.'

'I've got ideas for James Kennedy. Ideas he'll jump at it if I know his type.'

248

'Harry, for God's sake slow up. Bidding's one thing, slush money's something else. Look what happened to your Cayman cash when you tried to be too clever.'

Stone continued as if he had not been interrupted. 'I'm going to get Kennedy cornered. Dangle enough cash, let his greed grab it and then he's got nowhere else to wriggle but into my deal. That's the position I want him in by the time we leave today.'

Roger drew in a breath. 'It's your deal. So, okay, you pay for prestige. Not many would but it's your prestige not mine. And as for slush money ... well ... you get caught and you're locked up straight away.'

'You know as well as I do that the highest bidder doesn't always get the deal. It's the bits on the side that count.'

'Sure. But don't involve me in those bits. I don't want to know.' Roger took a newspaper from the seat rest and began to read it. It was the only way to stop Stone banging on.

After several hours of moody silence they entered the underground car park of a drab block on the edge of Fenfleet. Tension was building in Roger at Stone's hair-brained scheme, and they took the lift to James Kennedy's office suite in silence. There they were kept waiting for twenty minutes in a cold, sparse room.

Stone, becoming impatient, stood and paced, but he said nothing when a secretary came to lead them to Kennedy's office. As with the rest of the block it was austere, set with light brown papered walls bare of pictures and with chairs of cracked leather round a large table. Stone instantly approved.

James Kennedy was a large man, clumsily dressed in a green shirt, blue tie and pocket handkerchief that did not match. He greeted his visitors with a thin smile.

'Gentlemen, welcome to Fenfleet.'

'New place to me. So I thought it was time we met,' Stone replied.

'You come to see me or some of the properties? Some are close by.'

'See you, Mr Kennedy,' Stone said.

'Call me James, please.'

'Sure, James. And this is my adviser, Roger Garon. I take him everywhere. Especially when we're in for a big deal.'

'You do know the tender deadline is close. And we don't extend it,' Kennedy said.

'Don't want you to. Our tender will be in on time and it will be good,' Stone said. He managed a half smile. His thin lips moved upwards but grudgingly as if he had to show some deference to get his prize.

'Good, good. Last-minute bids are usually the best. Gives you more thinking time.' James laughed.

'James, like you we're businessmen so let's get to the point. We can talk here?' Stone raised his eyebrows.

'Nobody listens in this room but me and I have no tapes running,' James said easily as he clasped his hands in front of him in a satisfied gesture.

'We want to make this deal happen and there can be certain things in business which ... well oil it a bit. Discreetly you understand.'

'Always good to talk, Harry.'

'I want to see you right on this deal. If we get it then you get a bit, we get a bit. I'm sure you follow me.'

Stone stopped for a moment and stared into Kennedy's eyes. He saw no emotion and took that to mean that he should carry on.

'James, I know you'll understand we're the best people to carry out this contract for you. It will be without any fuss or problems to you personally and I guess you're happy to take the easy life like the rest of us. We've proved we can do it in other places. Roger will confirm we're the best at this game.'

'I know all that, Harry. I know your business background,

where you come from and how you operate. We check everybody before we deal with them.'

'Yes. Wouldn't we all.' Stone looked at Roger but their eyes did not meet.

'Let's have the details, let's have 'em on the table,' James said briskly.

'In return for me getting the deal you get a personal payment.'

Roger sat further back in his seat and saw a glint in James's eye that said he would bite at Stone's offer.

'How much are you offering? The bit I make I mean.' The question was blunt and expected by Stone.

'How much you looking for?'

'You're here to make the bid,' Kennedy said with a touch of tetchiness.

Stone raised his eyebrows. 'Six figures?'

'Six figures can be anything,' Kennedy snapped. 'How much are you offering?'

'A hundred grand,' Stone responded.

'Forget it. You're not in the race at that price.'

'Okay. Then I'll match anything anyone else can offer.'

'You're wasting my time and yours if you don't, Harry.'

'We agree then, I'll match anyone else. It's easy that way.'

'Not good enough,' Kennedy said sharply. 'You're in the hunt so you'd better fire the shots.'

'I'm here to help,' Stone said.

'You're here to get the deal, aren't you?'

'Sure. But straight tendering's no good to me. Or you.'

'The highest bidder gets it, Harry. You'll need to go high.'

'How many other bidders are there?' Stone asked.

'Plenty. These pubs are good properties. I guess you've seen the figures.'

Stone stared directly at James just to see if he would flinch.

'I want to warn you off any ideas of Switzerland,' he said.

'I don't know what you're talking about,' Kennedy replied.

'Look, James, sometimes in these deals people think money paid to places like secret Swiss accounts is the right thing. I know otherwise.'

James's face gave nothing away. 'Swiss accounts, offshore accounts, secret accounts, sound all right to me,' he said dryly.

'It's just not a good way forward if we're to do business.'

'Why not?'

'Take my advice. Only take cash. Used fivers or fifties.'

Kennedy fingered some papers on his desk. 'Even at £100,000 that's a hell of a lot of paper.'

'It's your deal,' Stone said. 'But you'll find a Swiss bank account difficult to use. I've tried 'em. Cash in your hand.' Stone waved a fifty pound note in the air.

'Okay, you make your point.'

'Something else important, James. Used notes aren't recorded, certainly not in my books. Anybody else offer you used notes?'

'No one's offered me anything,' James spat.

'Good. Keep the notes safe, spend 'em quietly, no flash cars all of a sudden, and nobody but the three of us in this room will know the deal.'

Roger said nothing, his face was tight and he stared at the floor. He had heard it all before, once even when it had ended in denials from Stone and his lawyer writing letters threatening libel action, and Stone running from the deal like a hunted hare. Roger shuddered at Stone's oily, plastic, false, undermining of his bait, James Kennedy.

'Come clean. How much are you offering me?' James asked.

'Two hundred grand nearer the right number?'

'It's better than a hundred. Still not enough.'

'I've told you I'll match anyone. So tell me and I'll beat it.'

'It's just you and me, Harry. We're on our own.'

'Sure,' Stone said. 'It's best that way. So can we talk about the deal itself, James?'

'Fine by me.'

'Whatever I pay you in used readies has to buy the deal for me. You understand that?'

James nodded again, perhaps out of his depth in this murky water.

Roger looked at James. He judged this guy was being bought. Easily.

'So with £200,000, or whatever it is you'll settle for, I can be sure I'll get your pubs? Sealed bids are no use to me.'

'You'll have to bid like the rest.'

'And the highest bidder gets it?'

'Harry, I can make recommendations. My lot'll listen to me. I've got influence but you'll have to go through the process. I can't change that.'

Roger saw that this guy was suddenly relishing the power offered and he was going to use it.

'This deal could make you rich, James. So give me some leads and it'll help me to cover you.'

James's face softened. He liked the idea of having cash and he spoke quickly.

'Trifoni Group, yourself and a consortium from France. The French will stand no chance whatever their price because my lot don't like 'em. But you and Trifoni? Well it might be tight so don't try to get away with it on the cheap. It won't work.'

'How much are Trifoni coming in at?' Roger asked. He did not expect an answer.

James leaned back in his chair and stared out of the window, measuring his words carefully. He'd got Stone on the run and he'd now keep it that way.

'You ask too many questions,' he said.

'We have to explore this together so we both win,' Stone said.

'Look. Trifoni have shown interest but I don't know their price. And would you expect me to tell you if I did know?'

'No,' Roger said. 'Any more than you'd tell them our price if you knew it.'

James laughed and sat further back in his chair. 'You know what makes it work for you, so stick that in. Then maybe I'll help it along. Cash talks.'

The ring of sarcasm hit Stone and Roger. James with his box of secrets was becoming difficult to prise open.

'I guarantee we will get our bid in on time,' Stone said. 'So the used fivers, where can I deliver them?'

'Let's agree how many first.'

'We will agree, James. Be sure of that.'

'Okay. But don't leave it too long.'

'Sure,' Stone said. 'I'll deliver what you want and where you want.'

'Future times we use the code word "Palm". Like greasing the palm.' And for a moment James smiled.

Roger again stared at James, disliking the man as much as he often disliked Harry Stone. The meeting had gone exactly as he had expected and he decided these two graspers deserved each other.

Stone fumbled for a moment in his jacket pocket and clumsily pulled out a small green box. He placed it on James's desk.

'From now on both of us have much to lose if we don't work together. Me a deal and you very usable cash. So I know you will accept this little gift. Just a deposit for the good times ahead shall we say. In gold.'

James snapped open the box and took out a pair of gold cufflinks. He held them to the light as if checking a twenty-pound note and then quickly put them in his pocket.

'As you say, Harry, a nice little deposit. Eh?'

There was no thank-you from James just the end of a

conversation which he saw as satisfactory. He knew there was more to come.

The parting was formal, not friendly. Roger, relieved it was over, drew in a breath as he shook James's wet hand. James Kennedy had shown he was greedy and Stone had fed his greed. And that was how it would be from here on.

In the car it was at least half an hour before Roger spoke. He had preferred the silence of his own thoughts.

'You didn't get much out of that guy.'

'What do you mean?' Stone snapped. ''Course I did. He's as hungry as a starving rat.'

'Numbers, Harry. How much feeds his greed? And anyway, do you really intend paying Kennedy his used fivers before we get the deal?'

'If it oils the deal, why not?'

'It's dangerous. He could walk away. And he probably will.'

'If he accepts the fivers that buys him in. For goodness' sake you know how these things work, Roger.'

'Yes. I know how they work.'

'The deal's not done with Kennedy yet but he's coming my way. You watch.'

'So once you've paid him he'll deliver?'

'Sure.'

'How do you know?'

'Our tender will be the highest. You forget too quickly the trouble I'm taking to get the Trifoni numbers. When Claire calls with the figures we just top them. Say fifty thousand more than Trifoni. Sound right?'

'You're getting carried away, Harry. This deal is worth so much and not dollops more. Fifty grand is a lot of cash, remember. And I've checked the figures for the number of people who use these pubs. They're not that strong. A lot of money's got to be spent to bring the punters in.'

'Yesterday's figures,' Stone snapped. 'Just the beginning.

And we'll grow with them. This might be my last big deal. The one I'll be remembered by. Okay?' A smirk of satisfaction that would have repelled even the most persistent questioner spread over Stone's face.

'I think it'll be the one you're forgotten by. You could lose a pile.'

Roger opened his mobile phone as it quivered to receive a call, happy to blot out any more conversation and Stone rested his head back, satisfied with his day's work. James was more pliable than he had thought he would be, he could be bought and there was hard cash tucked away safely in Arrow Hall that would buy him. To Stone the deal was as good as done.

An hour later, alone in his suite at Claridge's, whisky in hand, the phone rang three times before it made him stir. Stone put his whisky down slowly and grabbed the call. Whoever it was he would make it short.

'Yes?'

'This is the hotel reception desk, sir. We are aware of your security requirements but I have a Mrs McAvoy who wishes to speak to you. She says it's urgent. Do you wish to take the call?'

Stone immediately sat upright on the deep sofa. He had not expected his sister to call.

'Yes,' he said. 'Put her on.'

Jane spoke before he had time to say hello.

'This is your problem, Harry. Not mine.' Jane's voice was tight with anger.

'Jane. Hold on. Calm down.'

'Listen to me carefully. You'd better get your business problems sorted like quick and without involving me.'

'Jane? What's happened?'

There was a moment's silence before Jane continued.

'A bottle full of petrol through the front door at six o' clock this morning. That's what's happened.'

'No warning?'

'No warning. The note that came with it said that the next time there'll be a match attached to it.' Jane's voice trembled with emotion.

'Jane,' Stone said calmly, 'leave it to me. I'll get it sorted.'

'That's the trouble with you, Harry. You never get *anything* sorted.'

'I will this time. Anyway, I warned you of the danger didn't I?'

'Warnings are no good. If this happens again I go to the police. And I give them your name and address. That's what you'll get.'

Before he had a chance to respond Jane put the phone down. Stone sat still for several seconds. It was as if Drake and his thugs loitered around every corner and although he had blotted them out for the past few days he now recalled Anton's violent and bloody end. He stared at the phone, ran his hand through his hair, then thoughtfully picked his whisky up from the low table and sipped it slowly.

# 19

Light was streaming through the half-opened curtains and the bedroom was very quiet. Claire quickly came to, turned over and wondered where she was. It was seven-thirty, she was on her own and her skin was tight around her temples.

She flung the duvet aside, went to the bathroom and pulled a towel around her half-naked body. Without making a noise she crept to the kitchen expecting to find Rick eating breakfast or reading a newspaper. But all she found was a scribbled note.

> *Claire, sorry. Gone off for an early appointment with my accountant in the City. The housekeeper doesn't come until ten so help yourself to breakfast. Enjoyed last night. Hope you did too. See you in the office when you're ready.*
> *Rick.*

Claire blinked and frowned as if she had just woken from a dream. Her head pounded. The consequences of the previous evening suddenly became clear and in the stark light of the early morning she felt less than sure of herself. Dinner had been great. Rick, sophisticated and witty, was good company and The Ivy had lived up to its reputation for fine food, expensive wine and crisp service. But spending a night with Rick was not what she had planned. Claire had known from the start that she had to keep her distance from Rick, but now, sitting alone at the kitchen table, she felt hot as the dilemma hit her. What now for her mole-burrowing and betrayal? Her mouth felt dry. She took an orange carton from the fridge, made a quick breakfast of yoghurt and fresh melon with black coffee and then hurriedly dressed. Even after a shower, within forty-five minutes of waking she was ready to leave Rick's apartment.

But what should she do? Go back to Jennie's flat? Return to Arrow Hall? Cut off the whole deal and let Stone get on with it another way? Within a few minutes she made up her mind because she had little choice and she knew it.

Her head gradually clearing she took a taxi and was walking into the bright marble foyer at Trifoni within an hour and half of waking. But she was worried, flustered, and hardly in control of her emotions. What would she say to Rick when he came in later from his accountant? And what would he say to her? Would this new relationship with his temporary secretary mean she had to go?

In the quiet solitude of her own small office she rang Jennie Garon in Newbury. She needed to talk and urgent reassurance. The phone was answered quickly and Claire felt her tenseness relax as Jennie spoke.

'Claire, how are you?' she asked easily.

'Can we meet at lunchtime?'

'Are you all right?' Jennie asked. 'You sound upset.'

'Yes, I'm all right but I need to talk.'

'Are you sure everything's okay?' Jennie was perceptive. The tight tone of Claire's voice was unnatural and forced.

'Somewhere quiet, Jennie, please, for talking, not for eating. And it'll have to be quick,' Claire said.

'Yes, of course. I'm coming up to London for this evening. So what time?'

'Early. Half twelve?'

'We'll meet at the end of South Audley Street. On the corner. And I'll fix a light lunch. Anything I should know?' Jennie asked.

'It'll keep.'

'See you then. But in the meantime take care and wipe those tears from your eyes,' Jennie said.

There were no tears in Claire's eyes and her head had stopped aching, but she knew this impossible turn of events had to be sorted, and quickly. She looked at her desk, which was clear of papers and her screen switched off. Work would be impossible this morning. She hoped that the pernickety director would not summon her and drone on in his monotonous grey tone because she knew she would walk out if he did. And where would that lead?

In the small kitchen she made herself a cup of coffee and sipped it slowly. At her desk she reapplied her make-up, this time more carefully than she had in Rick's flat. She wanted to tame her wildly running emotions, calm herself, and look in control even if she did not feel it. Just in case Rick came in.

But then in the mirror her imagination saw an image of herself facing Harry Stone. His steely blue eyes were compelling her to finish off the dirty work for him, and she shuddered, wondering why she had let herself be lured into this dangerous web of deceit. Quickly she turned away, uneasy, and as she sipped her coffee she decided that the balance should tip away from Harry Stone and his devious nastiness that was designed to hit Rick, someone she was beginning to like, someone who gave her a feeling of mutual closeness.

*

Jennie flicked the phone off after Claire's call and she too thought for a moment as she walked into the garden, the phone still in her hand. Sure Claire was anxious – the tight voice told her that – and as if she had been looking into the same mirror as Claire the image of Harry Stone flashed before her. It had to be his meddling that was upsetting Claire, who else could bring something nasty without caring?

The sun was warm, the garden a pleasing array of colour with the scent of flowers wafting in the summer air as Jennie sat on a south-facing seat and tilted her eyes to the sky. But a moment later she punched in the numbers for Roger at his office.

Hearing Jennie's voice Roger sat up straight in his chair.

'Roger, you'd better tell me what's going on,' Jennie said firmly.

Roger was surprised but spoke calmly. 'Hey, darling, hold on a minute. You always know everything that's going on.'

'Roger, don't be obtuse. Claire's upset. Deeply upset I'd say.'

'So what's that got to do with me?'

'Harry Stone's scheming and Claire's hurting. That's what.'

'I only know what you know. Stone doesn't tell me everything.'

'I don't believe you. Claire has rung and asked to have lunch today. And her voice was trembling. She was emotional. She needs help. So before we meet I need to know more.' Jennie's tone became increasingly demanding as she spoke, leaving no room for argument.

'What can I tell you, darling? Claire's fine, with business running as normal.'

'In Harry Stone's language that means something underhand is going on. Claire's being used so what are you doing to stop it?'

'Jennie, please don't meddle in Stone's work. Whatever Claire's doing is her choice too and it just won't help for you or me to get involved. Anyway, there's nothing I can do.'

'Don't you understand that Claire's naïve? She's right out of her depth in this pool of sharks and now she's about to be devoured by the lot of them. And that's all because your mate Harry Stone lacks morals.'

'Honey, listen,' Roger said, trying to be conciliatory. 'If Claire doesn't like where she is she can always say no. You would.'

'You know damn well she can't say no. Not when Stone puts heavy pressure on. And from the sound of her voice that's just what he's doing now.'

'Please stay out of it, honey,' Roger said.

'I'm not staying out of it. I'm seeing Claire at lunchtime and I intend to find out what's troubling her. And then I shall make damn sure she's protected against the likes of Stone and anybody else come to that.'

'Stone's in the middle of a big deal. He needs Claire's help on this one, so go slowly. That's all I ask because there's a lot at stake.'

'No, I won't go slowly. Claire needs help and I'm going to give it.'

'Jennie, it'll all work out in the end. These things always do.'

'No. You go tell Harry Stone to lay off. And if I find anything nasty from Claire I'll open it up even if you won't.'

'I've already told Stone what I think, but it won't make him change course.'

'That's not good enough, so I'll do what I have to do,' Jennie said and put the phone down.

In the kitchen, overlooking the green expanse of garden, with a cup of tea in her hand, Jennie calmed down but decided Harry Stone had much to answer for by enfolding Claire into the twisted deal he was in the middle of. And to hell with what he might say if she shielded Claire or exposed him for the crook that he was.

Jennie left for the West End half an hour later and as arranged met Claire, who was already waiting with a strained, tired look in her eyes, on the corner of South Audley Street. What a contrast, Jennie thought, with only a few days ago when she had achieved an immediate transformation in

Claire's elegance and attractiveness. Something was amiss. Jennie took her arm as they walked a hundred yards to the restaurant.

'You look too tense,' she said.

'That's how I feel. It's all going too fast for me.'

Jennie smiled easily as the head waiter opened the door and led them to a table in an alcove towards the rear.

'Aperitifs, Mrs Garon?' the waiter enquired.

'No, just a bottle of Pouilly Fumé, well chilled.'

'Thanks for meeting at such short notice,' Claire said. 'Hope it hasn't upset your day.'

'I'm here to help. But you do look a bit bewildered. So what's going on?' Jennie's voice had a ring of sympathy that eased Claire's tenseness.

'It's time I stopped and got things sorted out. For starters, what I'm doing here in London.'

'Got a new job, that's what. And you look good wearing that suit,' Jennie said.

'The job's exciting, very busy, hectic even. Never thought I could get involved as I have and it was a bit different for me to have chunks of money to spend on clothes.'

'Shall we say Harry Stone was generous in that department.'

'Harry Stone's never generous,' Claire responded quickly. 'He does things for a reason, usually to suit his own plans.'

'Is that why I can see a worried look in your eyes? You're worried about what we spent?'

'No, I really don't care what we spent.'

'Spill it then.'

Claire sipped her wine and leaned forward in her chair. It was as if she had known Jennie for years and here there would be no shouting, arguing, manipulating, just sorting a growing problem that was leading Claire into something that she could not control.

'It's Rick Austin. You know, my temporary boss?'

'I don't know much about your arrangements. It's probably better I don't, particularly as it involves that horrible man Stone.'

'Everything involves Stone.'

'Okay, tell me what's happening and we'll see if I can help.'

'You remember the Stargel Agency?'

'Of course.'

'Well, they don't know it but they've helped me into some undercover work for Stone. Somehow he's arranged for me to work for Rick Austin, one of his competitors.'

'Whatever for?'

'To find inside information that he needs to corner a deal.'

'What you mean is that you're spying for Stone.'

'Yes. I hate that part of it. But it's now gone beyond simple rummaging for information.'

'Go on, Claire. Let's have it all.'

'Last night I had dinner with Rick.' Claire paused, waiting for a response from Jennie, but not even a smile appeared. She continued. 'He asked me out, I was flattered and I agreed. But I knew there was more to it than just dinner. I was so muddled I did wonder for a moment if he'd found my connection with Stone and he was taking me aside to send me packing. But I knew that was stupid. The world doesn't work like that. If he was going to sack me he'd do it in the office, have me marched out by security, and even maybe call the police. Dinner would never come into it. From the minute I first met Rick he's been looking me over and it's made me self-conscious, uneasy and jumpy. Even when my back's turned I know he's watching me. Not in an inquisitive sort of way but ... well I just don't know. And the day I joined him he took me to Geneva on a business trip. There was no work for me to do, he just wanted me to be there. Jennie, I think your style change has had an unexpected effect.' A tear crept into the corner of her eye.

Jennie sat back and watched Claire as the waiter served their food. She then spoke slowly.

'It didn't take much to bring out your natural colours and once that happened, well, the rest always follows. You became the real "you". A "you" that's been hidden under the cloak of Stone for too long. You should have got out into the world long ago. You've proved you can do it, so have *more* dinners with this Rick. Why not?'

'It's moving too fast. I'm only supposed to work for Rick for a few weeks. Find the information on the deal and then disappear back to Arrow Hall. But the longer I'm with Rick, the more dinners we have, the less easy it will be to walk out when the time comes.'

'Well, don't let that time come. Don't even think of Arrow Hall again.'

'You don't understand. Harry Stone expects me back, that was part of the deal, and anyway, Arrow Hall is where my home is.'

Jennie placed a hand on Claire's arm. 'I think you'd better tell me exactly what happened over dinner last night. Has this Rick got other ideas for you than work? Share with me what's making you so upset.'

'Dinner was boozy, plenty of champagne, a bottle or two of wine with good food, I can't really remember, and it was great fun being with Rick. But then we went on to a nightclub where we had more champagne, we danced, and the time slipped away so quickly the night was soon morning. It was late, about two, when we decided to go home. And I easily agreed it would be better if I stayed overnight at his flat. He said his housekeeper could be there if I wanted and I wouldn't be compromised. We both giggled and laughed at the idea.'

'So you went back to Rick's flat after dinner and dancing. What's wrong with that?'

More tears crept into Claire's eyes. She raised her napkin to her face and tried to turn away.

'You mean you slept with Rick last night?' Jennie pressed.

'Yes. I know it wasn't in the plan but...'

'Well, as I said, there's nothing wrong with that,' Jennie said. 'You're a grown-up girl and he's a grown-up man. So forget Stone, you do what you like.'

'That's not the problem. It's just that I'm ... well, betraying Rick's trust. I've gone in and found information for Stone and that makes me feel awful about where I am.'

'So what happened in the office this morning? Did you give the game away?'

Claire dabbed tears from her eyes and took a deep breath. 'I haven't seen him. Rick left to deal with business early this morning with his accountant in the City. But if I had, well, I don't know what might have happened.'

'Why shouldn't you have an affair with a prosperous businessman if that's what it is?' Jennie took a long thoughtful sip from her glass and looked hard at the Dover sole that was now confronting her.

'I have a feeling it could go on and develop into ... well, I don't really know what. But what do I do with Harry Stone if it goes that way? Do I betray Rick Austin for Harry Stone?'

'Walk out on Stone. That's what you do. You know my feelings about him and they aren't soft. He's using you, Claire, and if it gets you into trouble he'll deny he even knows you. By now those ought to be your feelings too.'

'It just isn't that easy. Harry Stone would betray me if I walk out. He'd let the world know what I had done. And what then?'

'I'll tell you what then. Stone only thinks of himself. So forget him. And as for living in Arrow Hall, I've only been there once but what I saw was too run down for you to have an apartment there. You've got a new exciting job and there's plenty of those going, and if you want to move to my flat it's yours for as long as you need it.'

'I've made up my mind I'm going to renovate Arrow Hall.

It needs money, Harry has already agreed to spend it with a bit of pushing, and I've started lining up architects. So once my work with Rick is finished I'm going back to get on with the work. It's part of me and I've just got to do it. Then we'll see from there.'

'Your choices are clear and only you know which way you should go. Pulling Arrow Hall back from the dust heap and Stone using you, or fun with Rick and the big world out there waiting for you. What do you really want?'

Claire wavered but she knew Jennie was right, she was being used, bullied, hustled into a nightmare beyond her control. Arrow Hall's pull was strong but there had to be limits to the price she would pay for seeing Stone splash his ill-earned cash on the restoration.

'There's something else,' Claire said.

Jennie looked up quickly.

'More? Tell me,' she said.

'I'm being followed.'

'Stalked? For God's sake, who by?'

'I don't know. Harry denies he knows anything about it. Maybe he's right this time, maybe it's Rick having me tailed.'

'And why should Rick want to do that?'

'To see if I'm genuine, of course. Find out who I really am.'

'Has anybody threatened you?'

'No.'

'Well it doesn't matter then.'

'It's a coloured girl. She's sometimes outside the flat and she even followed me to the office once.'

'Are you really sure it's not just your imagination?'

'No. I've seen her several times and this is for real,' Claire responded.

'That phone call when you came to the salon. Somebody looking for Harry Stone, wasn't it? Anything to do with that?'

'Probably. You do know he's hiding at Claridge's, and I can't get out of him why,' Claire said.

'Yes, Roger's been there. And that caused a row. But perhaps you should go to the police and report a stalker if you're that worried.'

'How can I? I've told lies to get a job just so I can spy on the man who employs me, and they'd blow me apart. They'd find out everything.'

'My advice is leave Harry Stone. Like now, not tomorrow, today. Get out and get on with your life,' Jennie said.

Claire was silent for a few moments, again considering the possibility.

'You don't know how many times I've thought about that. But what if Rick finds out what I'm up to? He may go to the police and where would that leave me? No job, no home, criminal record, and who'll employ me then?'

'You can't go on as you are. Stop it all now, don't give Stone anything you find in Rick's office, then you've not betrayed Rick. Walk away from it. Claire, you have got choices.'

Claire hesitated. Harry Stone or Rick Austin? It could not be both, that was obvious.

The silence was intense for a few moments as they both ate and drank. The restaurant was comfortable, slow in pace, and gradually Claire felt more relaxed, if only because her thoughts were becoming clearer.

Lunch took two hours and Claire had already decided she was not going back to Trifoni that afternoon. She had left a note on Rick's desk saying to call her at her flat if she was needed and even then, if he was busy, she would not care. There was always tomorrow, that would be different, a day she now felt she could face up to with confidence knowing that she could deal with the choices confronting her.

The restaurant gradually emptied. They finished the wine and a look from the head waiter said it was time to go.

'Promise me something. You'll enjoy Rick Austin if he asks you out again?'

'That's at the weekend,' Claire said with a smile on her lips.

'So soon?'

'A couple of days in the Cotswolds. Some entertaining so that Rick can get his hands on the Fenfleet deal before Stone has a chance. So don't tell Roger.'

Claire and Jennie laughed and a few moments later they parted. Claire promised to call Jennie and keep her up to date. She caught a cab for the short journey to the flat and on the way made up her mind that as soon as she got to the flat she would call Stone. She would give him what he deserved – information, but information skewed and slanted, just as he would do if he wanted to hide the truth.

As Claire left the cab at the flat's front door she instinctively looked around to see if the girl was loitering but she saw nothing unusual. Inside she considered what she would say to Stone. She knew his methods of questioning and probing, she had seen him use them many times trying to corner a deal, and she knew she had to sound as if she had conducted the deepest investigation on the Fenfleet contract.

She called Arrow Hall first, but there was no answer. Slightly relieved at this reprieve, she wondered where Anton was. He always answered the phone at Arrow Hall if she was not there. He had not contacted her for several days, which she found odd. He would normally have called by now to see if she was all right, like a protective father, and to make her laugh as he always did. Was Anton still in London with Stone or had he been sacked, chucked out without warning, no longer required as the errand boy? It could happen on a whim depending on Stone's mood of the day; it was the sort of thing he would do without feeling, hardly being aware that he'd been ruthless. Being away from Arrow Hall was allowing Claire to see more of the real Harry Stone, the ruthless manipulator, the underhand dealer, and the more she saw the less she liked.

She walked into the kitchen, a small intimate room fitted cosily but with little natural light and no view. The contrast with the large kitchen at Arrow Hall was stark, as was the change in the pattern and possibilities of her life.

She could not delay any further. With a deep breath she called Claridge's, choosing to ring reception rather than Stone's mobile.

Claire's tone was firm and controlled. 'I'd like to speak to Mr Harry Stone. Suite 404.'

'Just one moment please and I'll have you connected,' a woman's cultured voice responded.

The next few seconds felt like a very long time.

'I'm sorry, but there's no response from Mr Stone's suite. May I take a message for him?'

'Thank you, no,' Claire said. 'I'll call again later.'

There was a slight pause. 'Mr Stone is due to check out tomorrow.'

'I thought he'd already done that,' Claire said with an abruptness she almost regretted. She disconnected, sank onto the sofa and sighed. She realised that she really didn't care where Stone was or what might happen to him. What she had to tell him could wait.

# 20

Stone had made up his mind. He really had no choice. His voice was sharp as he called Cutlass from his suite.

'I need to go to Arrow Hall,' he said.

'That's dangerous, boss.'

'I know. But I'm going.'

'The place is being watched by the Rex Gang and that lot are ruthless when they're after something.'

'Things I got to do there so I'll take the risk.'

'What if I go first just to have a look?'

'No,' Stone snapped. 'I'm going today. But you better be there. Just in case it does get messy.'

'The Rex boys don't give chances. If they find you they'll hit you. They strike when they can. Hard.'

'I know all that crap, so don't keep on about it. Are you coming?'

'Sure, boss. And I'll bring one of my mates. You know what happened to Anton,' Cutlass said with relish.

'Shut up, Cutlass, that won't happen again.'

'You forget St Lucia too easily, Mr Stone. The Rex mob want money and they won't stop till they get it.'

'Okay. Bring your mate. But I don't want anyone getting in the way. As long as he can move faster than you and he's useful ... well, okay.'

Cutlass was not offended and he grunted happily.

'How soon, boss?'

'Meet me there in an hour. And be sober, be sharp.'

'Sure, boss. I won't be late. And maybe I'll stick a knife in my pocket,' Cutlass said.

Stone tried to ignore the comment but he felt his hair prickle on the back of his neck. He felt nervous at the thought of knives and after what had happened to Anton. But today he was driven by urgency. There were papers at Arrow Hall that told his life story via his dealings, papers that held too much lethal information to be discovered. If they were found by the likes of Drake, blackmail could bleed him dry more effectively than knives.

He called the concierge and ordered a chauffeured limo. It would be ready in fifteen minutes. He went down to the foyer and sat impatiently behind his newspaper. He wanted to get on with this, and even fifteen minutes was a long time for Harry Stone.

Stone's paranoia about being tailed subsided as they turned into the overgrown driveway of Arrow Hall an hour later. But even in his own backyard he was wary and, his work done, he would get out of there, out of reach of the hoods who wanted his money, or his blood.

He glanced at the garage block where Anton had lived. That would need clearing out, kept from prying eyes. No tracks from Hammersmith must lead to Arrow Hall. What would he tell Claire about Anton? An accident? She would soon be asking questions and the truth would hurt and frighten her.

Stone's mood plummeted at the decrepitude of Arrow Hall. Even the summer sun failed to lift the shabbiness of the old house and not for the first time Stone knew that he had to let Claire change it.

Cutlass was waiting with a fellow Jamaican in a dented Mercedes that looked as if it had always been driven hard and should soon be taken off the road. Through the lowered window Cutlass puffed cigarette smoke into the air with a look that hinted he was the driver of a luxury car.

'Don't just sit there, you idiot!' Stone shouted. 'We've got work to do.'

Cutlass did not respond but heaved himself from the car and slowly waddled across the gravel at a measured pace with his large friend close behind. Since St Lucia Cutlass had put on flab and both men wore stained T-shirts and discoloured jeans that hung below their pot bellies, their size appearing to make them incapable of any sustained physical movement.

Stone sent his driver off with a tip, turned his key in the lock, pushed the door ajar and then hesitated and stood back.

'Something's happened since I've been away. I can smell it,' Stone said. He waited for Cutlass to join him on the steps.

'What's up?' he asked.

'There's loose gravel on the steps. That's not normal.'

'Doesn't the postman come? Or the milkman?' Cutlass asked, trying to be helpful.

'Don't be more stupid and thick than you have to. It doesn't help.'

Cutlass did not understand and did not respond. Instead he went past Stone and into the hallway, fingering the knife in his pocket for reassurance.

He flicked the light switch, marched down the uncarpeted corridor and threw open the door to Stone's study. He peered inside and then entered the room, his mate following behind.

Stone followed cautiously and despite all his misgivings was not prepared for the shock when he saw his room. Only the large desk in the middle of the room stood upright, some of its drawers were open, some upturned on the floor. Chairs were toppled as if they had been thrown, the fabric of the two sofas was heavily slashed, and the sideboard was upside down, drinks bottles strewn across the floor.

Stone surveyed the room, a tight frown on his forehead. It was as if he was standing on the warm beach in St Lucia with dark clouds above and was seeing by the light of the moon the jagged remains of his hotel. He could not run from feeling the tightness of St Lucia closing in on him again.

Cutlass was standing by the desk. 'Boss, look at this.'

A long silver paper knife had been implanted with some force several inches into the desk's worn leather surface. The knife pinned a scrawled note to the green top, the paper hardly torn by the blade which was sharp as a razor. Cutlass took a dirty handkerchief from his pocket and with difficulty pulled the blade free and handed the note to Stone.

The lines on Stone's pale face were rigid as he took the note and snapped, 'You needn't worry about fingerprints. We all know who's been here.'

'But that knife is bloody lethal,' Cutlass said.

Stone knew the knife, it was his, and he stared at Cutlass, a defiant look in his eyes.

'You get round the rest of the house like quick and search every room. Make sure nobody's hiding anywhere. And if they are I want to see 'em. Got it?' he shouted.

Stone's temper was boiling, this was too close to tolerate and if he found anyone now he would personally let the blood flow from them.

Cutlass looked up from the desk and followed by his mate went off to search. This room was now a heap of junk, he thought. He could sense Stone's mood of swift revenge, just like St Lucia. He was sure no one would be lurking here, not even in the garden. The Rex gang would stand and fight, not hide in corners.

Left alone in the silence of his study Stone ran his hand across the leather top as if to soothe his agitation. Slowly he walked to the light of the window and read the note.

*Stone. Two hundred grand in used fivers on Monday. This time Victoria Tube. Platform two going east. Second waste bin from the stairs. Exactly 2.37. Remember your man at Hammersmith got killed when he played funny. And we know where your pretty woman is, so you hiding won't work. Pay up or else one of you'll get it.*

Stone's anger rippled roughly through him, clearing out any anxiety at returning to Arrow Hall and again he swore, this time loudly. He looked around the large trashed room and then peered through the wide French windows at the shrubbery at the end of the lawn.

The garden was still and peaceful. A light breeze ruffled the leaves of the beech tree that was beginning to turn autumnal brown and a rabbit scampered across the lawn into the sanctuary of the shrubs as if it knew that Stone was watching. Stone had looked from this window many times, it was the place where he had total control, it gave him comfort, and nobody was ever going to push him into running away from it, however nasty the threats they made. He would renovate the hall when he was ready, but never alter it.

Stone again held the note to the light. Action by Monday it demanded, just a weekend away. He picked up his diary from the floor and flicked the pages. The Fenfleet tender had to be in next Tuesday, four days away. Stone stood by his mutilated desk, his thoughts now concentrated on what was in front of him and he stooped to pick up a half-empty whisky bottle. What damage could be inflicted by this lot of thugs between now and four days' time that could hold him from the Fenfleet tender? And where would they strike?

Claire and Jane were both innocent of the real threat, they were easy targets to this lot if Stone played hard to get. But Stone knew he could do nothing to protect them, even warning them as he had tried with Jane would not help, and his thoughts quickly drifted to his own agenda.

Claire would soon find something on Fenfleet. Then he'd give wads of used fivers to James Kennedy. And why not then get the hell out of it until the Rex Gang were halted? His thoughts running fast and erratically, he stopped and picked up another bottle, anger still shooting through him.

'Cutlass!'

The noise echoed around the high-ceilinged room like a bell bringing children from the playground, and within a few seconds there was a rumble as Cutlass lumbered down the staircase. Breathless, his vest stained with sweat, he entered the study.

'Wesley's still searching but there ain't nobody up there. Do you want me to go in the garden, search the garage and the sheds?' Cutlass asked.

'No, you don't go anywhere or touch anything unless I tell you.'

'Shall I call Wesley down?'

'Yes. Then I need to talk to you. Alone. So you get Wesley down, go and sit in your car, keep your eyes open and I'll call you when I'm ready.'

'Something special, boss?'

'Something very special.'

Wesley rumbled down the stairs as heavily as Cutlass had done. Stone moved away from the odorous sweat of the two men and waited until they had shut the front door behind them before he picked up the scrawled note and stuffed it in his pocket.

Arrow Hall was no longer his safe house where he could scheme and manipulate people, where he could dream up the next deal that would make him money. It was a prison and the warder was Drake and his irrational, violent, druggie contract men in London. The break-in added urgency to Stone's reason for coming home.

He took a key from his pocket, unlocked a small cupboard under the stairs, switched a light on and after a quick inspection he breathed out heavily. The cupboard had been left untouched.

He knelt on the floor, removed a muddled bundle of papers into the hallway, and pulled up a thin strip of floorboarding. He sat back and gloated as he saw that the large piles of notes were still there. The settled dust told him that they had not been touched, so he didn't need to count them, he knew there would be £350,000 in used fifties. The thick wads were neatly piled together and elastic bands held separate bundles of £10,000 each. He fingered just twenty bundles to give him a total of £200,000 and tossed them quickly from the claustrophobic cupboard into the dim hallway.

He replaced the floorboard and rummaged in a bundle of papers on a small shelf hidden beneath the stair treads. From the middle he pulled five sheets concerning his Cayman account. He laid them on the floor and in the dim light clumsily fumbled through two box files. They held papers exposing how he had manipulated his special deals, going back over the past few years, deals that had given him cash to feed his money boxes in the Caymans and Jersey. His hand trembled as he removed papers that should always be hidden, just like the cash that flowed from them.

There was the Canyon project in Brighton that Roger had worked on but was unaware how Stone had manipulated it, and the sale of the business that dealt in exotic foreign sports cars in London's East End. Stone only kept records when he thought he might need to pursue somebody for money so these papers told stories in raw and vivid detail.

He opened a small plastic wallet and retrieved the details of his Jersey bank account which the inspector from the Revenue had uncovered. He had not touched it for five years, and the letters in the wallet, brown with age, gave addresses and names, a paper trail to the real source of the cash which had been paid in. The inspector would want to know all that, she would want to know if it really had anything to do with antiques. Stuffing the papers into his pocket Stone decided that he would shred the whole lot into tiny unreadable pieces and the one address he had promised the inspector – an office in Paris – he could now safely send because he had covered his tracks on that with his innocent lawyer, George Latham. He breathed out heavily, satisfied that he was now one step ahead. The password and code numbers to the Jersey account, something he never even tried to remember, he left in the wallet and replaced on the shelf.

Stone flipped open a passport resting on the same shelf and checked the details. He read: *Thomas, David, British Citizen, Born 18, 12, 51, Plaistow* alongside a photograph of himself. The document had cost him £5,000 when he acquired it five years ago through a contact in Soho and although he had never used it, it held a value greater than any insurance policy could ever provide. It was his escape route.

Stone roughly shuffled the other papers back into a pile, satisfied he had got what he wanted, and felt his shirt cling coldly to his sweaty back as he switched off the light of the cramped cupboard.

He securely locked the cupboard door, gathered the bundles of fifties and in his study placed the lot into an old leather case. The combination lock on the lid he reset to the word PALM. Although heavy, the case bulged only slightly. Satisfied, Stone walked to the French windows, took in a deep breath of fresh air and called Cutlass.

'You here, now, alone. Tell your mate to stay in the car and keep his eyes wide open.'

Cutlass appeared ten seconds later.

'Extortion. That's what they're trying to wrench from me. Extortion by blackmail,' Stone said.

'They're threatening violence?'

'Money first. Usual protection stuff. Otherwise somebody gets hit.'

'How much they demanding, Mr Stone?'

'Stop asking questions,' Stone replied irritably.

'What you want me to do?' Cutlass asked.

'I've got £200,000 in used fifties in this case and you've got to keep it safe for me. You tell no one else what you've got and you don't even try to open the case yourself unless I give my personal permission. Clear? If I find you've spent one penny of it on drink or anything else then you're dead. Remember that you did Drake over in St Lucia, you personally broke him up, so you'll find you've got some nasty enemies in London who'd like to tell you what they think of you if you ever forget it's my money. So you'll only use it my way. Your survival is now in my hands.'

Cutlass did not flinch at the threat given with venom by Stone in a loud voice and replied in his usual flat tone.

'Is this the ransom money? To be paid over if you're captured?'

The mere suggestion that he might be held against his will did not take long to sink in. He could be banged about, killed like Anton, with knives stuck into him with the same force used on his desk.

'If I'm held you pay up. Immediately. No questions. Just do it.'

'Yes, boss,' Cutlass said. 'I know what to do.'

Stone contemplated the gardens as he spoke, almost to himself. 'But I guarantee that won't happen. I'm cleverer than Drake and his Rex mob.'

'When they demand, the Rex Gang usually get, Mr Stone.'

'Not from me,' Stone replied easily.

'Where do they want the money delivered this time?'

'Victoria tube station. On Monday.'

'Do I go to Victoria for you? With the readies?' Cutlass asked.

'No. I'll tell you what to do when I'm ready,' Stone said.

'What if I just go and watch at Victoria? I've got nothing else on Monday.'

'You keep the money in your fat fist until I call.'

'Do they threaten your girl assistant? Or your sister? Are they okay?' There was a tinge of concern in Cutlass's questions.

'Don't interfere, Cutlass. You and me have to understand one thing. You do as I tell you and nothing more. My sister's fine. Claire's fine. They won't get them.'

'But the Rex boys know where they are. I heard all that in the club and that's dangerous, Mr Stone. We don't want any more knives stuck into people do we?'

'I fight this my way. You do exactly as I tell you, don't start getting smart again and you might live, otherwise you'll go like Anton.'

'Yes, boss,' Cutlass said nervously. 'I'll hold the cash safe for you.'

'You'd better or else. And when I want you I'll call.'

'Boss, I'll get some extra help. My mates'll see it as a great job to guard this place.'

'You were absolutely useless in St Lucia. You let that thug Drake stamp all over me so around Arrow Hall you'd better make it work.'

'But, Mr Stone ...' Cutlass began to protest.

'Get one of your mates up here to look out and I'll get real professionals to patrol too,' Stone interrupted, his voice sharp and decisive. 'But you can forget Victoria Tube. We're not going there. Got it?'

Cutlass had got it, and there was a definite sense of purpose in his stride as he left the ransacked study with the case full of notes tucked under his arm. The noise of flying gravel on the driveway as the old Mercedes spun its wheels spelt finality to the meeting and the house became deathly quiet, not even the whistle of wind or the tyres of cars on the road half a mile away penetrated the stillness.

Stone quickly scribbled a note to the taxman on Arrow Hall letterhead with the name and address of his lawyer's French associates, sealed it in a small envelope and stuck it in his pocket for posting. That was the end of the tax inquiry for him, it would kick that annoying bureaucracy off the pitch, and his shady deals he could now shred into history, hiding them forever from the world.

He thought of Claire. He needed her. He called her mobile. He tilted in his chair, held the phone away from his ear as it rang and faced the windows, his mind whirring with possibilities.

Claire saw Stone's number and she responded, her voice so low it was barely audible.

'Call you later,' she said. 'Got something else on at the moment.'

'But there's something I need to talk to you about,' he said.

Stone was cut dead. He threw the phone heavily onto the desk, ran his hand through his hair in frustration and swore. He wanted to warn her about Drake as he had Jane, but was she now deliberately avoiding him, or was she too busy helping to run the deals of Rick Austin at Trifoni Group?

'Damn Claire,' Stone said to himself as calculating ruthlessness filled him. He'd get the Fenfleet figures, then she was dispensable, and so what if Drake found her? He shuffled carelessly through the muddled pile of papers from the cupboard, found the tender for the Fenfleet contract and skimmed it as if it was the only thing in the world that now mattered to him. He would never admit it but Roger's own sums were not far off and even though he had his own ideas on how much to bid, only Claire could tell him for sure. And he'd get that from her soon.

Dusk was lingering, making his trashed study gloomy, and Stone was anxious to get away. He searched in his wallet and pocket. There were three credit cards and £500 in notes. He took £50, folded the notes in half and tossed them onto the desk. It was a teasing, empty gesture that gave Stone curious satisfaction and helped his determination set hard, a determination that Drake and his druggie London cousins would get no more.

A fierce penetrating look came into his eyes as he took from his pocket the note from the Rex mob with its way-out demands, tore it up into tiny pieces and scattered it across the floor. He had other ideas for spending £200,000, ideas that would make him a lot more in ready money.

He walked to the kitchen, drank a glass of cold water which came straight from the well in the garden, and momentarily felt refreshed. But sitting at the table where Anton had searched for a knife a few days ago, he felt isolated and alone. He called the XS security company in Chelmsford, who had some heavyweight guards he had heard about from Anton, who acted discreetly, and arranged for them to visit Arrow Hall.

'Three times a day and three times a night, patrol the outside and let me know if anyone has broken in or even come near the place,' he said to the girl on the other end of the phone. It made him feel better.

In the utility room he shredded the pile of secret papers, took a neat slug from a whisky bottle and then called a taxi. Impatiently he waited in total silence as daylight finally faded. Avoiding switching on the lights he stood in the shadow of the front door staring vacantly into the overgrown garden, searching for any movement. Not even the slightest breeze rustled the leaves in the trees at the edge of the lawn and the warm red glow that described an arc in the sky from the lights of the town two miles away gave Stone a momentary sense of protection from the nutters and druggies chasing him.

But, unable to speak to her, Stone did not know how that would be killed by the way Claire's life was now moving.

# 21

Driving the Porsche fast, Rick was unusually tense. It was Friday afternoon and he was going westward on the M4. The sun shone brightly onto the windscreen but it was not the dazzle which caused his deep frown.

'You got some friends who know where you are?' he said to Claire.

'Sometimes I think mobiles are a curse, we can never get away from them.'

Claire had just taken the call from Stone. She felt embarrassed at Rick's comment and slid lower into her seat.

'Just a girlfriend wanting a favour,' she lied.

'Sounded like you didn't want to talk to her, but don't worry about me. If it's girl talk I'll keep my ears closed.'

'I'll switch it off for the rest of the weekend, and I'm sure the Kennedys won't want interruptions to do with my girlfriends any more than you would,' Claire said.

Claire openly clicked her phone off and felt her pulse race. Something stupid like that could blow everything she was doing wide open and where would that lead?

'You must give me your number some time,' Rick said, the frown deepening over his eyes.

'It's ex-directory. I was once stalked, never again. You'll have to promise never to disclose it if I give it you,' Claire said. This was not a conversation to pursue in her present delicate position and she was pleased that it was Rick who changed the subject.

'I hope you're looking forward to luxuriating in a nice bit of the country,' he teased.

'Depends,' Claire said easily.

'Depends on what?'

'James Kennedy's wife. I've never met her, I've got to be nice to her for two whole days and I don't know what she's like. But if she's anything like her husband, well...'

'Just be yourself. No business talk. No Geneva, no Fenfleet. Just fun. Anyway, for me life's too short to do otherwise.' Claire liked his flippancy.

'What I don't understand is how on earth this weekend with Kennedy can help to seal the Fenfleet deal? Surely the deal's bigger than that.'

'Human nature, Claire. This guy wants to be cared for like a child. Give him some sweets and he might just say thank you. That's all. Surely you know how business works even if you don't agree with it? Anyway, do you know how much bribe money he's demanding to fill his account in Switzerland?'

'I thought Geneva wasn't on the menu tonight.'

'Sure it's not, but wouldn't you like to know about it?' Rick asked.

'Yes, of course.'

'Well, guess how much then.'

'I couldn't even start with people like Kennedy. I can see he's greedy, it's in his eyes, they're too close together and that meeting with his obnoxious lawyer in Geneva ... well what can I say?'

'Take a breath then because he's demanding £200,000.'

'To me that's a lot of money and I just hope it's worth it,' Claire said, trying to hide her excitement that the missing piece in the jigsaw for Stone was suddenly falling into place. She relaxed into the seat but could feel her heart pounding.

Rick continued, 'You obviously think money like that is too much?'

'How should I know? I'm not an expert in bribing.'

'No, not many people ever get caught up in this sordid

type of racket. So you just steer clear, Claire, and forget everything you hear from me.'

'So why are you telling me?'

'I don't know really. Let's leave it that you're a friendly face.' Rick laughed easily.

'And as a friendly face let me advise *you*. You don't like it, so you don't pay.'

'If I don't cough up I know what will happen. It's simple, the contract goes walkabout.'

'So tell Kennedy's boss, I bet he'd sort it,' Claire said with a hint of anger.

'He'd probably want some of it too. And if grassing got around you'd always be left out of the party for future business.' There was a pause. Rick seemed to be looking for support. He added, 'I feel this deal somehow going sour.'

'I'm not surprised. Deals like this should be left for Kennedy and his ilk, and everybody else should walk away,' Claire said quickly. She was drawn into this web of corruption but her comment was heartfelt, coming from her natural instinct.

Rick continued as if he had not heard her. 'An anonymous Swiss account doesn't help. Kennedy avoids tax, his name disappears in the web, and I have to explain if it goes wrong. You're right, it doesn't make sense.'

Concentrating on driving Rick glanced in the rear view mirror and his shoulders hunched with sudden tenseness.

'I really haven't worked out yet how Trifoni Group ticks,' Claire said.

'It doesn't tick unless I'm there. I make the deals work,' Rick said.

'Okay, so you're the one who takes all the decisions. Surely you have to consult someone else sometimes?'

'Only the bank manager if he calls. And that's only if I've got a really big deal on that needs lots of cash.' Rick shifted uneasily and again looked in the mirror.

'Did you tell anyone else at Trifoni that you're doing a deal with Kennedy? I mean £200,000 is a lot of money to be paid out just like that. Especially as a bribe.'

'It gets lost in the entertaining account.'

'Entertaining? Is that what you call it?'

'Entertaining. Consultancy fees. Call it what you like. But to a large business like ours it's peanuts. And as for the other directors, well, they wouldn't approve. So I just don't tell 'em. All they need to know is when I've got the deal, when I'm successful.'

'I've done some work for Mr Cuckney. He seems to know what's going on. Wouldn't he be interested?'

'Graham? He's the legal man. Puts into words what I agree, and the £200,000 for Kennedy is not put into words. So he won't know anything about it.'

'So you put your trust directly in Kennedy to deliver? From what I saw in Geneva I wouldn't give him an inch, and I'm surprised that you believe him enough to go out of your way this weekend,' Claire said.

'Sure, I don't trust him either, but what the hell, it's just a bit of petty cash splashed around. I pay up and keep my fingers crossed. Anyway, don't think of £200,000 when you meet Kennedy because that'll just spoil everything for you.'

'Does Kennedy get a fun weekend from everyone who wants to deal with him?' Claire asked. 'I mean, there has to be a limit to the time he can be away wallowing in somebody else's hospitality.'

'You sound cynical, Claire. From what I've seen that's unlike you.'

'No, just realistic.'

Sure Claire was realistic, she knew Stone would never entertain James Kennedy to a weekend away in the Cotswolds or anywhere else come to that, it was not his style, he did not have the time or patience for playing like that and if it needed sorting then he would get somebody else to do it. Like Roger Garon. In her mind she suddenly pictured Stone and her face flushed.

Her reverie was interrupted as Rick continued.

'The good news is Kennedy doesn't arrive until tomorrow morning. This evening's ours so let's make the most of it. Dinner and a few drinks, what about that?'

'Sure,' Claire said, and nestled firmly into her seat. She turned up the volume of the classical CD that was playing and closed her eyes, nodding easily to the music and the gentle vibration of the road. She did not notice Rick's expression.

Tenseness again tightened the lines on his forehead as he looked in the mirror. He said nothing but he had a growing and uncomfortable feeling that they were being followed, tailed by a red Suzuki 4x4 which had been in his mirror constantly over the last hour. Sure, that was nothing unusual on the motorway, even though he had pushed to a ton for a short stretch, but it now bugged him as he left the M4 and drove at speed on the B roads. He left the Suzuki trailing sometimes but it always reappeared when he slowed, never trying to overtake, as if it had a magnetic attraction to the rear of his Porsche.

Approaching the small town of Broadway in the Cotswolds the car came close to his bumper, almost edging his car forward, and Rick was tempted to stab on the brakes to warn it off. But on the narrow winding road there was no escaping it and even if he stopped he was sure the Suzuki would stop behind him. Very close.

Claire's eyes were closed as Rick accelerated easily on a straight stretch of the leafy road but she opened them as the Porsche gained an alarming speed and saw the trees flash by them as if they were in a tunnel.

'What's up?' she asked, seeing the frown on Rick's face his knuckles showing white as he gripped the wheel.

'We're being followed.'

The road ahead was now straight as far as the eye could see and there was nothing in front of them. Rick changed gear, pushed the pedal to the floor and the car gained more speed. Claire nervously gripped the seat belt that was restraining her.

'Rick. Not too fast.'

'I'll just shake them off,' he replied, the car responding quickly to his actions.

Neither spoke for several seconds and the music from the CD was lost in the rush of air that surrounded them.

Claire leaned over to switch the CD off. 'Who would want to follow you?'

'I haven't a clue,' Rick said as he slowed at the approach to a bend. 'But I'm damn sure that's what's happening.'

'Sure you're not imagining it?' Claire asked. She turned to look behind her but the rear window was too small to see clearly.

'Who knows? Anyway, everything's in order in my life, so it's not me they're after. What about you?' Rick asked with a teasingly nervous laugh.

'Me?' Claire responded, flustered at the suddenness of the question.

'Perhaps you've got a murky past I don't know about.'

The Porsche drew up behind a lorry billowing smoke that was impossible to pass. Rick took a sideways look at Claire but their eyes did not meet as she stared through the windscreen. For a shuddering moment the red Suzuki nudged close behind, again almost close enough to touch, and Rick involuntarily clutched the steering wheel tightly, this time in frustration.

Without turning to Rick, Claire spoke forcefully, stung by his comment. She felt the depth of her guilt which did not help her to keep calm.

'You should have checked me out before you took me on if you think I've got a murky past.'

'Sorry, Claire,' Rick said. 'I didn't mean it.'

Claire felt tense, not helped by Rick's throwaway comment, whether he meant it or not. Whoever was following was not after Rick. Of course she knew that. They were after her and if they got any closer the truth would tumble out in front of Rick.

The chase continued, but at a slower speed, for another half mile until Rick, with a quick flick of the gear lever, turned into a side road. It led to an ivy-clad hotel, welcoming in its aspect of calmness, a refuge from the high-speed chase on narrow roads. Rick expected the Suzuki to follow and he breathed an audible sigh of relief as he saw it accelerate past the turn-off.

'Thank God for that,' Rick said, and leaned back in his seat.

Claire's eyes were now wide, she was alert and she felt sweat on the palms of her hands. She took a deep breath to calm herself as they drove into the car park.

'Problem solved, nobody's following,' she managed hoarsely.

'Let's hope so,' Rick replied.

'Come on, Rick. Your eyes show you're tense, your hunched shoulders show you're tense. I think being followed was entirely in your imagination,' Claire said, determined to get the moment over quickly.

'In business you need imagination,' Rick said enigmatically.

'Let's leave it then. Let's forget it. Let's not add to the agony of dealing with Kennedy,' Claire replied lightly.

'Sure. Maybe I need a glass or two of champagne to start the weekend,' he said and put his arm around Claire's shoulders.

A porter collected their bags and followed them into the hotel. Dusk was falling and Claire felt a chill from the still air.

She tried to smile easily, she tried very hard to walk with

290

a natural step, but this whole charade was becoming unnatural. She did not really want to be here, cornered into a position where she felt awkward and would have to tread very carefully. The weekend filled her with apprehension. She had to meet again with the disgusting Kennedy, she had to keep Rick from suspecting anything was undermining his Trifoni empire.

They were given separate rooms.

'Just for show, for Mrs Kennedy, but that doesn't mean we'll need to use them both,' Rick said, putting his arm firmly on Claire's shoulder as they walked to the stairs.

For the next hour Claire needed to be on her own. In her room she flicked on her mobile to check for messages from Stone but found none. Then she called room service for a large gin and tonic to be brought to her room. Gradually she relaxed, helped by the aperitif and a long, hot bath. Lying on a chaise longue by the window and wrapped in a bathrobe she looked at the colourful hotel garden and flicked through a copy of *Country Life*. Arrow Hall should look like this she thought. Stone's promise to renovate the estate, to make it green, ordered, a place where she could wander, work and relax was becoming a top priority, a big thank-you for the tight corner he had squeezed her into.

As usual Claire dressed carefully. Tonight she had to look her best, she had to keep up her pretence of a wealthy young woman escorting a business partner. She put on the pearl necklace and the glistening surface of the pearls absorbed the light and sent back a gentle sparkle. It was the finishing touch and made her feel good. She was ready when Rick knocked at her door an hour later.

'You *do* look great,' he said as they walked to the bar. 'So you can leave it to me to see the rest of this evening keeps up to the mark.'

'Thank you, sir,' she responded lightly. 'Anyway, this is

a nice place you've brought me to. Pity that it might be spoilt by the business end of it all.'

'It won't be, promise. And sorry about my wild imagination this afternoon, I hope that doesn't get us off to a bad start.'

'Why should it?' Let's put it down to a hard week's work and leave it there.'

'Good, as you say, we'll leave it there.'

It was impossible to talk in the crowded bar, but seated at a corner table in the oak-panelled dining hall which had a gallery running the width of one end, they sipped champagne and Claire felt a million miles from Stone and Arrow Hall. But the enticing spell was broken as Rick sprang a question.

'Tell me about yourself, Claire. You're becoming a mystery to me.' He leaned forward and looked into Claire's eyes with no smile on his face.

It was the dreaded but expected question from Rick. For a few seconds she pretended to read the menu and then rested it on the table. A pretty girl played a harp gently in a corner of the room, there was a buzz of conversation and she returned Rick's gaze without flinching.

'Oh. So I'm a mystery? What an odd way to describe somebody who comes to help you at short notice.'

'It's never worked out like this before with everything fitting into place so easily.'

'So what do you want to know about me?' Claire asked.

'It's simple. You're introduced to me by an agency as someone who only works when she wants to and I would have thought that would make you hesitant, a bit slow in front of the word processor. But, Claire, you're efficient, you get through the day twice as quickly as anyone else I've employed, and you seem to take it all in your stride. So just tell me about yourself.'

'It's a bit late to start interviewing me now,' Claire said, hoping that with hedging Rick would change the subject.

292

'I'm not interviewing. I just want to know more about you. Our two paths meet by chance and it throws up somebody I like. What's wrong with that?'

'Nothing,' Clare answered.

'So let's have it on the table. I'm interested in you, I'd like to know a little bit more about your background, your family, your likes, dislikes, any interests outside work. Anything you'd like to tell me.'

'All you get is what you've already read on my CV,' Claire said. There was a glint in her eye, the champagne had relaxed her, and she smiled easily as she spoke. She was teasing, and Rick instantly saw it.

'For a very pretty girl you're too intense in your work. You've given me no hints that you have any boyfriends who take up your time and even when I've kept you so busy that you're late leaving the office you don't seem worried about missing anything outside work.'

'Sure I have boyfriends,' Claire said. 'But I don't let them get in the way when I've got work to do.'

'So what else do you do when you're not working?'

'Rick, you're getting off limits,' Claire said. 'Just take it I live life as it comes, I work when I want to and I don't think about it too often.' The lie fell easily from her lips but she felt she was convincing.

'You're right, I'm wrong to pry. But it's just that I'm ... well ... oh, forget it.'

Rick emptied his wine glass and ordered a bottle of Haut-Brion 1976, his favourite, very smooth, classic Bordeaux. But Claire covered her glass with her hand as the waiter poured, as if she knew where that might lead and Rick had a frown on his face as he spoke.

'Okay, you've got me cornered. I've got the message, So, I'll stop these questions and wait to see how you let slip your past.' Rick laughed as if in surrender to Claire.

'Playing hard to get is the way you should do business,'

Claire said and laughed too, momentarily feeling she could deal with any questions Rick might try on.

'That's good. I like it. So I'll let you negotiate with James Kennedy for me.'

'Rick, relax. You don't have to win against me.'

'Not trying to. It's just I'm impatient to see what you tell me.'

There was easy silence as they both tackled the food. The room hummed with gentle conversation and the harpist played beautifully. It would be possible to spend the evening here just eating, not talking, but watching the other people in their intimate groups. Claire would find just that worth the journey. Her thoughts were broken by a sudden penetrating stare from Rick.

'I have one last but very important question,' he said. 'Then no more quizzing. But promise to give me a truthful answer.'

'Try me,' Claire said easily.

'Will you come and work for me full-time?'

'Wait a minute,' Claire said. 'That's never been in the contract.'

'I'll increase your salary by fifty per cent. You'll get a car and expense allowance. Sometimes we travel, always first class, and you'll meet some nice people. They're not all like James Kennedy you know.' Rick was persuasive.

Claire stared at him in surprise. 'That sounds like a bribe to me,' she said.

'Call it what you like. It's a very serious offer.'

'I've never thought of working for anyone full-time. I just don't need to.' Claire said the words quickly but firmly as a way of putting Rick off.

'I know you don't need to work. But give it a try. You might just like it.'

'I don't think it would be a good idea,' Claire said, trying to fend off Rick's persistence. 'I might look disciplined but you've only seen me for a short while and I'm not always like that. I like to spend time in the shops.'

Rick drained his glass. 'I somehow knew that would be your answer.'

'Well, that settles it then,' Claire said easily.

'Yeh. I guess so. But you remain a mystery to me. Someone who doesn't quite fit the mould.'

'What mould are you thinking of?'

'You're just too good to be true. My luck doesn't always run this way.'

'Let it run tonight, Rick,' Claire said enticingly. 'I'm not here to stay.'

'No I guess not, but at least stay to help me through the hard work of Kennedy,' Rick said. 'And we can always keep in contact after that. Shall we leave it at that?'

Claire did not answer but laughed in response. Saying nothing suited her well and as for later ... well she would deal with that when it came. The harpist continued to play and Claire was drawn to look deeply into Rick's clear eyes. Suddenly she wanted to tell him everything. All that had happened since she had left Arrow Hall. Searching for information in his room, being followed, and Stone's plans which had started with the outfit and pearl necklace she was now wearing. She wanted to spill everything down to the last deceitful detail, get Stone out of her hair and then move on with a new life.

She kept the tears from her eyes and took another sip from her glass so that her hand momentarily hid the visible signs on her face that said she was uneasy with the game of deceit, a game she now had to see to its end.

Dinner finished, they took coffee in the lounge and Rick mellowed over a large vintage port. They talked of nothing in particular as the laziness of the evening enveloped them both. Claire tried not to look at Rick, knowing that the more their eyes met the more likely she was to give the wrong signal. Their being together this evening was not part of the plan, being followed was not part of the plan and Rick's job offer, tantalizing as it was, was not part of the plan. And what if he really did think she was too good to be true, an unsolved mystery entering his life by the back door? Claire smiled to herself at the odd, bizarre, reality that now confronted her. In that instant she began not to care what might follow.

Rick was enjoying his second port in a comfortable chair before a large open fireplace decorated with a basket of dried flowers. The buzz of conversation around them gradually died. Rick stood.

'Before we have a nightcap do you fancy a stroll in the night air, see the stars and feel the tranquillity of the place? Sometimes I go outside in London before I go to bed but it's different there. Anyway, it's too hot in here. I need air.'

'I'd like that. I'll go and get a coat from my room and see you in a minute,' Claire said as Rick helped her from the deep chair.

Her room was warm and the bed had been turned back exposing crisp white sheets. A perfumed smell from the fresh flowers that flowed over a low table filled the air and Claire wanted to linger. She sat on the side of the bed and hesitated by the phone for a moment.

She had taken an aperitif, champagne, several glasses of wine, she felt confident she could talk to Harry straight, so why not get it over with now? She could tell her own story in her own way. She could be forceful and deal with him on equal terms. Everything Trifoni Group was doing on the Fenfleet deal she now knew. A £200,000 claim and £1.5 million a year for the franchise fee was information which would surely satisfy Stone.

Suddenly she felt the power of her position, the power of information that Stone needed and that was now in her hands to give or withhold, the power of manipulation that it was her turn to use. And whatever she told Stone he would never know of the power that she was handling against him.

She clicked on her mobile. The temptation was strong – to get Stone out of her hair and start afresh with Rick. But suddenly she knew instinctively that if she called now Stone would quiz her deeply. How had she ferreted out this information? How did she know it was right? Where was she phoning from? And if she admitted she was enjoying herself in a classy hotel in her role as spy it would make him suspicious and the questioning would deepen. He could stay at Claridge's but for anyone else plush hotels were not on.

And then once he'd got the detail he needed from her he would push her to come back to Arrow Hall. Immediately. Having now got close to Rick, having seen a new fast-track world she could easily slip into, she knew that was something she did not yet want.

She looked at her watch. It was 11.35 and ten minutes already since she had left Rick just to get her coat. Time was not on her side and she knew it as she snapped her mobile off. She pulled her coat over her shoulders and felt light-headed as she walked down the stairs to join Rick in the cool night air.

Her hope that she could stay in the middle of the two powerful men, Rick Austin and Harry Stone, was misplaced. There would be a price to pay.

# 22

The air was sweet and the night still when Claire and Rick left the hotel. She breathed in large gulps to clear her foggy head and felt the refreshing contrast with the confined, stuffy space of the hotel lounge which had become oppressive. The smell of summer reminded her of the wild gardens at Arrow Hall, fresh, cool, stimulating in its own unconfined space.

Claire linked onto Rick's arm as they strolled slowly into the nearby village. They passed two antique shops, their windows well lit and enticing buyers with expensive bygone furniture. Claire found the quietness between them comforting, undemanding, timeless. Passing cars intermittently interrupted the silence, their headlights ablaze and throwing the road from darkness to brightness and back again like a photographer's flashbulb.

Claire received the first punch. The sharp karate chop to her neck, just like the one Stone had felt at his mother's funeral, stunned her, and her shoulder bag fell to the ground. She toppled into a thick thorny hedge that bordered the narrow pavement and it was several seconds before she looked up, unbelieving, her heart pounding. Instinctively she tried to pull herself free but a sharp twinge of pain in her neck made her cry out and momentarily she lay back in the thorns as they held her tightly. Dazed, staring blankly into the starry night sky, she heard Rick's shoes scuff noisily over the pavement as two hooded men hauled him away. He offered no resistance, he was not able to, and even his one desperate and hollow shout disappeared quickly into the thin night air.

The few undemanding moments Claire and Rick had enjoyed in the clear country air were snuffed out as easily as extinguishing a flickering candle. The footsteps that had come from behind had been silent, their owners unseen in the shadows, and the attack had happened with a ruthless suddenness. The stars which Rick had wanted to see were suddenly hidden behind a cloud and darkness soon engulfed him as he was roughly dragged away. Claire saw the attackers punching and kicking his helpless body sprawled across the pavement, his hands covering his head in a vain attempt to deflect the merciless blows.

A nightmare was tightly enfolding Claire, though she was desperate that it should not be true. Slowly she recovered her senses and oblivious to the pain from the thorns she tugged herself upright and for a moment stopped dead still, staring blankly into the darkness.

Instinctively she ran towards Rick, stumbling, her legs feeling like jelly, her head thumping. She was powerless, she screamed hoarsely, a useless gesture that bounced straight back at her as her voice was as a mere whisper in the sudden commotion of the street. Like Rick's first protesting shouts less than a minute ago it floated away on the gentle breeze that blew past the shadows and wafted away into the distant trees.

'Stop it!' she shouted. 'You'll kill him.'

The attackers, their faces hidden by their hoods, ignored the shout as Claire ran towards them. A grey anorak, like a huge shadow, moved to turn Rick's body over as if positioning it for the final thumping kick that landed in the middle of his spine. Rick was now no more than a stuffed gymnasium punch bag that would noiselessly swing with the force presented, offering no resistance.

'That one's for luck. It comes from Drake,' the dark anorak shouted. 'And Drake says to remember St Lucia. You're a bastard, Stone. You've had this coming so the rest is for not paying up the £200,000. Remember the funeral, remember your big place in Essex. Remember what happened when you sent somebody to interfere, and don't forget your sister down the East End. I don't fool around, I kill. So next time you'll feel a knife right up you where it hurts and it won't be just a soft kick in the balls.'

Claire froze, terrified, powerless, now close enough to hear the man's words tumble out with venom.

'That's not Harry Stone!' she shouted. 'It's Rick Austin! You've got the wrong man. If you want Stone go to Claridge's or Arrow Hall. But for God's sake leave us alone.'

Rick let out a long low groan, an unexpected noise from an inert body, as the two hooded men ran off. The extra darkness of a small alleyway that led from the main road behind two cottages soon engulfed them as if they had never been there, with total stillness returning to the main street as if nothing nasty, nothing dark and sinister had happened in this tranquil country village.

Tears fell heavily down Claire's cheeks. Sure this wasn't a dream, this was happening with a frightening, stark reality, a brutal picture of hatred which she did not understand. Utter helplessness swept like a tide through her as, silently, she bent over the inert body of Rick and a bruised, grotesquely swollen face with hair strewn over its forehead stared back at her.

A pain stabbed in her neck when she moved quickly and made her draw in her breath. Rick's unmoving, beaten body groaned as she rolled him onto his side and a stream of blood mixed with white bile dribbled from his mouth. His eyes were closed, a wide gash showed through the torn trousers of his right leg and it too oozed blood.

Rick's breathing came in little half-gasps like sobs without tears. She unbuttoned his torn shirt and through her own uncontrollable tears close to his face she whispered in a desperate voice.

'Rick, talk to me.'

Pulling away she waited for a moment but there was no response. She bent more closely over his face and pulled back a swollen and bruised eyelid but his eye looked blankly into space and did not even flicker.

'Oh my God,' she said. She checked his breathing, the twinge in her shoulder becoming a stabbing pain. The little gasps from Rick became shallower, flowing blood making a red smudge on his chin. Claire shuddered, stunned, and fumbled for her mobile. But she had left it in her hotel room so that she wouldn't be bothered any more that night by Stone.

Her sobbing increased as she realised this is what she had led Rick into and it was made worse as she felt utterly helpless at the viciousness and unprovoked suddenness of the attack. The rough words of the masked attackers frightened her as they again echoed in her ears. They thought they were beating Stone. Surely nobody could mistake Rick Austin for Harry Stone? They looked different and they were different. But Stone's name had been shouted loudly by the thugs, they knew what they were after and that was Stone, beaten to within inches of his life. No, it was not a dream, she had heard it loud and clear and of course so had Rick.

Help came quickly. Without Claire moving from the unconscious and bleeding Rick a passing motorist saw the scene in his headlights as she bent over the prostrate body. He pulled over, shone his headlights on the couple and saw wide-eyed fright on Claire's face as she stood up. Then he looked down to Rick and saw blood around his mouth and shredded and red stained clothing from his head to his legs.

'Good God. What's happened?' he asked.

Claire held her breath trying to compose herself. 'We were suddenly set on by two men. They threw me into a bush and they beat Rick until he was unconscious.'

'These guys gone?'

'They ran off. That way,' she said, pointing uselessly down a side alley.

'Is your friend breathing?'

Claire sobbed and just nodded her head.

'Okay, darling. Just stay quietly. Looks like your friend's taken a bit of a bashing, but we'll soon get him to a hospital.'

He took his phone from his pocket and called 999. Claire heard him describe it as an 'accident' and she wanted to shout that it wasn't. It was a vicious attack. She knelt again by Rick's side, gently lifted his head and placed her coat as a cushion underneath. For a moment the driver watched and he then took a rug from his car and wrapped it round Claire's shivering shoulders. He took her by the elbow and led her to his car, opened the door and helped her into the front passenger seat.

Claire sobbed, now uncontrollably, too shocked to talk and she sat shaking and staring at Rick's fragile, broken body.

It took just seven minutes for both police and ambulance to be at the scene, by which time a small crowd of other motorists had begun to gather but were pushed back from their gawping by a policeman. There was disbelief in the paramedics' eyes as they saw Rick's unmoving body. Sure they had seen worse on the motorway but it was a scene they did not expect to witness in this quiet backwater. His face was blotched, with bruises swelling both eyes, blood had congealed in a dark stain around his mouth and a few gasps clutching at the air were the only sign that he was alive.

'Okay,' the chief said. 'Let's get moving. This gentleman needs help.'

The paramedics quickly found Rick's pulse, put a neck brace around his head and then skilfully eased him onto a stretcher. There was no noise from Rick, not even a groan, he was a dead weight casualty who could make no response.

Claire was helped from the front seat of the car, still trembling. She watched mesmerised as Rick was lifted into the ambulance.

'So how did this happen?' the policeman asked.

Claire sobbed and put her head in her hands. She was unable to reply. The policeman saw the trauma and did not press for an answer as there would be time for that later. He took Claire's arm, helped her to a seat in the ambulance and with Rick lying behind her she again buried her head in her hands, her body shaking as if she was cold. She was offered a bottle of water but could not hold it and it slipped to the floor.

The ambulance doors closed noisily and with lights flashing it quickly took its passengers through the country lanes to a hospital some twelve miles away in Cheltenham. Claire tried to close her eyes but she could not look away as the paramedics adjusted the oxygen mask over Rick's face, fixed a saline drip into his left arm and took his pulse several times on the journey. She could hear the cold, controlled chatter on the radio as A&E were alerted to receive their next patient but there was still no noise or resistance from Rick and his totally inert body again made Claire tremble, now more with fright than anger.

The journey was fast and short along the twisting roads. As they reached the hospital Claire was feeling no pain in her shoulder, only a vacant numbness, a numbness that covered her whole body, a numbness that made her want to believe that this was still a nightmare from which she could wake. But the jolting of the ambulance as it swerved into the A&E bay told her differently, told her that her spying for Stone was coming unstuck as easily as a blade slicing through unprotected skin. In that instant she knew the work of these thugs could sink her and Stone if Rick ever found the truth of the beating, a truth that had been shouted directly at him.

Rick was wheeled out first from the ambulance with an urgent but controlled speed. Claire watched as the trolley moved away from her, she wanted to follow it, to stay with Rick and then to say she was sorry for what had happened. But all she could do was to sit alone in the ambulance, rigid, and shiver in the coolness of the evening.

A policewoman held her arm as she climbed from the ambulance. The officer was not much older than Claire and she smiled as she led her to the emergency entrance.

'We'll get you checked out first and then I shall have to ask some questions. Do you feel up to it?'

'I'll try,' Claire said, controlling her tears. 'But I really don't know what it's all about.'

Dishevelled and dirty, Claire dabbed her handkerchief at her eyes. As she entered the clinical and bright atmosphere of the hospital emergency room there was a dizziness in her head and a ringing in her ears. She automatically held out her hand to grab the arm of the policewoman. But she missed.

Seconds later her legs crumpled beneath her. As she started to fall backwards onto the shiny floor the officer caught her and helped her to a prostrate position in the middle of the corridor. Claire had fainted.

She came to in a bed tucked into a corner of the A&E ward of the hospital. She felt hot, her head throbbed as she moved to turn over and she blinked, disbelieving. The same policewoman who had helped her was sitting beside the bed.

'How're you feeling?' she asked.

'What's happening?'

'Don't worry. You're safe here.'

'Where am I?'

'Just relax. You don't have to move or get up.'

Claire looked around the small room with its polished floor and bright lights and it all flooded back. Yes, something very nasty had happened and as she tried to move the pain in her neck reminded her of what it was.

'It's Claire Watts isn't it?' The question was tentative but firm.

'Oh my God. Yes. How's Rick? Rick Austin. He was with me and they brought him to the hospital in the same ambulance.'

'Yes, Claire. We know that. How do you feel?' she asked for the second time.

'I'm fine,' Then she screeched a loud, 'Ouch!' as she tried to sit up and the pain stabbed in her neck. Sitting more upright she continued, 'But I must know what's happened to Rick.'

'Please, Claire, just relax, and let's see if we can find out what's going on here.'

'Yes, but Rick was beaten. Is he dead?'

The policewoman ignored the question, she did not know the answer anyway, and continued. 'Right now I need to ask some questions. We've got to find out who did this.'

Claire closed her eyes and let her head fall to the pillow. She knew she was cornered and had to submit to questioning. Should she get it over with, tell all about her duplicity and then run from here? It would all come out anyway, she was not good at lying, she felt numb and frightened, wanted to get this whole ghastly spying business finished. She suddenly wanted to wind the clock back and start again her life as it normally ran at Arrow Hall.

'Would you like to get up and have a bath or are you feeling okay to talk now? Obviously the sooner we get onto your attackers the better,' the policewoman coaxed.

Claire took a sip of water from the glass beside her bed and nodded as she sat more upright. She still felt dizzy.

'We were mugged,' she volunteered.

'Well, let's check that.' There was an inflexion of authority in the policewoman's voice. 'Would you mind going through your handbag and purse and let's see if anything's missing.'

The policewoman handed Claire her bag from a locker at the end of the bed and her hands trembled as she undid her purse and checked its contents.

'Do you know how much cash you had?'

'Not really. I never carry much anyway.' Questioning made her feel hot and again the urge to get up from the bed and run was compelling.

'We put your necklace in your bag. It looks expensive and it wouldn't have been difficult for a mugger to pull it off.'

For a moment Claire continued to fumble in her bag. She found her credit cards, fingered the pearl necklace from Stone and felt confused.

'I'm sure everything's here,' she said croakily. 'And anyway they didn't touch my bag. All they did was push me in a bush.'

'Yes. That's why we don't think this is a simple case of mugging. A woman with a handbag is an easy target. I don't think they were after you.'

'I've never been hit like that before,' Claire said, feeling her neck. 'Whatever they were after, it hurt.'

'Tell me, what is your connection with Mr Austin? We don't give secrets away so you can be open with me,' the policewoman said.

'Rick is my boss. I work for him and we were to entertain clients for a weekend. I'm not married and he's not married,' Claire said indignantly.

'I'm sorry, Claire, but we have to ask to get the full picture.'

Claire knew the full picture and she closed her eyes. Again it was tempting to get it all over with and confess her spying to this friendly policewoman. James Kennedy and his wife were due tomorrow and what would now happen with them? Tears came into her eyes.

'I'd like to check your identity and address?'

'I'm Claire Watts, you already know that,' she said.

'And your address?'

'43a, Grenville Street, SW1.'

The policewoman looked up after she had finished writing it down in her notepad.

'Your driving licence has an address in Essex. Somewhere called Arrow Hall isn't it? We saw that when we were checking your bag after you fainted.'

'I've moved. Only last week and I've not yet had a chance to notify my change of address. Does it matter?'

'It's the least of your worries just now. But make sure you do it before too long. Do you live in London alone?'

'Yes. I rent the flat from some people I know.'

Claire tried to sit upright as the policewoman scrutinised the Knightsbridge address she had written in her notebook. Just another part of the jigsaw that did not yet fit.

'It's odd your attackers didn't take money,' the policewoman persisted. 'That's the usual stunt. And muggers don't usually rough people up like they have Mr Austin. Then again, we haven't had a mugging in the village of Broadway before. It's prosperous but too far in the country and too genteel for that.' She spoke as if she felt that Claire would automatically understand.

'I've told you, I'm not missing anything. My watch, jewellery, money, credit cards are all there. Perhaps they took some of Rick's money. Perhaps that's what they were after and they were interrupted by a passing car as they were beating him for it. He's not the type who would give it up easily.'

'What about mobile phones? Did you have one with you? That's what muggers often go for.'

'I left mine in the hotel room. Don't know about Rick's. Never heard him use it but I've only worked for him for a short while so I don't know everything.'

'We'll check all that. The witness from the car who stopped

to help you says he didn't see your attackers. But, Claire is there anything more you can say as you were there?'

'All I saw was two of them wearing hoods. Big, six foot at least, and after they hit me on the neck and pushed me into the bush I ran towards them. I screamed to leave Rick alone. But they kept on kicking, punching and shouting at him.'

'Are you all right?' A hovering nurse approached the bed and gave the policewoman a look that said she had to stop this questioning. Her experience saw the glazed look in Claire's eyes as if her patient was about to faint again.

'Yes, I'm fine.' Claire dabbed her face with a tissue.

The policewoman continued, not put off by the nurse's stare.

'Just a few other things, then we'll leave it for the moment. Do you remember anything being said to you or to Mr Austin by the attackers? Any demands for money? Or anything else come to that? We need to know anything which might lead us to these thugs.'

Claire felt the sharp edge of the charade she was playing and it reduced the ache in her neck to no more than an irritation. Again she remembered that the thugs had shouted Stone's name at Rick as they kicked him and of course no demands for money or anything else were made. This was just a very ugly revenge attack by thugs who meant business.

Wondering what she should say, Claire looked through the window to the darkness outside. There were times when darkness enfolded Arrow Hall, but there everything was familiar, normal, in its right place, and at that moment she believed it to be the best place on earth. Her voice trembled as she replied.

'I remember very little. Everything happened so quickly. One minute we were walking along together and the next ... well it's a blur, a nightmare. I was stunned when they hit me and they said nothing that I could hear, they just beat Rick like he was not human and then ran away like cowards.'

'Can you say any more about the attackers? Were they coloured or white?'

'They were hooded, so I couldn't see their faces. Or their hair.'

'Anything else they were wearing? Anything distinctive?'

'Grey anoraks. Dirty jeans. Heavy boots. I can see them now.'

'And they both laid into Rick Austin together? One holding, the other hitting, or both hacking away together?'

'What difference does that make? He had no chance. They came from behind, dragged him away and I just saw him lying on the pavement with his hands over his head. They kicked him hard, not caring where the blows landed. It was awful.' Claire was now feeling annoyed at the questions and it showed in her tone.

The policewoman looked at Claire's pallid face. She had not got much and from experience she knew there was no point in probing further. At least not just now. This was the outcome she had expected and now was no time to linger. She stood and prepared to leave.

'Thanks for your help,' she said. 'I hope the scratches and bruises soon heal. We've a few things to check and we'll let you know how we get on with the investigations.'

Claire detected a hint of disbelief about the whole night's events on the face of the policewoman. It was as if she knew Claire was holding back and that she had been unable to tease the real story out of her.

Claire's guilt returned with her blatant lying which was there only to protect her own underhand betrayal of trust. She suddenly remembered the awful picture of pulling Rick's swollen eyelids back as he lay motionless on the dark, hard pavement and she had found no response, not even a flicker of life. She stretched and jerked the bell cord over the bed. The nurse quickly appeared at the curtain.

'The police have gone. I hope they didn't upset you too much with their quizzing because I know how persistent they can be. We see a lot of them in here. Anyway, I need to check your blood pressure before you get up.'

The nurse quickly and efficiently took the reading and smiled in satisfaction. 'That's fine and nothing's broken, I can tell you that,' she said. 'But you may want to take it easy for a few days. Those bruises on your shoulder will make you ache.'

'I want to see Rick Austin,' she said. 'He was unconscious when we came in the ambulance.'

'Take it easy, Claire.'

'But how is Rick?'

'I'll get the doctor as soon as he's finished with another patient. He'll tell you Mr Austin's condition,' the nurse responded.

'But how is he?' Tears came to Claire's eyes as she spoke.

'I'm afraid you must wait for the doctor. You just relax for a few more minutes and then we'll let you know what we can.'

The nurse disappeared and Claire eased herself from the bed. She sat in a chair facing the window and for a couple of minutes tried to calm herself in these strange surroundings. She combed her ruffled hair, washed her sweaty hands in a small basin and as she looked in the mirror she saw a red scratch on her left cheek. She touched it and withdrew her hand as if it might infect her.

A few minutes later the nurse returned with a middle-aged, balding doctor. Businesslike in his white coat and half-moon glasses perched at the end of his nose his manner said he knew exactly what he was doing, just as Rick commanded attention when he was giving instructions, Claire thought. There was something in the brisk air of authority on the doctor's face that made Claire suddenly tense. He would say it as it was.

'This is Dr Douglas,' the nurse said. 'Can I get you a cup of tea or anything to eat?'

'Thank you, no. All I want to know is how Rick is.'

Dr Douglas half smiled as he looked Claire straight in the face. It was as if he had a professional interest in the scratch on her cheek.

'Miss Watts, your friend is not well and from the scan we are still investigating his condition. But we plan an urgent operation within the next few hours to relieve pressure that may be on his brain from injuries to his skull and we need to repair a puncture to his right lung. He has a broken tibia and femur that also need attention. Then we will keep him in intensive care for as long as it takes. His condition is difficult and we need to make it stable but...'

'Emergency operation?' Claire echoed. 'Is he that badly hurt?'

'He remains unconscious. He has taken some severe blows to the head and over the rest of his body and it is difficult to tell at this stage what permanent damage may have been done. There were also some knife wounds that did the damage to his lung and although they have gone dangerously close to the heart luckily for him they didn't reach that organ.'

Dr Douglas saw the tension in Claire's face but did not relax his professionally intense manner of detachment. If people got themselves into trouble it was not his problem.

'Will he recover?' Claire blurted.

'Mr Austin is in good health generally and we shall carry out another whole body scan as soon as we can and then we'll know more after that.'

Tears filled Claire's eyes. 'That's awful,' she said. 'Stab wounds as well. I didn't see any knives.'

'I suggest you call tomorrow when we shall probably have some more news.' He glanced at the nurse who was hovering at the end of the bed. It was time for him to move on around the ward.

The encounter left Claire feeling numb, the colour had left her face as she was stunned by the news of Rick's condition and drained of emotion. She had not seen the stab wounds, just the blood that flowed from them, but the thought made her shiver and her face became prickly, hot. She felt unable to speak. Rick was not somebody in any fantasy dream she could ever imagine as being unconscious, in intensive care, utterly helpless, as he was the one in control, confident of what was happening. It was too early to think clearly but this nightmare she already knew had cast its spell because of Stone.

The nurse spoke gently. 'Why don't you freshen up and we'll call a cab to take you home? Your personal things are in the locker and you might want to check that they're okay.'

'I've done that already with the police,' Claire said.

'I hope they haven't upset you with their questioning. They weren't too aggressive were they?'

'No, it was all gentle, routine even.' Claire breathed in heavily, no it wasn't routine, she knew that.

'Good. Call tomorrow evening to see how things are with Mr Austin but do try to take some rest before then.'

Claire washed and put on some make-up, deliberately taking her time. She looked in the small mirror over the basin and saw the scratches on her face. As she turned from the mirror she again remembered Rick's blotched, swollen face and tears welled into her eyes and a strong determination began to grip her. She was only here for Harry Stone with his selfish, arrogant scheme and this was what it had led her to. Harry Stone had to answer for this. From hereon her life as far as Stone was concerned had to change. And that payback would come soon.

She left the hospital in a taxi an hour later and directed the driver to the hotel. It was a bright summer's morning but she felt tired, drained of rational thought. She knew sleep would never come as she silently sat in the back of the cab. Would the hotel receptionist ask her questions when she picked up the keys to their rooms? Why was she coming back so early in the morning and on her own? Surely news of the attack would have spread like a forest fire by now and Claire was in no mood to face more questioning however gentle it might be.

She gave a large tip to the cab driver and walked slowly to reception. At the desk a young girl, too bright at this time of day for her mood, handed her the room keys without question. Claire kept her face turned away so that the scratches would not be seen. She felt lethargic and in no mood to hurry and she climbed the few stairs to her room, still dazed from the horrors of the previous evening. She knew she had to face up to difficult decisions. Where should she go? What should she plan to limit the damage from Rick's beating? She collapsed on the bed, closed her eyes and, out of sheer exhaustion, slept.

Four hours later, feeling heavy-eyed and with growing anger directed at Stone, she methodically packed her clothes and then did the same in Rick's room. Nestling on the bedside table she found Rick's keys to the Porsche and for a moment she held them before she called reception for their bags to be brought down to the car. She wanted to get away from this place.

At reception she cancelled the rooms for the next two nights, settled the account with her credit card and forced a smile. She turned away as the receptionist enquiringly glanced at her scratched face. A question hovered on the girl's lips but she said nothing.

'Have a Mr and Mrs Kennedy checked in yet?' Claire asked.

The receptionist took a quick look at the computer screen. 'Yes. About an hour ago,' she said.

Claire hesitated. She wanted to get away without seeing them.

'Can I leave a message?'

'Of course.'

'Please tell them Mr Austin has had to make a sudden change to his plans. We'll call them later to explain.'

The receptionist nodded as she wrote it down. She then smiled at Claire, now openly intrigued by the puffy scratches on her face but again her discretion prevailed as Claire turned away and walked down the narrow hallway. The place had been disrupted by a visit from the police only an hour ago but the manager had told her to keep calm, and make sure the guests were not disturbed too much. There would be gossip later but now it was time to get on with her work.

Relieved that no questions had been fired at her Claire followed the porter to Rick's car. Halfway down the path to the car park she saw James Kennedy. His wife was walking a step behind him. Claire turned away quickly but Kennedy recognised her immediately and smiled.

'Ah. We find you at last.' He held out his arm to bar Claire's passage.

The porter continued with the bags towards the car and Claire watched as he moved into the colourful garden, desperately wanting to follow him.

'The receptionist rang your room and there was no answer. So we thought you might have decided to go home without us.' Kennedy laughed loudly but a moment later he saw the tight look on Claire's unsmiling face and the deep scratches on her cheek.

'It's not like that at all. We've had an accident,' Claire said, her voice hoarse.

The smile left Kennedy's face. 'What sort of accident?'

'Rick's unconscious, in hospital in Cheltenham. He was taken there last night after we were both mugged. He's

314

badly hurt.' Tears rolled down Claire's cheeks and her voice croaked from the tightness in her throat.

Mrs Kennedy's eyes widened with genuine concern. She was a well-built woman in her late forties with coarse blonde hair.

'My dear, that is too bad. Were you not hurt too?' She stared at the puffy scratch on Claire's cheek.

'Just some scratches when I was pushed in a bush. But they beat Rick. Hard. Kicks and even a knife.' More tears came into Claire's eye and she began to turn away.

'Have the police been told?' Kennedy asked, his tone demanding.

'Yes, of course they know. But they haven't been able to talk to Rick yet. He's still unconscious.'

Kennedy turned away and breathed out heavily. 'So this leaves the weekend up the creek,' he said. 'We've come all this way and there's nobody to meet with us.'

Claire scowled and blood rushed to her face in a moment of uncontrolled anger.

'You stay on. Drink as much champagne as you like and send the bill to Rick. He's expecting it after all.'

Mrs Kennedy turned to her husband and glared at him. 'James, calm down. Can't you see Claire's upset and if Rick's in hospital shouldn't we go to see him?'

'No. You can't. No visitors allowed. Rick's unconscious and he wouldn't know you if he saw you.' There was fiery sarcasm in Claire's voice and she began to walk away towards the car park.

'Where are you going?' Kennedy asked, more softly this time.

'If you really want to know, back to London. I have no intention of staying here without Rick. And I'll only come back tomorrow to see if he's still alive,' Claire shouted, her face flushed with anger, her fists clenched and her lips pursed. For a moment she stood still.

'Where does this leave Rick's bid for the contract?' Kennedy's tone was suddenly businesslike.

'How should I know? I don't give a damn about it. And if that's all that's on your mind at this time, well...'

Kennedy interrupted. 'Bids by next Tuesday. It can't be extended. You do know about the deal I presume? And you do remember Geneva?'

'Yes. I remember Geneva,' Claire responded. 'I remember Geneva for one thing. You did all the demanding with your fat lawyer intimidating Rick. Isn't that a fair summary?' Now several paces away Claire stared at Kennedy, unable to control her increasing anger.

'You shouldn't be talking to me like that,' Kennedy said. 'Who else at Trifoni Group can I talk to about this?'

'There's no one else. No one in their right mind would want to get involved in your sleazy ways.'

Kennedy was unruffled by Claire's sharpness. Sleaze was a not a concept he understood anyway. 'Well, that puts Rick firmly out of the race,' he said. 'A bid without the Geneva end of the deal, whatever you want to call it, won't work. I'll make sure of that.'

Mrs Kennedy, speechless and embarrassed at the unexpected spat, put her hand on her husband's arm to slow him but Kennedy just turned away and stared into the garden, a brooding scowl creasing his eyes.

Claire walked quickly away without looking back, leaving the Kennedys stunned, standing as if stranded on a mudflat with the tide flowing inexorably around them. More eager than ever to get out of the place, away from the greedy, uncouth, unfeeling Kennedy, the sight of Rick unconscious on the dark pavement flashed before Claire's eyes. She shuddered but it fuelled her growing determination that Stone would get the Fenfleet contract. Whatever the price and whatever happened to her.

# 23

Claire was never an aggressive driver but, her anger now raging, she pushed the accelerator pedal hard as she rode the free-flowing outside lane towards London. The Porsche responded easily. She switched to cruise control.

At the first service area Claire filled the Porsche with petrol, drove to the car park, got out and breathed in the air as she walked amongst the cars. Her neck ached but was soothed by the sun on her face and she stopped for a moment. Her anger with Kennedy had long gone, replaced with a satisfied determination to get even with Harry Stone, to follow a plan, secret to her, that had been taking root in the past week.

She walked slowly back to the car, slammed the door heavily and then sat still for a minute. Tension was growing in her neck, her shoulder ached and loneliness engulfed her. There was only one place she could find sympathy and support to carry through a confrontation with Stone and on her mobile she called Jennie before she drove from the services. The call was diverted from the Newbury number and Jennie answered it in her salon. Although it was a Saturday she was at work and by the sound of her harassed tone not entirely enjoying it.

'Claire. I'm sorry. I can't talk now.'

'That's a pity,' Claire responded.

'Are you all right? You sound flat. Your voice is distant.'

'I'm fine. Fine. I'd just like a chat.'

'Just a moment,' Jennie said. 'Let me answer the other phone.'

Claire heard the ring in the distance and then Jennie's voice. She waited a few minutes. It was like being in a queue and Claire did not like it. Suddenly Jennie returned.

'Sorry about that. Tell me what's been happening,' Jennie said.

Claire gabbled into the phone quickly, she cried as she spoke, her words came out incoherently, disjointed, and the full horror of her story was lost in the distance between them. Jennie, only half listening, gave little reaction, and anyway she was busy with a difficult client taking up a sunny Saturday when she would have preferred to be in her garden, cutting flowers that she would arrange in the house. Claire had called when Jennie had other things on her mind.

Then the mobile crackled with an echo that made conversation impossible and after a moment the line went dead. In frustration Claire switched it off. She had only wanted to talk and she was left with an overwhelming disappointment, as if she had been rejected. She pushed at speed onto the motorway where the London-bound traffic was getting denser and concentrated on the road.

The West End on a summer Saturday was not busy and Claire drove to an underground car park just off Park Lane where she paid three days rent in advance. Their overnight bags she hid in the locked boot.

Before she left the car she rang Anton's number at Arrow Hall. No answer came so she rang his mobile and got the message that it was no longer valid as a number. Claire needed protection and Anton was the one person she knew who could give it. But why didn't he answer? Where was he?

Deflated, apprehensive, she looked around the concrete claustrophobic car park where every noise echoed, increasing its volume, but her determination to confront Stone was growing and she wanted to see him. Like now.

She walked quickly from the concrete tomb and in the sunlight of Park Lane took a cab to Liverpool Street. Growing frustration turned to deep irritation which gnawed into her as she waited three quarters of an hour for the next train to Arrow Hall. It was an hour after getting on a slow train that she walked the mile and a half from the country station to the mansion with the sun dimly shining on her back. It was dipping over the horizon with an inevitability that said this world was certain and although it reinforced her love for Arrow Hall she was now sure the affair with the old house had to change. Harry Stone had unwittingly intervened.

She had taken this walk through the country lanes with their grassy verges and high hedges many times but today it was all different. She felt ragged, desperately tired, but she was driven to put right the sharp unfairness suddenly intruding into her life. The overgrown drive that led to the house loomed a few minutes later and Claire did not see one of Cutlass's mates well hidden in what was once a small gardener's shed but like the rest of Arrow Hall now crumbling into a rambling mess. Cutlass's mate, a hidden guard, lifted his head lazily from the canvas deckchair that supported his wide body and let Claire pass without question. He flicked open another can of beer to ease his disappointment that nobody more menacing had turned up in the last few hours.

Claire let herself into Arrow Hall by the western side door and in the small hallway it was quiet, musty from damp, but a feeling of safety surrounded her. She made her way to Stone's study. Without thinking she knocked but it was so light it was barely audible and as she entered the large room she sensed the stale, dusty air that hung heavily. Having been away for some days it came to her fresh as if it was part of Stone himself.

Claire shuddered, stunned by the chaos and upset. Stone had done little clearing up, some rare books that had been bought with the house when he acquired it littered a corner near the large French windows.

Standing uncertainly in the doorway Claire saw Stone himself, sitting at his desk, the only furniture upright in the large room, an impassive look of defiance on his face. He was on the phone, listening, which was unusual for him. People rarely rang Stone, he always called them and usually spoke loudly. The small noise which Claire had made when she entered the room made him swing round and look towards the door. A flicker of welcome appeared in his narrowed eyes.

'Roger, Claire's just arrived,' he said, breaking across further conversation. 'We'll talk again later when she's told me all. And then the tender goes in. I think the deal is on.'

There was no goodbye as Stone threw the phone onto his desk.

'Sit down,' he commanded.

'What's happened here?' Claire asked, surveying the upturned furniture.

'Nothing to worry you,' Stone said.

'It does worry me. I've been away a few days and this mess erupts.'

Stone stood as Claire walked to his desk. 'You've been a long time coming,' he said.

'It hasn't been easy. But now I'm here and we've got to talk.'

She turned a chair upright, placed it close to Stone's desk and stared into his eyes. There was an edge of a smile, a gesture that often came when Stone felt his manipulation was showing results.

'You'd better be bringing me some good news,' Stone said.

'We have to get a few things straight first,' Claire replied firmly. 'Then I'll give you the information you want. Then your deal can be on.'

'Get a few things straight?' Stone echoed.

'That's right, that's what I said.'

'That talk's unlike you. What's biting?'

'Rick Austin's been beaten and stabbed. To within an inch of his life. He's in hospital. Unconscious. He might still die.'

'What's that got to do with me?'

'The thugs who did the beating thought they were smashing you up.'

'How do you know that?'

'They shouted about St Lucia and revenge for Drake. They said you hadn't paid them some money. What do you know about that?'

'Nothing.' The smile had now gone completely from Stone's face.

'I don't believe you,' Claire said angrily.

Stone waved his hand in the air. He had no answer and he knew it.

Claire's stare intensified. 'You know I've been followed these last few days. You did nothing about it. Why?'

Stone became annoyed. 'I could tell you all about St Lucia and Drake but it won't mean a damn thing. It was a deal that went badly wrong. I lost a lot of cash, Drake got beaten up and blames me for it. So he takes revenge. Got it?'

'Is Drake the reason you ran away to Claridge's? Was he chasing you then?' The question hit hard.

'I didn't *run away*. The Fenfleet deal was easier to work on from Claridge's. It's more central.' Stone disliked Claire's sudden perceptiveness.

'But Rick Austin got hit with kicks and a knife meant for you. He probably heard them call your name too.'

'What do the police know?'

'Nothing yet. But if you don't listen now they'll hear the lot.'

Claire relished the distinct look of unease on Stone's face.

321

'Can't you see what I'm having to deal with? Drake's thugs did this,' Stone said.

'Why didn't you tell me about Drake?' Claire asked. 'Why didn't you warn me all this could happen?'

'I had no reason to.'

'Come off it. You knew something nasty was going on. And all the time you kept quiet.'

'Why not? You're working away from all this mess. And anyway how could I know they'd take Rick Austin out?'

'You should have known.'

'Claire. It's over. You're safe.' Again Stone tried to smile but abandoned it after a moment.

'That's not good enough!' Claire shouted. She looked at Stone, she was becoming hot, infuriated at his calmness and she wanted to hit him and see a river of blood flow as it had from Rick.

Stone did not answer. He was cornered, he knew it, so he kept quiet.

'When the police questioned me I lied to them. I lied about where I live and what I heard when Rick was beaten. They haven't spoken to Rick yet but they'll follow him up and he might tell them everything. That's if he lives.'

'Listen, Drake wanted money or violence. He's had his violence and he's picked the wrong man. So forget it.'

'If Rick dies there'll be a murder hunt. What then?' Claire's voice was forceful through her tears.

'You just keep on denying you know anything. And if he dies, well that closes it.'

'You're just too callous, too cold to be real!' she shouted. 'It'll catch up with you and hit where you won't like it. Don't you know that?'

'What's happened can't be altered. Besides there's other things to think about.'

There was silence. But Claire could see that the lines

were tightening around Stone's mouth and her own inner rage was growing.

'Let's talk the numbers on the Fenfleet deal. There's only two days left for the tender to be in and I've been paying you to get those for me. So what've you found?'

'I make the demands first.'

'What do you mean? Not so fast. I've just told you there's only two days to go.'

'I'm not going to let Rick's beating get past you that easily.'

'Well, you're okay. That's all that matters.'

Claire rose from her chair and spoke in a tone she had never used with Stone before. She was dominant and she was loud.

'There's no business until you do what I ask,' she said.

Stone's eyebrows arched as he leaned back in his chair. 'What is it?' he snapped.

'What do you intend to do to catch those thugs? This Drake lot.'

'There's nothing I can do. I don't know where they are.'

'Right. I'll be forced to tell the police the whole story. The Trifoni deception, your underhand dealings. I don't care about myself but I do about Rick.'

'Claire, Claire. It's not like you to want revenge.'

'I've lied to the police about it all. I've told them I thought it was a senseless mugging. So I want out but on my own terms not yours.'

'And out is revenge?'

'I don't want *revenge*. Just justice. Justice for Rick Austin.'

'You know that's not how I operate. I keep away from the police and their officious ways. They've never been any good to me. I work through the back door.'

'Okay. Work through the *back door* but I still want justice. You get no information on the Fenfleet contract until I know what you're going to do.'

Stone thought for a moment and looked anxious, his face ashen grey.

Claire knew that if he had been hit like Rick Austin he would have taken revenge. But she also knew that he would not have done it himself, he was too squeamish for that. The *back door* was definitely Stone's way of working and if she had to force him through that door now, she would.

'Okay. I'll get Drake for you.'

'Good. You know what I want and I expect you to get it.'

'But you've got to keep your story straight with the police. They mustn't know of St Lucia. And as for you spying on Rick Austin ... well, if we're caught lots of things'll unravel. Both for you and for me,' Stone said.

'Where's Anton? Has he left you?' Claire asked suddenly.

'Anton's dead.'

'Dead?' The stark word hit Claire. She moved back from Stone's desk.

'He got in a fight last week. He was knifed.'

'By Drake's thugs?'

'Yes.'

'Why didn't you tell me?'

'Didn't want to frighten you.'

Claire sat down again and let out a gasp of breath. She desperately wanted to hit Stone as he sat smugly in his chair.

'And what have you done about Anton's death?' she asked.

'Nothing.'

'Nothing! Somebody gets killed working for you and you do nothing about it?'

'We can't have the police crawling all over. Haven't I just told you that?'

'So they meant to kill Rick Austin too?' Claire's face turned red and her eyes widened.

'They wouldn't kill Rick Austin any more than they'd kill

me. They just want my money and if they kill me ... well that turns off the supply.'

'These people have got to be stopped and I want to know how you're going to do it.'

Stone fingered the silver paper knife on his desk and the sharpness of its edge prompted him to action like a cornered animal fighting back. 'All right. I know someone who can tell the police all about Anton's death. He knows what happened and he'll do it as a tip-off. Anonymously.' Stone's tone was low.

'A tip-off? What good's that?'

'It's the way to play it so that the police can solve the crime without knowing about you and me. Or Rick Austin. That enough?'

'I'm pleased to hear you think Anton's death is a *crime*,' Claire said sarcastically. 'Just remember Rick Austin's beating is a crime too and it might also become a death. Then you'll have two deaths on your conscience if you have any left.'

'I've told you I'll get it done, so leave it there,' Stone snapped.

Claire looked at Stone's troubled expression and was satisfied she had made a mark on him. Unusually he was listening, and he was yielding to her demands. But Claire had not finished.

'Get on with it then,' she said. 'Like now.'

Stone's face showed an expression of distaste as if he had swallowed an astringent drug. Claire saw the deep scar in the leather desk top. Something sharp had bitten into it.

'How did that happen?' she asked, placing her finger over the mark.

Stone said nothing.

'Is this the only room that's been done over?' Claire asked.

'I haven't been round the house. Does it matter?'

'What about my flat?' Claire asked.

'Don't know. Haven't been up there, you go and look if you want to, but we need to move on like quickly,' Stone replied sharply.

'You don't care what happens to anyone else as long as you're all right. Your eyes give you away, they're shifty, they always have been and they're even worse today.'

'Claire, what's biting at you? I said we gotta move on and that's what I mean. Okay?'

'On to what?'

'You've got to tell me the Fenfleet figures. I want that deal.'

'You get no figures from me until you talk to your police informer. I want to sit here right in front of you and hear it all spilled out in tiny detail.'

Stone stared at Claire as if he disbelieved her. He was not used to being spoken to like that and it hit him like a thud to the stomach. He ran his fingers through his hair, left his chair and started to pace as if he wanted out. Claire's unexpected and pointed sharpness made him uneasy.

A moment later Stone grabbed the phone and walked to the window. He was angry, cornered by someone he had always believed to be soft and pliable, and it showed. He punched in Cutlass's number and waited.

'That you, Cutlass?'

Satisfied he was connected to the right man, Stone faced Claire, replaced the phone on his desk and switched on the conference speaker. He spoke slowly and quietly.

'Here's another chance for you to earn some money.'

'My man's watching your house isn't he?'

'If you say so,' Stone said disinterestedly, not listening. 'But nobody's been here since they bust it up. So instead we go find them.'

'You pay me, then I do it,' Cutlass replied.

'You know where the Rex lot are. You know who they are.'

'They're dangerous, boss. I told you that. Leave 'em alone.'

'I want them shopped. Grassed to the police.'

'Wait a minute, I can't do that. They'd kill me. Just like they did your mate Anton.'

'Cutlass, listen. This deal is anonymous. That means nobody knows who does the grassing and nobody else gets killed.'

'They have ways of finding out,' Cutlass argued.

'You should have bloody well completed the job in St Lucia. Then all this wouldn't be necessary.'

There was silence for a moment as Cutlass thought. He was unsure. Stone continued.

'You call the police saying who the killers of Anton were. Tell 'em you know of the Rex Gang. Where they hang out and what they do with drugs. Confirm it was a drugs killing. And remember this mustn't lead back to Arrow Hall. If it does you don't get paid and they'll get you.'

'You ask too much, Mr Stone,' Cutlass protested.

Stone cut in. 'I want it done quickly. That means tomorrow latest.'

'I can't do it,' Cutlass replied firmly. 'I don't mind a fight at any time but the Rex mob stop at nothing. Nothing.'

'How much do I have to pay you to get the job done?' Stone asked.

There was silence for a moment as Cutlass considered an obvious opportunity.

'Enough to get back to Jamaica where I've got mates to protect me. This is really dangerous work you're asking for.'

'How much?' Stone persisted.

'Twenty grand,' Cutlass replied.

'You get results and it's fifteen.'

'It might take time. The police don't always bite at the first offer.'

'Don't give me the problems, Cutlass. You know what I

want. Just go and do it. And quickly, not your fat lazy slow way.'

There had been a sharp edge to Stone's voice that Claire knew all too well and she sat upright in her chair, satisfied that she had pushed him to the limit. She would take the rest whatever he might try to throw at her.

Stone looked up and stabbed a finger towards Claire. 'Just remember. You've had very expensive new clothes. Now you've got your own way too. If this goes wrong...'

'Hang on,' Claire interrupted. 'You forget too easily about Rick Austin. I've also got some very painful bruises I didn't expect. It should be you lying in that hospital bed fighting for life. Not him. You couldn't face that could you?'

'Shut it, Claire,' Stone said sharply. 'I want the Fenfleet figures. What've you found?'

With the facts clearly in her memory Claire spoke with a confidence that she thought she would not find.

'There's a bank account in Geneva opened for James Kennedy with £200,000 going in from Trifoni. The account is under the control of a Dr le Borge, some sort of lawyer. Here's the address.' She placed a slip of paper on the desk. Stone made a note on a small pad.

'And the big one? How much are Rick Austin and his Trifoni lot offering for the contract? What's the size of their real money?'

Claire paused before answering, knowing this had to sound convincing. She was not used to lying and this lie would be gross, premeditated, widening the gap between fact and fiction.

'They're offering £2.25 million fixed for the next two years and then it goes up each year by a minimum of ten per cent. So the more they take from the pubs the more they pay, like a ratchet that keeps on going upwards was how Rick described it to me.'

Stone again made notes on the pad. He showed no

emotion. This was how he faced opponents when he was negotiating, when he wanted to give nothing away, but it did not unnerve Claire, she had seen it all before and she continued with an outward show of confidence that hid her inner turmoil.

'There's one other thing Trifoni have offered I think you should know about.'

Stone nodded.

'However bad business gets, they won't seek renegotiation of the deal. They'll stick with it so long as Fenfleet don't open other pubs nearby.'

'Anything else for Kennedy?'

'Entertaining. Holiday hotel accounts paid in Mauritius. And some crates of champagne delivered.'

'I'm not interested in trivial stuff. I can beat all that crap.' For a moment Stone looked satisfied.

Claire breathed out. She had now said all she wanted to. But Stone continued.

'How did you find all this information?' he asked.

'Why do you question what I've told you?'

'I'm reading your thoughts. You look confident in what you've said. I want to know you are.'

'What do you think I've been doing these last few days? Where do you think I've been?' There was tetchiness and irritation in Claire's voice. It made Stone look up.

'Okay, okay, don't get bitchy about it. I only asked.'

'That's what I've found. You've had it all.'

'Look, all I asked is, are you sure the information's correct? There were no false trails?'

'I ploughed through Rick Austin's desk myself. I risked getting caught with spy cameras all around the place and then I got chucked in a bush watching Rick get done over. Isn't that good enough?'

Stone smiled.

'We'll agree you've earned your new clothes. Okay?'

Stone scanned the figures on his pad. Claire left her chair, went to the sideboard and tidied the disarranged bottles noisily as if to distract Stone from his thinking. She would stick to her story but there could now be argument, tetchiness, if he in any way doubted the figures as feasible, as the true numbers that would make it pay for Trifoni Group and she was in no mood for that.

'Anything else you got to tell me?' he asked.

'No. What are you expecting?'

'Nothing,' Stone said.

He scratched the back of his neck, and took another long calculating look at the figures he had written down as if to check that he had got it right.

'Do you know how much Roger Garon says the deal is worth?' Stone asked.

'No.'

'Only £1.5 million.'

'Why are you telling me that?'

'Just that Trifoni's figures are a hell of a lot higher than I expected.'

'Well, you know how these things work.'

'Did you find the detail on drink and food sales Trifoni are expecting from the Fenfleet pubs? It goes to the guts of these numbers.'

'No,' Claire said quickly. 'That was all stored in Rick Austin's computer and I couldn't get into it without passwords. You know what passwords are don't you?' she added sarcastically.

Stone stared at Claire as if about to lose his temper.

'This isn't complete. I need those figures to check Trifoni's bid.'

'I'm not going back to find them, I've done all I can and that's it,' Claire said, returning his stare straight into his steely blue eyes.

'I always thought you were more efficient than that,' Stone

said and he threw his notepad across his desk with a noisy thud.

Claire walked quickly to the door and took a long last look at Stone's face. It was devoid of expression with just creased lines on his forehead. His mood was dangerous. It was time to get out, time to avoid more quizzing from Stone as he digested and then distrusted the figures. And to hell with Stone, she needed time to calm down so she could help Rick and deal with the police if they came again.

Was Rick still alive? She suddenly thought of the man she had spent a night with. She wanted more.

She walked quickly along the gloomy hallway to the stairs that led to her flat where she looked in each room, sadness tingeing every movement. This flat had been her home for eight years and as the lowering sun shone through the windows it left a warm feeling. Mayfair was fine, elegant, but it was small, confining, and Arrow Hall, even with its decrepitude, was where she was comfortable, safe and herself.

Claire selected some of her favourite clothes, quickly packed them neatly in a case and on her mobile called a cab to take her to the station. She wanted out quickly and she was not sure when she would be back.

As he heard the front door close half an hour later Stone walked round his study deep in thought. He grabbed the whisky bottle, poured a drink and stood at the closed French windows. Staring into the wild garden was a habit that had grown stronger since he had returned from St Lucia, and what he saw now made him edgy and insecure.

In his threadbare green jumper, with heavily creased corduroy trousers, hands in his pockets, he looked as dowdy as the room. His mood was tense and now was the time to make a binding, difficult decision. He had sunk over $3 million from his Cayman account into St Lucia and lost the lot to thugs who were still striking at him. Wary, like a cat stalking, he had already decided he was not going to let it happen again. The Fenfleet deal had to be different.

Stone's tension increased, his mood becoming belligerent and dark as with a sudden jerk he picked up the phone and punched the digits for Roger Garon. He waited only a few seconds before it was answered.

'Roger, we got the deal,' he said firmly.

'What do you mean we got the deal? You haven't put the tender in yet.'

'Look, I've got the information we need. I've got all the numbers from Claire. She's given me the bribes and I know the Trifoni Group tender money, so with James Kennedy in our pocket we're there.'

'I wish you luck because that's all a bit quick. You sure you got everything?' Roger responded.

'Why not?'

'It's sometimes the figures you *don't* know that are important. The bits you've not been told.'

'I've got enough,' Stone said.

'Tell me then.'

'Kennedy gets £200,000 from Trifoni. Swiss account in Geneva. You know the trail. It'll be billed as consultancy services or some other jargon, anyway something to make it look legal.'

'Yeh, we guessed that, it's nothing new. But too much for my liking just to feed the greed,' Roger said.

'This is a big deal. It'll take big money.'

'What else?' There was disinterest in Roger's voice.

'Entertaining. Hotel accounts. Crates of champagne. Usual cheap jack stuff when somebody thinks they're important.'

'Yes. Everybody thinks they're important in these deals so don't let it go to your head too.'

'Don't be so irritable and tetchy, Roger. You put me onto Fenfleet and you know it'll be a good one.'

'Okay, so how much is the cash down? How much are Trifoni giving to Fenfleet for the deal?' Roger asked.

'It's big, Roger. Two and a quarter million a year for two years. Some increases in later years. And payment guaranteed each year even if customers stop spending.'

'That's crazy. Way out. Forget it at that price.'

'You made a lot of assumptions when you did your sums. You could have been wrong about how quickly the pubs will grow. Anyway, I keep on telling you you're a downtrodden pessimist.'

'Have you seen Trifoni's calculations? Do you know their assumptions on what sales each property will get? Important stuff, eh? Has Claire found all that out?'

'No, and I don't need it. My gut feeling tells me what's right.'

'Perhaps Rick Austin and Trifoni need the deal more than you do. So let them lose money together without you.'

'Never,' Stone snapped. 'You know damn well that this deal will be stuffed with cash, pound notes, coins. You never been to a pub? That's how they pay in pubs and that's what I'm after. So let's take it seriously, Roger.'

'Okay. Believe those figures from Claire. But remember my calculations showed £1.5 million. Max. So two and a quarter, forget it.'

'They came from Claire direct to me. Claire's not stupid. She's loyal. I trust her. She knows how I work. Isn't that enough?'

'Yes, if you say so,' Roger replied, but inside he knew differently. Jennie had spoken to Roger about Claire often. Claire was the girl in the middle. And where could that lead? Jennie at least was perceptive even if Stone wasn't.

'Are you sure Claire's not been found out at Trifoni? You know marching in like that and then marching out suddenly isn't exactly straightforward,' Roger said.

Stone hesitated, measuring carefully what he would tell

Roger about Claire's visit to Arrow Hall. Most of it he would keep back as if nothing had happened.

'Claire's now finished at Trifoni. Rick Austin got done over yesterday by some nasties who thought they were bashing at me, he's in hospital so she won't be going back, she has no reason to, so we can now wrap it all up.'

'You wrap it up your way then, Harry. That tender price is stupid and you know it. You're being blinded by something I find difficult to understand. And do you know where Rick Austin, landed in hospital mistaken for you, might lead?'

Roger did not get a response from Stone. The phone clicked as Stone ended the conversation.

Stone leaned back in his chair as far as it would tilt and took a slug from his whisky glass. He rested his head and stared at the oak beam that ran the length of the ceiling, looking vacantly for an answer. Arrogance stopped him from admitting it to Roger but he too was puzzled over the figures. The more he looked at them the more surprised he was at the size of the offer Trifoni was prepared to make. It was huge. Were there other facts that Claire had not found? After scanning again his own calculations Stone placed them in a desk drawer as if to finish them off by shutting them away. In his normal sneering way he made up his mind. He had quizzed Claire, he had looked hard into her eyes – she was telling the truth as she knew it. He swung his chair round and then walked to the window. He knew better than Roger, he had first-hand facts that didn't lie.

A flock of geese flew over the garden in a V-shape towards the coast, a signal almost that it was now time for him to get the tender into Fenfleet so that Kennedy and his hangers-on could see how good it was. As he finalised the figures and put the papers in an envelope he knew everything he had planned was working out and with a top-up from the whisky bottle a wide grin crossed his face. The Fenfleet deal and the cash that flowed from it was now his for the taking.

Moments later Stone shouted for Claire. Patiently he waited two minutes and then swore loudly as he remembered that she had gone to sort out the mess of Rick Austin. Outside it was now dark, inside it was cold, and without Claire Arrow Hall felt a lonely, forgotten place. Suddenly Stone saw the danger that lurked through it all, starkly understood his position and shivered.

# 24

There was nervousness in Claire's step. She waited in a queue at the busy reception desk for two minutes, and began to feel the heat overpowering her but her hands stayed cold and clammy in the clinical atmosphere. There was a visitors' card to sign as part of the hospital security and her hand shook as she replaced the pen, then the noise and bustle rang in her ears as she looked around carefully after she was given directions to intensive care on the sixth floor.

The lift was wide enough to take a bed but she was alone and she felt enclosed and claustrophobic. Of course she remembered fainting last time she was here and her brain went into overdrive as she did not want it to happen again. Eagerly she left the lift onto a carpeted landing when its doors opened a few seconds later and at the end of a long gleaming corridor she found the sister's door. Claire knocked tentatively and then walked into the small office.

'I'm looking for a Mr Rick Austin. He was admitted two days ago.'

The ward sister, whose badge identified her as Sister Davies, was a middle-aged woman Claire had not seen before. She looked up from her paperwork. Her face softened with a smile.

'Are you a relative?' she asked.

'No. My name is Claire Watts. I was with Mr Austin when he had his accident and I came in the ambulance.'

'I'm afraid you can't see him. Only close relatives are allowed in,' Sister Davies said in a firm tone.

'Why on earth only relatives? I was attacked too, you know, and I need to find out how he is. Anyway the police will want to see me again and I can't possibly deal with them without knowing how Rick is.'

Sister Davies pulled a file of notes from a cabinet and read them for a moment. Removing her glasses she looked at Claire with a controlled professional stare. She then again flicked over the pages of her notes, this time reading more closely, and finally, sitting uneasily further forward in her chair, she spoke without looking at Claire.

'Mr Austin is very poorly, Miss Watts. In fact he's still unconscious.'

'Still unconscious? Oh my God.'

Sister Davies' smile had now gone and she stood. Outbursts like Claire's she had heard before.

'Mr Austin had a heavy blow to his head. Brain scans show a blood clot.'

'I've got to see him.'

'His condition is constantly monitored and he's receiving the best attention possible.'

'And how long will he be like that?'

'Sometimes it can be days. Sometimes a lot longer.'

'He's not going to die is he?'

She did not reply. She did not know how to. But she saw the look of lined anguish on Claire's face. Her complexion was pallid, drained of blood and the nurse's trained eye told her that this visitor was in a state of very high anxiety and nervousness. There were counsellors who usually took the burden of dealing with these situations but with natural instinct overtaking her she spoke soothingly, a hint of compassion in her professional tone.

'Sit down for a moment.' She indicated a chair facing her.

Claire's eyes were red, heavy with dark marks underneath, her cheeks blotchy, and her hair, usually brushed carefully into place, was windswept. Taking the seat offered her she looked around apprehensively, expecting a policewoman or someone else to appear to quiz her and she clasped her hands tightly. Her heightened state of tension did not go away.

'Can I get you a cup of tea or some water?'

'No. I'm fine,' Claire said. 'But the whole mess has all been such a shock, something I'm not used to.'

'Yes. I'm sure. But you have to understand we cannot let Mr Austin receive visitors which might interfere with his treatment. He is not a well man.'

'I've come from London to visit. I work closely with Rick so surely I can see him.'

Sister Davies smiled. 'Please call before you come again because we have a responsibility for the welfare of Mr Austin and it would not be appropriate for you to see him now. When you call, ask for my extension and I'll let you know how he's doing before you visit.'

'So there's no point in my hanging on here? There's nothing else anyone can tell me?'

'Mr Austin is in capable hands. You can be sure everything for his care will be done.'

'You will tell me if he's going to die won't you?' Claire pleaded.

'Miss Watts, there's nothing more I can say that will help you, so tomorrow evening before seven give me a call. Extension 614 will find me. We'll see how things are then. In the meantime take it easy and get some rest.'

Claire rose to leave, her hands clenched tightly, and she hovered for a moment. Something else was deflecting her thoughts. Rest was the last thing that concerned her at that moment as she spoke, her voice hoarse.

'The police questioned me about the attack. I don't know if they've found anyone yet and I can still see what they did to Rick, but will he remember anything about the horror of the beating when he regains consciousness? Will he remember all that went on?'

'You mustn't worry yourself about such details now. They just don't matter and there's plenty of time for the police to do what they have to do later when Mr Austin's condition improves.'

'The police wanted answers when we came in the ambulance. The attack was awful, it all happened so quickly, I ran to help but I couldn't, and Rick just moaned.' Claire's thoughts were jumbled and she spoke in a torrent.

'If you're not ready to face questioning then let your doctor know. We need to get priorities right and that means Mr Austin's condition and your own are more important. So the police'll have to wait until you're both fit.'

Sister Davies' voice was emphatic and gave comfort to Claire. After Jennie not taking her call, walking out on James Kennedy and a row with Harry Stone she felt not many people had been on her side in the last few days.

'I'm sure you're right. But it's funny how you always feel pressure from the police even when you're the victim,' Claire said.

'Take my advice and don't worry yourself about catching these people who did this to you. Get yourself fit first, then tackle the investigation.'

'I do so desperately need to know that Rick will be okay at the end of all this and that he won't hold it against me,' Claire said as tears crept into her eyes.

'Are you sure I can't get you a cup of tea?' the nurse asked.

'Thank you, no.' Claire opened the door to the small room with a sudden urge to leave. She felt weak, unable to focus on the problems in front of her and even though the police had gone she knew they would come again.

'I'll call,' Claire said. The bright light and clinical smell of the hospital made her voice tremble.

'Yes. Take care and drive safely,' were the words Claire heard as she closed the door of the small office.

Claire was now in a hurry. She took the lift to the ground floor, walked quickly to the car park, her shins aching with the exertion, and once cocooned inside Rick's Porsche she sat still for a few minutes, breathing heavily, tired and tense.

Over her shoulder Claire looked to the sixth floor of the building. Somewhere in there Rick was barely alive and next time she came...

She turned her gaze resolutely away, started the car and a few moments later cautiously drove from the hospital. Easily she found the motorway, took the eastbound route for London, put on cruise control and let the car do the rest. Soothing music from the CD caressed her thoughts but there was still the tugging question hard in front of her. What would happen if Rick died?

*

It was getting dark as Stone entered the front door of Arrow Hall. Checked out from Claridge's by midday a limo had brought him back to Arrow Hall and he had called in at the Sportsman pub, his nearest local which he hardly ever frequented, for a sandwich and a glass of wine which he found undrinkable. He wanted solitude and he found it. Nobody spoke to him, nobody knew him as he sat alone in a corner of the sparse but cosy bar, and after a short walk along the lane to Arrow Hall with his own solitude still enclosing him, he was still unsure.

In the hallway he flicked on the chandelier lights, the brightness momentarily making him blink. Suddenly the phone rang. There was no Claire to kill the noise, there was no Anton to see that Arrow Hall was safe, but unlike his last visit the smell of the place was benign.

Stone swore loudly as he pushed into his large study and

340

saw again the ugly, uncleared chaos caused by Drake's intrusion. A trickle of light percolated through the windows past the heavy curtains and Stone picked up the phone from his desk angrily as he stared at the torn sofa and books all over the floor.

'Is that Mr Harry Stone?' The accent was pure Birmingham.

'Yeh,' Stone replied.

'My client tells me that by now you should have decided how much you're offering.'

'What's this about?' Stone asked sharply.

'You have seen palm trees, Mr Stone. You know all about their fruits.'

Stone was momentarily puzzled. Drake's cousins were Cockney, this was a Brummy accent but suddenly the code word 'palm' clicked and he became excited.

'Yeh. What about £225,000 to buy the palm trees your client wants?' Stone said quickly, and grabbed a pencil and a piece of paper.

'That sounds good. You're well in the game at that price against what anyone else might offer, so listen to this. Hire a green Ford Fiesta, drive to the first service station on the M3 leading to Southampton and park in the corner at the back, away from the shops. You'd better be there at precisely ten o'clock tomorrow morning and have the money ready for easy checking as there won't be time for hanging around.'

The phone went dead abruptly and Stone stood erect, a smile covering his face. The call had come much more quickly than he had expected. He dialled 1471 to trace its origin but had no luck – number withheld. He barged his way to the kitchen and flooded it with light. The Glenfiddich whisky bottle was in a cupboard, he took it out and poured himself a large measure which he gulped neat as a celebration, even a thank you to Claire for getting the right figures. Stone sat at the kitchen table and took in a big breath.

Everything he had done for the Fenfleet contract had been right.

He finished his whisky and poured another. Like a little child he could not control himself any longer – had to tell someone. Even though it was evening he called Roger Garon.

'Roger, it's moving,' he said.

'Everything's moving, so what's new with you that you need to call me at this time of day?' Roger replied.

'Just listen,' Stone said tetchily. 'I've had a phone call from palm, that's palm as in hand, and just to remind you, it's the code word we agreed with Kennedy.' Stone paused and then continued quickly. 'He wants me to deliver the palm gift tomorrow and I've agreed £225,000. Just ten per cent of the price. There's always a tip of ten per cent,' Stone added.

'Crikey, Harry, how can you? Your starting price is way out in the stratosphere. Two and a quarter million down payment for two years is outrageous and you're mad to offer that much. Harry, stop and think again because you've got this one really wrong.'

'We'll see who's right. In time.'

'Do you intend to deliver the palm gift to James Kennedy before you get the deal?'

'Why not? Kennedy can't play false on this one. Not now. He does us, we do him.'

'So where do you deliver this large parcel of readies?'

'Motorway services on the M3. Anonymous job. I'll send Cutlass.'

'You amaze me how you can play with £225,000 just like that. No records, no receipts, perhaps no deal, I don't believe what I'm hearing.'

'That's how the system works. Just think of what I'll make under the contract. After this there'll be money in the bank in case I want another one. And remember you introduced me to this.'

'For the very last time, Harry, listen. You're offering too much. If you get Fenfleet pubs you'll lose heavily and just so that you remember what I've said I don't want anything more to do with this deal. I might have led you to it but I've given you advice which you've ignored so now you're on your own. And that's final. Finished.'

'You forget Claire's told me the facts. If Trifoni and Rick Austin can make it pay at that price then there's something wrong if I can't. Got it, Roger?'

'I've got it all right,' Roger said wearily. 'But get something from Kennedy for the £225,000 you're giving him. That's big money and even bigger if you don't get the deal.'

'Don't be stupid. You know he'll never admit he's had it. It's a chance I have to take.'

'So Kennedy gets the cash, does a runner and then denies he ever had it? That doesn't sound much of a deal to me.'

Stone remained silent for a moment as if he was uncertain. He looked up and stared thoughtfully around the large kitchen and, alone in the old house, felt the darkness of the evening creeping in on him.

'I'll let you know how it goes,' Stone said.

'Yes, please do,' Roger responded with mounting sarcasm.

'One other thing,' Stone said. 'The tender's going in. In the post today.'

'The full price, Harry?'

'Yeh. The full price. Just higher than Trifoni are bidding.'

'Good luck, Harry,' Roger said. 'You'll need it more than you ever have on this one.'

'It's not luck, it's judgement, instinct, gut feel, call it what you like. Anyway I haven't used your useless methods. Insider info is what makes this work.' Stone's loud voice echoed around the bare walls and floors of the kitchen.

'It's your money. But don't come back to me in a year's time and tell me it's not working. I won't listen.'

'Goodbye, Roger. I'll come to you if I ever need you.

And that won't be in a year's time. Probably not in two years' time either.'

Stone did not wait for a reply as he put the phone down heavily. He felt annoyed. Roger was too negative and the bill he had now received from Jennie Garon for Claire's makeover was outrageous. Services £5,500, new clothes £10,500 and jewellery £6,000. And then Roger's own bill to come, plus expenses. This was not what Stone had meant when he had suggested a makeover for Claire.

Stone suddenly felt enclosed by the dingy hallway with its dark oak panelling and threadbare carpet. Then he remembered. Of course. He had promised Claire he would spend money renovating that too. Just two steps down the hallway he knew he wanted her back.

Darkness was enveloping the house but Stone went into the garden from a side door and walked to the decaying summer house on the edge of the lawn. There was a window left permanently open on its hook. Stone peered inside and saw the large body of Cutlass's mate. His snores came loudly, reverberating against the wooden walls as he slept in a garden chair. Stone walked to the front of the shack, opened the door angrily and shook the sleeping body of the large Jamaican. He woke with a start, lumbered to his feet and blinked as if the light was bright. Two empty beer cans were on the floor and they rattled noisily as his foot hit them.

'Get out, you useless fat waster!' Stone said. 'You're finished here and I don't want to see you again. You wouldn't know how to guard a rat's hole.'

The Jamaican had no chance to reply before Stone stamped off back to the house. He was agitated. He was furious. He still did not trust Drake with his London thugs and he wanted them kept away.

In the house Stone sat again at the kitchen table, grabbed the phone and punched in the number for the security company in Chelmsford he had put on the job of guarding Arrow Hall.

'How many times you been around?' he asked quickly. 'Are you coming at night as well in the day?'

After hastily scrabbling through papers a few seconds later a woman answered. 'Three times every twenty-four hours. Our guards look around the house and walk round the gardens, and there's nothing suspicious reported.'

'So you haven't seen a coloured guy sleeping in the summer house? You're as useless as the rest of them,' Stone snapped and threw the phone into a waste bin in a corner.

He sat for only a few seconds and then with growing irritation walked around the room. That simple activity eased his tension, he recovered the phone, looked at it as if defying it to say something he did not want to hear, and pressed the numbers for Cutlass.

'You're a blithering fool,' Stone said. 'You say you'll guard Arrow Hall and all you do is send me some slob of a cowboy who sleeps on the job.'

'But, Mr Stone...' Cutlass started.

Stone cut him off. 'I've sent him away. You want to get paid then you gotta produce something better for me from now on.'

There was silence from Cutlass. He knew how his friends worked if they could get away with it, and sleeping on the job was something they were used to.

'Get one of your bouncer mates up here like smart. Someone who can stay alert and alive. And remember I'll check on what they do.' Stone spoke aggressively.

'Sure, boss. But it can be boring just hanging around waiting...'

'I don't want to hear that crap. Get on with it like you haven't done before and don't ask questions. Anyway, I need to know if you grassed to the police about Anton's death yet. You done what we agreed?'

345

'Yeh. Did it yesterday. It took two calls, but still don't know if they're biting at it.'

'Did you remember they record phone calls when they think they're interesting? No names? No addresses? Was that the way you did it?'

'I know how to grass. And I did it my way. I used two phone boxes. One up West and one in north London. Okay?'

'I'll want results,' Stone said.

'I want the £15,000 you promised as payment,' Cutlass said. 'I need to get out of here.'

'You still got the £200,000, Cutlass? Still got it safe?'

'Yeh. It's under the bed.'

'Good, because now's the time to deliver it.'

'Deliver it?' Cutlass echoed. 'I've given you results on grassing haven't I? Now I need to get paid.'

'You'll get paid. Like any other deal I do. But first you gotta deliver money for me.'

'That wasn't in the deal, Mr Stone. I need money to get away now. The Rex lot are probably looking for me already.'

'Get a green Fiesta. Hire it for a couple of days. And not in your own name,' Stone replied, ignoring Cutlass's plea.

'You mean a false license?'

'If you haven't got one, borrow one,' Stone replied irritably.

'Who pays for the car?'

'I do. In cash when you've done the job.'

'Mr Stone, I've already done what you asked.'

'Not quite. You're still paying back for St Lucia, remember? Come to Arrow Hall now. Tonight. You'll get another £25,000 to go with the £200,000 you've got under the bed. You deliver that little packet then you come back and get your pay-off. You understand all that?'

There was silence for a moment.

'Okay, boss. You're paying me. But deliver where?'

'You take the £225,000 to a service station on the M3,

346

Junction 4. Tomorrow morning. Be there at ten o'clock sharp. You park in the back row away from other cars and sit in the car until somebody comes. And then you hand the cash over when they give the password. Got it?'

'Password? You don't understand the Rex boys. They aren't into passwords.'

'For God's sake listen,' Stone snapped. 'The password is "palm". You just understand that nothing is handed over without that word first.'

'How can I do this when I've just grassed on 'em? They'll kill me.'

'They don't know you. Your grassing was anonymous wasn't it?'

Cutlass considered for a moment. 'Mr Stone, you are being careful I hope. The Rex boys won't leave you alone. They'll still go hunting for you, especially when they know the police have been informed.'

'They've already mistaken me for someone else, they think they've already hit me. And can't you see we give them some money that'll keep 'em satisfied.'

Stone lied, it came easily, particularly as Cutlass would never know the money was not going anywhere near the Rex mob but was a bribe for a new deal and he was just the delivery postman.

'You didn't pay Drake in St Lucia. Why now?' Cutlass persisted in his ignorance.

'No more questions, Cutlass. You do as I say if you want to get paid.'

'The Rex lot won't stop there, boss. Once they've got the smell of your protection money they'll keep on coming back for bigger sniffs. You sure this is right?'

'Shut it,' Stone said forcefully. 'You just do what you're told and I guarantee you'll be okay.'

Impatience was overtaking Stone and in his usual abrupt manner he cut the call short. Let Cutlass think that it was going to the Rex mob as blackmail, pay him his fat fee for the simple task of delivering a bribe to a greedy employee on an ego trip, and then Fenfleet pubs would be well sealed. And Cutlass, running to Jamaica, would never know which job he had done.

Stone paced the tiled floor of the kitchen making a scraping noise. He would be alert for Cutlass coming to get the £25,000 cash, then he would lock himself in securely, flooding the place with light. Momentarily it made him feel safe against Drake and the Rex mob, they had been violent with Rick Austin and they would not strike again. But as he paced and the gloom of the early evening penetrated the whole house, he suddenly felt enclosed by an unseen menace. He was alone, the house was unguarded, and it was beginning to rain.

# 25

That night Stone slept at Arrow Hall with no more noise to disturb him than the creaking of the house in a wind that also rustled the trees. His sleep was light, fitful, and twice he got up to peer through the heavy, drawn curtains. He was fully awake and restless just before dawn.

The post arrived at eight o'clock and he grabbed ten envelopes from the box at the gate and shuffled them into a heap on the kitchen table. At the top of the pile was a brown envelope containing a letter from the Revenue. He had dismissed this threat as blocked and his heart skipped as he scanned its contents. He did not read every word, he never did in any letter however important, but he breathed out heavily. Two facts from the letter stuck to him like glue.

Fines, back tax, interest would be £85,000 coupled with a note that he had not been cooperative at the meetings so far. It made him hot and angry and for a moment he wondered why he had not chucked everything into his Cayman account, away from any prying eyes. But his temper calmed as he read further.

It said the inquiry was ongoing and the £85,000 demand was for undeclared income arising in Jersey. Further inquiries would depend on the information from Paris on the source of funds deposited in Jersey. And Stone was confident Paris would cover for him, after all, he had done them a favour when needed.

He thought of the demand for £85,000 again and swore to himself, but then decided it was a price worth paying as at least it would keep that bureaucracy happy and get them out of his hair. He wandered to the cupboard under the stairs and found the papers containing his passwords and PIN numbers for the Jersey account. There was still money there and without memorising the detail he locked it firmly away for future reference, contented that a bundle of cash still remained hidden under the floorboards.

The rest of the morning he spent tidying his study from the mess left by the Rex thugs. With no Anton to help he found it heavy work and by midday he was hot, aching from the exertion. In the kitchen he fumbled with some bread and cheese which he ate slowly to avoid indigestion and then just before two o'clock he could wait no longer. He rang Cutlass. He needed to know.

'You got the cash handed over?'

'Yes, boss. But the guy had long hair, a moustache, and a leather jacket. And he was white. The Rex boys are all Caribs. You ever seen a Jamaican with long hair? You sure I've given the cash to the right lot?'

'Did the leather jacket give the password before you handed over the loot?'

'It was all quick. The man was on his own, he came to the car before I'd stopped the engine and flashed a piece of paper right in my face with the word "palm" written on it.'

'That's all you need to know. The money's gone, you're back home, you've earned your £15,000 so now forget it and take your fat arse off to Jamaica.'

'Yeh, I'm gonna do that after I've been to Arrow Hall to get my pay-off. You're not gonna back out now are you, Mr Stone?'

'I keep my word. It's hidden away here, yours for when you come.' Stone breathed out heavily as he put the phone down, knowing that the final piece of the jigsaw that would get the Fenfleet deal was now in place.

Stone was feeling tired from lack of sleep and he was irritable. He was now committed to finding large sums of cash to make Fenfleet work, and a tinge of doubt began to set in. Not for the first time in the last forty-eight hours he had a nagging thought that would not go away. Had he thrown too much at the Fenfleet contract? Would the deal earn as much as he thought? Kennedy had his money but could he be trusted to deliver? Stone ran his hand through his hair. The atmosphere was heavy, hot and stuffy. He rested his head on the high back of his chair and the word 'Fenfleet' wouldn't leave his mind, as if it had more to tell him that would bring surprises.

Stone shuffled some papers on the Fenfleet deal, looked again through his figures and those that Roger had given to him as if searching for a clue that would make it all work. But he was unable to concentrate, and his thoughts wandered to Claire, her absence from Arrow Hall, the spying work she had done for him, Rick Austin and the unlikely strong words she had used against him.

Closing his eyes Stone made a decision. Renovating Arrow Hall, and soon, would be the enticement to get Claire back. He knew of no other way to mend the rift in their dealings. Something Stone rarely did was to go to Claire's flat in the west wing of the house but he now wanted reassurance, he wanted to see if she had cleared it and left it forever because that was what it felt like in the oppressive silence of the house.

He took the stairs two at a time, paused on the landing and looked through the long low window onto the gravel driveway. With fresh eyes he saw the ramshackle picture which without Anton would only get worse.

Weeds had smothered most of the gravel except for puddles where car wheels had made dents and kept it clear. Rabbits had pockmarked the lawn with their holes and brambles grew where lush grass had once flourished. Yeh, let's get on with it, he thought, and to hell with what it might cost to bring it back to life.

Stone turned away from the window and knocked on Claire's door twice as if she might be there. There was no answer and he didn't expect one. Unknown to Claire Stone had a duplicate key and he released the lock. Quietly and slowly he pushed the door open and walked into the sitting room, a place he had not been to for several years. It was tidy, it was chic, with antique and modern furniture blending easily, and pictures, family photographs and dried flowers giving the room life. Why not let Claire start with her flat, where she could dictate everything down to the last detail? Cautiously Stone peered into the bedroom. He breathed out heavily as he saw that things remained that were personal to Claire. Things that she would surely come back to. The photographs of her mother and sister in Australia, a silver-backed hand mirror and brush. Her wardrobe still held her clothes in neat rows and except for the utter quiet it was as if she had never left.

Stone's moment of panic ended. Her flat was intact just as she had left it and of course she had not really gone away, how could she? This was her home. He ambled back down the stairs and into his study. There he picked up the phone and dialled Claire's mobile number. She answered almost immediately.

'Have Trifoni Group put in the Fenfleet bid yet?' he asked.

'Yes. One of the other directors dealt with it today. I rang to find out.' Claire lied but it came easily. She knew nothing had happened, she knew the time had passed and that the tender document was still in Rick's desk. This was Rick's own deal and nobody else at Trifoni would handle it. But why tell Harry Stone that?

'How much?' Stone snapped.

'£2.25 million.' Being at the end of a phone hid the

flush that came to her cheeks and the giveaway frown did not show, but she caught her breath in a moment of anxiety.

'And have they paid cash into that fancy account in Geneva?'

'No.' Claire breathed out easily, the truth being more her style.

Stone continued more slowly, his voice relaxed, as again he felt he was winning. 'Claire, I want you to give in your notice today at Trifoni. You're now done with them and there's letters and all sorts piling up here. It's about time we got back to normal.'

'I won't walk out on Rick just like that. He's still in hospital. Yesterday he was unconscious, in intensive care. And what if he heard the attackers when they shouted your name at him? Don't you remember what I told you?'

Stone thought for a moment but his natural instinct took over. 'All we do is to deny it. Tell Rick he heard incorrectly if he questions it.'

'But the police know my address as Arrow Hall. It's on my driving licence.'

'Nothing we can do about that.'

'That's the trouble with you. But I'll never forget the horrible thrashing Rick suffered, and I can't carry on like nothing has happened.'

'You still worried about getting those thugs caught who roughed him up?'

'You need to see Rick Austin in his hospital bed to understand how I feel. Nobody's hit you have they?'

Stone remembered. He'd run and he'd hidden. But he wouldn't admit it. Ever.

'Claire, listen. It's time for you to come back,' Stone snapped. 'I didn't pay Jennie Garon's grossly inflated bill to help you stay away.'

'I went to Trifoni as a temp but that doesn't mean I don't

finish the job. Until I know Rick's recovering and find out what he heard ... well I don't move. And that's final.'

Claire's tone was forceful and Stone momentarily held the phone away from his ear. 'I can't let you do that. Temporary is temporary isn't it?'

There was arrogance in Stone's voice, the usual arrogance he used to intimidate or bully when he wanted something. Claire had heard it often but she was now fired by the whole deal to answer back. And nothing Stone said would change that.

'You don't see it do you? Rick Austin will suspect something if I walk out now. Especially after what he's been through.'

'Tell him you found something permanent. Tell him you've had to go off somewhere else. For God's sake, Claire, it happens all the time and you know what to do.'

'No. That's not possible. And it's time you came to your senses and lived in the real world. Anyway, Rick is not up to hearing *anything*, let alone lies.'

The tetchiness in Claire's voice continued and nervousness and tension now showed in her eyes, but Stone did not see this and continued in a more persuasive tone.

'So let's say sometime next week. That's giving you a few more days.'

'I'll come if and when I'm ready,' Claire said. 'And not before.'

This time it was Claire who put the phone down on Stone. She was standing in the middle of the sitting room of Jennie's flat and she breathed out heavily as she flopped into a chair, in no mood to listen to Stone's demanding arrogance. One day soon there were certain things he had to know, she wanted to shout them at him now, but she would pick her time for that when she would be able to gloat at his severe discomfort.

She left Stone alone, his eyes narrowed, and from that

instant he knew times were changing. Fenfleet pubs again flashed into his mind. Had he fixed it all too far?

*

Claire walked to Rick's office early the next morning. It was empty, and there were no awkward questions, not even from the security guard at the front entrance. She was able to clear her desk without interruption. Within an hour she walked out of the Trifoni building purposely, looking closely into each of the miniature cameras that pointed at her intrusively and satisfied that she had completed her work.

Early that afternoon she busied herself in Jennie's apartment. She was meticulous in her own flat at Arrow Hall and she now tidied Jennie's few snug and comfortable rooms in Knightsbridge, even though she knew that Jennie would always send in a contract cleaner to go through the place. Although she did not know where she was going to go, Claire then laid her clothes out on the bed in the small bedroom so that she could pack them easily. When she was ready the flat could be handed back to Jennie just as she had found it. She liked to be prepared and she wanted to remember this place as an unhurried haven in which she had felt secure.

Claire walked down the stairs warily and then locked the front door with care as if there could still be loiterers around. Without looking up and down the street she walked the few blocks to a small hairstyling salon on the corner of a nearby Mayfair road where she had made an appointment for her hair to be styled, a repeat of what Jennie had arranged for her a few days before. It was something she had not treated herself to for some years while she lived at Arrow Hall and the occasion now made her feel good. She looked in the salon mirror, saw the scratches on her face and felt the ache in her shoulder but she was refreshed, ready to deal with the difficult task ahead. It was two hours later that she returned to Jennie's flat and settled down in front of the television.

Jennie's call came at seven that evening.

'We got cut off the other day and Roger's told me of your problems. I'd like to talk. Are you doing anything tomorrow evening?' Jennie asked.

Claire relaxed at the sound of a friendly, familiar voice.

'Big problems, Jennie. I hoped you might ring.'

'So what about tomorrow?' Jennie pressed.

'Yes. Of course. Where?'

'Come over to Newbury. Let's have some supper. It'll be informal. Just Roger and me. And if you want to stay the night...'

A tear came into Claire's eye. This was the help she had not expected. She had much to tell Jennie and perhaps she had some news for Roger too.

'What time?'

'As early as you like.'

Claire left for Newbury late afternoon the next day. The roads were busy, but driving Rick's powerful Porsche was effortless with no strain on her bruised shoulder. Within an hour she had found Jennie's house as directed and drove into the wide driveway. Inevitably the contrast with Arrow Hall immediately hit her.

Roger's greeting was as warm as Jennie's as he handed Claire a gin and tonic a quarter of an hour later. Claire settled into a large armchair and gazed at the colourful garden, fresh from recent rain, the reds of geraniums contrasting with immature silver birch trees dotted around. She sipped her drink and savoured the moment. She was with people who would understand, the ache of Rick's injuries and her own bruising she no longer felt, knowing she could soon talk freely.

'You look tired,' Jennie remarked.

'It's been scary, awful, exhausting. Arrow Hall, Claridge's, the Cotswolds, hospitals. It's turned out pretty bloody, even my worst nightmare could not have been like this and I've still got a big problem to sort.'

'Rick Austin still not good?' Roger asked.

'He's unconscious, and the hospital won't tell me if he'll recover.'

'The police ought to sort it,' Jennie said. 'I mean, it's the type of thing you expect in London not the Cotswolds.'

'Maybe they will. Who knows? But I don't want too many questions from them,' Claire said.

'What is the powerful Harry Stone doing about it?' Jennie asked with sarcasm.

'He doesn't care. Nothing worries him. He might get some justice for Rick's beating which was meant for him but that's all,' Claire said.

'Claire, you have something on your mind. I can see it by the far-away look that keeps coming into your eyes. Come on, let's have it.' Jennie's coaxing led Claire easily.

Sipping her drink, she spoke slowly. 'I'm in the middle of something that's getting really nasty and I'm just not used to it. And I'm not sure I know how to face Harry with what I've got to tell him.'

'What do you have to face him with?'

'He needs to know what I've done. He needs to know where he stands. So I'm going to Arrow Hall to tell him everything.'

'What do you mean what you've *done*?' Jennie asked.

'I can't leave it as it is. It's unfinished. Not only with Rick but with the Fenfleet deal too.'

'Whatever's happening, it sounds too messy for my liking,' Jennie said. 'So great, go and do what you need to do.'

Claire frowned. 'Harry's got to listen to me like he has never done before,' she said.

'About the real facts on the Fenfleet contract?' Roger asked.

'Yes.'

'So what did you really find in Rick Austin's office? What was his real deal?' Roger's voice was not intimidating but Claire was a little nervous of him.

'Why do you ask?'

'I don't believe the figures you gave Harry Stone on the tender.'

'Why not?'

'They don't add up. Look, Claire I've been here before, I know what makes money.'

Claire arched her eyebrows for a moment, indicating she was uncertain.

'I had to teach Harry a lesson,' she said. 'He's used me, Rick got beaten to a pulp instead of him, and if he's gone into the tender too high, well it just shows how his greedy fear has won.'

'You mean that £2.25 million isn't the Trifoni Group figure?'

'No. Nowhere near it.'

'So what did they offer?'

'Nothing. Rick Austin's still in a hospital bed and they pulled out.'

'Sure. But if Rick Austin had been up and about what would their bid have been?'

'About £1.5 million. Max.'

'And guarantees?'

'No guarantees. I made that up. It sounded more plausible that way.'

'And Harry took the bait like a kid in a sweetie shop.' Roger laughed loudly and took a long sip from his whisky as if to enjoy the moment even more.

'What will this do to Harry?' Claire asked.

'Lose him a lot of money. He invested heavily into St

Lucia. That's gone. And now this. But I told him the figures didn't add up. I told him to walk away from it at that price and leave it to Trifoni. But Harry's ego is big. Too big to keep him stable.' Roger took another thoughtful sip from his drink. 'You do know that Harry has been awarded the deal?' he asked.

'So soon?'

'Yes. Rang me to tell me this morning. Kennedy obviously thought it was too good to lose so they snapped it up like quick. Before anybody could change their minds.'

'Was Harry pleased?'

'You know Harry. He doesn't show his emotions.'

'Perhaps I've done the wrong thing in rigging it,' Claire said.

'Don't have sympathy for that guy,' Roger responded. 'You know by now he has no sympathy for anyone else.'

Jennie laid a comforting hand on Claire's shoulder. 'You do realise you're one of the very few people who've pulled the wool over Harry Stone in the past few years? And got away with it,' she said, smiling.

'I haven't told him yet, the real figures I mean. Nor have I got away with it. Then there's Rick, with his life hanging on a thread.'

'You mean you're going to let Harry *know* you gave him false information?' Roger asked incredulously.

'Yes,' Claire responded firmly.

'I wouldn't do that. You never know how Harry will take it and your life will never be the same again afterwards, he'll see to that. So my strong advice is let him lose his money, keep your distance and see what happens. Even I tried to stop him and he wouldn't listen.' Roger leaned forward, uncomfortable at the idea of Claire confessing.

But Claire persisted. 'No, I have to face him and I'm not going to run away from that, whatever the consequences.'

'You're very brave, Claire,' Jennie said. 'But be careful, very careful.'

'Well, he can't get violent. He's got too much to lose if the police come snooping and I would then tell them everything if I really had to.'

'Stone's dangerous,' said Roger. 'Look how he let Anton be killed. And he didn't care. And haven't you seen how he always deals with problems at a distance which leaves him out of the front line.'

'I can handle it, you just watch,' Claire said.

There was silence in the large elegant room for a few seconds. Roger rose, refilled Claire's glass and as he handed it to her he looked thoughtfully through the windows to the lawn where the sun was now disappearing. It was slowly sinking into his consciousness how easily Claire had plotted and led Stone into the ruinous trap of Fenfleet pubs and of course that meant this deal was far from done.

'Before you were hit, how was it developing with Rick Austin?' Jennie asked slowly.

'I told you everything at lunch the other day. Last weekend could have been good but that's now gone and I guess finished with Rick at death's door,' Claire replied.

'So you've got to get away from Arrow Hall,' Jennie said, sharpness in her voice.

'Yes. I know. But where do I go? I've been the Judas, stolen information from Rick. Valuable insider stuff. Isn't that a criminal offence?'

'What does Rick know?'

'Nothing yet. But he might.'

'You're not going to tell him as well as Harry are you?'

'No. But he could uncover it all. If the police are clever enough to trace who smashed him up then he'll know all right.'

'Listen, Claire. Whatever information you might have taken and twisted hasn't harmed Rick or Trifoni Group,'

Roger said. 'All it's done is kill off Harry for a while and for God's sake that's no bad thing and it's about time.'

'But I've led Rick into this bust up. Let him get smashed up as if he was a punch bag.'

'And the police investigation, where are they with that?' Jennie asked.

'They've asked me but all I've given is a false address, your flat, but it's not a murder hunt yet. I told them it's just a mugging. But will they believe that?'

Jennie sighed. 'I don't know,' she said. 'But just lie low and be careful what you say.'

'If Rick recovers and remembers nothing, it's a mugging.'

'Will you have dinner again with Rick if he recovers?' Jennie asked.

'It all depends.'

'On what?'

'I'll tell you when I've seen Harry.'

Claire's eyes became watery but she tried to hold back a tear. Her drink gave her courage, though she was sure that the confrontation with Stone would be volatile. Her thoughts quickly flashed to Rick. She wanted to see him again, not in a hospital bed but strong, in control, as she had briefly known him, and the image pushed her determination harder into dealing with the unfeeling nastiness of Stone.

Claire looked at Roger. With his long legs stretching from his deep armchair he had a satisfied smirk on his face as the evening now washed past him and he drank more whisky. They both knew beating Stone was not easy. Roger had tried it several times and never won. But Claire would show him the damage she would bring to Stone, cash that would drain from him, wearing away his ego over the next few years as easily as dripping water reshaping soft sandstone. He would find his fear of getting beaten to the Fenfleet deal came at great cost.

Roger suddenly sat more upright as reality hit and he

remembered he had seen Stone get nasty and ruthless when provoked, especially if losing money was involved.

'I'm not sure you should go to Arrow Hall. Not on your own,' Roger said.

'Roger, listen. I'm going. That's it,' Claire said firmly.

'Your straight face says you're determined so who am I to stop you? But I'll watch from a distance. Yes?' Roger sipped his whisky, relaxed more deeply and Harry Stone suddenly became a whole universe away, of significance no more.

Claire stayed the night in Newbury, sleeping heavily and waking late, refreshed, and even eager to get moving and face Stone with the true facts on Fenfleet. She left Roger and Jennie before midday and drove Rick's Porsche to a secure storage off Park Lane. She took her two CDs from the player in the boot, checked to see there was nothing else personal to her and then carefully sealed the keys in an envelope with the car park ticket and posted it to the Trifoni Group offices.

She walked the short distance to Jennie's flat and called the hospital. The connection to Sister Davies' office took five minutes. Holding the mobile Claire's hands became cold and clammy, the long wait increasing her anxiety and she felt her heart rate increase. This call would decide her future.

Claire went to the window and stared at the street below as she waited. It was empty, no one was watching the flat. She guessed that Stone had put pressure in the right place as she had demanded.

'Miss Watts? It's Sister Davies. Do you want to visit Mr Austin?'

Relief washed over Claire at this.

'I can see him, how is he?'

'I'm sure you'll understand that we need to talk face to face, so please come.'

'Is Rick awake?'

'Please, no questions until you get here.'

'Can I come right away? Like now?'

'Yes, we'll make an exception to the visiting rules. Come as soon as you're ready.'

'It'll take me a couple of hours.'

'Hurrying won't make any difference to Mr Austin's condition so take your time.'

Rick was still alive! It stirred something inside her, an inner toughness that came when she was pushed too far and which would not let her walk away from the ugly bits of life. Unlike Stone, Claire could face problems head on.

Within ten minutes she was ready to leave. She called a private taxi service that she knew Stone had used before, packed an overnight bag in case she needed to stay with Rick and then waited for exactly an hour before the driver arrived and they headed for the motorway.

An hour later she entered Sister Davies' cluttered office

'You look a little better than the last time you visited,' the nurse said. 'But you look very tired. I hope you're taking care of yourself.'

'I'm not worried about myself, just Rick. Tell me what's going on. Please, I do need to know.'

'Sit down for a minute, get your breath back and then I'll give you the full picture.'

Claire's face went white. This was not what she had expected. She wanted to see Rick, desperately, but she sat down and looked helplessly at Sister Davies.

'How is he?' Claire pleaded.

'Well, he's regained consciousness. That's a start. A blood clot has been removed, we believe without permanent damage. But he's far from well, you must understand that. You can see him, but I'm afraid I can't let you stay long. Ten minutes at the most.'

The door to Rick's room was open. He was lying on top

of the bed, totally still in a grey gown, and as he heard the noise of somebody entering he tried to turn his head. The strained look in his red eyes set into the swollen blotchy, bandaged face said the effort was very painful for him. Claire held the back of a chair tightly, not knowing what to say, unsure that she could stop herself from fainting, and there was silence.

Sister Davies interrupted. 'I'll leave you,' she said. 'But I'll be back in a few minutes.' She then methodically tidied the end of the bed as if it was a ritual she had to perform before she left.

Claire sat in the chair and stared at Rick. White bandages swathed his head and his left eye was heavily swollen. His lips were puffy.

'Rick, what can I say?' Claire said, a tight hoarseness in her throat.

'I've had a long sleep.' Rick's voice was a low growl and hardly audible.

'Yes. It's been a little while.'

'The doctor tells me it's been four days. It feels like four months. How are you?'

'Couple of scratches. Nothing serious.'

Claire stared into Rick's eyes but she detected no hostility, nothing that would tell her he understood the real meaning of the attack. Rick was still very ill and even to talk he had to grind out the words from the back of his throat. Perhaps she should leave straight away, come back in a couple of weeks, as even five minutes with Rick like this would be too long.

'What happened?' Rick rasped. 'The police've come twice today.'

'They asked you questions?'

'I don't understand but they want to know how it happened, how I got hit.'

'Oh.'

'They asked if there's somebody who doesn't like me out there. Something about revenge,' Rick said slowly.

'There's nothing I can add,' Claire said softly.

'Who do I know who would want to hit me that hard?' Rick mused.

'Did they ask anything else?'

Rick slightly moved his head but his eyes did not focus on Claire. 'Told me they had questioned you too,' he said.

'Yes. I told them we were mugged.'

'Mugged. Yeh that's it. Did you lose anything?'

'No. Only my dignity.' Claire tried a smile.

'I have a fuzzy memory of being followed,' Rick said. 'I was driving and there was a car close up our tail. Is that right?'

'Rick, no...'

'Being followed,' Rick said with a drawl as if he was drifting into sleep.

'Well I didn't see it,' Claire said, looking away but now determined come what may to stick to that denial.

'I find it difficult to remember anything,' Rick said. He tried to move his legs in the bed to find a more comfortable position and screwed his face with pain. 'It's all such a bloody blur but the doctor says maybe it'll all come back to me. Maybe sometime.'

Sister Davies suddenly put her head around the door.

'I'm afraid time is up. Mr Austin now needs to rest but I'm sure there'll be another time,' she said.

Claire rose quickly, pleased at the interruption. 'Yes, there'll be another time,' she said.

Rick tried to move again, tightening his face with the effort. 'Don't leave it too long before you come again. There's other things we need to talk to about,' Rick said. 'Didn't we have some business to do?'

Claire did not answer but hovered uncertainly until Sister Davies led her to the door.

'I think you've had enough for one day, Mr Austin,' she said. 'What with the police interrogation. And Dr Edwards is due to call and he'll demand you rest.'

Claire took a last look at Rick's inert body just as she had when he was lying blood spattered and unconscious in the road. She felt as helpless now as she had then.

'Yes, I'll come again,' she said, holding back a tear. But she did not know when that would be, she was unsure about making any promises and she did not want to talk to Rick about any other business, whatever that might be, especially as she had blotted James Kennedy from her thoughts. She raised her hand in a small wave as she left the sparse room and she thought she saw a flicker of a smile come to Rick's hideously distorted face.

Claire followed Sister Davies down the corridor without looking back. In the office she sat tentatively and took a deep breath to calm the disquiet that showed in her eyes. She looked at the nurse as if she needed help.

'Rick's not good is he?' she asked.

'He's had major surgery but he's strong and should pull through. Concussion is his main problem. Broken bones will heal in time but it may take a while for his memory of the attack to come back. Possibly it never will.'

'He remembered me,' Claire said.

'I think you figure differently in his life,' she said enigmatically.

'What a mess all this is,' Claire said.

'Nasty is the best word. But it's over and hopefully you're both on the mend.'

'Rick's memory still worries me though,' Claire said. 'Surely he can't lose it just like that.'

'Are you worried because of his business?'

'Maybe. When he gets back to his desk his memory will be vital. It is for all of us.'

'Let it take its time,' Sister Davies soothed.

'Should I come back to visit soon?'

'If Mr Austin wants you to come then I suggest you come. I'm sure your presence will help his recovery. After all, he's not had any other visitors apart from the police.' The smile had gone from Sister Davies' face. She added, 'I've told the police not to come again as Mr Austin is just not up to it and his recovery is far more important than the police probing. They're unlikely to get anything from him while he's here.'

Claire's frown relaxed. It was what she wanted to hear.

'They certainly haven't asked me anything else,' she said. 'And anyway there's nothing I could add to what they already know.'

As if being chased, Claire suddenly rose to leave. She forced a short smile as she moved to the door.

'Thank you for being so helpful and understanding,' she said. 'Yes, I'll come back. And of course whatever I can do to help Rick I'll do.'

There was a tear in her eye as she left the office without looking back. As she walked down the corridor towards the stairs she knew her visit had been too short. Too short to feel the closeness with Rick which she had wanted. But how could it have been otherwise as she knew their closeness was now a million miles apart and even though she desperately hoped a new bridge could someday be built to Rick she could not be sure how she could handle it or whether it would work. She would always have to hide her deceit which had led him into this awful mess.

Claire took the train back to London and then a taxi to the Knightsbridge flat. It was early evening and a wave of tiredness swept through her as she entered the front door. This would be her last time here. She had come to like the place as if it was personal to her and she was unsure where she would stay next, where she would call home. All she knew for certain was that her settled, comfortable way of life had now changed and that her work at Trifoni was finished. Tomorrow she would face Stone in a meeting that would be volatile, a confrontation she had never been tempted into before but which was now inevitable.

Her tiredness waning she sat up late that evening and watched a film, and then did not sleep easily. She woke several times and each time her mind whirled around Rick and his bandaged, swollen face and then settled on the same question. At Arrow Hall tomorrow, how would she tell Harry the stark truth of the Fenfleet deal? Would her voice tremble, would she shake and hide from his icy stare? The visit could not now be stopped, she wouldn't let it, but in the middle of the dark night Stone's cold ruthlessness told her it could be a reckless thing to do.

But as the dawn gradually brought light to her bedroom Claire's thoughts again hardened and her own steely determination took hold. She had been pushed too far by Stone and what had she to lose? She dressed purposefully and as she looked in the mirror decided that she would not let the confrontation with Harry control her future. This would be her last chance to get to him, let him see what his total greed had brought him. She fingered the exquisite pearl necklace she had bought with his money and held it to her neck as if it was a ransom she could demand from him. For a moment she felt curiously at ease.

Claire took an early train from Liverpool Street which, running against the commuter crowd, was empty. As the train gathered speed she flicked open a tabloid newspaper and the headline on the third page startled her.

## SUSPECT ARRESTED FOR HAMMERSMITH MURDER

She read the bold print quickly. The timing and the place of the murder with the description of the victim fitted with what Stone had told her of Anton's death. Suddenly she felt this newspaper report was part of her life, she knew the victim and, as she read it, it was as if the violent thug attack on Rick was all happening again. The column finished with a sentence on a suspected drugs gang which was operating in the East End of London. Claire shivered as she read the words and then a tear crept down her cheek as she read that the victim had still not been identified. Anton's death was as anonymous as Stone would have wanted.

Claire rested the paper on the seat and stared through the window. She sat brooding in the empty carriage, not even noticing the lush greenness of the fields and trees which usually captivated her. Today was always going to be different but Claire now felt numbness and no satisfaction for Rick or Anton from what she had read. Anton had gone and he wouldn't come back. Rick was still alive but she had a nagging doubt her life would continue with him, and where would she be after today?

She left the train at Chelmsford and walked the short distance to an office in a tall building that overlooked a small river. She had an appointment to keep, a project she had started but now felt, because of all the twists and turns of the last few days, and despite strong feeling for its outcome, she would not see through.

It was just after 9.00 a.m. when she pushed through the glass front doors and was quickly shown into an elegant, modern office. Keith Kent, an architect who knew old buildings, understood how they were built, their history, and had a reputation for his thoroughness in researching them, met her warmly. The tenseness of the early morning left Claire's face, colour came to her cheeks and she was momentarily excited.

'You were right, Arrow Hall's in a sorry state,' Kent said.

'It's not gone too far to be pulled back, has it?' Claire asked.

'No. But it'll cost some money to put right. Big money.'

369

'Harry Stone is a wealthy man,' Claire said.

'Whatever he spends will be a good investment. Property like Arrow Hall is irreplaceable and renovated it'll stand out like a gem. Especially if all the land round about is landscaped.'

Kent turned away to a drawer and removed several large sheets of thick paper. He placed them on the table in front of Claire and she took a long interested look at the colour-washed drawing on the top. The neatly arranged landscape led her eye to Arrow Hall standing like a respected statue surrounded by disciplined nature. She flicked over the sheet to the next page. The lake, once part of the moat, was shown dredged and replenished and the water gleamed with the reflected greenness of willow trees that drooped over its edge. Claire gasped. This was a tantalising look into the future.

'You'd like to see my thoughts on the inside?' Kent asked.

'Wait a moment,' Claire said. 'I'd like to soak up the outside first. How long would this work take?'

'Trees take a while to grow. But the lake and the lawns and other landscaping ... well, if we started soon next spring could be interesting. It'll take a while to develop but quickly it'll look good. And a lot better than it is now.'

Claire and Kent laughed. They both knew that the present decrepit state was sticking a thumb into the face of history, a sacrilege that should haunt those responsible for it. A minute later Claire flicked to the next sheet. It was Stone's room.

Claire stood up and took a step back. 'How do you do it?' she asked.

'That room made me weep when I saw it,' Kent said.

For a horrid moment Claire wondered if Drake had done his menacing work there before the architect had been. Kent looked at her and saw the unease in her face.

'It just needs restoring. A lick of paint, new wallpaper,

new carpets, new curtains. And if you do that this is what you'll get.' He pointed to the drawing in front of Claire.

'It just needs restoring,' Claire echoed.

'Yes. It's a nice room. Faces south and east. But its present furnishings and decoration ... well what can I say? The whole lot is just too gloomy. I know it's an old house but that doesn't mean it's got to be morbid and depressing.'

'No, no,' Claire said.

'I liked the French windows,' Kent said. 'They have character, they let some light into the room and from the garden they let you look in. They give a perspective of the whole history of the house.'

Claire sat and clasped her hands. Kent had put into words her thoughts on those windows that she had often looked through. Thoughts that she had tried to hide but which she knew were true. The coincidence gave her an eerie feeling.

'Please send all these to Mr Stone at Arrow Hall,' Claire said. 'I'll need to talk to him about them.'

'Sure,' Kent said. 'But do *you* like them?'

'If only we could do it now.'

'We won't hurry it,' Kent said. 'After all, Arrow Hall is several hundred years old and a few months delay now won't make any difference.'

Claire had seen a glimpse of the future, a picture she had wanted for a long time, but uncertainty over the possibilities of making that dream real had grown and the doubt would weigh heavily on her over the next few hours.

Twenty minutes later she left Kent's office by cab, a mixture of excitement and rage driving her forward. She directed the driver to Arrow Hall and felt coldness as she suddenly remembered the horror of the killing of Anton that she had read in the paper earlier that morning. Then there was the inert body of Rick that she had seen only yesterday in a hospital bed, with his croaky voice and uncomprehending memory of what had happened. Claire looked out of the car window but could not feel any peace from the green unspoiled countryside around her.

Suddenly a police car overtook the cab, its whining siren penetrating her ears. It disappeared around a bend in the road ahead.

Two minutes later they came to the narrowing lane that led to the gated driveway of Arrow Hall. Suddenly Claire felt numbness. It was the same feeling that she had felt when she had watched helplessly as Rick was beaten.

She asked the cab driver to stop. She did not know why but she wanted to walk down the lane to the house alone. Perhaps she just wanted to release the tension that was now in her head, the throbbing that had happened before when she had to face Stone.

She stopped and took a deep breath as she looked at the wild flowers that were growing on the grass verge that bordered a ditch. High trees now shielded the lane from the road where she had left the cab and a picture of Arrow Hall came to her eye. If it was restored to only half what she had seen in Kent's office she would be satisfied. But Stone was a difficult man to handle. Anton's death and Rick's beating had been avenged and she cried easily in the still air as she walked slowly along the quiet lane. Had she demanded too much from Stone?

The sun suddenly turned dull as if a mist had risen from the damp grass and Claire felt suddenly cold. She pulled her coat more closely around her. The lane took a sharp curve before Arrow Hall came into sight and Claire walked more purposefully. She began to summon up her mental energy for the next hour which would be critical to the rest of her life.

Claire walked faster until she reached the iron gates coated in years of green mould that announced the entrance to Arrow Hall. On the widening road she suddenly stopped.

The sight that confronted her was one she had hoped she would never see. Arrow Hall was ablaze with roaring flames. Smoke helped the red spikes upwards, polluting the morning air, like great forks reaching into the sky. Desperately she ran down the driveway. This was her home. She had personal things here that she wanted to save.

Two firemen were desperately hacking at the front door of the old house. But its aged oak did not yield easily. Suddenly it gave in and a gust of dark smoke poured out into the morning air.

He appeared like a ghost. Through the confusion that was in front of her Claire saw Stone across the garden. He was in his threadbare sweater, shouting with wild anger at a fireman. She could not hear what he was saying but it was Harry Stone as she knew him. Demanding and threatening. Then Claire saw a large Jamaican sidle towards Stone. The two men stood and watched motionless as there was a loud explosion. The fire was taking its terrible toll.

Claire approached Stone but he did not see her.

'You know who's done this?' Stone shouted to the Jamaican.

'I can guess, boss. I knew they wouldn't stop even if they received a bit of money. You should have paid Drake in St Lucia.'

'But I got more money in there, stuffed under the stairs and all sorts of papers that tell me where other cash is banked and how to get hold of it!' Stone shouted back.

Suddenly Stone noticed Claire as she moved cautiously towards him.

'Thank God you're back,' he shouted.

Claire remained silent as Stone came closer and she saw a wild look in his eyes. This was Stone in a defiant, dangerous, mood.

'We've got work to do. We've got to rebuild this lot. I need you back to help me.'

Instantly Claire shouted back. 'No that's not how it's

going to be. You're going to listen to me. You don't need me here. Arrow Hall'll never be the same now.'

A puff of dark acrid smoke blew over them and they both inched away on the gravel.

'What the hell are you talking about?' Stone demanded.

'Fenfleet,' Claire said.

There was only a short pause before Stone screamed, 'The price that got me the deal?'

There was no response from Claire but she saw the immediate rage in Stone's contorted face which for a fleeting second flashed red. A beam in Arrow Hall over his study suddenly cracked in the fire sending a dense cloud through the French doors. Harry Stone stared incredulously at the burning building, agitated and broken.

Claire turned away, a tear blurring her vision of Arrow Hall. Walking quickly to the waiting cab, she manipulated her mobile to call Sister Davies at Rick's hospital.

In that instant she knew where she wanted to be and where she was going.